To Claire and Mark – thank you both. I have marvellous neighbours. Xx

A special thank you to Richard Luke and Jamielee Thornley – photographer and make-up artist.

To the amazing Dr J C D Wells who fixed the pain in my neck which enabled me to finish this novel, thank you so much. Dr Julian Tomkinson thank you also for taking care of my health. Thank you.

Listening to music whilst writing helps me with the creative flow. My tastes are wide but The Cranberries, Stereophonics, The Goo Goo Dolls, Fleetwood Mac, Of Monsters And Men, Pink and Alanis Morissette, to name but a few have pulsed down my earphones continuously whilst writing this novel.

Lastly my Granddad and Grandma – even though they passed many years ago I think of them both almost every day and hope they are watching over me smiling. Yes, I'm happy at last, it took me a long time but I did it! Much love and many, many fond memories but most of all thank you for the amazing memories of my childhood I have, the holidays to the caravan, the apple picking and Granddad your garden. You both sit firmly in my heart and I miss you both so much. I created Eve in your memory – John Thomas and Evelyn Watson. xx

To PublishAmerica – wow thank you so much for having the confidence in my work. I have loved creating Jesse and Amy and the guidance you have offered has helped me every step of the way. You have helped me realise a dream in bringing Jesse and Amy to life for readers everywhere to hopefully fall in love with and enjoy.

THE EYES
PROLOGUE

The smile that played softly on her lips was for real this time. Could she really go through with this? That chance meeting that had sent her spiraling into an unfamiliar world and as she asked herself for the hundredth time that day - was she really doing the right thing - her foot pressed down just a little harder on the accelerator as she sped towards her destination.

It was one thing sending flirty, arousing, not to mention risky texts, another actually going through with what they had discussed, what she needed and wanted so badly, what she had deprived herself of for the last four years. Was she actually strong enough to carry this on? Amy felt the warmth spread across her cheekbones as she remembered the messages where she had been so brave, so explicit.

Pulling into the car park, her mind and body in turmoil, Amy reached for her mobile phone.

'I'm outside babe. x' Her hand hovered over the send button debating whether to press it or not as last minute doubts flooded through her brain. Wouldn't it be best if she just drove home and forgot he had ever existed? Biting down hard on her bottom lip and closing her eyes for the briefest moment she allowed her finger to snake once more over the key. Inhaling deeply feelings of courage began washing over her as she remembered her friend's words. Taking as much air as possible into her lungs Amy pressed the send key. She could feel her heart rate increasing, the thud pounding in her ears and as she tried to control her breathing she knew there was no turning back. Amy was taking her first courageous steps and from somewhere deep inside her she drew the strength to exorcise the doubts firmly away, expunging them for the time being.

'Shit!' She exclaimed what the hell had she done! Was she really capable of going ahead with this liaison, this one night stand? Could she really see it through? Years and years of self-doubt and loathing, not to mention the vile words that had been spoken to her over the years began to invade her brain. 'No!' She said a little half-heartedly. 'I can do this!'

Looking around she knew it was too late to retreat; too late to be the coward she so desperately wanted to be as last minute nerves began to pitch about in her stomach. As she saw him approach her car and reach for the door, a glorious, sexy smile upon his handsome face, his dark, wavy hair just as she remembered it, she closed her eyes for a brief second, fighting back the nausea as the waves of sickness threatened to overtake her.

Swallowing hard she turned to look at the man who was now seated beside her and pushing her nervousness and doubts once more to the recesses of her mind she felt that genuine smile caress her lips once again.

CHAPTER ONE

'Do you want me to get that hun?' Amy asked jumping up from the sofa to answer the knock on her friend's door.

'Please.' Shouted back Jen, who was busy in the kitchen making the two friends a hot drink and no doubt preparing one of her usual delicious snacks.

Opening the door Amy was met by what she thought were the most amazing pair of eyes she had ever seen. Not blue, not brown, she couldn't quite make out their colour as he stood before her on the door step, a gentle smile playing at his perfect lips.

'Oh hi Jesse,' Jen called as she suddenly appeared by Amy's side. 'Come on in, Rick is just in the bath, I'm sure he won't be long. This is Amy, my friend, by the way.'

Amy mumbled a timid hi before sitting herself back down on the cream leather sofa surrounded by the cushions that she felt somehow defended and shielded her from this man who had her heart racing in her chest. What the hell was the matter with her? She was a strong, independent woman, a mature woman and yet this friend of Rick's was having this strange and unusual effect on her. Thank god she wasn't stood up because Amy was positive her knees would be shaking uncontrollably and she would fall flat on her arse!

As they struck up casual conversation Amy could feel her whole body beginning to tense, the muscles across her shoulders were beginning to tremble under the strain and as she shifted position she deliberately sat on her shaking hands. Every time she glanced in Jesse's direction or he uttered a word she was drawn to the pull of his mesmerizing, magnetic eyes. Damn, why couldn't she make out their colour? Perhaps if she stood and moved a little closer....... 'No!!!!' Her subconscious screamed at her. 'Be cool!'

'So are those beautiful flowers in the kitchen for your girlfriend?' She found herself asking in a bid to try and strike up some sort of normal conversation and hide her obvious nervousness.

When she had arrived at Jen's house and walked into the kitchen,

Amy had immediately noticed a breathtaking bouquet of red roses stood on the counter top and naturally presumed that her friend's new man had bought them for her. After giving her the third degree Jen informed Amy that a friend of Rick's had bought them for his girlfriend and left them whilst he had gone into town shopping.

'No.' Jesse laughed in response. 'I don't have a girlfriend.' Amy couldn't help but notice his smile as she felt her eyes once again being drawn to his young, handsome face.

Amy felt herself blush at his response and wanted to pinch herself hard to banish the thoughts that were slowly creeping around her brain. Jesse was casually leaning against the door frame and as she sneaked another quick glance in his direction from under her long, black eyelashes and heavy fringe, she took in fully the tall, dark brown haired man with what she could only imagine was a perfectly toned physique. His lips were full and enticing, his smile light up not only his eyes but his entire face and as he looked in her direction she felt the blush begin all over again as his eyes met hers briefly. He was captivatingly handsome; his face perfect and as she secretly studied him she noticed the small dimple in the centre of his chin, god how she wanted to put her finger there, to feel how his skin felt beneath her fingertips. She closed her eyes for a second as images of her running her hands through his wavy, tousled hair overtook her brain. Jesse was simply delicious.

Amy became aware that she was holding her breath as the pain began to spread across her chest and her lungs silently protested from deep within. She felt as if the last tiny portion of air was being sucked out of her and knew she had to make her escape quickly, out of sight of this mesmerizing man she had met only moments ago. Fidgeting she moved her legs to stand, praying that they would not betray her just as Rick appeared rubbing his head with a towel as he descended the staircase.

'Alright mate, give me 5 to get dressed.' He said, addressing his friend who was still leisurely leaning against the door frame unaware of the effect he was having on Amy.

Turning, with a casual, sexy smile on his face Jesse followed Rick out of the room.

Amy felt the whoosh of air leave her lungs and as she fought to catch up with her breathing she turned with worried eyes towards her friend.

'What the hell is up with you?' Jen whispered.

'Friggin hell Jen, what's wrong with me?' Amy replied, a puzzled look spreading across her pretty face. She had grabbed hold of one of the many cushions that adorned the leather sofa and was now fingering the tiny sequins with nervous, shaky fingers.

Bursting into laughter Jen looked closely at her friend and knew that finally she had completed the circle; finally she was able to feel again. Jen had been worried for a while about her dearest friend but seeing her flustered like this she knew that Amy was finally ready to fully live again.

'Will you please put my cushion down and breathe for god's sake. Your colour is fluctuating between crimson red and a deathly grey. Here, finish your drink.' Jen said, handing Amy the cup she had previously set down on the coffee table.

'Thanks hun.' Amy muttered in reply, not daring to meet her friend's eyes, afraid of what she may reveal but more afraid of what she was feeling. The emotions swirling throughout her body and mind stunned her, never before had a man had this effect upon her.

'Someone has the hots for Jesse.' Jen teased, grabbing the cushion out of Amy's hands. 'Shit Amy, you've pulled half the bleedin sequins off!' She laughed inspecting the cushion carefully before tossing it onto the other sofa.

'Jen, I'm so sorry, I'll buy you a new one and the answer to your statement is no I do not!' Amy replied with a passion which was just a touch to fierce.

'Whatever!' Her friend replied. 'I think I know you better sometimes than you know your bloody self! I mean, look at you, you're a mess woman.' Jen giggled.

'Sssshhh, will you keep your voice down please Jen.' Amy pleaded looking around, afraid that Rick or worse still Jesse would over hear their conversation.

'It's ok, I heard the back door, they've gone outside. I asked Rick if he would smash up that old wooden cabinet that I moved out of the shed ready for the kids to use for their bonfire.' Jen reassured her, a satisfactory smile upon her glowing face.

'I better get going hun.' Amy had finally managed to compose herself once more and felt as if she was back in charge of her emotions and body. For a brief moment, whilst Jesse had been present in the room, something had overtook Amy, something strange and alien to her, something that had her nerves jangling and her whole body on fire. The butterflies that were busy skitting to and fro in her belly were beginning to make her feel nauseous and so making a conscious effort to try and slow her breathing down she eventually succeeded in calming herself sufficiently enough to make her escape.

'Ok sweetie, oh and by the way he knows how to massage you know.' Jen wore a devilish grin on her attractive face as she gently teased her little friend.

'Piss off Jen; I'm not having any indecent thoughts about your son's friend! I forbid it!'

'Yeah, yeah, whatever.' Jen replied, the laughter still edging into her voice.

As the two women walked out into the garden Amy was aware that Jesse was stood only inches from her and as the heat began its journey once again across her cheekbones and chest she grabbed her friend's arm and ushered her quickly out of the gate shouting a mumbled goodbye in Rick's and Jesse's direction.

After giving one another a warm hug Amy got into her car to begin the journey home. Turning the music on loud she shook her head violently as she forced herself to concentrate making a firm decision to put Jesse and his sexy eyes completely out of her head.

CHAPTER TWO

The following week passed by uneventfully. Amy and Jen spoke to one another every day and even joked about Jesse. Remembering their conversation Amy asked how Jen knew he could give a good massage.

'I was joking Amy. It was funny watching you blush.' Jen had informed her. 'Don't tell me you thought I had personal knowledge!' Jen screamed as she chuckled down the phone.

'I don't know.' She laughed back. 'I wouldn't put anything past you honey bunny.' Amy chuckled.

Amy made some rude comments which Jen found hysterical and totally out of character but seeing and hearing her friend smile and laugh again made everything worthwhile for her. Amy had once had a great passion for life and had touched many people's hearts over the years but gradually she had lost that special spark and withered under the cruelty of a manipulative and controlling man for almost twenty years. Now, with nearly a year of independence and freedom under her belt Jen felt that her friend was ready to fly again and who better than with someone she knew. Yes, it was definitely time for Amy to have some fun and Jen was just the person to make sure she did!

'Do you know that if I carry on this conversation with you I will need a cold shower?' Amy exclaimed to her dearest friend during one particular telephone call.

'Well you started it!' Jen retorted, laughing.

'I did not! You said that you dropped Rick off and had seen Jesse and that he was all dirty and muddy after playing football, so I think you stand corrected Mrs, you started it!' Amy laughed, blushing furiously on the other end of the telephone.

'Yes but tell me you didn't actually visualize him Amy.' Jen was laughing so much her stomach was beginning to hurt. 'Tell me that you didn't visualize him all dirty, stripping off his clothes slowly and stepping into the hot, steamy shower? Tell me you didn't visualize him soaping that fit, young body up...'

'STOP!' Amy pleaded as she tried unsuccessfully to force the disturbing images out of her brain as vision after vision assaulted her. First she imagined his eyes, those sexy, magnetic eyes. Next him removing his clothes exposing his fit, lean torso…… 'You encouraged me!' Amy replied emphatically. 'If I remember your exact words you said, and I quote, "Oh just think, Jesse all dirty and muddy getting into the shower. Just imagine him soaping himself up! So Jen, you put the idea in my bloody head!' She chuckled, closing her eyes in a bid to force the image of Jesse from her mind.

'Ok, I admit it, I said it.' Jen replied, the words coming out in gasps as she tried not to laugh. 'But you just admit lady that your thoughts are disgusting, in fact, they are downright filthy and fit for the sewer where Jesse is concerned!'

'You are leading me astray, do you know that?' Amy laughed back refusing to admit that the thoughts she was now encountering again were disturbing her so much. Visions of Jesse flooded her head as she remembered how drawn she had been to him, his eyes.

'Mmmm I think you will find that you are leading yourself astray hun. All these conversations and subsequent cold showers.'

The two women laughed so hard they both had tears running down their faces.

'Right, I better go and get some sleep Jen.' Amy laughed. 'I'm knackered after this conversation.'

'Ok Sweetie, may a hundred dirty dreams fill you're beautiful head tonight.' Jen giggled in response.

'You are encourage able, do you know that! Amy exclaimed, trying to quell the laughter that was threatening to escape at any minute.

'Night Sweetie, sweet dreams.' Jen replied hanging up the phone before Amy could respond.

As she lay back against the soft, feather pillow Amy sighed softly to herself. Her life had changed so much over the last 12 months. Her ex-husband, Paul, had forbidden her to see or contact Jen after a dispute between the two and Amy being the ever, faithful and controlled wife had done as her spouse had bid and banished her dear friend from her life. For nearly four years the two women had not uttered a word to one another but as soon as Amy had secured her escape, Jen was the first person she contacted. She had missed her best mate over the years and often took out photographs of the pair when Paul was not around; reminiscing about the time they had spent together. Now, the pair where virtually inseparable and Amy couldn't have been happier, a part of the jigsaw that was her life had been firmly put back in its place, forever to stay there.

CHAPTER THREE

With a little over a week before Bonfire Night to go Amy reached for her phone as she heard it beep signaling a message from her Facebook account.

'Jesse Clayton wants to be friends on Facebook. Reply 'Add' or 'Deny.'

Feeling courageous Amy typed out 'Add' before typing out a private message to him.....

'Feeling brave Mr Clayton?'

'Very brave. Came the reply in the form of a text message.

'Shit!' Amy threw her mobile phone onto the sofa and stared at it, suddenly petrified of this small piece of technology. Putting her finger in to her mouth she nibbled softly on the nail. What the hell was she doing, he was almost half her age! She had two daughters almost his age she quickly thought to herself. Chloe, her eldest child was 20 and Bethany, her youngest, 17; shouldn't she be acting more responsibly, she questioned silently?

Picking the phone back up she debated what to reply. What could she say? 'God you have amazing eyes and I want sex with you because I can't help my dirty, sewer of a mind. By the way I don't know what the hell is wrong with me; this is not like me at all!'

'Aaarrgghhh, what is the matter with you woman!' Stamping her feet firmly on the ground like a two year old having a temper tantrum she resolved to be in control once again and stop being so pathetic.

'You can do this.' She told herself firmly. 'You deserve this, you deserve some fun.' As an image of Jesse's eyes entered her mind she remembered the conversations that had taken place between herself and Jen. Positive comments had also been made by Jesse to her son, Rick and so taking a much needed deep breath she typed out her reply.

Over the next week texts were sent back and forth. As the days passed the messages grew more explicit and sexual but Amy was always conscious of the fact that she was older and therefore could make him uncomfortable, perhaps for him this was just a bit of banter, something to pass the time, a joke with his mates. For her this was the much needed release she required to free her finally from her horrific past.

'I don't want to make you feel uncomfortable in any way Jesse.' She text, trying to test the situation.

I'm fine.' He quickly replied, adding a smiling face to the end of his message.

Feeling happier Amy gave in to the temptation that had presented itself to her and by Wednesday that week they had decided to meet up on the Saturday which coincidently was Bonfire Night. Jesse had promised to attend a firework display and then go to the local pub for a few drinks after with his mates and so they arranged that Amy would pick him up from the pub.

'So what would you like to do on Saturday? x' Amy seductively text summoning a tiny morsel of courage from somewhere deep within her.

'What did you have in mind? x' He text back.

'Well I was thinking a game of monopoly. x' She joked, enjoying the new feelings of flirting as she hit the send button.

'Do I look as if I play board games? x'

Wow, she was amazed, he was so young and yet so forward and a damn sight braver than she was! The days couldn't pass quickly enough for Amy, the anticipation and nerves growing with every hour that passed, the doubts paying her a visit, just to bring her back to reality.

They had the whole "safe sex-pregnancy talk" with Amy confiding in Jesse that she had been tested after her husband and she had not had any sexual partners since and she certainly couldn't get pregnant. Jesse more or less assured her of the same and so feeling comfortable that she wasn't risking her sexual health and trusting his word Amy decided that if Jesse didn't want to use condoms that would be fine with her. She had ensured that Chloe and Bethany would be out of the house for the night and now as she sat in her car with this young man and the irresistible pull of his eyes beside her she wished she had been able to have a few glasses of her favourite rose wine for courage.

CHAPTER FOUR

The drive home seemed endless for Amy as she tried to resist looking at those magnetic eyes. The air was heavy with sexual tension and chemistry, Amy not daring to look at Jesse for too long, refusing to meet his eyes with her own for fear of losing control of her car. The sensations she had experienced since their paths crossed had dumbfounded her and she knew that the only way to quell the bewildered and muddled thoughts that had been charging through her head was to go through with the meeting and find out a little more about this captivating, handsome, young man.

Once in the confines of her house she quickly reached for the nearest bottle of alcohol she could lay her hands on. Downing one shot after another she felt the tequila sting the back of her throat before she swallowed and allowed the heat of the spirit to warm her insides. Every nerve in her body appeared to be jangling and she had to hold the glass firmly to prevent her hands from shaking.

'What colour are his eyes?' The silent question ran around her head as she peeped at him from underneath her eyelashes. The distance between them seemed so small as she leant back against the cabinet, Jesse on the other side of the kitchen.

For a brief moment she gazed into his eyes and felt herself drawn towards him. Walking slowly, she took a deep, calming breath as she felt the effects of the alcohol begin to take hold of her body. Reaching him, she stood on her tiptoes. Closing her eyes she tilted her face up to his, their lips meeting briefly as she parted her mouth to welcome the tip of his tongue. Sensations swirled around her head as he picked her up gently and sat her on the counter top. His hands came up to her hair, gripping her head lightly on either side, his fingers gently loosing themselves in her thick, chestnut hair as once again he kissed her, deeper this time, claiming her mouth as his own which she gladly surrendered. Amy was lost, totally without a care in the world she reached for him and pulled him closer to her all thoughts of what she was embarking on abandoned, cast away without a second looking back.

Amy didn't know how they ended up on the sofa but she knew that this was where she wanted to be. She felt his strong hands exploring her body, long, slow movements with only the pads of his fingertips as he traced her contours and discovered what lay beneath the sheer fabric that encased her form. Small moans escaped her parted lips which he once again claimed and covered with his own. The way he kissed her left her breathless and wanting more. She knew that she was ready for this man, ready to accept him as desire took over and she allowed herself to give in to the pleasure he was lavishing upon her. As she felt his fingertips travel down her body to their ultimate goal she experienced the first powerful stirrings of lust and ached for him to touch her intimately. Parting her legs she gasped in surprise as he touched her deep within, his fingers weaving an unexpected magic. She could feel how warm and ready she was for him as she lay back and allowed the feelings he was creating to wash over her, his thumb was deliciously teasing and stroking her clitoris, his fingers caressing her deep inside. Jesse slowly built up the tempo, his young, expert fingers moving quickly, massaging her insides as he moved them in and out of her. She felt his lips slowly tracing the contours of the sides of her neck, her shoulders, trailing their way down her body until he captured her left nipple and began to suck making the tiny bud rise and stand proud. Amy began to feel the first delectable waves of an orgasm; the deep, penetrating rhythm over took her body and as she felt herself begin to contract around his talented fingers she rode with abandonment the deeply fulfilling and unexpected sensations that raged throughout her.

As she came down from the spellbinding, earth shattering orgasm she looked up and saw Jesse smiling at her, his fingers trailing an exquisite path across her flat stomach. Amazement was clearly evident in her eyes, in fact, her whole body was silently betraying her, making her feel alive and wanton, sexy and brave. Amy had long ago forgotten how heavenly a man's touch could be and fuck did this man know what he was doing!

She wanted, no she needed to feel him inside her. Amy was reveling in the sensual feelings that enveloped her body. The slightest touch seemed magnified, as his strong but soft hands reached for her neck she threw her head back and arched with desire as his lips followed their tantalizing path, creating a fire like sensation on her soft tanned skin. As she felt his presence between her legs she moved her hips slightly to allow him to enter her. Feeling his hands on the small indentation of her back Amy rose to meet him, as she held her breath waiting she could feel the minute trembling of her lips, the ache that spread throughout her body was welcoming as she reached for him, drawing him towards her so the intense hunger she felt could be sated at last.

The air was pungent with the perfume of their aroused bodies as Jesse continued to pleasure her, the body that was ripe and so very ready for this man, the body that was crying out for his touch, that wanted again and again to be satisfied.

'I want to taste you,' she whispered as she trailed her lips slowly up his neck, gently nibbling the exposed skin. Slowly he carried on moving inside her, his hard cock creating a fiery path which she was positive was going to make her explode.

Shifting slightly Amy reluctantly released herself from him and slowly kissed her way down his body. Taking him deep within her mouth she could taste herself upon him, sighing softly she seductively ran her tongue around him relishing the feel of this man, knowing her only aim was to pleasure him with this delicious sexual act. Gazing up at him she knew he must be able to read the lust that was clearly evident in her eyes. Taking her time Amy moved her mouth to the tip of his erect cock once again whilst teasing him with provocative glances.

Slowly she slid as much of him into her mouth as she could, gently moaning with pleasure as she felt him right at the back of her throat. Amy heard his breath quickening as she slowly withdrew before taking him once again into her mouth sucking and licking him, her fingers and mouth working in unison she knew that before long she would feel his warm, salty maleness in her mouth.

'I want to come inside you.' Jesse hissed through clenched teeth.

Releasing him from her mouth Amy lay back down on the sofa

and gently reached for him, pulling Jesse down towards her. As he claimed her once again her breath caught in her throat as she moaned out in pleasure, her body responding to every movement Jesse made. Wrapping her legs around his back she allowed the sensations to once again course through her body, each succulent, delicious pulse filling her with complete wonder. As she exploded around him she cried out as wave after delicious wave took over. His steel like cock filled her entirely as Amy relished the fullness she felt as he continued to move and thrust into her in a way that no man had ever before.

CHAPTER FIVE

Waking the next morning Amy turned to look at the man lay beside her. It had been a while since a man had lain in her bed but somehow it all had felt so right. Jesse was on his stomach, his handsome face buried in the soft, feather pillow. Listening to the sound of his shallow breaths she felt the new but now all too familiar stirrings inside her and knew that this man had awakened something deep within her that had been dormant for so long. His body had been like heaven to touch and was as she had first thought, young, firm and athletic. A slow, warm sexy smile caressed her face as she remembered how they had discovered one another's bodies and the heights of passion that he had created so easily within her. Smiling softly she realised that Jesse had managed to accomplish something that the other three men from her past had never, he had given her the most amazing, most delicious orgasms with his cock planted deep within her, he was good, no, he was very good!

Sliding gently from the bed so as not to wake him, she tiptoed across the cream carpet making her way to the bathroom. Closing the door quietly behind her Amy closely inspected her face in the mirror. Her cheeks were flushed and her blue eyes held a glint and sparkle she had not seen for many years. Gingerly stretching she felt the previously unused muscles aching in her body, a welcoming, delicious ache that no amount of exercise other than raw, passionate sex could have inflicted. It had been nearly 5am when they both had collapsed; totally satisfied into bed and now it was almost midday!

After quickly brushing her teeth and washing her face Amy reached for her short, black dressing gown that hung on the back of the bathroom door. Shrugging into it she crept back into the bedroom to find Jesse lazily smiling at her.

'Good morning.' Amy whispered, returning his smile.

'Good morning babe. What time is it?' Those eyes, even after all their sexual athletics the night before, Amy still found herself responding to him, wanting him once again.

'It's almost 12.' She could feel her chest constricting as his hand reached out and leisurely stroked her leg. 'Do you want anything to eat or drink?' Amy knew she had to make a fast exit out of the bedroom before she got carried away and allowed the heat that was rapidly spreading throughout her body to take over.

'Please babe, have you got any eggs?'

'Yes, what would you like Jesse?' Amy pushed herself up from the bed in order to put a little bit of distance between them. Fuck he was so captivating, his eyes so.....

'Mmmm let's see, scrambled eggs on toast please but why don't you come back to bed for a while.' Jesse was grinning at her, a sexy, cheeky grin that she couldn't resist.

Sighing softly Amy went into his outstretched arms, welcoming the sensuality that was once again washing over her.

Rolling her gently on to her back Jesse's fingers and lips once again began their journey, their sole destination to bring her gratification. She felt her arms reach up to him as her own fingers entangled in his hair and she brought his face down to hers. The delicious, little pulses that ran throughout her body overtook once again as he satisfied her beyond anything she thought was possible. As he entered her she felt the irresistible pull of his eyes and marveled once again at how someone so young could satisfy her so completely.

Where had this man been all her life?....... Amy knew the answer but decided to ignore it. That was for another time, because she knew with absolute certainty that after today had ended she would begin to question herself, but, for now, she was willing to give into the abundance of new feelings and experiences that were overtaking her body and mind.

'Please don't look at me like that.' Amy mumbled, refusing to meet his stare. 'I can't look at your eyes for too long....' Her words trailed off as Jesse claimed her mouth as his own, his lips scorching hers every time they touched.

'What's wrong with my eyes?' He breathed in response as he kissed the sides of her neck.

'I don't know, I can't explain it.' Amy replied feeling the blood course to her cheeks once again. 'What colour are they? I can't....'

'Ssssshhh let's talk later.' Jesse huskily replied, his fingertips gently circling her belly button creating tiny explosions deep within her.

'Oh fuck.' Was the only reply Amy could manage as she felt his fingers move lower.

As he took her once again Amy wailed loudly as feeling after feeling assaulted her body.

'Oh….. My…… God!' She shouted out as the deep pulsating rhythm overtook her and she melted once again into the welcoming orgasm.

CHAPTER SIX

Driving Jesse home was fast becoming one of the hardest things that Amy had ever experienced. So many emotions ran through her brain and ravaged body and she knew that she would forever cherish the night before, take out the memories when she needed them, revel in the joy that he had brought to her and then put them away again for another time. She hadn't had an easy life, the last twenty years had been a nightmare that she had found hard to escape but her ex-husband was now in prison, she was safe at last.

'Are you ok babe?' Jesse asked sensing she was deep in thought.

Pulling up at the traffic lights Amy turned to him and nodded her head, not daring to allow any words to escape her mouth. Smiling she reached out her hand and touched the side of his face.

'Thank you Jesse.' She uttered in a hushed tone. He would never know how much the previous night had meant to her, how much she had risked daring to go through with the meeting that she somehow now knew would change her and her life for the better. One fleeting night with a young, handsome man had made her finally feel like a woman again.

'Anytime.' He replied smiling at her. 'If you turn left after the lights that's my street.' He added, those eyes once again playing with her, reaching out to her.

Looking away she prayed that the lights would change quickly and was relieved when they signaled green so she could once again concentrate on the road ahead.

Drawing to a stop in front of his home he reached out to her, drawing her into his arms he kissed her one final time.

'I will text you.' he whispered into her ear before reaching for the door handle and exiting the car.

As she drove away Amy finally felt able to breathe freely again. Part of her wanted so badly to turn the car around and go back to him, the pull of those eyes, that man, but as reality crept in she knew that was not an option and so she decided to go and visit Jen, Amy desperately needed to confide in her friend and hopefully make sense of what she was feeling. Reaching her fingers slowly up to her mouth she caressed her swollen lips, lips that only moments before had been kissed by that wonderful man, Jesse. As visions of the night before entered her mind once again she fought desperately to force them from her. The way he touched her had sent her spiraling into a world so unfamiliar. The mere thought of him had her wanting him all over again and the powerful high she was experiencing was something that she had never felt or experienced before.

CHAPTER SEVEN

'Are you home?' Amy had stopped off at the petrol station and was now on the phone to her friend.

'Yes, I am home Sweetie, how did it go? Come on tell me all about it.' Jen sounded excited on the other end of the telephone. She had spent an anxious night, pacing back and forth, worried that her friend had perhaps taken on a little more than she could actually deal with. She had desperately wanted to text Amy just to make sure that she was ok but Jen's sensible side knew that Jesse was a gentleman and her friend was in safe hands and so she eventually fell into a troublesome sleep at about 2am.

'I am on my way round now, I will tell you all about it hun.' Amy was laughing at her friend's enthusiasm.

'Ok, see you in a bit.' Jen replied. 'And I want all the gossip, every detail Mrs, do you hear!'

'I hear you.' Amy giggled hanging up the phone.

Knocking on her friend's door ten minutes later Amy knew she was going to face a severe interrogation. Jen would want to know everything and would instantly suspect if Amy was keeping anything from her. They had been friends a long time and Amy often wondered if even her ex-husband had known her as thoroughly as Jen did. She had a way of knowing what Amy needed and despite their brief time apart, they had always been there for one another. When Jen had split from her boyfriend of 5 years Amy had been there to support her friend and wipe her tears when she cried. Jen was a beautiful woman inside and out and Amy wanted so desperately for her to find happiness and the new man in her life, David, seemed to be providing her friend with everything she needed. Jen craved emotion, all she wanted was to be loved for herself and Amy secretly thought that David was a very lucky man indeed! What worried her was that her friend seemed to be caught up in a whirlwind romance and although she had tried to rein her in Amy could see how happy and content her mate was and so gave in and watched with happiness as Jen became more and more smitten with the new man in her life.

'Well, come on, dish it!' Jen grabbed Amy in a bear like embrace and kissed her on the cheek. 'You look as if you have had a very long night.' She giggled, drawing back a little to inspect her friend closely.

'Oh, I don't know where to start Jen.' Amy exclaimed.

'Well, as the song goes Sweetie, "at the very beginning."' Amy couldn't help but laugh at her friend who was now doing a little jig across her living room floor whilst belting out the tune from The Sound Of Music.

'Will you behave and put the kettle on, you mad woman!' Amy tried to distract her friend whilst she collected her scrambled thoughts together.

'I nearly didn't go Jen, I was so nervous but I can honestly say I don't know why. I thought it would be awkward, ok sex is one thing but actual conversation with someone you hardly know, plus him being in my house, well, that is another! Now combine all that with the fact that he is a lot younger than me and I was so worried about my body. I've not had, well you know…. consensual sex for a long time Jen and I was with Paul for nearly twenty years and here I am at my age doing god knows what with a man half my fuckin age!' Amy knew she was rambling as her worries tumbled out and she grasped her friend's hand.

'What do you mean you silly woman!' Jen retorted. 'Have you looked in the mirror lately, you have a better body than most 20 year olds! Sex is sex Amy, you never lose the knack but it sure has hell can get better.' She laughed. 'Anyway, what I want to know is was he a fumbling idiot like you thought he would be?' Trust Jen to want to get down and dirty but she appreciated the kind words that her friend had spoken in order to boost her self-confidence.

'Actually, no he wasn't Jen; I had the best sex I have ever experienced in my whole bloody life and I mean the best!'

'Woooo, way to go girlie, I am so pleased for you. I honestly thought I was going to have problems with you!' Jen laughed.

'What do you mean problems?' Amy replied.

'Well, you kept saying "Oh, no Jen, no man will ever sleep in my bed again. Oh, no Jen I don't want a man, I'm happy being on my own." See, what an utter crock of shit!' She laughed.

Amy burst out laughing remembering the words only to vividly that she herself had spoken a few weeks before whilst they had been sunning themselves by the pool in Majorca. Her first girly holiday had been a blast and the two women had come back firmly glued at the hip.

'I know, I know. All I can say in my defense is it must be his eyes! Shit! I don't even know what colour they are because I can't feckin look at him for long enough!' Amy exclaimed.

'Well, all I can say is it's about bloody time! So, come on what's he like in the sack?' Jen pulled her tongue out at her friend before turning to finish the hot drinks.

'God, you are so bloody crude at times, do you know that?' Amy couldn't control the laughter that escaped her mouth. Over the last year Amy had begun to piece herself back together again as a woman but she was still blissfully shy and unconfident.

'Call me crude, I don't care, I just want to know EVERYTHING.' Jen squealed.

'Jen, he awoke something in me that I thought was long gone. Let's just say he is very talented in ALL departments.'

'Wooooooooo Hooooooooo.' Shouted Jen. 'Do you know how friggin pleased I am for you Miss Sahara.

'Do one with the Miss Sahara Jen! You can no longer call me that, it was more of, shall we say, a bloody rain forest.' Amy brought up her hands in despair, had she actually just said that out loud?

'Now who is being crude?' Jen guffawed.

'Shut up! In my defense I've had hardly any sleep, the best fucking sex ever and my head is very firmly up my arse!' Amy replied laughing. 'What the hell have I done Jen?' She added the laughter slowly disappearing from her voice.

'Just get on with it for Christ's sake!' Jen replied, frustration written all over her pretty face. 'It's sex Amy and remember age is a number!' Jen finished, wagging her finger in Amy's direction.

Amy regaled Jen with the events of the night before, giving her just enough information to satisfy her curiosity but holding back some of the more intimate details. Jen may be her closest friend but how could she even begin to tell her that she had, only hours before, experienced her very first orgasm by penetration, the delicious, deep and relentless penetration of Jesse's hard, young cock. She could feel the all too familiar blush spreading across her cheeks as she remembered the way Jesse had ignited her body.

'Ok, now, an important question Amy. How are you going to go back to wine now you have had champagne?' Jen asked. 'And why the bloody hell are you blushing?' She added laughing.

'What do you mean hun?' Amy replied, knowing exactly which direction her friend was heading in whilst also choosing to ignore her question over the crimson colour of her skin.

'God, do I need to spell it out for you? You said it was the best sex ever. Now we both know he is younger than you so now you have had champagne do you think you can give that up and settle for a more mature wine?'

'Of course I can!' Amy retorted, not entirely convinced herself with the words she uttered. The sex had been good, no the sex had been fanfuckintastic!

'We shall see.' Jen replied a pensive look on her face as she swept her hair back from her eyes.

'Listen Jen, this cannot go anywhere, it was just sex - two consenting adults having a very, very good time and I might add the best fucking sex ever!' Amy shrieked in horror as she realised what she had just said out loud.

'So are you not seeing him again then?' Jen quizzed, a smirk playing at the corners of her mouth. She knew Amy well and a little bit more of Jesse would do her the world of good. She couldn't actually believe the transformation that sat before her, yes Amy looked worn out but her skin glowed and even though her eyes were sleepy Jen could detect a faint sparkle in her vivid blue irises'.

'I don't know Jen. Let's put this in perspective. He is nearly half my age, my eldest daughter is not much younger, plus he is your son's friend. Yes, he is very talented and gave me multiple orgasms and yes

I could definitely spend another night like that but let's just see what happens, a relationship this is not!'

Amy knew she had to be firm with her friend; Jen was a romantic and thought everyone should be in love and she didn't want her getting this confused. Just because she had met a wonderful man and was totally smitten did not mean that it was the same for Amy besides, she was happy being on her own, loved her new single life and independence. She was like a little bird that had been caged for years and she loved the feeling that spreading her wings had given her.

'It's sex Jen, just sex. Good, hot, very satisfying sex but it is just sex. I admit I was wrong when I said no man would ever get into my bed again Jen but my life, my heart and my head are off limits.' She stated, pointing to her chest and head. 'I've tried too fucking hard, cried too many tears; I just couldn't do that to myself ever again! My independence is everything to me Jen, I was told how to act, talk, and dress for so many years. I was only allowed friends who Paul okayed and when he thought I was getting too close he took them away from me. I'm finally my own person Jen; no man will ever dictate to me or own me again!' Amy cried as she angrily wiped the tears from her cheeks with the back of her hands.

'Ok, ok. I will shut up now.' Jen replied knowing she was perhaps pushing her friend a little too far. Her scars ran deep, her hurt and pain had lasted too long and as Jen finally accepted with a heavy heart that her friend would never love or be loved again she felt the sadness flow throughout her. Every woman deserved to be loved and it broke Jen's heart that the beautiful, kind, soft natured woman before her would never allow herself to be cherished. Her ex, the bastard, could rot in his prison cell for all she cared.

Smiling at her friend, oblivious of the thoughts and feelings that Jen was experiencing, Amy felt as if she had made herself and the situation between her and Jesse clear.

As Amy rose from the chair her friend burst out laughing.

'What's the matter Sweetie, you are walking funny.'

'Jen, will you get lost! I 've found muscles in my body that I didn't know bloody existed!' Amy said as she rubbed her aching, sore thighs.

'Wow, he must have been good then, have your legs over your head did he?'

Bursting into laughter the two women hugged one another tightly.

'I really am pleased for you Amy; you deserve this after everything you have been through.'

'Yes, you are right, I do!' Amy replied, not wanting to think of the past. 'Right, I had better get a move on hun. Are we still going to the pub tomorrow?'

'You bet your arse we are Sweetie. Get your glad rags on because it's piss up time!' Jen replied giggling.

Amy was still chuckling when she got home. Walking upstairs she glanced at the unmade bed. The smell of sex was heavy in the air, the stains evident on the ebony sheets where only a couple of hours before they had lain pleasuring one another. Yes, champagne was excellent she thought, champagne was very, very excellent indeed and Jesse was an exceptional year.

CHAPTER EIGHT

That night as she lay in her bed alone Amy tried to relax and closed her eyes. Immediately visions of Jesse entered her mind and despite her tired and sore body she felt her desire for him grow slowly within her. As she fidgeted with the pillows in a bid to get herself comfortable Amy felt herself beginning to respond to the kinky images her mind was casting and flitting about, tempting her from deep within.

'Shit! What the hell is wrong with me?' She exclaimed to herself. Her body was aching and sore, the muscles in her legs taunt from the previous night yet her secret place was on fire, craving for Jesse's touch. As her hand stroked down from her neck she felt the peaks of her nipples, so hard, yearning for his mouth. Placing her forefinger and thumb to her lips she wet the tips with her saliva before reaching once again to twirl the delicate buds in-between them, increasing the pressure as her passion mounted. Trailing her fingers further south images of him positioned above her flew through her mind and as the tips of her fingers connected with her clitoris she felt how wet she was. Trying to mimic the motion of Jesse's fingers Amy's orgasm approached quickly, her sex contracting around her as she pushed her digits as deep as she could, Jesse's image and the hot sex engraved in her mind.

Amy tossed and turned in her bed that night, her dreams passionate and vivid, filled with the events of the night before which she knew would soon seem like a distant memory. She wondered often that night what Jesse was doing, was he thinking the same things as she but as quickly as the thoughts entered her head she dismissed them with a determination she thought was impossible. What amazed her most was how much he had satisfied her, her ex-husband had been an ok lover but as the intimidation and cruelty had grown her needs had withered until finally she had closed her heart, body and mind to him. As time had passed Paul had begun to use her body whenever he wanted, beating and raping her repeatedly until totally crumpled she had succumbed to his demands without complaint. He had berated her for her lack of enthusiasm, telling her that she was ugly and that no one would ever want her and how grateful she should be to him because he was willing to put up with her. Paul had used every negative word or comment he could to inflict pain on her but this just made her withdraw even further away from him until completely shut off she had endured the daily abuse from him silently until he went too far.

She couldn't actually believe that just a little over a year had passed since that day, the day when she finally realized that she couldn't take anymore. The day she had snapped and faced her husband for the very first time only to wake up weeks later in the hospital after he had beaten and raped her to near death. Their relationship had never been perfect, oh yes, they had happy moments but as the years went on the abuse escalated, the attacks growing more vicious with every rise of his clenched fist. Amy had spent many an hour in the emergency room, making up excuses for the cuts, bruises and broken bones to the nurses and doctors, her husband looming over her, making sure she never revealed the ugly truth. The injuries soon healed and then the beating and verbal onslaught would commence all over again until Amy felt that there was no way out of the life she had been dealt, she was trapped, smothered and totally under his control and so the icicle was thrust very firmly and securely into her heart and Amy was determined that it would never, ever be removed.

That final attack and the weeks leading up to it had ended her marriage and years of abuse. When she had woken from the coma she had willingly given the police a statement and with the support of the domestic violence unit she had given evidence against the man she had once promised to love forever. The constant verbal abuse, the vicious beatings and the cruel, violent rapes were now a thing of the past.

Paul was found guilty and sent to prison whilst Amy was given a restraining order in a bid to try and protect her from him when he was released from prison. Part of the divorce settlement was that he was to receive just over £60,000, Amy never thought or cared about the money, she was just relieved that her years of being abused were finally over and as she slowly began to rebuild her life she realized that although it would probably take her forever to heal, she would never allow another man into her life. How wrong would those words prove to be?

Amy remembered how she had hardly slept at night during her years with the man who became her tormentor. Lying on the very edge of her side of the bed silent tears had drained her already tired and shattered, beaten body. She knew she was trapped, there was no way out, she was destined to stay with this monster for the rest of her life. Perhaps he would beat her so badly that it would all end for her, sometimes she had prayed for that....

Her life had changed so much since then. At first it had been difficult, fear had invaded even the simplest of thoughts and actions. Amy got into the habit of snatching a few hours' sleep during the day, the darkness and loneliness of the night petrified her as she lay awake listening to every sound. Images of Paul escaping from prison and coming back to finally accomplish what he had so obviously wanted took over her mind. As time moved on she gradually learnt to sleep at night only to be awoken by nightmares so vivid she was left shaking uncontrollably, tears of anguish soaking her crumpled pillow. Amy knew the psychological damage would take years to heal, perhaps never, the deep, mental scars were clearly evident for the world to see at first but as time moved on she began to welcome each day with a smile and vowed to herself that she would make a better life for herself and her daughter's.

CHAPTER NINE

Jesse and Amy exchanged texts for the next few days and it was during this time that she made one of the biggest and bravest decisions of her life.

'Do you fancy going away for a couple of night's babe? x' She dared to ask by text.

The reply came back and Amy screwed her eyes shut not wanting to reveal his answer in case it was a refusal. Summoning up the courage she picked up her mobile phone with trembling fingers.

'What did you have in mind? x' His reply was short but straight to the point and Amy blushed as she again remembered the way his hands had felt on her body, the way his rock hard cock had brought her so much gratification, the way his lips had trailed soft, tantalizing, seductive kisses over every part of her sex starved body but most of all the way his mouth had claimed hers and somehow made it his own.

'A surprise :) xx.' She replied.

'Ok, yes, I'm game for that. x' Amy couldn't help but smile at her phone like a stupid teenager. The sex had been mind blowing and she wanted more, much more.

'Leave it with me. x' She hit the send button with determination.

Picking up her laptop she logged in and did a quick search on Google.

"Cottages to rent in the Lake District."

Scouring through the search list Amy selected a couple of options. Clicking on the first one a beautiful, very old stone cottage graced the screen. As she read the description Amy's first thought was wow.

"Gateway Cottage is a charming, luxury 17th century cottage and is equipped to an exceptionally high standard.

This lovely, rural cottage is situated down a quiet, cobbled lane and sits in its very own extensive gardens. The small village has two good pubs and a shop that stocks any necessary essentials.

The stable style front door of the cottage opens up into the wonderful, expansive kitchen and dining area. This lovely room is further highlighted by 2 adorable window-love seats which overlook the extensive gardens. The fully equipped kitchen has a brand new built in electric, fan oven, gas hob, separate fridge & freezer, washing machine, clothes dryer, dishwasher; microwave with 2nd oven built into it, and every kitchen utensils and piece of equipment you could possibly want to make your stay a very comfortable and enjoyable one.

The bright, sunny but cozy lounge has two brand new, sumptuous soft leather Italian sofas which are set around the roaring log fire. The French doors are south facing and look out into the private, enclosed, secluded garden which has a loveseat for two plus other garden furniture and a barbeque which is stored in the outside building. The lounge, as previously mentioned, has a lovely, original stone fireplace and lots of antiques. There is a television, DVD, CD player and radio plus a small collection of DVD's for your viewing pleasure. In the nook, under the stairs, you will notice a built in bookshelf with an array of books. During the day the lounge gets lots of sun and at night time it's a lovely cozy room to relax in front of the roaring log fire."

Amy had read enough! The log fire secured the deal for her and as she reached for her phone she felt that genuine smile once again as she pictured Jesse and his wonderful, sexy eyes.

Speaking to the owner she found that the cottage was available to rent for the next two nights. After quickly texting Chloe and Bethany Amy reached into her handbag to secure the booking with her debit card.

'Can you be ready for 1pm babe?' Now she couldn't help but smile, a smile which light up her entire face. She, Amy Lucas, was about to embark on an adventure, an adventure that had her stomach pitching and rolling about with nerves and excitement.

Amy was amazed at how game he was, after all, he hardly knew her yet was willing to spend the next two nights in her company. A finger of doubt began to stab at her brain – she hardly knew him! What if he turned out to be some sort of weirdo? A cottage in the middle of nowhere, was she insane? Having him in her home was risky enough but going to a cottage out in the sticks.......

'Fuck it!' She shouted into the empty space. 'I can do this, I want to do this, I need this.'

Running up the stairs she hastily grabbed a bag and started throwing in clothes and toiletries. Looking at her perfectly made up bed she reached for the black fur throw that lay underneath the mountain of decorative pillows. That would be perfect for in front of the fire she thought, a shy smile on her face.

As she ran the bath thoughts of his hands and lips roaming all over her body overtook her mind and as images of his eyes flooded her brain she knew that despite his age he was certainly all man.

'A man that knew how to please her very thoroughly.' She whispered to herself.

Amy ensured both her daughter's would be fine before starting the drive to Jesse's house to pick him up. She couldn't hold back the excitement she was feeling, this wasn't only an adventure for Jesse but for her also. She was stepping into unfamiliar waters, into territory completely alien to her. Part of her knew that what she was about to embark on was wrong but how could something that was wrong feel so right. Jesse made her feel like a woman again and so shoving every niggling little doubt out of her mind she carried on, exhilaration and nerves coursing throughout her body.

Approaching his house she reached for her mobile phone and dialed his number.

'I'm here.' Her mouth was suddenly dry as she fought to force the words out of her parched lips.

'Ok, I'm coming.' He replied disconnecting the call.

Amy watched as he walked up the driveway from his house towards her car, his overnight brown leather bag flung casually over his shoulder, a smile on his handsome face as the gravel beneath his feet crunched noisily. Opening the back door and placing his bag onto the seat she turned to look at him. It was the first time she had seen him since Bonfire night and as he returned her gaze she felt that very familiar magnetic pull of those amazing, sexy eyes.

Seating himself beside her, curiosity overtook him.

'Where are we going babe?' He questioned as he reached for her to place a tender kiss on her lips.

Reaching for the booking form and directions that she had printed off from the internet earlier she handed them to him, her hand briefly touching his fingertips. Immediately she felt the electricity and sexual pull of him, this almost stranger, a stranger that knew almost every inch of her body intimately. Amy raised her eyes to look at him briefly feeling the blush begin to take over her face as the heat spread rapidly throughout her body. Taking a deep breath she turned her attention back to the navigation system, pushing the kinky images from her mind for the time being.

Yes, this was going to be a very exciting two nights she thought to herself, a very promising two nights. Bring on the champagne!

CHAPTER TEN

Arriving at the cottage Amy and Jesse unloaded the car. Earlier that day, before she had picked Jesse up, Amy had been to the supermarket and bought plenty of food to keep the ever hungry man fed. She had been amazed at his enormous appetite. After demolishing the scrambled eggs and toast, the morning after Bonfire Night, he had gone on to eat a bowl of cereal only for an hour later to declare he was hungry again. Amy wanted to make sure that he didn't feel hungry during their stay, plus she secretly hoped they would both work up healthy appetites with lots of hot, passionate sex.

What's for tea?' He asked as he delved into the grocery bags piling the contents onto the work surface. Amy opened the refrigerator door and began to place the assortment of food on to the shelves. Moving to the other side of the kitchen she opened one of the wooden cabinet doors and began to place the rest of the groceries onto the bottom shelf.

'Well I drove us here so I thought you could cook.' She joked in reply, turning her head in his direction to see his reaction.

'No problem.' He replied gathering the bags together and tossing them into a drawer before disappearing into the fridge to inspect the contents.

'Well, I will leave you to it.' Amy replied. 'I'm off to investigate.' She added throwing a shy smile in his direction before disappearing up the staircase.

After familiarizing herself with the cottage Amy returned to the kitchen and hopped up onto one of the high, wooden stools that were placed around the breakfast bar watching with interest as Jesse began to cook their meal. Yet again he amazed her; he was not only talented in the bedroom but also in the kitchen. He was expertly cooking them steak with potatoes and vegetables and a peppercorn sauce.

'Oh I bet you burn the sauce.' Amy teased; fluttering her eyes at him in what she hoped was a suggestive and sexy manner, instantly berating herself silently as her shy nature returned with a vengeance.

'I bet I don't.' He replied, diligently stirring the creamy sauce whilst giving her a smile and a look that sent her heart beating wildly. She could hear and feel the thudding in her chest as the all too familiar heat began to spread across her face and chest before weaving its naughty path down in-between her legs. How the hell was he doing this?

Reaching for her bag in a bid to distract herself from the thoughts that were now overpowering her brain and body, Amy withdrew a plastic container and waved it in Jesse's direction.

'Guess what I've got for later?' A cheeky smile played easily on her mouth as she continued to wave her hand in front of him.

'What are they?' Jesse asked a puzzled look on his face.

'Sexual position playing cards, they were a divorce present from a friend.'

As Jesse reached for the cards Amy playfully waved his hand away.

'Now, now Mr Clayton, watch that sauce.' She playfully teased, moving her hand away from his outstretched one.

'The sauce will be fine.' he replied reaching out and grabbing the cards from her. As he carefully inspected them, turning each one over, he began to laugh. Looking up he noticed the deep, crimson blush that had spread across Amy's face which only made him laugh louder. She was peeping at him from behind her heavy fridge, not able to meet his eyes. 'I think we are going to have lots of fun Amy.' There was that "look" again, the one that stopped her dead and had the blood coursing through her body at an alarming rate. Damn he was so feckin hot!

'I wonder how many of the fifty two we can accomplish in two days.' She laughed nervously, desperately trying to hide her blushes and appear confident to the younger man before her.

Turning around to finish cooking the food Jesse smiled; a smile that drew her attention once again to his sexy, irresistible eyes.

'Your eyes drive me bloody mad, do you know that!' She whispered quietly.

Giving her a look that she thought would stop her heart from beating he turned his attention back to the food and began to plate up their dinner.

Amy found the food delicious, almost as delicious as the man seated at her side. They had decided to sit in the living room and as they ate in almost silence she wondered again how the next two days would unfold. She knew that she had stepped out and taken a huge risk but the sex and Jesse were too good to resist and even if after the two days it all ended, she knew that for the rest of her life she would remember the time she spent with him and how good he had made her feel about herself once again. The little bird that had been caged for so long was slowly and gently unfurling her delicate wings and testing the air for flight.

The anticipation made it difficult to swallow the mouthwatering food. As she cut up her steak she sneaked a sideways glance at Jesse and their eyes met. Gulping down the food before she choked she felt the blush spread once again across her cheekbones.

'Your eyes.' She whispered delicately.

'What about my eyes.' Jesse was looking at her so intensely that she had to look away.

'They drive me crazy.' Amy was beginning to feel uncomfortable as the heat began to spread throughout her body. Reaching for the remote control she flicked through the channels on the small television in a desperate bid to banish the thoughts that were creeping through her mind. What was this obsession that haunted her, how could a man's eyes have such an effect on her? She had never experienced anything like this before and knew that one look, one glance; the slightest touch could send her toppling over the edge.

Finishing the meal Amy collected the plates and placed them in the dishwasher. She could feel the nerves in her body begin to play their game, dancing and weaving, making her doubt herself once again. She looked over at the breakfast bar and spotted the discarded cards; smiling to herself she stood to her full height of just over five foot, puffing out her chest in a bid to install some confidence in herself she made her way to the bottom of the staircase before calling out to Jesse.

'I am just going upstairs babe, I have a surprise for you.'

'Oh yeh, what's that then?' Jesse appeared in the doorway an irresistible, sexy grin adorned his face. 'Is it something sexy to wear like we discussed?' He asked, that look once again in his eyes.

The day after their initial meeting they had continued to text one another. Jesse had casually mentioned that he liked kinky underwear and so smiling to herself, Amy paused before answering him.

'You will see.' She smiled seductively at him before walking up the stairs in the direction of the cottage's bathroom.

Gripping hold of the sink to steady herself Amy studied her face carefully in the mirror.

'Come on you can do this!' She told her reflection. Her stomach was churning, nerves were making her feel sick and she noticed that most of the colour had drained from her face. Closing her eyes she leant against the cool mirror as beads of sweat began to form on her brow and upper lip.

'Come on Amy, you have got a hot, sexy man downstairs who wants to fuck you til the sun comes up and then some, get a fucking grip you shit bag!' Pushing herself away from the mirror with a determination she didn't realise she possessed Amy pointed a trembling finger at her reflection.

'Just do it for fuck's sake girl.'

Taking a much needed gulp of air Amy reached for her bag and withdrew the contents. Earlier that day when she had been to the supermarket she had also nipped into the local lingerie shop. Pulling out the outrageously kinky, black, lace, crotch less body stocking Amy giggled to herself. Her stomach was still performing the god awful somersaults and so without another moments thought she began to undress before stepping into the shower.

CHAPTER ELEVEN

Taking a deep breath Amy descended the stairs to find Jesse seated at the breakfast bar. The look on his face as he took in the sexy outfit and high heeled black shiny boots that adorned her petite frame was priceless. Tiny little doubts had entered her mind earlier when she had walked into the shop to purchase something to wear but she knew these were not because of Jesse but down to the mental abuse she had suffered. Paul had done a very good job of shattering her self-confidence and so the look of pure lust that was clearly evident on Jesse's face was just what she needed.

'Wow!' Jesse exclaimed, a boyish yet sexy grin spread across his face and lit up those hot, steamy, sexy eyes.

Feeling nervous again Amy covered the distance between them quickly, the heels of her boots clicking noisily as she walked towards him on the slate floor.

'Do you approve Mr Clayton?' She asked in a low, husky voice, her eyes cast downwards to the floor.

'Oh Miss Lucas, yes!' Came his sexy reply.

Reaching bravely for the cards Amy opened the plastic container. Her tiny fingers were shaking so hard that she sent the contents and the container flying across the breakfast bar.

'Shit!' She exclaimed, as she felt the all too familiar burning begin once again as the blushes overtook her body claiming not only her face but her neck and chest.

'Are you nervous?' Jesse asked, reaching out for her hand.

'A little.' She quietly replied as she splayed her hands across the counter to collect the troublesome cards, not raising her eyes as she knew he would be watching her.

'Don't be, you look soooooo sexy.' His hands brushed over her behind causing her to inhale sharply, biting her top lip softly.

'So, which ones do you like?' She turned into his arms and closed her eyes briefly, enjoying the sensations that were now rippling throughout her tiny body as she inhaled the scent of him and felt his hands trail alluringly over her.

Taking the cards from her outstretched hand Jesse began to go through them one by one.

'Mmm I like the look of this one.' He murmured sexily, tossing one of the cards to the side.

'Shit!' Amy secretly thought as she gazed at him leaning against the counter. 'He is a fuckin hot piece of male ass!' Her responsible side scowled at her, this was not her character at all! Her body felt alive as visions of him inside her banished any rational thoughts she may have had.

Picking it up a small laugh escaped Amy's mouth as she looked at the sexual position depicted. The kitchen had two long counter tops and so the "Counter Top" card should be a breeze to accomplish. Although more advanced in years, Amy had led a very sheltered sex life, almost hating any physical contact before meeting Jesse. This young, very hot man was about to change all that and boy was she looking forward to it. The cards were meant as a bit of fun but Amy secretly knew that she needed something to hide her inexperience from this very talented young man.

They continued to look through the cards, selecting the ones they fancied trying out first.

'Well, we have our work cut out for us for the next two nights Jesse.' Amy nervously giggled.

'Better get started then.' he replied as he easily picked her up and carried her into the living room. Amy was squealing with delight as carried her through the kitchen in his strong arms.

As he placed her on one of the soft, leather brown sofas Amy saw the flicker of the roaring fire.

'Wow, you light the fire.' Amy was staring at the orange flames as they danced around in the hearth, hypnotized by their movement.

'I did it whilst you were upstairs babe.' He replied as his hands reached out and drew her to him.

His soft lips met her willing ones and as they kissed Amy felt as if once again her heart was about to stop beating. This was complete and utter madness but as his lips trailed down her neck and he lavished the soft skin with tantalizing kisses whilst gently drawing her flesh into his mouth all her self-confidence issues and doubts disappeared once again as her body was suddenly reborn, the heat spreading at an alarming rate as it coursed from the tip of her toes to the top of her head, saturating every inch of her in it's warm, seductive path.

Moving swiftly she straddled him, never loosing eye contact she placed her hands tenderly on the sides of his face before bending her neck so their lips could meet once again. Amy knew she could only hold his gaze for seconds, any longer and she would be putty in his hands and despite her need and want for him the icicle would always remain firmly stabbed in her heart, that she was sure of. This was sex. Hot, steamy, mind blowing sex! She was older but in his arms, his lips on her skin, age suddenly became just a number as their bodies molded into one.

'I love kissing you,' she whispered in to his ear, the tip of her tongue flicking out to tease his ear lobe.

'You turn me on so much,' he murmured back, his hands reaching into her chestnut hair before bringing her lips back down to his. She felt his hands leave her head and begin their trail over her shoulders and slowly down her back, their pace almost unbearable as his fingertips connected fleetingly with her torso.

Desire overtook Amy as she hungrily reached for his hands with her own, their mouths meet as they tasted and explored one another she heard the sound of her own and Jesse's breathing escalating as their need for one another grew with every passing second.

'How do you do this to me Jesse?' She asked a little bewildered, her hands all over him, her lips seeking out his.

No reply was necessary as their hands began their journey of seduction. Reaching up Jesse slid the delicate lace fabric from her shoulders exposing her breasts. As he took her left nipple into his mouth and gently sucked she arched her back as the raw hunger that was now rippling throughout her body engulfed her. Looking up their eyes met briefly and Amy heard the sharp intake of air she made as Jesse bent his head once again to deliver the same ecstatic sensations to her right nipple. His tongue swirled around the nerve filled bud sending maddening little pulses deep down, straight to her groin.

Their hands roamed over each other's bodies and as she reached down to unbutton his pants she felt how hard he was and knew she wanted to feel him inside her and in her mouth with a fervor that was unsurpassable.

Never taking her eyes away from him she rose to her feet, gripping the sides of his jeans she tucked them down before completely removing them. Reaching up she trailed her fingers delicately along the waistband of his grey, tight fitting Calvin Klein boxer shorts.

'Fuck!' She silently thought. 'He's a god! This man before me is perfect!'

Softly she moved one finger to the inside of the band before slowly moving it side to side, dipping down just a little further to feel the head of his hard, swollen cock.

'These have got to come off!' She declared, removing them swiftly with strangely deft hands.

Straddling him once again she felt him between her legs and knew that no matter how much she wanted him she had to hold back just a little while longer. What Amy really wanted was to grab his hard cock in her hand and push herself down on to him so he filled her as only he could then fuck him so she could relieve some of the sexual frustration and tension that had been building up since she had picked him up! Suddenly the little bird was soaring, high in the sky, feeling the wind in her wings as she rose higher and higher.

'Hold back, hold back Amy.' She silently cursed to herself as she made an effort to slow her racing heart.

Reaching for the hem of his t shirt she tucked it up as he raised his arms to aid its removal she sighed as his firm, lean, tanned torso was revealed. Her hands were all over his bare skin as she reveled in the feel of his young, firm flesh. Fuck he was so sexy, so damn fucking sexy, Amy thought to herself. The way her hands glided over his smooth body and his back, wow, she was going to explode!

Reaching for her Jesse gathered her into his arms before smoothly laying her down so he was positioned over her, his lips so close to hers. Reaching up he gently brushed her hair away from her blue eyes,

eyes that she knew burned with a fierce passion for this man. Amy had always worn a heavy fringe; it was her way of defending herself somehow and hiding her feelings, fears and the scar. This gentlest of touches left her feeling vulnerable so reaching up she quickly ruffled her hair back into place and prayed he didn't notice.

'You need to catch up.' His husky voice only increased the sexual, raw emotions that were starting to course through her once again.

Taking hold of the black lace he drew the fabric down her body slowly, his lips following their path until Amy lay naked before him. As his fingers trailed along her skin she felt the fire increasing until finally he sought out her secret place. Teasing her with his fingers he gently stroked her and as she felt herself arch with desire she begged for him to take her.

'Please Jesse.' She pleaded. 'Please. I want to feel you inside me.'

As he placed himself above her she closed her eyes with sweet anticipation.

'Not yet.' He whispered into her ear, his breath sending tiny ripples straight to her groin.

'Please!' Her eyes flew open, lust written all over her face as she began to squirm beneath him.

'No.' Never taking his eyes away from her he moved himself down her body, replacing his fingers with his mouth.

'Oh....My.....Feckin.....God!' She cried as his mouth connected with her sex.

Amy felt as if she was about to explode as she felt his fingers and tongue on her throbbing clitoris. Jesse lazily trailed his tongue around her swollen bud before taking it into his mouth and sucking gently. His fingers were teasing her entrance and as she tried to move he pinned her down gently.

'Not yet.' He sexily scolded her. 'I want to make you come with my mouth.'

No further words were necessary as Amy forgot her embarrassment and gave in to the delicious sensations that Jesse was creating with his tongue and fingers. Slowly he placed two fingers inside her, stretching her, caressing the inner walls of her vagina whilst his tongue weaved its own special kind of magic on her clitoris.

Small ripples began to pulse through her as she lay back and gave herself up to his mouth, the delicious sensations overtaking and as she came she moaned loudly her hands clenched into fists at her sides, afraid to touch Jesse in case she inflicted pain upon him, her passion was that intense and burning.

Looking up from in-between her legs he gave her a lazy, sexy smile and "that look" again with his eyes. Placing her hands on either side of his head she gently pulled him up her body until she could taste herself on his soft lips.

'I want you Jesse.' She breathed. 'I want you so much.'

Drawing himself back he positioned himself over her. His eyes burning into hers and as he entered her she came again, long, heavenly waves washing over her as he rode her hard, his cock filling her deeply and completely.

'Oh…. My…. God!' She called out as he lifted her legs and placed them on his chest. Amy felt him so deep within her, each stroke creating a heat so intense that she felt as if she would stop breathing, the sensations rampaged her entire being as she called out again and again in pure ecstasy, the deep contractions of her orgasm taking over her body making her shudder beneath him.

The Eyes 49

CHAPTER TWELVE

'I haven't finished with you yet.' Jesse whispered in her ear as he unhurriedly teased her neck with his lips and fingers. 'Turn over.' He instructed gently.

Lying on her stomach Amy wondered what on earth he was going to do, tiny shreds of fear travelled up her spine as her imagination shot off wildly in all directions. As she felt his fingertips begin to caress her back she began to relax and willingly gave in to the sensations he was creating throughout her body as he gently kneaded her muscles with his expert fingers.

'Lift your arse up, I want to fuck you from behind.' Shit his voice was so sexy; it made her feel wild and brave as his words echoed around her head.

Doing as she was bid Amy raised herself onto her knees. She felt exposed as she felt Jesse move slightly back.

'Jesse.' She whispered, reaching out for him.

'Amy you have a very, very sexy arse.' Jesse said, his fingers brushing the soft flesh of her behind seductively. 'And your legs…..' His voice trailed off as his fingers leisurely stroked the back of her thighs, tempting her, teasing her as he moved his fingers up and down, fleetingly touching her intimately before withdrawing back to her legs and bottom once more. Amy felt the intense heat snaking its way throughout her body as each touch sent her further and further towards the edge, spiraling out of control she bite her fist hard to quell the screams of passion that so desperately wanted to escape from her body.

'Please Jesse, I want to feel you!' Amy screamed not sure how much more she could take.

'So impatient.' He replied as he thrust his fingers inside of her, spreading them apart he massaged her secret, warm, wet place as she grinded herself back onto him.

Gasping loudly Amy concentrated hard on the movement of his fingers and knew that if he carried on the sweet rhythm he was creating she would explode around them within seconds. Sensing her rising desire Jesse withdrew his fingers.

Don't, please don't stop!' Amy wailed. 'Jesse!'

'Sssshhh.' Jesse instructed as he slammed into her hard, his steel cock plunging deep within her making her detonate around him in long, fathomless waves. Again she cried out words of pleasure as he continued to thrust into her making her come again and again. Amy matched every thrust with her own, opening up, allowing him access to the very depths of her inner self. As she felt his pace quicken and his hands tighten around her hips she knew he was almost there and so grinding back onto him she rode her own waves until she felt the first spasms of his orgasm. As he ejaculated deep within her she felt the warm semen explode, clenching her vaginal muscles with every ounce of strength she possessed she held him tight, draining every last drop of orgasm out of Jesse's body.

They collapsed in a heap, their breathing sharp and ragged as each fought to control their gasping lungs. Shifting onto his back, Jesse gathered her into his arms taking her with him so her head lay across his chest. She could hear his heart hammering as she lightly rested her head, gently placing her hand over it so she could feel the centre of his body beat.

'How do you do it babe?' She asked a bewildered look on her face. Never in all her years had she been so utterly satisfied, so completely and utterly fucked.

'I just do.' He replied. 'I have a knack.' A cheeky smile spread across his face which glowed with the reflection of the flames from the roaring fire.

'Have you had a sex instructor?' She joked bursting into laughter.

'No!' He laughed back.

She could still hear the steady beating of his heart and as she gazed at the burning fire Amy felt as if she had gone to heaven. As she watched the orange flickers disappear up the chimney her mind and body were united in peace, a peace she had craved for many, many years.

'I feel so relaxed.' She murmured, her eyes closing as the heat from the fire washed over her body.

Jesse squeezed her lightly.

'Are you hungry Jesse?' She asked, raising her head to look at his handsome face. There was that dimple again and god how she still wanted to stick her finger in it.

A grin was quick to appear on his lips.

'What do you think!?' He replied.

'I don't know why I bother asking babe. Do you want me to make you something to eat?' She laughed. Glancing at the clock she noticed just over four hours had passed since they had eaten. 'My god!' She exclaimed. 'Have you seen the time? I didn't realize we had been err mm... busy for so long.' She giggled as she felt herself begin to blush.

Stretching leisurely she slowly got up from the floor and wandered into the kitchen, picking up the discarded clothes as she went she shrugged into Jesse's t shirt.

'Do you want a drink?' She called. 'I'm having a beer.'

Jesse sauntered naked into the kitchen, his magnificent, toned and athletic body sending shivers up her spine once again not to mention the all too familiar heat that was rapidly making its journey across her face and chest.

'Can you please put some clothes on?' Amy cried, trying to avoid looking at him. 'You are just too much!'

Laughing Jesse sat down on one of the stools.

'No and please babe, I'll have a beer too.' He replied. 'So how many of these do you thing we have accomplished?' He was waving the cards in her direction.

'I don't know.' She laughed. 'Let me just finish making these sandwiches and we can go through them.' Averting her eyes from his intense ones she set about making the food.

The atmosphere was light and jovial as they sat and ate whilst leafing through the playing cards. Amy was acutely aware of the damned fact that Jesse was sat opposite her naked and so the red, hot fire of her blushes stayed firmly in place, scorching her face and chest.

'Mmmm I guess we have made a good start babe.' Amy giggled taking a large gulp of her beer. She was trying her best to remain calm but failing miserably due to the fact that she couldn't quite shut off the images that were dancing around her head.

'Well, we still have this counter top teaser card Amy.' He replied, leaning forward and running his hands slowly over the smooth, black work surface.

Placing her bottle of beer down, she took hold of the card from his outstretched hands. Waving it in front of him Amy jumped up and sat on the work counter. Feeling a sudden surge of bravery she spread her legs slowly and seductively, beckoning to Jesse with her finger.

'Come here babe.' She whispered as she leisurely ran her fingertips up and down her thighs before pushing her legs forcefully wider for him.

As he came towards her she grabbed him by the arms pulling him in-between her legs. Wrapping her tanned limbs around his waist Amy pulled him closer to her, her lips seeking his, desire heavy in her eyes as she reached down and guided his erect cock towards her. As she felt him enter her slowly she moaned loudly as once again he possessed and filled her body completely.

CHAPTER THIRTEEN

The pair never left the cottage for two days and spent their entire time pleasuring one another totally. They had talked too and Amy was once again surprised by Jesse. He was not only handsome but shit he had brains too. They had covered a variety of subjects and Amy had even felt confident enough to share a little about herself. Usually she was a very shy and private person, keeping her woes to herself but as Jesse had gently probed her, asking her questions about her marriage and earlier life she had opened up just a little and was surprised that it wasn't as painful as she originally thought it would be. She knew that it was Jesse's gentle way of encouraging her but she didn't want to reveal too much, Jesse would run for the hills, of that she was certain. This was a fling, sex; he didn't need to know about her past. He was so young and Amy knew that her past had to stay firmly locked away. They were her scars to wear, not his and there was no way that Amy was going to put any of her heartbreaking past onto this wonderful, young man. He was untainted and Amy decided firmly, no matter how hard he tried, no matter how persuasive his questioning became, that he would stay that way. There were times that even she couldn't bear her past life and the horrific memories it held. No! Her scars and her's alone.

As Amy checked around the cottage on their last morning to make sure she had packed everything she felt a sudden sadness wash over her. She had experienced something very new, something very magical and intense and as she watched Jesse descend the staircase she hoped they would be able to meet again.

'Have you got everything you brought babe?' She asked, smiling softly at him.

'Yes and I checked the bedroom and the bathroom, everything is packed.' Jesse replied.

'Time to go then I guess.' Amy tried to force herself to smile. This was goodbye but she had enjoyed the time she had spent with Jesse and didn't want it to end just yet. She was having the time of her life and Jesse made her smile….. oh the orgasms, she could never forget the mind blowing orgasms that had shattered her tiny body.

'What's the matter babe?' Jesse asked, expertly reading the expression on her face as he came towards her, his hands reaching for hers.

'I have had the best time of my life Jesse, thank you. I will never forget this and I guess I'm sad that it has to end.' She replied bending her head to cast her eyes towards the floor.

'This is just the beginning.' He replied, hooking his finger underneath her chin to softly raise her head. 'I like this, this situation, its sweet. Once we are home I would like to see you again Amy, we are having a good time, enjoying one another's company so why the hell not.' Jesse said, smiling at her.

Amy felt her stomach lurch and the grin that was now on her face made her blue eyes light up, the sparkle returning brightly.

'I would like that Jesse.' She said. 'I would like that very much.' Holding on to his hands she closed the space between them, standing on her tiptoes she placed her arms around his neck, gently placing her lips on his for the briefest of kisses. 'I guess it is time to go now.'

CHAPTER FOURTEEN

During the journey home Amy's mobile phone sprang to life. For the last two days the reception had been virtually nonexistent and so she had turned it off knowing that both her daughters were safe and banished it to the realms of her handbag.

'Bloody hell, 19 text messages!' She exclaimed as her phone continued to beep relentlessly.

'Who are they all from?' Jesse laughed in reply, fiddling with his own mobile as it too came to live.

'One guess and speak of the devil.' She replied as her phone began to ring. Pulling over to the side of the road Amy answered her mobile.

'Hello Jen.' She said turning to smile at Jesse.

'Oh hello, and just where the hell have you been? Why haven't you been answering your phone Mrs?' Jen huffed, clearly angry that she hadn't been able to reach her friend although Amy knew that really she had been afraid that something was wrong.

Amy heard the laughter escaping from her lips.

'Erm, I have been somewhere with no phone reception Jen.' She giggled in response.

'Oh yeh! Who with? Oh don't tell me, Jesse!' Amy could hear the excitement in Jen's voice and started to feel the first stirrings of a blush begin to creep across her cheeks.

'Yes with Jesse.' She replied, trying to keep her voice steady.

Turning to look at the man beside her briefly, Amy noticed he was smiling.

'Hello Jen.' He shouted into the phone.

'Right Amy, I want all the details, you better get your skinny butt round here pronto!' Jen said the excitement clearly evident in her voice. 'Oh and tell Jesse I said hi back.'

'Ok, ok.' Amy giggled in response. 'We are on our way home. I will probably be another hour or so.'

'Good, drive fast but drive safe. I can't bloody wait!' She exclaimed.

Laughing Amy hung up the phone and turned to Jesse.

'Don't worry I won't tell her everything, some things are meant to be private. Is that alright with you?' Amy didn't want Jesse to think that she would divulge all the intimate details to her dearest friend although now she thought about it she wondered what tales Jessie would tell to his own friends.

'Of course.' He smiled in response. 'And Amy, what happens between us is between us, I won't be discussing this with my mates.' He astounded her, how the hell did he know what she had been thinking only moments before!

They chatted for the remainder of the journey home and as Amy once again pulled the car up in front of Jesse's house she felt the familiar pull of him. Leaning towards him she gently kissed him goodbye.

'I'll text you later.' He said before planting another quick kiss on her ready lips.

'Bye Jesse and thank you.' She whispered reaching her hand out to touch his.

'No, thank you Amy. I've had a really good time with you.' He replied squeezing her hand as he kissed her once again on the tip of her nose before opening the car door.

As she watched him walk up the driveway to his home she wanted to follow him, pull him into her arms for one last kiss.

'Damn those sexy eyes!' She exclaimed to herself.

Releasing the handbrake she took one last glance before driving off to visit her friend.

Amy was greeted by a smiling, laughing Jen who couldn't seem to sit still.

'Well?' Jen asked, placing her hands on her hips in mock exasperation. Earlier she could have practically throttled her little friend, now, well, the look on Amy's face told her that everything was well in her friend's world.

'Well what?' Amy threw back, a devilish smile on her face, knowing full well that she was tormenting her best friend.

'You sod off for two nights, come back with that god forsaken fucking twinkle in your bloody eyes and sit there and say well what!

Where did you go for starters?' Jen was now bobbing up and down on the sofa, crossing and uncrossing her legs.

'Why can't you sit bloody still?' Amy chuckled. 'Do you need to pee?' She joked, a mock expression of shock on her face.

'Because I'm excited you moron!' She replied.

Amy began to tell Jen all about the cottage, explaining in detail the old, wooden beams and open fire. It had been the most charming and beautiful building that Amy had ever seen and she had committed every room to memory.

'Will you just get on with it, please!' Jen wailed. 'I don't want a fucking floor plan of the cottage; I want to know what you and Jesse got up to, I want to know about the sex!' She declared, beginning to get more than a little frustrated at Amy.

'We had mind blowing, wonderful sex! There are you satisfied?' Amy grinned, unable to keep her new adventure to herself any longer. What she really wanted to say was 'Fuck me Jen, he blew me out of the fucking water! Shit that man is talented and I want more of his delicious, hard, steel like cock if you don't mind!' Pinching herself secretly Amy silently vowed to be good.

'No!' Jen retorted. 'But it's a start.'

'You are bad, do you know that Jen.' Amy laughed, unable to hide her excitement. She was travelling down a new path and for now it felt like the path to heaven.

'I know, I know but hey, my best mate has landed herself a hunk, a young hunk at that. My friend, who said that no man would ever get near her again! I feel like Mrs Match Maker.' Jen laughed.

'What can I say in my defense?' Amy replied, throwing her hands up in the air. 'I have said it before; it's his bloody eyes, which are green by the way! Most of the time I find myself having to look away from him.' Amy sighed as images of Jesse coursed into her mind. Finally she had been able to meet his gaze for long enough to determine the colour of those sexy, wonderful eyes. They were an amazing shade of emerald green that smoldered when he wore his "special look" and light up whenever he smiled. Whenever he looked at her something deep within Amy would stir, that was why she had to force herself to look away. She liked him, she wanted him, he made her feel alive and sexy, but the icicle was still firmly in her heart and nothing would make her change her mind and allow her heart to open to another man.

'Well I'm just glad that you are smiling again hun. It's so good to see you happy, genuinely happy I mean. I guess that is what multiple orgasms do for you hey.' She joked.

Amy was about to reply when her phone bleeped signaling a message had arrived. Reaching for it she felt the blush spread across her face.

'Oh, I'm guessing from the expression on your face and the colour of your cheeks that the text is from the one and only Jesse!' Jen was rolling about on the sofa laughing so hard that tears were rolling down her face.

'Piss off Jen!' Amy retorted turning her back to her friend to try and hide the small smile that was threatening to escape.

'Well what is he saying, tell me, don't be so bloody spiteful?' Jen said trying to wear her best serious expression on her beautiful face.

'Not telling you.' Amy replied a smirk on her face as she swirled around to face her friend.

'Bitch! You are sooo mean; you are depriving me of the juicy stuff.' Jen huffed, stamping her feet loudly, her mouth set in a grim line.

Re-reading the message Amy debated on whether to share it with her friend.

'He just said he had an amazing time, that's all.' Amy divulged.

'So why the blush Mrs.' Jen retorted knowing full well that Amy was hiding something from her.

'I don't know! Perhaps because every time I fucking think of him I want to jump him and have mad, passionate sex! There I have said it, are you satisfied? And please stop with the Mrs, its Miss now!' Amy giggled.

'Very!' Came Jen's fast reply. 'Seriously Amy, do you know how good it is to see you happy, the sparkle has come back into your eyes, look how blue they look, how alive.' Jen leaned forward and grabbed her friend in a tight embrace. 'I just want you to be happy Amy.' She mumbled, tears of emotion glistening in her eyes. 'You are a very special woman Amy and deserve a bit of happiness; this is your time to flourish and bloom Sweetie.'

'Will you be quiet woman! You're going to have me crying in a minute.' Amy tried to make the conversation light again as she tried to fight back the tears that were threatening to fall. 'Well I had better be going Jen and the answer to your unspoken question is yes, the icicle is definitely still there, and stay it friggin will!'

'You are no fun at all, do you know that Amy? You remember these words Mrs. One day that icicle will melt and those tungsten walls will come crashing down around your tiny size two feet!'

'Pft, whatever!' Amy snorted in reply, dismissing Jen's silly idea straight away. Jesse was great, he had brought her body alive and created feelings and sensations that had her mind in turmoil but never again would a man have her heart, it was hers and hers alone.

The two women hugged tightly both smiling, Jen because her friend seemed happy at last and Amy because she felt the happiest she had in years.

CHAPTER FIFTEEN

As the weeks passed by Amy and Jesse continued to see one another and Saturday nights became their own private time together. Chloe and Bethany both had boyfriends so that left Amy with the house to herself during the weekends. Every week the pair would make plans for their evening together, Amy often surprising Jesse with some new, sexy lingerie she had purchased.

'You look happy mum.' Bethany said as she poked her head around her mother's bedroom door. 'Are you seeing Jesse tonight?' She asked.

'Yes I am baby girl.' Amy responded, the smile ever present now on her face which had delicately changed over the last few weeks, she looked happy but most of all her face wore the gentle expression of peace.

Amy had decided to keep her daughter's and Jesse separate, not wanting to expose her children to the new and exciting life she was leading. This was her own private time, her own world where she was able to laugh and enjoy Jesse's company not to mention the fabulous sex they had. She had sat both the girls down when she had returned from the cottage and told them about Jesse. At first they had both been shocked at the age gap but seeing their mother so happy after all the years of abuse and misery they both decided that maybe it wasn't such a bad situation after all.

Doubts had become second nature to Amy since meeting Jesse. She constantly worried about the age gap wondering what on earth Jesse saw when he looked at her. She would agonize for days after seeing him but then as soon as those magnetic, enticing green eyes looked at her once again they all melted away, disappearing, totally forgotten until the next finger of doubt stabbed hurtfully at her brain, reminding her that she should really be acting more responsibly.

For the last few years Amy had occasionally smoking cannabis to help the pain in her back. The violent attacks that she had suffered at the hands of her husband had permanently injured her lower spine with two discs collapsing trapping the nerves. For days she would be in agony, hardly able to function until she had discovered, with the advice of her friend the medicinal, analgesic properties of this wonderful plant. Since meeting Jesse and finding out that he also enjoyed the occasional smoke they had enjoyed getting high together and Amy had been amazed at how relaxed and passionate the sex had become, Jesse took her to new heights and each encounter left her breathless and wanting more. Every emotion and feeling became highly tuned but for Amy the relaxing benefits of the marijuana helped her self-confidence, her shyness almost totally disappearing when she had smoked the marvelous plant.

As Christmas approached Amy had never felt happier with her life. Her daughter's had grown into beautiful, young women with lives of their own, her ex-husband was still in prison and so her and Jesse found that they were spending more and more time together, often meeting during the week as well as maintaining their Saturday night liaison.

'I can't seem to get enough of you.' She murmured as she lay in his arms after they had finished satisfying one another for hours.

'Me neither.' He replied, squeezing her softly to him.

As Amy snuggled into him she felt herself drifting off to sleep, a blissful, welcoming sleep where nightmares were banished and pleasant dreams visited, all thoughts and memories of her past life and the torment and pain she had experienced firmly shut away.

Life was good these days, Amy always seemed to be either smiling or laughing and she knew the reason for this was Jesse, the man with the most captivating, green, sexy eyes she had ever seen, the man who satisfied her beyond her wildest dreams; marijuana or not, the man who was slowly but surely gaining her trust and dare she even say it, her heart.........

For the last week Amy had battled with her feelings and analyzing them had become second nature to her. As she picked apart her thoughts and emotions she knew that she was falling in love with Jesse and even though she tried to fight every single one of them she knew that it was impossible, their paths had crossed for a reason and who was she to deprive herself of what she was feeling? This amazing man with his breathtaking eyes and kind, gentle nature had captured her heart; a heart that had been broken and hurt but a heart that she now knew could love and feel again. Jesse, with his kind and gentle ways, had gradually melted the icicle and the tungsten walls were slowly but surely falling down leaving her heart, soul and mind free to experience love once again.

Amy daily tormented herself with her thoughts and with just a little under a week before Christmas she decided to confide in her best friend, her sole confident for advice on what she should do.

'Jen, I am in trouble, big trouble!' Amy cried. 'I need help!'

'What do you mean honey?' Her friend replied, a concerned look on her face. 'Fuck me! Don't tell me you are pregnant!'

'Jen you moron, I had a bleedin hysterectomy after I had Bethany, it's bloody impossible for me to get pregnant but seriously I am falling for him Jen.' Amy whispered the last part which was almost inaudible to her friend. 'And I don't know what the hell to do! Part of me wants to carry on but a bigger part wants to run as far away as I can, as fast as I can. I'm scared Jen, he's too young!'

'I don't understand what the problem is Sweetie.' Jen replied. He is a good man who treats you well, makes you smile, and gives you the most amazing orgasms. Why are you tormenting yourself like this?' Jen grabbed hold of her friend's hand in a bid to instill some confidence in her.

'Oh I don't know Jen!' Amy replied emphatically. 'It all comes back to the age gap. Again and again it's all about the age! What the hell am I doing?' She questioned, tears forming in her blue eyes. 'I should know better at my age!'

'I'll tell you what you are doing. You are having the time of your life, enjoying the company of a man, having a sex life, laughing, smiling, need I go on? Listen honey, age is just a number.'

'I know, I know.' Amy responded. 'But he is so bloody young. This could never work Jen.'

'Why not?' Jen replied, a stern look on her face. How could she make her little friend understand? The transformation in the woman before her astounded Jen and all she had ever wanted for Amy was peace and happiness and finally that was within her reach.

'Because of the age difference, I mean come on Jen, think about it.' Amy could feel the tears of frustration that had been forming in her eyes begin to run steadily down her face. 'Fuck why does he have to be so young, in every other way he seems bloody perfect!'

'Do you want my advice Amy?' Jen asked, reaching for her friends other hand and taking it firmly in her own.

'Please, I can't think straight.' Amy cried. 'I don't know what to do Jen.'

'Do you want to tell him how you feel Amy?' Jen questioned hoping that her friend was brave enough to say yes, she needed this, fuck she deserved this!

'Hell, I don't know. Part of me wants to be honest with him but a bigger part is so afraid that I will scare him away. I have always been honest with him Jen, which at times has been hard, especially when he has asked me about my past. I'm not even sure what I am feeling, I'm so afraid Jen.' Tears began to flow steadily down Amy's face as she allowed the misery to overtake her. 'When I'm with him I am so happy, we get on so well and no, it's not just about the sex. When I'm not with him I actually miss him Jen, how the fuck has this happened to me, why have I allowed myself to fall like this?' Amy sobbed.

Where was the strong, independent woman that she had fought so hard to create, the woman that would never allow another man to hurt her? Amy pleaded silently for her to return so she may banish this soft natured, brave and sexy woman that had slowly replaced her.

'If you keep this inside, to yourself, it is going to burn you Amy. Tell him, Jesse is wise beyond his years honey but leave it until after Christmas, it's a sentimental bloody time as it is.' Jen wore a satisfied smile on her face feeling as if she had solved all of Amy's problems with her one single sentence.

'Ok, I will, I promise Jen. You say he is "wise beyond his years" well I only hope that perhaps he may have realized how I feel to make this a bit easier on me. I'm literally shitting myself Jen.' Amy declared as her hands began to shake violently.

When she had embarked on this new and exciting adventure she was determined to keep Jesse at arm's length. As she had grown to know him and his gentle nature it hadn't been difficult to fall and falling hard she was. Her thoughts were tumbling around her, not making any sense whatsoever as she plummeted towards what she could only conclude would end with her heart being broken.

'Have you any idea how he feels Amy?' Jen asked quietly. 'Mind you.' She added. 'You are a bit dense when it comes to men!'

'No and thanks a bloody lot!' Replied Amy, the frustration clearly evident in her voice and on her face. 'The way he looks at me, the way he kisses me, oh fuck Jen, I just don't friggin know, I'm no expert! For all I know this all could be a game to him – "Oh look at me, I'm shagging an older woman, I mean he has called me a "milf" on more than one occasion! Hell Jen what am I doing?' Amy was becoming hysterical as a foreign sense of reality began to peck away at her. Could it be possible that for Jesse she was merely a conquest, something to brag and cheapen to his mates?

'Calm down Sweetie.' Jen replied, grasping her friend in a bear like embrace. 'Everything will be fine, things happen for a reason and I'm positive you will be fine, you just need a massive injection of self-confidence Miss.' Amy couldn't help but smile as Jen said "Miss."

'I will be fine. I can do this; I am going to do this!' Amy jumped up from the sofa dragging her friend with her. 'I am in love Jen…. Jen I'm fucking in love!' She shouted as she wiped away the remains of the tears she had shed just moments earlier.

'Yes you can Amy.' Jen replied. 'You just remember lady, you deserve this. You have been through that much shit, had your confidence destroyed so badly and frankly spent the last God knows how many years being beaten the shit out of. Yes, you can do this. One word Sweetie, one word, ENJOY.'

As Amy left Jen's her worries seemed a little easier. She would tell Jesse how she felt after the festive period had past; she just hoped he didn't run a mile. Since first meeting Jesse she had changed so much as a person and a woman. The smile that light up her blue eyes was genuine, not the dull, forced smile of years gone by. Her confidence had soared although there were still times that she looked in the mirror and wondered what Jesse saw in her. As soon as he began touching her body the flames overtook the doubts, yes, she was going to reveal her feelings to him but for now they had to remain a secret, her secret. She, Amy Lucas was in love with champagne.

CHAPTER SIXTEEN

'Chloe, Mark is here.' Amy shouted up the stairs as she walked to the front door. 'Hi Mark, I thing Chloe is almost ready.' She laughed walking back into the living room.

'Coming.' Chloe yelled down the stairs. 'Two minutes.' She added.

As Chloe appeared in the living room she noticed the special look that Mark threw her way and knew that her daughter was deeply adored by him.

Hugging her daughter close to her Amy whispered into her ear.

'I love you so much. You look beautiful.' Her long, dark hair hung in soft waves, her dark eyes looked sensational with the smoky make up she had applied. Standing back, Amy eyes swept over her eldest child.

'You look stunning, that dress is perfect for you Chloe.' The short, figure hugging midnight blue dress suited her tiny frame perfectly.

'Thanks Mum.' She replied. 'I love you so much, have a wonderful time tonight, you deserve it and you look beautiful.'

Taking her daughter once more into her arms Amy gave her a final hug.

'You too baby cakes. See you tomorrow. Look after her Mark.' She added, reaching out to give him a hug also. 'Have a good time tonight and Merry Christmas.'

Waving goodbye to the young couple Amy sighed softly to herself. Her daughters were her world. She had tried her best to protect them over the years but feelings of guilt would always sit heavily in her heart. She could have been a better parent, she could have been stronger.......

Shaking her head to banish the negative thoughts from her mind she checked her watch and gasped as she noticed the time.

'Bethany have you got everything you need?' Amy shouted up the stairs. 'Please hurry up, I'm running late as it is baby girl.' She added picking up her bags.

'Coming.' Bethany yelled in reply.

'For God's sake Bethany, how bloody long does it take one little person to get ready!' Amy laughed as Bethany came sauntering down the stairs in her high heeled shoes. 'You look amazing.' She added as she studied her daughter carefully. Her long, chestnut hair was wound into a tight bun which sat on top of her head, her dress was short and fitted, the vivid red colour suiting her perfectly, matching the lipstick she wore on her pouting mouth.

'Thank you mum, I can't wait to get to the party, it's going to be epic.' She said, excitedly clapping her hands together.

Amy looked at her youngest daughter, pride and love written all over her peaceful face.

'Well let's get going shall we.' Amy replied. 'Now have you got everything and have you turned off your hair straighteners Bethany?'

'Yes mum, don't worry.' Bethany replied as the women walked towards the front door.

As Amy reversed off the driveway Bethany turned and smiled at her mother.

'Mum, this is the first Christmas Eve we have all spent apart and I just want to say you look beautiful and I hope you have a really good time tonight.'

Stepping on the brake and unclipping her seatbelt, Amy turned and gathered her youngest daughter into her arms, cradling her to her chest, inhaling the scent from her hair.

'Thank you Bethany, that means a lot.' She murmured. 'Right let's get going.' She said releasing her daughter before fastening her seatbelt once again and releasing the handbrake.

Twenty minutes later, after dropping Bethany at her boyfriend's Amy was finally on her way to the hotel that they had booked for the night. Excitement coursed through her body as she felt the very familiar sensations she experienced every time she thought about Jesse. Amy knew she had allowed him to break down each of her walls and it had been so painless except for the torment she put herself through on a daily basis over the age difference. She completely trusted Jesse and knew he would never hurt her physically, her heart was a different matter, that lay, very delicately in his hands and as she remembered her promise to Jen she knew it was only a matter of days now before she told him how she felt, she only hoped that for tonight she could keep her mouth firmly shut.

As she pulled into the hotel car park her mobile phone sprang to life. Reaching into her handbag she retrieved her phone and found a missed call from Jen followed by five texts messages.

'Jen, are you ok?' She asked as her friend answered her return call almost immediately.

'Yes honey, I just wanted to say have a lovely evening but remember not tonight Amy, wait beautiful lady, be patient.' Jen closed her eyes whilst she waited for her friend's reply and prayed that she would do the right thing.

'I promise.' Amy replied. 'Thank you Jen, you are a good friend and I love you to pieces.'

'I love you more.' Jen laughed in response. 'Now go and have a good time and make sure Jesse gives you plenty of those mind blowing fucking orgasms. We will see you tomorrow.'

'Ho ho friggin ho. Merry Christmas to me, let's hope my own personal St. Nick brings me lots and lots of orgasms cos I sure have my stockings on ready to go.' Amy giggled in response.

'Bad, bad girl!' Jen laughed. 'Now go and check into that bleedin hotel, I don't want to hear from you until tomorrow. Merry Christmas Sweetie.'

'Merry Christmas honey and have a good night yourself Jen. We will be there about 2ish tomorrow, is that ok with you all?' Jen and David had invited Amy and the girls for their Christmas day lunch and Amy was really looking forward to sitting around the table with their families the next day but first she had a wonderful night alone with Jesse in a beautiful hotel and she planned on making the most of it.

'That's fine. Have a good night. Love you.' Before Amy could respond Jen hung up the phone.

As she walked into the hotel foyer Amy noticed the huge, twinkling Christmas tree and decorations that adorned the lobby and smiled to herself, now it felt like Christmas.

'Hi, I have a booking under the name of Clayton and Lucas.' Amy said, smiling at the waiting receptionist.

'One minute please Mrs Lucas.' The receptionist replied before turning her attention to the computer screen that sat in front of her. 'Here we are. Would you care to set up a tab for your room?'

'Yes please. What time are you working until?' Amy asked feeling sorry that the pretty, young, red headed woman was not out on the town celebrating the festive season with her friends.

'Midnight.' She replied handing Amy the key to the room whilst giving her the directions to locate it. 'Once you have opened the door you will notice a small box on the left wall, insert the card and the lights will come on automatically.'

'Thank you and Merry Christmas. I hope you get some time off so you can enjoy it.' Amy smiled softly at the receptionist before picking up her overnight bag.

Following the directions given to her Amy walked across the marble foyer, her shiny, black stilettos tapping loudly as she walked. As she took the corridor to the left the rhythmic noise from her shoes disappeared as her feet hit the brown and beige checked carpet. Glancing up at the doors she searched for room 29 and realised she was practically stood next to it.

Inserting the card into the lock Amy opened the door and stepped back in amazement as the lights came on and she took in the size of the enormous bed.

'Wow!' She said out loud to herself as she sprang across the room, dropping her bags on the floor before diving on to the bed like a child.

Reaching for her mobile phone she typed out a quick message to Jesse.

'Hi baby, wow! You want to see the size of the bed in this room!!!!! Xxx'

His reply was swift.

'Hi babyyyyyyyy, I'm on my way! What room number are we in? xx'

'29, I can't wait to see you. xx' She replied a wide smile adorned her face. She loved this man, she Amy Lucas, was in love! Who would have thought it was possible?

CHAPTER SEVENTEEN

The knock on the door sent the usual butterflies swimming about her tummy. Taking a large gulp of air Amy opened the door to Jesse.

'Hi you.' She said shyly, looking up at him through her long, black eyelashes and heavy fringe.

'Hi yourself.' Jesse replied before picking her up and planting a soft kiss on her eager, waiting lips. 'You smell gorgeous.' He murmured into her ear.

'You don't smell too bad yourself Mr Clayton.' Amy giggled in response.

'Such a nice sound.' Jesse breathed, his lips trailing up and down the side of her neck.

'What's a nice sound?' She replied, a puzzled look on her face.

'You laughing and giggling, it's cute.' He said as he gently lay her down on the bed. 'Wow! You weren't joking when you said it was enormous.' He added bouncing backwards and forwards to see if it squeaked.

'No squeaks, already checked.' Amy grinned, her giggles becoming uncontrollable because of her nerves.

Reaching towards her face, he gently stroked back the stray hair that had fallen across her eyes and Amy felt her arms instinctively go around his neck before her fingers trailed up into his hair. She loved the feel of his soft hair between her fingertips. Pulling him towards her their lips met and as he kissed her deeply Amy felt every nerve disappear as her heart opened for this very special man.

'God I love this man so much.' Amy secretly thought as their eyes briefly met. His mesmerizing, sexy, green to her bewildered, smitten blue.

As she felt his fingertips and lips begin their journey of seduction, Amy sighed softly.

'You turn me on so much.' She breathed into his ear, softly nibbling the lobe before trailing her soft lips down the side of his neck. 'What are you doing to me?' She cried out delicately.

'The same thing you are doing to me Amy.' Jesse replied as his fingers lazily began to trail across her stomach. 'This needs to come off!' She could feel the heated path that he was creating as he ran his index finger down the centre of her blouse. Slowly, without taking his eyes from hers, he unbuttoned the delicate fabric. Amy couldn't stand the heat from his eyes so throwing her arm across her own she closed them, surrendering herself completely to his tender touch.

'This is new.' His voice was husky and low as he peeled back her blouse to reveal the new lingerie she had bought especially for tonight.

'For you.' She breathed. Uncertainty had flitted across her mind when she had found the exquisite bra and matching panty set but the silky, black fabric had felt so good on her skin when she tried them on that she was unable to resist. Amy was silently pleased that Jesse liked it, she wanted to please him in every way possible, this was the man she had fallen in love with after all.

Moving his fingers to her breasts Jesse traced the outline of the bra, his fingers sending tingling sensations right to her sex. As he slowly placed one finger inside the cup she gasped as the soft pad met her bare skin. Every time he touched her she felt an intense fire deep within her belly, a fire that never seemed to want to go out, shit she wanted him so badly.

She knew he was teasing her, not quite touching her nipple he drew leisurely figures of eight, the pad of his fingertip only briefly grazing her bud as it completed its journey, only for him to start all over again.

'Please Jesse.' She begged, her eyes seeking his for the briefest moment.

'Please what Amy?' He replied, gazing once again into her blue eyes with his smoldering green ones.

'Touch me.' She whispered throwing back her head and closing her eyes.

She felt his lips brush against the exposed skin of her neck. Pulling her up so she was seated, he grabbed her hair, tilting her head gently to the side.

'I am going to kiss you here, and here, and here.' He said sexily whilst delicately touching various parts of her neck lightly with the pad of his finger.

Amy threw herself back on the bed and surrendered her exposed skin to his lips willingly.

'Stand up baby.' Jesse whispered into her ear.

Obeying Amy stood on shaky legs and watched in wonder as he slowly walked around her, his hands trailing across her body, igniting her secret place.

'Everywhere I touch with these.' He breathed as he brought his fingertips up to her lips. 'I am going to kiss.' Reaching greedily for his forefinger she placed it on her partially open lips, flicking her tongue out she drew it into the depths of her mouth, rolling her tongue around the pad.

'You are so sexy.' Jesse mumbled into her hair. 'So fucking sexy!'

'Oh Jesse. I want you.' Her need for him was so great she practically clung to him.

Reaching for the belt on his pants she unbuckled it swiftly before reaching for the buttons. Sinking to her knees before him, she undid them one by one, her fingers teasing him this time. Hearing his sharp intake of breath Amy placed her fore and middle finger inside the waistband of his boxer shorts and began running them tantalizingly across the front, her fingers dipping down briefly to touch the head of his already rock hard cock.

'Not yet Amy.' He instructed gently as he placed his hands on both sides of her head and carefully guided her up until she was standing before him. Bending quickly he removed his pants and socks before scooping her up and placing her back on the bed, his hand cradling her head tenderly as he lay her down beneath him.

Their lips met each hungry for the other as the passion built. Amy couldn't get enough of this man, he ignited her body like no other and made her feel sensations that she had never experienced before. Her whole body felt as if it was on fire, her heart ready to explode in her chest.

As they unhurriedly undressed one another Jesse kept to his word, his fingers touching every part of her, his mouth following the fiery blaze that his digits created wherever they touched. As he stroked sensually down her leg he reached for her foot, repositioning himself on the bed he gazed into her eyes.

'I love your tiny feet.' He said, bending his head to place delicate little kisses up her instep. Amy wriggled in response, the tiny kisses creating an almost uncomfortable sensation between her legs. 'So small and perfect.' He added running his finger along her crimson red painted nails before increasing the pressure as he stroked down the arch of her foot.

Reaching for him, Amy drew him close to her once again, needing to close the distance between them.

'I want to feel you inside me.' She said, her whole body conveying her desperate longing for him.

'All in good time, Miss Lucas.' He replied, a lazy smile caressing his handsome, young face as his hands began their path of seduction once again.

Taking her nipple into his mouth he sucked hard causing Amy to gasp out with an almost painful like pleasure.

'You like that, don't you.' Jesse asked, bending his head once again. His hands and lips seemed to be everywhere.

'Yes.' Amy hissed through clenched teeth. His warm breath felt delicious on her erect nipple as he blew softly before taking her once again into his mouth. Jesse sucked again before flicking his tongue rapidly over the swollen bud.

'I think this one is lonely.' He said briefly touching her right nipple before taking it quickly into his mouth. She could feel his teeth grazing her as his mouth worked its magic.

'Shit!' Amy shouted out, her body arching and dipping in response to his touch, as his mouth continued to assault her nipples.

As his hands travelled down her body Amy was positive she was about to explode. The heat his touch created was almost unbearable and as his expert fingers sought out her hidden place she felt the beginnings of her first Christmas Eve orgasm building slowly within her.

'So wet, so ready for me.' Jesse said into her ear whilst planting sweet little kisses on her neck before bending once more to tease and arouse her nipples.

Amy was in complete awe of this man. Her body was alive, every nerve tingling, every fibre filled to the brim with the intense heat that was rapidly spreading throughout her petite body.

Cupping her sex with his hand he began to move his thumb over her clitoris, his index and middle finger buried deep inside her, massaging her, bringing her so close but then withdrawing just as she was about to topple over the edge.

'Please Jesse.' She pleaded. 'Please, I want you inside me.'

Giving into her demands, Jesse removed his boxer shorts and thrust into her with a force that sent her body into a myriad of convulsions. As she exploded around him he continued to ride her, his big, powerful cock draining every last nanogram of orgasm out of her.

'Turn over.' He instructed, his voice laden with lust.

'No, I want to taste you; I want your cock in my mouth.' Amy demanded demurely.

Moving down his body with her mouth she placed dainty kisses around his belly button before taking him firmly in her hand, guiding him into her mouth. Amy was immediately rewarded with Jesse's sharp intake of breath as he hissed between clenched teeth. She had never enjoyed performing fellatio before but with Jesse it was different, she loved the taste and feel of his hard cock in her mouth, relished and preened in the pleasure that she was able to bring this wonderful man. This little bird was certainly unfurling and spreading her wings and boy was she flying, in fact she was soaring, soaring high towards God knows where but, she didn't care, this was right, it felt right. She had given her heart willingly to this amazing, special man, bringing him pleasure was her only goal and so taking him deep into her mouth she began the sensual torment with her tongue and lips.

'Oh babe, you know just what I like.' Jesse gazed into her eyes as she seductively glanced at him whilst running her tongue around the bell shaped end of his cock.

'You taste so good.' She whispered closing her eyes to avoid the intense gaze from his smoldering green ones. Bending her neck to allow his cock full access to her mouth she took him once again, clasping her mouth firmly around him, her tongue assaulting him, making his heart race wildly and his hips thrust forward as his hands became lost in her hair.

'Enough!' Jesse reached for her, gently turning her onto her stomach. As he entered her from behind his hands reached for hers, placing them above her head he grasped them firmly with his own as he thrust once more into her she collapsed as yet another intense orgasm washed over her. Her muscles clenched around him, holding him tight as wave after wave ravished her body.

'Jesse…… Oh Jesse…..' She cried out in pure ecstasy as her body stiffened in response to the contractions that were still raging.

'Oh baby, you feel so good.' Jesse shouted out.

'I want you in my mouth again. I want to taste your come.'

Moving from on top of her Jesse once again turned her over, his gaze one of bewilderment as their eyes meet.

'Amy.' That sole word created a passion in her that was so intense she thought she would erupt; she loved it when he spoke her name so softly when their bodies were united, their only goal to bring one another pleasure.

Placing her mouth near his ear she murmured to him.

'Adios. Hasta que nos volvamos a encontrar.' Goodbye. Until we meet again.

'You speak Spanish.' He asked huskily. 'Now that is sexy!' He declared.

'Gracias, eres muy amable.' She replied, the foreign language slipping off her tongue.

Gliding down his body she took him once again in her mouth, her fingertips caressing his balls as she slid her hand and mouth up and down his handsome, hard cock. She took him deep into her mouth, her tongue running deliciously around the end, sucking and licking. His fingers were wound in her hair and as she continued to assault him with her lips, tongue and hands she felt his hips thrust up to meet her. Increasing the tempo she sucked harder and felt the first explosion hit the back of her throat. Fuck, he tasted good, the warm sperm glided easily down her throat as he exploded again and again, emptying himself into her ready and eager mouth.

CHAPTER EIGHTEEN

'Wow!' Jesse's breathing was beginning to slow. 'Babe that was….'

'I know.' Amy replied dreamily. 'It just keeps getting better and better.'

'You can say that again!' Jesse replied, his voice husky and low as his breathing slowly returned to normal.

'Ok, it keeps getting better and better.' She laughed.

'You are such a tit!' Jesse declared, laughing along with her. 'I'm starving.'

'How did I know you were going to say that?' Amy chuckled. 'Forever hungry hey Mr Clayton?'

'Hungry for you Miss Lucas and your pussy.' Jesse sexily replied, his hands that had been drawing lazy patterns across her back suddenly reached for her behind. 'You have got one sexy ass and a very sexy pussy.'

Swatting him playfully Amy stretched before getting out of bed. Compliments and kind words would always be difficult for her to understand but even harder for her to accept.

'So what do you fancy?' She asked holding up the room service menu before diving back on to the bed and into his outstretched arms.

'Your pussy.' He cheekily replied, a devilish grin upon his face. 'And where did you learn to speak Spanish by the way.' He added.

'Will you behave and at school!' Amy scolded; a sexy grin was plastered firmly across her face. 'It probably didn't even make any sense, it just seemed right for the moment.' She felt the blush spread across her face immediately.

'Behave! Me Behave! I don't think so.' He laughed gathering Amy into his arms, laying her back on the bed. 'Ready for round two Miss Lucas and your Spanish sounded mighty sexy to me, I don't care if it was correct.'

Winding her arms around his neck she drew him once more to her and as their lips met she closed her eyes and gave in to the sensations he was once more lavishing on her body.

As he brought her to climax after climax she called out his name, clinging to him with a fervor she didn't know she possessed. When he finally emptied himself once again into her she tightened herself around him, clasping his cock hard inside her as she rode the crests of her own orgasm to the very end.

Lying in his arms, her head resting on his chest she smiled to herself. If only he knew, she thought. As she was about to speak and break the peaceful silence her mobile phone began to beep.

'Sorry Jesse, I have to get that, it could be one of the girls.' She said, reluctantly removing herself from his embrace.

'It's fine baby.' He dreamily replied, a faraway look in his eyes.

Reaching for her mobile phone Amy laughed as she read the message from Jen.

'Hope you are having a good time. Remember, mum's the word until after Christmas. Have a wonderful, sex filled night and hope Santa brings you lots and lots of orgasms. x'

'What's funny babe.' Jesse asked, propping himself up on one elbow, his eyes searching her face.

'It's Jen.' She replied. 'She said she hopes Santa brings me lots and lots of orgasms.' Amy blushed as she recited the part of the message she could to Jesse. 'Now, what about some food?' She questioned in a bid to distract him from the text whilst locking her mobile phone and putting it back into her handbag.

Reaching for the menu they both selected what they wanted and Jesse rang their order through whilst Amy grabbed a quick shower. As she soaped her body Amy heard the bathroom door open and then close again. She felt his presence draw nearer in the cubicle and turned as he placed his hands gently on her shoulders.

'Here, let me do that.' He breathed as he reached for the shower gel. Squirting some of the liquid into his hands he rubbed them together to produce a rich lather which he leisurely stroked over her body. 'Turn around.' He whispered, his hands gently gliding up and down her arms.

Amy was quick to oblige and closed her eyes as she focused on his hands and the soapy gel as he bent and washed first one foot, then the other, slowly running his hands up her legs, pausing briefly before delving to her inner thighs, increasing the pressure making Amy gasp out loud.

'There, you will do.' He said, abruptly removing his hands before slapping her on the arse playfully.

'My turn.' Amy said, reclaiming the shower gel, a smirk playfully resting on her lips.

Pumping some into her hands she moved them over his lean, athletic, young body, fuck, he was heaven to touch and she couldn't literally get enough of him. As she washed his stomach she noticed he was becoming hard again, sighing softly she dropped to her knees and took him in her mouth.

'Oh Amy.' Moving swiftly he turned off the shower before grabbing a towel and wrapping it around her. Reaching for an identical one for himself he quickly wrapped it around his waist. 'It's my turn to taste you.' Picking her up Jesse carried her back to the bed, sitting her down on the edge. Reaching up he placed his hands on her shoulders and gently nudged her backwards until she was lying flat on her back. Immediately he dipped his head as his hands gently parted her legs and she gasped out in pleasure as his tongue and fingers connected with her sex. Throwing her arm across her face she gave into the sensations he was busily creating, his tongue moving expertly over her clitoris, his fingers inside her, stroking her, making her gasp for breath. As she began to climb the mountain of climax once again there was a loud knock on the door followed by a man's voice.

'Room service.'

'Fuck, shit, fuck shit!' Amy declared, scrambling about, her orgasm forgotten as panic set in.

Grinning Jesse stood up.

'To be continued Miss Lucas.' He muttered sexily as he walked towards the door, grabbing a bathrobe on the way.

Flustered and embarrassed, Amy jumped up from the bed and ran into the bathroom, locking the door firmly behind her. As she walked towards the sink she could clearly see her reflection in the steamy mirror above. Her skin was flushed, her hair wild but her eyes... they sparkled, not the glint they had worn for the last few weeks but a real sexy sparkle. Smiling she gently stroked her swollen lips with her middle finger. How she had changed, her body, her mind, her whole outlook on life. She was in love and although she wanted to scream her feelings out for the world to hear she knew that her secret needed to be held close to her heart for just a while longer. She loved Mr Champagne, yes, she, Amy Lucas was in love.

CHAPTER NINETEEN

'Merry Christmas Jesse.' Amy murmured as she lay cocooned in his arms.

'Merry Christmas babe.' Jesse replied, his fingers trailing up and down her arm reducing her to a state of complete and utter relaxation.

It was almost 3am. They had enjoyed one another's bodies for hours. Amy was amazed at how she responded to him, every touch, every kiss seemed magnified and intense, every time he entered her she was blown away with the feelings that swam around her body and mind. Her heart was his and as she nuzzled closer to him that secret smile played on her lips once again.

She desperately wanted to tell him how she felt as she lay with her head on his chest. She could hear his heart steadily beating and knew that this would forever be her "special place," a place that no matter how stressed her life became she could escape to and reminisce, secure and safe, knowing that this wonderful man had stepped into her life at exactly the right time. He had helped her to heal and feel again until the icicle had melted, banished forever. Yes, Jesse made her feel safe and that astounded her. Closing her eyes she allowed sleep to take over and as she sank into the darkness she snuggled closer into Jesse, that secret smile very firmly planted on her untroubled, carefree, peaceful face.

CHAPTER TWENTY

'Merry Christmas. Ho ho ho.' Amy laughed as she walked into David's and Jen's kitchen wearing a ridiculous Santa hat perched on top of her chestnut hair. Grabbing Jen in a tight embrace Amy hugged her friend close to her.

'Merry Christmas Amy.' David said as he came towards the two women. 'Can I get in on this Xmas cuddle?'

'Of course.' Amy said, releasing herself from Jen and opening her arms to invite David. 'Merry Christmas David.'

'Did you have a good night?' David asked a slight twinkle in his eyes.

'Well I'm guessing from the look on her face and the sparkle in her eyes that she did!' Jen replied, laughing loudly. 'Where's Chloe by the way?'

'She is with Mark honey, Bethany has nipped up to the loo but I bet she is with Caitlin in her room.' Amy replied, referring to Jen's six year old daughter. 'Right, do you need any help?' She asked looking at the chaotic disruption before her.

'Oh please honey. David can you finish setting the table please? And where the bloody hell are the kids? They can help too.' Jen replied.

Removing her coat and hanging it in the utility room Amy rolled up her sleeves and began to peel and chop some carrots. Christmas carols played softly in the background creating a happy, festive atmosphere.

'So how did it go?' Jen asked as the two women busily prepared the food side by side.

'Oh Jen, he is wonderful. I spent my first Christmas Eve in over 20 years happy and in the arms of a man I love. No arguments, no violence, no threats, it was a night I will forever hold close to my heart.' Tears began to form in Amy's eyes as she tried to convey her innermost feelings to her dearest friend. 'And no, I didn't tell him.' She added softly.

'Hey now, no tears!' Demanded Jen. 'It's bloody Christmas Amy.

I am so glad you didn't tell him though honey. When are you seeing him again?' She asked, rubbing her friend's shoulders.

'They aren't tears of sadness Jen, I'm much too happy to feel sad. It's not just the sex either.' Amy replied, grabbing a piece of kitchen towel to wipe the tears from her smiling face. 'He has changed me so much, opened my heart and mind. He has taught me to trust and feel again….' Amy's voice trailed off as she closed her eyes and took a deep breath. 'Jen, I never thought I would say this but I have found a man who I am falling deeper and deeper in love with every time we meet, a man who I rejoice at having in my life. Why do you ask when I am seeing him again honey?' Amy finished.

'Why the sad look then?' Jen questioned as she watched her friend's happy, beautiful face turn to one that was full of sorrow. 'And so you can tell him how you feel. You need to share this with him Amy.'

'What's the point? I mean, what's the point in even continuing with it? We can't go anywhere.'

'And why are you saying that?' Jen responded. Amy noticed the cross look that was gradually taking over her friend's face as her eyebrows furrowed in despair.

'Because of the age difference.' Amy replied quietly, casting her eyes towards the floor.

'Bullshit! Age. Number. Fuck it all Amy, you love him that should be all that matters.'

'I know, I know.' Amy replied. 'But let's look at this realistically. I'm a grown woman, he is a young man. Yes, I love him, perhaps more than I even fucking realize myself but shit Jen we honestly can't go anywhere, I mean, how would you feel if Rick brought home a woman twice his age?' Amy knew she was being unfair, her friend was merely offering her words of comfort but Amy was becoming increasingly frustrated with her friend's indifference to the age gap between herself and Jesse. Why couldn't she understand?

'Let me think about what you have just said.' Jen responded. 'I don't want to answer your question off the top of my head, I want to think about this and then respond truthfully.'

'That is what I love about you Jen. You won't feed me bullshit just because it's what you think I want or need to hear. You are a true friend. Now, let's forget about all the love sick talk and have some feckin fun!' Amy drew Jen into her arms. 'You really are a good friend you know Jen.'

'Shut up or you will have me crying.' Jen laughed, wiping the last few stray tears from her friend's eyes with her fingers.

'Right, let's sort this food out, I am starving!' Amy giggled. 'I have worked up quite an appetite.' She said grinning.

'Mmmmm, I bet you bloody did you saucy mare.' Jen laughed in response. 'Kids! Kids! Get your backsides down here and help please, Christmas dinner is not going to cook itself nor get onto the table!' Jen had moved to the bottom of the staircase and was now hollering as if her life depended on it.

As the kids came hurtling down the stairs Amy began to laugh.

'What's up with you?' Jen asked, turning to look at her friend.

'You certainly rounded them all up quickly Jen. How are they all getting on?' Amy asked.

Amy had been concerned when Jen had announced she was moving in with David. They had only been dating for three months when the pair decided that they could not spend another night apart and so Jen had packed up all hers and Caitlin's belongings and moved in with him. Her eldest daughter, Leanne, was moving in after the festive period and Rick had decided to stay at home but today they were all present and hanging around the kitchen causing chaos.

'They all seem to be getting along fine.' Jen answered. 'It has been bloody hard though Amy, trying to bring two families together is not a task I recommend.

Amy looked closely at her friend, studying her facial expression in detail. She looked content and happy and as she glanced across the room she caught David looking at her friend with what she could only interpret as a look of complete and utter devotion and love.

'Ok everyone, do you all want to take your seats.' Jen instructed as the two women began to carry the various serving platters to the large, mahogany table.

'Oh Jen, it's beautiful.' Bethany said. 'Caitlin, look at the little silver stars.' Bethany had developed a lovely bond with little Caitlin and it made both women smile as they watched the two together.

'You are really good with her.' Jen said taking hold of Bethany's hand. 'At least I know who to call if I need a babysitter.' She joked.

'Anytime.' Bethany responded laughing whilst letting Caitlin take hold of her free hand.

'How's Jesse?' Rick asked Amy, a smirk on his face.

'He's fine, have you not seen him?' She asked blushing furiously.

'Nah, he's never around these days, I wonder why?' The twinkle in his eyes and the grin on his face caused Amy's blush to deepen until her skin felt as if it was literally on fire.

'Rick, leave Amy alone.' Jen chuckled.

Laughing Rick walked off towards the table, glancing over at Amy one last time he winked.

'Piss off.' She mouthed to him, her grin matching his.

As the group tucked into the magnificent meal all conversation of love and hope was shelved away. For Amy, Christmas that year would be a period of time she would never, ever forget. For many years she had lived an almost miserable existence, now she was surrounded by people who loved and cared for her deeply. As she picked up her wine glass to join in the festive toast that David was busily rambling Amy smiled once more, yes, her life had changed so much, for the first time in a very long time she was blissfully content and finally at peace.

CHAPTER TWENTY-ONE

'Well I have thought about your question.' Amy knew that it would only be a matter of hours before Jen rang her. They hadn't left until late the previous day after consuming, what in Amy's opinion, was a large amount of food and too much alcohol. It was now 7am on Boxing Day and the loud ringing of her phone had woken Amy out of a very peaceful sleep where Jesse had visited in her dreams.

'And......' Amy asked, her eyes shut tightly, afraid of what her friend was going to say.

'Ok. If Rick brought home.. erm..... shall we say a more mature lady.' Jen began to chuckle.

'Will you be bloody sensible for once; this is my life we are talking about!' Amy sulkily replied.

'Keep your knickers on lady! Jen retorted. 'Right, if Rick brought home an older woman I honestly feel that at first I would be shocked but and I say this with a capital B U and T, I would want to get to know her, find out what she is about and most certainly give her a chance. Now, I know you, I know that you haven't got a bad fibre in your body but as a mother to a man roughly the same age I can honestly and truthfully say that I wouldn't be arsed. I should hope that I have instilled enough values and raised my son to know that any woman he gets involved with will be his choice and his alone and that I have done a good enough job in raising him so he knows who to give his heart to and who not to, regardless of age. Does that make sense Sweetie?' Jen finished.

Amy listened carefully to what her friend was saying.

'So, you wouldn't want to punch the living hell out of her then?' Amy asked as her friend's words slowly sank in to her foggy brain.

'No! I trust my son; I trust that he will make the right decisions during the course of his life. Who am I to tell him who to love and who not to?'

'I hear you honey.' Amy responded. 'God I wish you were Jesse's mum.' She laughed halfheartedly. 'This really worries me Jen; his parents would hate me before even meeting me.' She cried. 'I'm not a bad person Jen, I would never do anything to hurt Jesse, he means the world to me.' Amy knew her heart would eventually be broken but to hurt Jesse in anyway was something she could never do. She cherished him, wanted good things for him but most of all she wanted to be free to love him.

Jen could sense the misery in her friend's voice.

'Listen Amy. My advice is this…. Be brave; tell the man you love him for Christ's sake! Stop worrying about the what if's and just friggin do it. You are beautiful, intelligent and a lovely person to know.'

'Ok, ok. I guess I am just going to have to follow my heart and not my stupid brain.' Amy replied, trying to convince herself that she was following the correct path.

'Yes! Now don't let me down. If you need me you know where I am. Be brave beautiful lady.'

As Amy lay back down she wondered what Jesse's reaction would be. Picking up her mobile she rang Jen back.

'It's me again. How will I know when the time is right Jen?' She cried. 'What if he walks away?'

'It's a chance you have to take Amy. Have you any idea at all how he feels?' Surely there were signs there for her friend to read but Jen knew she was very naïve where men were concerned.

'No! The way he looks at me, well, oh fuck Jen, I just don't know!' Amy could feel tears of frustration brimming in her eyes and as she blinked they tumbled down her face. 'I'm scared Jen.' She whispered. 'This could all be something completely different to him Jen, for him, and I'm going to be blunt, I could just be a…… well you know what I mean.' Amy finished, unable to force the word from her mouth.

'Don't be. What is the worst that could possibly happen?' Jen asked.

'Not seeing him again. I could lose him Jen.' Amy responded. Now the tears of frustration were tears of misery. 'I have never felt like this before.'

'Take a chance Amy, take a chance. Be brave my little bird.' Jen encouraged softly, hoping that Amy would listen to her.

Hanging up the phone once again Amy curled herself into a tight ball and closed her eyes tightly to prevent any further tears from forming. Deep in thought she reached for her mobile as it beeped signaling a message had arrived.

'Hi baby, did you sleep well. Sorry I didn't text you last night but I was wasted :) Did you have a good day yesterday? xx' Jesse, oh just what she needed.

Wiping the last bit of moisture from her face she felt the smile begin to develop. God, he made her so happy, she thought to herself.

'Good morning babe. Too much food, far too much alcohol and a banging head to show for it :) How was your day? Did you have a good time? xx' She replied.

As she waited for his reply she ambled down the stairs and into the kitchen. Switching on the kettle she reached for her favourite mug before spooning in the coffee and sugar.

'It was good thanks. Are you busy? xx' He asked.

Amy closed her eyes and leant against the kitchen sink, the cool stainless steel providing a welcome relief from the heat that was quickly spreading throughout her body. This time, it wasn't the usual warmth that was created with sexual longing and passion but a surge of red hot panic that was rapidly overtaking her body and mind.

Remembering Jen's words she reached for her mobile phone. "Be brave," she had said.

'Easy for her to say!' Amy shouted into thin air. Typing out her reply slowly she hesitated before sending the message. She was about to take a very big step and she was petrified.

'No, just chilling today babe. xx' She text back.

'Are the girls out tonight? xx' His reply was swift.

All common sense seemed to leave Amy's body as she firmly decided to follow her heart, a heart that now belonged to the wonderful Jesse.

'Yes, Chloe is with Mark and Bethany is at her boyfriend's, Adam, until tomorrow night. Would you like me to cook? xx' Amy responded, her heart was racing as feelings of nausea began to develop deep within her stomach.

Popping a piece of bread into the toaster, Amy picked up her cup and sat at the table. Waiting for her toast and Jesse's reply she hoped that if she had something to eat it would stop her insides from churning.

'Sweet. I can be there in about an hour.' He replied.

'Shit.' Exclaimed Amy, catching sight of her reflection in the metal of the toaster she gasped and flew up the stairs, her toast and coffee forgotten.

CHAPTER TWENTY TWO

'Hello you.' Jesse said, brushing his lips against hers as she stood before him in the hallway.

'Hello.' Amy replied, standing on her tiptoes so she could put her arms around his neck. 'You are up and out early!' She joked.

Swatting her playful on the behind Jesse followed her into the kitchen.

'I wanted to see you last night, in fact I was going to get a taxi but then I fell asleep on the sofa.' Jesse said, running his lips up and down the side of her neck.

The delicious little pulses began their journey once again as all thoughts of panic and frustration disappeared. The butterflies were still performing somersaults in her stomach but she knew that was because she was in love. Every time she saw Jesse they would begin their acrobatics, from that first day, when they met at Jen's till now, they never quieted down and Amy welcomed them with open arms because she now knew it meant that she was feeling again.

'Would you like anything to eat or drink Jesse?' She asked as she delicately extracted herself from his embrace.

Your pussy.' Came his seductive reply.

Laughing Amy reached for his hand, taking it in her own she studied his fingertips closely, her fingernail gracefully tracing the patterns of his prints, her eyes cast downwards.

'Bed then.' She said taking his index finger into her mouth suggestively.

'Bed then.' He replied huskily.

As they walked into the living room towards the stairs, Jesse grabbed hold of her encircling her with his arms. She could feel his erection pressing into the small of her back and immediately felt the warmth spread between her legs.

'Mmmm let's not go to bed. Let's stay down here on the sofa.' Jesse whispered into her ear, his lips teasing her neck softly as he ran them up and down her bare skin.

Turning herself around Amy looked for a few antagonizing seconds into his eyes.

'If only I could read his bloody mind.' She thought to herself. Studying his eyes she tried to read what they were conveying.

'You look so serious all of a sudden.' Jesse remarked as he picked her up easily in his arms and carried her to the sofa.

Just as Amy was about to respond Jesse silenced her with his lips. As she responded to their touch she felt her hands go up to his head, her fingers imbedding themselves in his soft, dark brown hair and as he deepened the kiss she silently reprimanded herself for the doubts that had invaded her mind.

'I love kissing you.' She breathed. Jesse's response was to deepen the kiss even more until Amy thought her heart would stop. Pulling back she placed her hands on either side of his handsome, young face. 'You are so handsome Jesse.' She quietly voiced her eyes searching his face.

As Jesse pulled her towards him she held back.

'What's the matter?' He asked, concern written across his beautiful face as he looked carefully at the tiny woman before him.

'I'm in trouble Jesse.' She said in the smallest of voices. 'I'm in big trouble.' Casting her eyes swiftly downwards she avoided the intensity of his gaze.

'What do you mean Amy? Why are you in trouble?' He replied, his fingers softly brushing her cheeks. 'Are you ok?' He questioned reaching for her once again, wanting to cocoon her in his arms.

'No Jesse, I'm not ok. I'm in trouble.' She replied, pushing herself away again as she tried to increase the distance between them. Amy was used to rejection but had never experienced the feelings of fear that now gripped every ounce of her body as she suddenly realised that her happiness depended on how the next few minutes played out.

'What do you mean you are in trouble, you keep saying that and I don't understand? Please tell me Amy. You are worrying me now.' Usually she was so ready to be enveloped in his arms, Jesse was now sensing that Amy was in distress and he didn't like the way it made him feel. Reaching for her one again he held her close. 'Please tell me.' He asked again softly.

'I am falling for you Jesse.' Amy couldn't meet his eyes. She was busy plucking some imaginary thread from her skirt with nervous fingers, her eyes refusing to meet his. Removing herself from his arms she stood quickly, walking away from him and into the kitchen, fear clearly evident on her face. The colour had drained from her skin, her palms were hot and sweaty, tiny beads of moisture gathered on her top lip and her heart was beating wildly in her chest.

As she heard Jesse follow her into the kitchen she immediately turned around to face him, tears in her eyes, her heart on her sleeve.

'I'm sorry.' She mumbled, looking down at her feet which appeared to have developed a mind of their own as they twitched and twisted on the cold, tiled floor.

'Why are you sorry Amy?' Jesse asked gently, walking towards her.

'I should have kept my big mouth shut.' She replied. Reaching for her face she felt his fingertips wipe away the tears.

'And why should you have kept your "big mouth shut?" He responded, his voice the merest whisper.

Shit, why couldn't she see what he was feeling in his eyes? Those sexy fucking green eyes, yes, it was their fault. If she hadn't have been so stupidly mesmerized by them she wouldn't be in this situation now.

'Jesse... I....' The words refused to tumble out.

'Amy, I have been waiting for this, waiting for these words.' Jesse smiled at her. Reaching for her hands he placed them in his own.

'Whattt.........' Why the fuck couldn't she speak!

'Amy, if you hadn't of said them, I would. I feel the same.' Raising her right hand to his lips he softly brushed the knuckles with a kiss.

'What?....' Again the words refused to flow. Shaking her head Amy tried to understand what the man she loved was trying to convey to her.

'You heard me Amy.' Gathering her into his arms he hooked his finger under her chin and tilted her head back. His sexy, magnetic eyes reached deep into hers and as she felt her heart rate increase she smiled. Slowly the smile reached her eyes until she was beaming as finally his words registered deep within her brain.

'Really!' She passionately cried, clinging to him, drawing him as close to her as was possible.

'Really.' Jesse replied, forcing her gently back a little so he could smile at her and see her face.

'Wow!' Was all she could reply as she tried to meet his eyes with her own.

Without another word he scooped her up into his arms and carried her up the stairs.

CHAPTER TWENTY THREE

Lying her gently on the bed, Jesse stood back to remove his shoes. As his hands moved up to the buckle of his belt Amy reached out to stop him.

'I want to do that please.' She whispered quietly, her cheeks flaming their usual crimson colour.

Never taking his eyes from her face he sank down beside her, propping himself up on his elbow. With his free hand he swept her hair from out of her eyes before planting a tiny, delicate kiss on the tip of her nose.

Amy needed no further encouragement, her lips quickly sought his as she reached for his hair and moaned with a pleasure she never thought possible as their lips met and his tongue found hers.

Running his fingers along her jawline he whispered in her ear. Three little words....

'I want you.'

Amy drew him towards her, ready to accept this man that she had only moments before bared her heart to. As she ran her tongue up the side of his neck she gently nibbled his earlobe.

'And I want you.'

With a fierce passion he grasped her, kissing her deeply, his tongue exploring the inner confines of her mouth. They moaned in unison as he slowly withdrew his lips and gazed into her wide, blue eyes before once again taking her mouth with his own. As he grabbed her silky, chestnut hair and tilted her head to the side, exposing the sweet, soft skin of her neck she called out his name in a whisper.

'Jesse.' Releasing her hair he gazed into her eyes, a sexy, hot smile on his adorable, ever so kissable lips.

Moving his hand down her leg he began to twirl his finger lightly across her flesh sending sparks straight to her sex. Amy threw her head back and moaned loudly wanting to feel this man she loved inside her as the aching and longing spread throughout her.

'God I want you. I want to feel you inside me Jesse.'

Pushing his lips back down on to hers she closed her eyes and surrendered to the delicious sensations he was creating throughout her body. As his hand travelled further up her leg she shifted slightly to allow him access to her dark, secret place.

'So wet, so ready for me and no knickers Amy. How sexy…..' He breathed into her mouth as his lips claimed hers once again.

Totally under his spell, all her fears and doubts banished, Amy gave herself completely to Jesse. As his fingers expertly wove their very own kind of magic she felt herself open to him. As if sensing the change in her Jesse increased the pressure of his fingers and lips sending her deliciously over the edge. As each delectable wave swept through her she felt herself open up just a little bit more as the scars she had worn so bravely for so many years vanished, never to be given a second thought by this courageous woman again.

Placing her hand on his stomach she ran her fingers along it until they came into contact with his belt. A quick tug and then pull in the opposite direction made quick work of the buckle. As her fingers snaked around the buttons on his jeans she felt his steely cock. Fuck he was so hard. She wanted him. She wanted him inside her, in her mouth, in her hands. She wanted to feel him shoot his warm sperm deep into her pussy. God he turned her on.

Jumping up Jesse quickly removed his pants and t shirt before pulling her gently to her feet.

'Mmmm I think these need to come off.' He said waving his hand at her clothes.

Reaching for the hem of her shirt he tucked it upwards. As he drew the material over her head the clips fell from her chestnut hair which fell in waves to her shoulders.

'I love your hair like this.' He said, taking a strand between his fingers. Loosely he held it, letting it slide slowly. As the last tendril past between his long, masculine fingers he watched it drop, following its trail with his lips.

Amy inhaled sharply, her head tilting as far back as it would allow. Pushing her gentle back onto the bed he leaned over her supporting his weight on his hands.

'Put me inside you babe.' He breathed, never taking his eyes from hers.

As she reached for him she felt her hands begin to tremble. She loved this man; she really loved this amazing, special man with the sexiest eyes she had ever seen. Guiding him to her she felt the moisture between her legs and as he slowly pushed himself into her she called out.

'I love you.' Three little words of her own.

'I have been waiting for you to say that as well.' Jesse whispered softly into her ear. 'I love you too Amy.'

Pushing his cock deep inside her she called out his name, clinging to him as yet another mind blowing orgasm swept throughout her body. As each wave crashed through her it became joined somehow with her emotions, her heart, uniting her whole body along with her mind. She was completely open to this man, his for the taking.

'I'm going to make love to you then I'm going to ruin you.' He hissed through clenched teeth as she moved position, releasing him from her before moving her head down to take his cock in her mouth.

'I love tasting myself on you.' She murmured as she took him deep to the back of her throat, her tongue and fingers building up the pressure as she grasped him firmly before withdrawing him until just the tip was between her soft, wet lips. His moan of pleasure ignited Amy's passion further. As she gazed into his sexy eyes she felt the fiery fingers of desire completely overtake her. Bending her neck once again she teased the bell shaped end of his hard cock with the tip of her tongue, running it around him before taking him once again into her warm, wet, eager mouth. As she increased the suction she withdrew slowly drawing his foreskin up with her lips before quickly pushing him back into the depths of her mouth. Jesse gasped loudly, drawing some much needed air into his deprived lungs.

'Fuck, you know just how I like it.' His voice sizzled with pure emotion as an almost animalistic groan escaped from the back of his throat.

'I love doing this to you, I want to give you pleasure.' Amy replied as she blew gently on him before running her tongue around the stiff head. 'You feel so good in my mouth.'

Reaching for her, Jesse guided her back to him, his lips seeking hers once again. Pushing her onto her back he began to trail his lips over her stomach and breasts, teasing her nipples until they were rock hard little buds of desire. Her whole body craved for his touch, the feel of his lips on her skin and as he continued to pleasure her she sank back against the soft pillows and gave herself to him completely.

'I am going to ruin you.' He repeated as he continued to torment her nipples.

'Bring it Clayton.' She sexily teased.

'Oh Amy......' He buried his face into her shoulder, his lips tantalizingly brushing against her skin. The fierce heat he was creating travelled straight down to her secret, warm, wet place.

'Please Jesse.' She begged. His fingers moved down in-between her legs and as the tips connected with her waiting clitoris she felt the convulsions building deep within her.

'Not yet.' He murmured.

'Please Jesse.' She pleaded once again.

As his lips sought hers he gently inserted his index and middle finger into her. As he massaged her inner walls she closed her eyes and sank into the pleasure. Sensing her desire building once again Jesse removed his fingers.

'Please.......... Jesse, pleaseeeeeee.' She pleaded, her eyes flying open as he moved.

Positioning himself above her he entered her with an almost painful slowness. Gripping him tightly with her pelvic muscles she savored the fullness he created whenever he was inside her.

'What do you want Amy?' He hissed, his eyes seeking hers.

Fuck he was so sexy. Her body was alight, her eyes wide and filled with love for this man.

'You.' Came her one worded reply.

A deep, almost animal like growl emitted from deep within Jesse's throat.

'Fuck I want you.' He shouted as he thrust himself into her. 'Wrap me up babe.' He whispered.

Convulsion after convulsion swamped her tiny body as she wrapped her legs and arms tightly around him. Flesh upon flesh, lips upon lips, fingers upon fingers.

'I love you.' She screamed out as her heart, body, mind and soul opened up once again to let him in.

As Jesse galloped towards his own climax he took Amy along with him, pushing her to her very limits, draining every last bit of orgasm out of her body. As he emptied himself into her he called out.

'I love you Amy.'

CHAPTER TWENTY FOUR

As they lay wrapped in one another's bodies Amy marveled at the feelings that had overtaken her.

'Amazing.' She dreamily murmured.

'Amazing.' Jesse echoed.

'Do you fancy going away somewhere Jesse?' Amy asked, extracting herself from him reluctantly whilst propping herself up on her elbow so she could gaze into his sexy eyes for the few seconds her body would allow her to.

'Where did you have in mind?' He replied, meeting her gaze whilst smiling softly.

'Well, I have a couple of places in mind.' She answered looking away. She hadn't quite got the knack yet of holding Jesse's smoldering looks for longer than a few seconds. 'Chloe and Mark go to a lovely little place. It's besides a canal and has beautiful and really cute little thatched cottages. In the deluxe rooms they have a wet room and massive jacuzzi.... I will show you.' She said as she rose from the bed to go and retrieve her laptop.

'Sounds sick.' Jesse replied. 'What other place do you have in mind?' He asked a sexy smile plastered on his handsome face as he reached for the packet of cigarettes and lighter from the cabinet that stood beside the bed.

'Amsterdam.' She answered nervously, sitting back down on the bed. 'What do you think? I have never been before and would really love to go with you.' Amy was biting her bottom lip as she waited for his answer.

'Yes!' Jesse replied excitedly. 'I have never been either, well not to stay there. Let's go.' He joked, standing up. 'What time is the flight?' He laughed.

As Amy looked at him she felt the surge of emotions infiltrate her once again. His body was heaven to look at, tanned and so toned, his stomach flat and his arse......

'One minute.' She said, reaching for her black, short robe. Putting it on, she quickly tied the belt before leaving the room. Returning with the laptop she plonked herself down on the bed beside Jesse and waited for it to spring to life.

'I'm excited.' She laughed as she quickly typed "Amsterdam" into the search engine.

'Me too babe.' He replied. 'When would you want to go Amy?' He asked, his fingers busily stroking her leg.

'I'm not sure baby.' She responded. 'But the sooner the better! How much notice do you have to give work to book some holidays?' She queried, playfully swatting his hand away. 'I can't concentrate Jesse.' She laughed as she saw his bottom lip stick out.

'A week, two tops. What about you?' He replied, his lips now a brilliant smile as his fingers once again reached for her thigh.

'I can muddle things around and practically go whenever.' Amy answered, playfully swiping his hand away again. 'I need to concentrate.' She giggled. 'And you are putting me off!'

Amy ran her small secretarial business from home and knew that it would be easy enough to juggle her workload to allow her to have a few days holiday. Jesse was a joiner and worked for a large firm so she knew he would need to organize holiday leave with his boss, Larry.

'Amsterdam. The land of tulips, clogs, sex and marijuana.' She laughed.

'Woo.' Jesse shouted. 'So when can we go?' He asked.

'I can book it now.' She replied. 'But don't you need to speak with your boss first?'

Amy secretly had a feeling that Larry would gladly grant Jesse the few days holiday that he needed to go to Amsterdam. She really wanted to meet Jesse's boss, he sounded a character and appeared, to her, to be reliving his youth through what he considered to be his young protégée. Larry was happily married with five kids and had built his business by sheer determination and stubbornness until he had created his own small empire. Four times a year he would jet off to his favourite place, Las Vegas whilst his wife did her own thing and vacationed with her girlfriends.

Reaching for his mobile phone Jesse made a quick call.

'Yeh, I need four days off, is that ok?' Jesse smiled and Amy hoped he had received the ok for the time off. She knew that Jesse was disturbing his boss on Boxing Day but they had a close relationship both professionally and as friends. Hanging up the phone he turned to her. 'Let's go!'

Looking through the list of city break options the pair decided on an early morning flight and The Greenhouse Effect hotel.

'It will give us an extra day more or less.' Amy said as she inputted the card details. 'There booked!' She rejoiced, putting the laptop to one side she reached for Jesse's outstretched arms. 'We are going to Amsterdam.'

In less than ten days Amy would step onto Dutch soil for the first time in her life. As Jesse's hands began to explore her once again Amy closed her eyes. Wow she had fallen in love with champagne and what an excellent year it was, she secretly thought. And we are going to friggin Amsterfuckindam!

CHAPTER TWENTY FIVE

'Well?' Jen asked. After nearly dying with frustration she had eventually gotten into her car and drove to Amy's. 'I have rang you four times and sent you God knows how many fuckin texts. Why haven't you answered me?' Jen cried.

'Calm down.' Amy chuckled. 'I have been busy.' She said a wicked, sexy grin played at the corners of her mouth.

'Well, you look happy, in fact you are friggin glowing girl.' Jen responded, flinging her arms around her friend. 'Truly, are you ok Amy?' She asked, standing back to closely examine her friend's face. She had been so worried about her little mate. She was vulnerable and scared but silently Jen admired her outstanding bravery. If she had suffered half as much as Amy had she would never have welcomed another man into her life. Amy had fallen hard and Jen had thought at one point that she would break but her little soldier had heaved up her worn out shoulders, thrust out her chest and carried on.

'Jen, I am fanfuckintastic!' Amy shouted. 'I am in love and guess what?' She teased, loving the frustrated, wanton look on her friend's face as she held back just a little while longer.

'WHAT? Will you please tell me?' Jen shouted unable to contain her excitement.

'I told him I was in trouble; that I had fallen for him. I was so scared Jen, I really thought he would walk, but he didn't, he feels the same way.' Amy rejoiced throwing her hands up she clapped into thin air. 'Did you hear me? He feels the same way.'

'I hear you, I hear you.' Jen laughed. 'Bloody hell Amy, what are you going to do now?'

'I don't know and I don't care Jen.' Amy responded. 'I am taking each day as it comes and making the most of it.'

Jen looked closely at her friend and grabbed her into her arms pulling her close.

'I am so happy for you Amy.' She gushed. 'You really do deserve this you know.'

'I'm not sure deserve is the correct word.' Amy replied. 'I'm just me, little, old Amy.'

'Little, old Amy who is in love with a hot, young, sexy little fucker.' Jen laughed.

'Oh, by the way, we are going to Amsterdam Jen.' Amy spurted out, excitement making her words tumble out.

'What? When?' Jen questioned, amazement written all over her face.

'In ten days!' Amy replied, jumping up and down. 'The city of sex, here I come.' She sang.

'Bloody hell, you don't waste much time Mrs, do you?' Jen responded.

'Miss! If you don't mind.' Amy joked.

'Miss, sorry I keep forgetting. Mrs just seems to roll off my tongue so easily.' Jen said.

'What's the point in dragging my feet?' Amy replied. 'I made a decision over a year ago that once I was free I would never put off anything again. It took me so many years to break away Jen and I never want to be that feeble, crumpled, pathetic woman EVER again!'

Jen drew her friend to her breast, hugging her tightly.

'Amy you are free. Paul is behind bars, he can't hurt you anymore and you are certainly not pathetic. You had a hard time and Sweetie; you don't know how much I admire your bravery. You stuck with it for so long and he almost killed you.....' Her words trailed off as she remembered the stories that Amy had recited to her when they walked back into each other's lives again.

'Let's not talk about all that.' Amy pleaded. 'That is my past and although Jesse, or anyone else for that matter, could never change it, he has helped me build a happy present for myself. Who knows what the future holds but I honestly don't give a shit. I wake up every morning with a genuine smile plastered across my stupid face.' She smiled.

'I know Amy. I know. All I want is for you to be happy and you don't know how good it makes me feel to see you like this.' Pushing Amy from her embrace gently she surveyed her from her tiny size two feet, to the tip of her head. Have you lost weight?' She asked. 'Your body seems more toned.'

'Fucking hell Jen, if you got up to half the sexual athletics that we do you wouldn't need the bloody gym.' Amy laughed in response.

'I get my fair share.' She retorted a slightly pained expression flitted across her perfect face.

Jen was a very attractive woman and when the two went out on the town men would flock around her. She had an easy and open personality that drew the male species to her. With her dark brown, almost ebony hair which had been recently cut into a trendy bob and her tall, slim body she was a magnet for the opposite sex.

'What?' Amy asked, noticing the look immediately. 'What's the matter Jen, tell me.'

'Oh, I don't know Amy.' Jen wailed. 'You know me, always looking for excitement, always wanting that little bit extra. I love David, truly I do, but I can't get Him out of my head!' Jen was now busily running anxious hands through her hair.

"Him!" How Amy despised "Him." Jen's ex had decided once again to up and leave when the going got tough, leaving Jen a broken, dejected woman. She knew that Jen loved him deeply, knew that she regarded him as her soul mate but Amy had never quite taken to him, something in his dark, mysterious eyes terrified her. Now David, well he was lovely, a warm, sunny man who had a face like a cherub and a smile that light up his big, blue eyes. Amy had liked him as soon as they met and as the whirlwind romance developed she hoped her dearest friend would finally forget the demons of her past and settle down.

'Jen, you have to forget about "Him." Amy pleaded. 'He will only bring you heartache again. Protect yourself honey, guard your heart and make it strong again. David will look after you Jen; you can see it every time he looks at you. Friggin hell, the man adores you. Put "Him" out of your head, please, for me. David worships you; I know he will treasure your heart.' Amy cried, hoping her words would embed themselves into Jen's brain.

'It's so hard Amy.' Jen wailed. 'I loved him with every part of me, honestly I did. I would have done anything for that man.'

'I know how you feel Jen, finally I can relate to your feelings. If we had been having this conversation two years ago I would be looking at you now with a very puzzled expression.'

'I'm so happy for you Amy. Look at us both; we are like a pair of silly teenagers.' Jen laughed, wiping the tears of frustration from her face angrily with the sleeve of her jacket.

'I am in a wonderful place in my life Jen and now I'm free to love unashamedly now he knows my secret.' She grinned.

'I know.' Jen replied. 'Shit, last night I was so worried about you but I guess I finally realised that if you needed me you would ring.' Jen had found it very difficult to settle the night before knowing that her friend was about to embark on something that frightened even her. Amy was vulnerable, yes she had become stronger over time and the change in her since meeting Jesse was remarkable but her heart was weak and had been hurt so badly. Her friend had finally found peace and anyone looking at Amy now would easily see she was a different woman from years past. Happiness was the only thing that Jen wanted for her friend and seeing the look in her eyes, the smile on her face Jen knew she had finally found what she deserved.

'He loves me too.' Amy jumped up and down excitedly. 'He loves me too.' She repeated.

Jen smiled dearly at her friend. She had come so far and healed so well. Jen knew that in the recesses of Amy's mind lurked the dark, horrible past that almost killed her, a past that had been filled with violence, rape and unkindness. Her friend had broken free and Jen was silently rejoicing that Rick's friend had knocked on the door that day.

'Can I show you something?' Amy asked grabbing her friend's hand and leading her up the stairs to her bedroom.

'Oh, what is it?' Jen asked excitement evident in her voice as she followed her friend.

Handing Jen the piece of paper she retrieved from her cabinet, Amy sat down on the bed whilst her friend read what she had wrote in her elegant handwriting.

"HOW DO I KNOW IF I AM IN LOVE????????????

If you are truly in love there is no mistaking it. – *TRUE!!!! OR IS IT??? SHIT!!! I WOULDN'T BE WRITING THIS IF I KNEW THE FECKIN ANSWER!!!!*

It becomes so overwhelming that it seems to take you completely away. – *TRUE!!!! I'M NOT TAKEN AWAY, I'M BLOWN AWAY!!!!!*

Have you ever experienced something so intense, so completely complete, so absolutely infatuating that you disappear within yourself? Yes, then that I'm afraid is love. - *OH SHIT!!!!!!!!!!! FUCK!!*

When you are with that someone and they are all you can see, feel... you lose yourself in that someone and become a part of them, you're complete when they are around. – *OH FUCK!!!!!! SHIT!!! HELP!!!!*

It's scary... – *DAMN FRIGGIN RIGHT IT IS, I AM SHITTING MYSELF!!!!!*

BUT there is no other feeling like it in the whole, wide world. – *WELL I CERTAINLY HAVE NEVER FELT LIKE THIS BEFORE* – *OH SHIT AGAIN!!!!! – HELPPPPPPP!!!!!*

When you first open your eyes after waking in the morning and within moments he is all you begin thinking about, the images so strong you almost feel as if he is there with you. – *YIP! YOU SURE CAN SAY THAT AGAIN!!!!! HE'S ALWAYS ON MY BLOODY MIND!!!*

When you go to bed and your bed is empty, even though you're in it it's still empty because they have left such a void. Your bed only fills right when he is in it. – *I REALLY MISS HIM WHEN HE ISN'T HERE – MY BED IS LONELY WITHOUT HIM!!!!!*

When you wear his shirt you can smell his fragrance. OH DEAR, I NEED COMMITTING. I CAN'T SLEEP WHEN HE ISN'T HERE AND CUDDLE UP TO THE PILLOW WHERE HIS HEAD HAS LAIN, INHALING HIS DELICIOUS JESSE SMELL!!!!!

You're captivated, helpless, and out of control. Caught up in a tornado of a dream that you never want to wake up from. Everyday tasks take double the effort as you think about him, wanting him, needing him. DOUBLE FUCK!!!! I'M WELL AND TRULLY FUCKING FUCKED!!!!!

I GUESS I AM IN LOVE!!!!!!!

'Amy this is somehow so beautiful.' Jen flicked away the tears that had begun to flow down her face. 'You have got it bad girly.'

'Tell me about it!' Amy replied. 'I want this for you Jen; I want you to feel like this.'

Jen looked at her friend sadly; a lonely tear trickling down her cheek.

'I have felt like that Amy.' She whispered her voice small and sad.

'And you will feel it again!' Amy replied emphatically. 'Give David a chance Jen, he's a keeper and you can have a wonderful life together if you just give him that little bit more.'

'I have nothing left to give.' Jen replied, tears of sadness now cascading down her face.

'Dig deep Jen and you will find it.' Amy advised. 'Just please give him a chance.'

Placing the piece of paper onto the bed, Jen reached for her friend's hands.

'I will try.' She quietly replied. 'I can't promise Amy but I will try.'

'Good!' Amy replied. 'Now, come on you, we are going shopping, I need to buy some new kinky underwear and we can stop off at the pub if you want, I think a stiffy is in order.' Amy laughed.

'Dirty, dirty mind!' Jen guffawed.

Laughing Amy handed her friend the box of tissues.

'Dry you bleedin eyes and sort your mascara out, you are doing a very good impression of Alice Cooper there.' Amy howled.

'Fuck you!' Jen replied, laughing hard. As she walked towards the mirror she shrieked loudly. 'Bloody hell, I think I need to put a note in my diary. "When visiting Amy always wear waterproof mascara." Jen joked. 'Give me five minutes to repair this mess and I'm all yours.'

Leaving her friend to tidy her face up Amy walked down the stairs and into the kitchen. She noticed her mobile phone flashing and reached for it smiling when she saw the message from Jesse.

'Boo sexy mama. What are you up to today? xx' He wrote.

'Hello there sexy eyes. I'm going shopping for some new underwear. xx ;)' She replied adding a cheeky smiley face with its tongue hanging out at the end.

'For weekend. xx' He replied.

'For Amsterdam. xx' She replied.

'Kinky. I can't wait. xx'

'Me neither. Maybe I will show you before we go but then again maybe I won't. xx' She teased.

'Naughty. xxx' He replied.

'Spank me! xxx' Amy bit her lip as she wondered if perhaps she had gone too far. Hell no, this was the man she loved and he loved her!

'Now that is kinky! xx' Came his speedy reply. Amy wished she could see his eyes right at that moment. He brought out the playful side to her character and as each day passed Amy's personality blossomed more and more, as Jen walked into the kitchen Amy turned, the biggest smile ever, firmly in place.

Telling Jesse she would speak to him later she picked up her coat and bag, checking that she had her purse and debit cards the two women walked towards the front door.

'Ready for some kinky underwear shopping?' Amy winked.

'Let's go.' Jen laughed in response. 'Got to keep that champagne interested Sweetie.'

Champagne. Well he certainly knew how to blow her cork and make her explode, she secretly thought, that ever present genuine smile gracing her happy, untroubled face.

CHAPTER TWENTY SIX

As they joined the queue to check in Amy thought her insides would literally burst with excitement. The days had flown by. Jesse and Amy had spent New Year's Eve together, a night that Amy had always hated. In the past it simply meant the beginning of a new year of torment, this one had been special; to Amy it symbolized the birth of a new year of happiness and peace.

Chloe and Bethany were with their boyfriends and had both wished their mother a fab trip. Now she was stood at the side of the most amazing, handsome, sexy man on the planet and they were flying to Amsterdam within the next hour or so.

Shoveling on her feet Jesse threw her a slightly puzzled look.

'Do you need a wee?' He asked, a sexy grin beginning to reach his eyes. 'I could come with you, we could have airport sex.' Reaching out he kissed the tip of her nose as she felt the butterflies begin in her stomach and the blush spread across her cheeks.

'Oh! How naughty.' She replied. 'And no I don't need a wee, I'm just really excited.'

'So no airport sex?' He winked, sticking out his bottom lip in a mock like sulk.

Amy could feel her heart rate increasing as the blood was forced to pump around her body at an alarming rate.

'Are you wet baby? I bet you are soaking wet.' He whispered into her ear. 'Have you got any knickers on?' He added a devilish grin on his perfect lips.

'Yes I am wet and no I haven't got any knickers on.' She replied through gritted teeth as her eyes scanned the people around her, sure that someone would sense her embarrassment. Her cheeks were on fire as her eyes fleetingly met his.

'That's my girl.' He mouthed. Bending towards her ear he whispered again quietly. 'When we have checked in I think we need to explore the airport, don't you?' He asked, arching one perfect eyebrow in her direction, a sexy look in his green eyes.

Gulping hard Amy tried to control the fierce blush that had invaded her upper body.

'You are bad, very bad!' She replied in a whisper, pointing a finger at his chest.

'Oh baby, you don't know how bad I can be.' The words were laced with sensuality and promise and Amy felt the muscles in her secret place begin to spasm.

'Will you behave?!' She pleaded quietly. 'I can't cope, I'm going dizzy!'

Laughing Jesse reached for her behind. Placing his hand firmly on her right arse cheek he bent towards her, his eyes searching for hers.

'No, I want you.' He breathed a passionate sexy look in his amazing eyes as he reached for her hand. 'I am sure Doctor Jesse can sort out that dizziness for you.' Planting a swift kiss on her cheek he reached for their bags as the queue moved forward.

Amy hoped that the waiting people moved slowly. Her face was crimson, tiny beads of perspiration gathered on her top lip and as she bit down hard to try and quell the sensations that were now running wildly throughout her body she tasted the droplet of blood that burst from the injury she had caused.

'You can't keep doing this to me.' She hissed between her teeth. 'It's not fair Jesse.' She pleaded. 'I have bitten my lip. Ouch!'

'You have the same effect on me Amy. I look at you and want you, I can't help it. Here have a drink of this water.' He replied offering the bottle that he magically produced from his bag out to her.

'Thank you.' She responded taking a large gulp of the cool liquid.

As the attendant beckoned for them to approach the desk Amy fumbled about with her passport and ticket in a bid to hide the embarrassment that was clearly written all over her face.

Trying to collect her thoughts and senses Amy looked at her straight in the eye, searching for the look that she constantly scrutinized people's faces for. The look of disgust......

When they had first ventured out into the big, scary world together Amy was apprehensive thinking that everyone around them would stare. She often expected to hear comments but as she handed her passport and ticket to the waiting attendant the only thing she saw was a genuine smile.

'Have you got any luggage to check in?' She asked. 'Can I also draw your attention to the statement in green below?' The blonde haired woman in the navy blue uniform pointed to the front of her desk.

Casting her eyes downwards Amy read the large writing.

'No, we have no luggage to check in and yes I packed my hand luggage myself.' Amy smiled pleasantly at the woman as she wrestled with the sensations that still lurked in the pit of her stomach.

'And you sir?' She asked, directing her attention and most dazzling smile at Jesse. Amy noticed the appreciative look she gave him and was surprised when she began to feel jealous.

'The same.' He replied. 'I have no luggage, just this.' He lifted his brown, leather bag up for the woman to inspect.'

Inputting their details into her computer system she quickly checked them in.

'Your flight boards in 45 minutes from gate number 2.' She instructed whilst pointing to the left. 'Have a good trip.'

'Thank you.' Amy and Jesse replied in unison.

Picking up their bags they strolled across the airport in the direction she had pointed them in.

'Airport sex?' Jesse asked. 'We have 45 minutes, I'm sure I can make you come at least twice in that time.' He added his voice low.

'Let's go.' Amy replied, marching off in the direction of the public toilets, suddenly feeling very brave. 'I can't actually believe I am about to do this Jesse!' She added smiling at him.

As they reached their destination Amy walked through the doors of the female toilets, her heart hammering in her chest. Walking to the mirrors above the sinks she was relieved to find all but one of the toilets empty. One of the black, wooden cubicle doors was firmly shut and so as Jesse walked in on quiet feet she placed her finger on her lips.

'Sssssshhhh.' She mouthed, pointing at the cubicle.

Smiling Jesse reached out for her hand.

'Come with me.' He whispered leading her into the cubicle furthest away.

Their hands were on one another as soon as he locked the door. Amy raised her left leg and positioned it on the closed toilet seat as Jesse's fingers sought her out.

'Amy!' He withdrew his fingers.

'Don't.' She hissed. 'Please Jesse don't tease.' She begged quietly, aware that someone was literally a few feet away from them.

'You are so wet.' He huskily replied thrusting his fingers into her once again, his thumb rubbing her clitoris faster and faster. As she climaxed Amy felt her right leg buckle from under her, grabbing hold of his shoulders she rode out her orgasm pushing his fingers deeper inside her.

'Turn around.' He commanded.

Obeying she faced the wall. As she heard him unbuckle his belt and drop his trousers she began to turn around. Grasping her hands in his own he placed them above her head before sliding himself effortlessly into her.

'Aarrrgghhh.' She moaned in pleasure.

'Sssshhhhh.' Jesse whispered into her ear as he began to slowly move in and out of her.

Biting down hard on her arm to quell the noises of pleasure she gave into the sensations that his cock began to create inside her. As Jesse felt the first convulsions of her orgasm he thrust deep within her shooting his warm sperm into her warm, cavern of sexuality.

'Oh…..My…..God!' She cried out, not caring if anyone heard her.

'I love you.' He said quietly into her hair.

'I love you too Jesse.' She replied her voice husky and filled with spent lust.

CHAPTER TWENTY SEVEN

'We have to fasten our seatbelts.' Jesse said as he gentle nudged Amy awake.

'Shit, I am so sorry baby.' She dreamily replied wiping the last dregs of stubborn sleep from her eyes.' 'How long was I asleep for?'

'Don't say sorry baby.' He replied taking hold of her hand. 'The music must have sent you to sleep.' He smiled. 'And about thirty minutes.' He added kissing the tip of her nose.

After the plane was securely in the air, Jesse had retrieved his IPod from his pocket. Handing one ear bud to Amy he deposited the other in his own ear. Together they listened to Bob Marley singing about one love and one heart until Amy must have drifted off into a pleasant sleep.

'I am so excited.' Jesse said a beaming smile on his handsome, young face.

'Me too babe.' She replied, matching his smile with a dazzlingly one of her own.

As the plane landed smoothly on the runway Amy squealed with childish delight.

'We're here!' She said a little too loudly. The couple sat across the aisle from them both turned and smiled in Amy's direction. 'Sorry.' She mouthed unable to wipe the stupid grin from her face.

As they waited for the passages to shuffle down the walkway Jesse reached up to the overhead locker for their bags.

'Here you go babe.' He said, smiling at Amy whilst holding out her bag.

'Thank you Jesse.' Amy replied, the ridiculous smile spreading wider and wider by the second.

Making their way to the exit they began to walk through the tunnel which connected the plane to the airport.

'We are in Holland.' She declared excitedly.

'Yes, we are in Holland but we are going to Amsterdam!' Jesse replied, wearing an equally outlandish grin on his young, handsome face.

Although Jesse had never stayed in Amsterdam he had flown to Schiphol airport when he was a teenager on route to the States.

'Can you remember which way to go?' Amy asked.

'Not really.' Jesse replied. 'I do know the train station is in the airport so once we are through here it shouldn't be too difficult to find.

The pair followed the signs to take them through the Dutch customs. Once their passports had been checked they took the escalator down to the train station. Approaching the ticket window Amy asked the waiting clerk for two tickets to Central station which lay in the heart of Amsterdam.

'Which platform does the train leave from please?' She asked the friendly clerk, relieved that he spoke good English.

'Platform 12 ma'am.' He replied.

'Thank you.' Amy said as she took the tickets from the cold, metal tray under the window.

They quickly found the signs which directed them to the platform and waited patiently for their train.

As an announcement crackled through the loud speaker system Amy jumped not recognizing the language.

'It sounds funny.' She laughed not being able to understand a word that had been spoken.

As the train pulled into the station Amy's mouth opened wide. The locomotive looked brand new and as they walked inside she realised it had stairs to an upper level.

'Shit Jesse.' She turned to look at him. 'The train has a bloody upstairs.'

Laughing Jesse followed her as she went to explore. Selecting two seats they sat and waited for the big train to move out of the station. Reaching for her mobile phone Amy plugged in her earphones and offered one to Jesse.

Amy gazed through the window in awe and was astounded to see some familiar stores. Carpet Right, Halfords and even a Kwik Fit. The rail line ran along a canal and she was fascinated by the large trawlers that carried cars and various other goods up and down the murky water.

'A windmill.' She shouted. 'Look Jesse, a windmill.' Amy was aware that her fellow passengers were looking in her direction but she really didn't care, she was too excited, this was her first time in Holland after all.

Graffiti graced every imaginable surface, big, colourful exhibitions of art work flashed past as the train took them closer to their destination.

'How long did the clerk say the train took?' Jesse asked.

'Not very long.' Amy replied. 'Surely the next station should be Central.'

'Excuse me.' The man seated opposite Jesse gently intruded their conversation. 'Did you say Central station?'

'Yes.' Jesse replied.

'You are on the wrong train.' The kindly Dutch man responded. 'You are heading into the south of Holland.'

'No!' Declared Jesse. 'How much further is the next station, do you know please?' He asked the stranger.

'The next station is coming up. Someone should be able to direct you to the correct train from there.' He replied.

'Thank you so much.' Amy and Jesse gushed in unison as they picked up their bags and headed towards the exit.

'Bloody stupid ticket man!' Amy said exasperation clearly evident in her voice. She was in a strange country and the language was foreign to her and very difficult to understand. 'Thank God for Jesse.' She silently thought as a tiny part of her old, unsure self began to reappear.

'It's ok, we will find the correct train babe, don't worry.' He reassured her taking hold of her tiny hand in his own.

As the pair dismounted they stopped the first person they came across, hoping the man would speak English.

'Excuse me.' Jesse said tapping the man lightly on the shoulder. 'Do you know which platform we go to for a train to Central station?'

'Of course.' The friendly man replied in almost perfect English. 'Follow me.'

As they made their way through the crowded train station Amy struggled to keep up with the two men, her little legs moving as fast as they could as they weaved in-between waiting passengers.

'Here you go. The train will be along in approximately ten minutes.' The Dutch man said. Amy stifled a giggle as the man struggled to say "approximately."

'Thank you so much.' Jesse replied shaking his hand.

'Yes, thank you, we would have been totally lost without your help.' Amy added smiling kindly at the helpful stranger.

'You are very welcome, have a nice holiday.' He said before promptly marching off to no doubt complete his own journey.

'Phew, thank heavens for him.' Amy remarked fighting to catch her breath.

The big locomotive pulled slowly into the station, its brakes squealing loudly as it drew to a halt and as they once again took their seats they both smiled at one another knowing that this time they were heading straight for the heart of Amsterdam.

CHAPTER TWENTY EIGHT

As they walked into the first coffee shop they spotted, Amy breathed a huge sigh of relief. She hadn't expected to see the huge amount of people on bicycles, peddling furiously, tinkling their little bells whenever a pedestrian crossed their path. The shop was literally across the road from Central station but Amy had nearly collided with four different cyclists whilst they covered the short distance.

The coffee shop was named "The Doors." The red canopy that hung over the front of the shop looked years old but Amy fell in love as soon as she walked into the entrance. The interior was shabbily painted in an off white colour but on the walls were giant posters of Jim Morrison. Jesse was thrilled; he had a wide and very eclectic taste in music which at first had amazed Amy. None of the modern crap that boomed, the lyrics hard to distinguish, Jesse preferred The Ramones, The Doors and just about all of Amy's favourite bands.

'This is surreal.' She whispered quietly to Jesse as she took in the scene before her. The shop was crowded; men and women were openly smoking cannabis whilst passing the time with pleasant conversation. To Amy everyone looked relaxed and chilled and she secretly wondered why the rest of the world didn't follow this unique and interesting life, surely the planet would be a much happier and peaceful place.

Walking up to the counter Jesse asked to see the menu. The shop keeper was clearly stoned and Amy giggled as the full reality hit her.

'We are in Amsterdam!' She excitedly reminded Jesse. 'Amsterfuckindam!'

Laughing he pressed the large red button that the attendant pointed to which lit up an old wooden case with glass on top. Inside there were various different types of marijuana.

'Wow, so much to choose from.' Amy remarked. 'Where the hell do we start?'

'What would you recommend?' Jesse asked the waiting man.

'It all depends what type of high you want.' He replied. 'Sativa or indica. For sativa I would recommend the haze, for indica, the cheeze although we do have a winning bud called "The Doors."

'Let's try "The Doors." Is that also a sativa?' Jesse asked.

'Yes, it sure is.' Replied the man.

As he went to fetch their purchase Amy sat down at one of the old, round, dark wood tables. She watched in complete fascination, whilst running her fingers along the deep grooves of the table top, as the man seated opposite her began to roll his joint. As he reached for his lighter the puzzled look on her face grew.

'Why is he setting fire to it?' Amy asked Jesse in a quiet voice as he joined her and took the seat opposite.

'He is back rolling babe.' Jesse replied. 'I will make one and teach you.' He smiled, squirming his bottom around on the tiny, red leather stool. 'This is not the comfiest of seats you know.'

Amy laughed and watched in amazement as Jesse began to roll their first Amsterdam joint. As he light the end of the flimsy cigarette paper she watched as the flames consumed the excess, leaving a perfectly made joint.

'Wow!' She remarked. 'Fascinating.'

As she took the potent smoke from Jesse's outreached fingers she dragged deeply, filling her lungs with the acrid plant.

'So different.' She observed. 'Not at all like the crap back in England.'

'This is sweet.' Jesse grinned as Jim Morrison's voice came over the speaker system singing People Are Strange in his laid back, poetic voice.

'I'm guessing you like it in here.' Amy smiled.

'Like it, I love it!' He replied. 'So what's the plan of action sexy bum?' He asked, grinning from ear to ear.

'I'm not fussed.' She replied. 'Whatever you want to do sexy eyes.' She laughed returning the compliment and using her favourite pet name for him.

'Well, I think we should smoke this.' He said passing the joint once again to Amy. 'Then go and find the hotel, unpack and then go and explore. I want to try and find The Resin Bar, I've been told its sick!'

'The Resin Bar it is.' Amy laughed, her enthusiasm matching his perfectly.

The two sat in contended silence as they finished smoking the potent herb. Amy had felt the effects of the sweet smelling plant almost immediately and as she took her last pull she reached across the battered table and lightly touched Jesse's arm.

'Thank you.' She whispered a dreamy look in her eyes. 'I love you.' She mouthed silently to him.

'I love you.' He whispered back.

CHAPTER TWENTY NINE

Amy dawdled as they made their way to the hotel. Her eyes couldn't move at a fast enough pace to take in her surroundings as Jesse strode along the cobbled streets, his long, athletic legs covering the distance quickly. Stopping she inhaled deeply, closing her eyes…. she never wanted to forget this moment. Imprinting it to the depths of her mind she opened her eyes to find Jesse starring at her.

'What are you doing?' He asked, cheekily laughing.

'I'm making sure that I forever remember this exact location.' She said, spreading her arms out before her. 'I mean Jesse, look at this place! It's amazing!' As she span around she took a few minutes to truly appreciate the city of Amsterdam. The canal was almost still, colourful barges gently floated on its surface and as she walked to the centre of the arched bridge she heard the now familiar sound of a cyclist's bell.

'Shit!' She exclaimed as she quickly dodged out of the way, the bicycle almost grazing her leg. 'That was close.' She laughed. Jesse knew the effects of the marijuana were kicking in as Amy doubled up, holding her stomach whilst the laughter rang from her body. Jesse suddenly lunged forward, grabbing her arm whilst hauling her out of the way of yet another bike.

'You are going to get yourself killed.' He joked, her infectious laughter suddenly attacking him.

Picking up their discarded bags the two made their way along the narrow cobbled streets to the hotel. Amy was finding it difficult to keep up with Jesse as she tried to suppress the laughter that so badly wanted to escape her lips.

'Jesse.' She called making him abruptly stop before her. 'I can't keep up.' She chuckled. 'And I can't stop bloody laughing, what's the matter with me?' She asked, trying to keep a straight face but failing atrociously.

'You're high babe.' He laughed. 'High on Amsterdam weed.'

Committing his smile and face to her memory Amy tried her best to quell the giggles that were again building up inside her body.

'We are going to have a fab time.' She declared. 'Bring it on Amsterdam, I am ready.' She shouted into the air.

'Come on you.' Jesse chuckled. 'It will be tomorrow by the time we find the hotel at this rate.'

"No more drugs for that woman." Amy said, doing her best Dietrich Hassler impression. Face Off was her favourite movie and she knew almost all the lines she had watched it that many times. Whenever Nicholas Cage said the line "Peach, I could eat a peach for hours," Amy would literally squirm in her seat. Not that she fancied Nicholas Cage, it was the way the outstanding actor spoke the words. They were always guaranteed to send a tiny tingle up her spine.

Standing up Amy straightened her left hand; bringing it up to her eyebrow she threw a mock salute in Jesse's direction.

'Yes Sir.' She grinned, slapping her feet together before bending to retrieve her bag once again.

Laughing they finally found their hotel. As they unlocked the door and walked into their room the pair burst out laughing. Amy had read on the website that each room had been decorated in an individual theme, their room "Arabian Nights," had dark purple and orange walls which were decorated with cheap pieces of Far Eastern art. Above the double bed she spotted a vibrant orange piece of almost sheer fabric that had been fastened to resemble a canopy. On either side of the bed hung large, multi coloured glass lights, these were secured to the ceiling with heavy chains and as she reached for the switch and turned one on she stood back a huge smile on her face.

'Wow!' She exclaimed. 'Jesse, come look at this.' She called out.

Turning around she saw Jesse closely inspected the pictures on the wall. As he reached for one he glanced in Amy's direction.

'This.' He said. 'Is being turned around!' As he grabbed the two bottom corners Amy burst out laughing as she looked at the picture of a woman with an elephant's head.

'Ewwwww, now that is ugly! She said, as she collapsed on the bed, her laughter causing her to grab her knees as the pain shot across her stomach. Tears ran down her face as she continued to roll about the

bed, her breath coming in huge rasps between the laughter. 'I......
can't........breathe.......Amy said.'

Joining her on the bed Jesse grabbed her. Placing one hand in her
hair he gently drew her head backwards, placing his lips on hers. As
his tongue began its discovery of her mouth Amy felt her lust for him
overtake the laughter. With a tongue as eager as his she pulled him
even closer, her hands in his hair as she felt the moisture begin to
develop between her thighs.

His hands made short work of her clothes, lying back on the bed
Amy watched him take off his shoes and socks and begin to undress.
His strong hands reached for the hem of his t shirt and with eyes
transfixed she inhaled sharply as he removed it exposing his athletic
torso, the smooth, tanned skin that she longed to touch and kiss. Shit,
he turned her on, she wanted him with a passion so fierce it sent her
dizzy and as he reached for his belt she felt her breath catch in her
throat. He was beautiful, so handsome and his eyes.........

'Sexy eyes.' She breathed.

With an almost deliberate slowness Jesse removed his jeans to
reveal a tight fitting pair of white boxer shorts. Amy felt her teeth sink
into her lower lip as she noticed how hard his cock was as it strained
against the smooth material.

'I want you.' Her words reaching out to caress him as they lingered
in the air.

Moving towards the bed Jesse smiled at her sexily, the look in his
eyes was difficult to meet and so sitting up on her knees she reached
for him her fingers once again disappearing into his silky, brown hair
as she brought his lips to hers. She loved kissing him and knew that
one day, maybe not too far away; Jesse would be able to bring her to
orgasm with just his lips on hers. Never had she experienced the deep
feelings and sensations he created within her when his mouth was on
hers.

'Yes.' She silently thought. 'It's not too far away.' Amy closed her
eyes and as Jesse tilted her head to the side to kiss her exposed neck
she murmured her special three words.

'I love you.'

CHAPTER THIRTY

Her mouth encircled the tip of him, her tongue cupping the back of his cock, holding Jesse firmly in place. Sliding her lips over her teeth she moved her mouth further down taking as much of him as she could into her mouth. Hearing him moan she slowly reversed her actions until once again only the very end of him was between her moist lips. Grasping him tightly with her left hand she began to suck hard, as she felt him tense she released him and ran her tongue around the head, randomly flicking then caressing him, her desire growing, her sex wet and ready for him. He tasted so good. As she increased the pressure of her hand whilst continuing to gratify him with her lips, tongue and inner mouth she heard him moan once again, his body tensing periodically as he fought to contain his impending orgasm. Her mouth was driving him wild as she continued to pleasure him, their moans of ecstasy filling the room.

Reaching between her legs with her free hand Amy began to massage her clitoris. As her fingers circled slowly Jesse opened his eyes.

'Are you playing with yourself?' He asked. His green eyes smoldered as they burnt into hers.

'Yes.' She breathed; a blush beginning to spread across her cheeks as embarrassment began to overtake the passion.

'Now that is sexy!' Jesse seductively declared his eyes on hers, reaching deep into her heart.

Bending her head she took him into her mouth once again. With a tentative hand she began to pleasure herself. As she took him deep she thrust two fingers into her wet pussy.

'Oh My God!' Jesse shouted. Bringing her head up, he grasped her shoulders and roughly pushed her back onto the bed. As he entered her his mesmerizing eyes burned into hers. 'Fuck I want you.' He hissed.

Thrusting into her Amy felt her hunger for him spread throughout her body. The tiny ripples of desire snaked their way around her secret place, each touch magnified, drawing her deeper and deeper under his spell. As gigantic swells overtook her Amy cried out, her fingernails digging into Jesse's back as she called out his name over and over again.

Reaching for her legs Jesse drew them up so they were positioned on his shoulders. Amy felt his cock deep within her and as he began to move once again she felt her heart miss a tiny beat as her breath became trapped in her lungs.

'Could she possibly feel any more for this man?' The silent words swam about her foggy brain and as she felt herself open to him she once again called out his name over and over again as the sweet agony of her orgasm pulsed throughout her.

CHAPTER THIRTY ONE

Amy tried to tame her "thoroughly fucked" hair in the steamy mirror of the bathroom. She had considered washing it whilst taking a shower but didn't want to waste the precious time they had in this magical city drying it. As she secured it with a clip Jesse approached her, playfully slapping her on the arse.

'Naughty.' Amy giggled.

'Oh Miss Lucas, I am going to show you just how naughty I can be.' Jesse sexily threatened that brooding, sensual look that sent her giddy burning deep within his eyes.

'Now stop your shenanigans.' Amy wagged her finger at him. Reaching out and snatching it with his own he took it into his mouth flicking his tongue over the tip.

Amy felt her eyes widen as she tried to meet and hold his eyes as the sensations from his tongue on her finger connecting with her secret place.

'Jesse.' Her voice was the barest whisper.

Abruptly letting go of her finger Jesse laughed as he walked back into the bedroom.

Stomping after him Amy stood before him, her hands perched at her tiny waist.

'Now that was BAD!' She pouted.

'What?' Jesse said innocently, "that look" in his eyes.

'You know what!' Amy replied sticking out her bottom lip as she sulked like a petulant child.

'Let's go and explore.' He said a self-assured look on his face.

'Pft! You know exactly what you do to me Clayton!' Amy tried her best to look annoyed.

As the laughter began to bubble in her stomach she noticed Jesse was already holding his sides trying to contain his own chuckles.

'Let's go smoke some weed.' Amy said picking up her bag whilst trying not to look at Jesse. He had her a tumbling, mumbling, dizzy wreck and boy did he know it! 'I will get you back.' She declared, trying to throw him a smoldering look of her own.

'I'm sure you will Amy.' Jesse laughed, slapping her on the arse once more.

As Amy locked the door to their room Jesse pulled out the street map from his pocket.

'Where would you like to go first?' He asked busily consulting his map.

'Why don't we try the coffee shop here first and then go and find The Resin Bar?' Amy offered in reply.

'Sounds like a plan.' Jesse enthusiastically replied.

Walking down the steep, narrow staircase they opened the door that led directly to the street. Taking the white door to the right they entered The Greenhouse Effect coffee shop. Again Amy gasped as she glanced at the people sat at the bar smoking their various different types of marijuana.

'Would she ever get used to this.' She silently thought as they walked to the back of the shop to consult the menu.

'What shall we get?' Jesse asked as he looked down at Amy.

'Lemon haze?' She suggested, standing on her tiptoes so she didn't look quite so small next to him.

As a young girl Amy had been a competitive dancer. Her training schedule, before a competition was grueling, rising at 5.30am Amy would be at the dance studio for a couple of hours before school, she would then study for her exams until the bell rang at 3.30 when she would run the short distance back to the studio to train again until 7pm. All those hours of training and pointing her small feet in the elegant dancer's pose that was demanded of her had left her with a habit of standing on her tiptoes constantly. It also helped make her look taller, especially when she wore flat shoes. At just over five feet tall Jesse towered above her at an impressive height of just under six feet.

Picking up their purchase the pair selected a table in the middle of the shop. As Amy took in her surroundings once again she realised it still hadn't quite sunk in. The city was surreal and they had only been here a few hours and sampled such a small portion. She couldn't wait for it to go dark so they could explore the Red Light District. They had watched a policing documentary series before they arrived and to Amy it just didn't look real. She wanted to see it all for herself, the women in the windows, the tourists. So far, as they had walked to their hotel she had continually noticed the smell of marijuana heavy in the air every time the door of a coffee shop opened.

'This is a truly fantastic place'. She declared taking the joint from Jesse's outreached fingers. I think I could live here.' She said dreamily, the effects of the plant beginning to wash her body and mind in an almost cleansing way. Amy found that she could completely shut out her past when she was stoned and although she had originally discovered the plant to aid with her pain relief she enjoyed the serenity it provided her as it gently took away her fears and insecurities.

'Are you hungry?' Jesse asked.

'Famished.' Amy replied rubbing her stomach. 'I think the munchies are setting in.' She giggled.

Finishing their smoke and drinks Jesse and Amy made their way out of the coffee shop. As the fresh air hit her Amy reached out for the wall to support herself.

'Shit, I feel really dizzy.' She exclaimed. The colour was slowly beginning to seep from her face leaving her a sickly, pale colour.

'Are you ok?' Jesse asked as he gently rubbed her shoulders whilst helping to keep her on her feet.

'I will be fine, it's easing a little now.' She replied as she tested the strength in her legs. 'Yes, I'm good.' She declared. 'Let's go.'

'Are you sure?' Jesse responded, concern clearly evident on his handsome face.

'Jesse, honestly I am fine.' Amy reassured him stroking his arm.

Satisfied that she was ok Jesse retrieved the map from his pocket consulting it closely once again.

'If we walk down this street and keep going until we reach here.' Jesse pointed to a road on the map.

'I haven't got a clue.' Amy replied. Map reading had never been a particular hobby or strength of hers but she was glad that Jesse appeared to be very talented at it. As she silently wondered where he had learnt to map read so well he turned to look at her.

'My dad was in the Royal Air Force.' He said answering her unspoken question.

'How the hell do you do that?' She asked, stopping to look closely at him to inspect his face. 'How are you able to answer questions I have not even asked?' It wasn't the first time that Jesse appeared to read her mind.

'I have a knack.' He grinned.

'Pft.' Amy replied starting to walk once again in the direction pointed out by Jesse.

Their hotel was ideally situated on the edge of the Red Light District. Jesse calculated that it would take them approximately twenty minutes to cover the distance from Warmoestraat, the street that housed The Greenhouse Effect to Hekelved where The Resin Bar was situated.

As they walked the crowded, cobbled streets of Amsterdam Amy fell in love all over again with the magical city, despite nearly getting knocked over by a passing cyclist again.

'Crap! They are everywhere.' She remarked as she carefully dodged another two bicycles as they hurtled down the narrow street, their little bells peeling out to warn pedestrians.

'You'll get used to it.' Jesse chuckled. 'Watch out Amy! Here comes another parade of bikes.' He warned.

Darting to the side of the pavement she dissolved into a laughing mess once again as the marijuana induced a fit of chuckling that she just couldn't stop.

'I'm having the best time!' She declared. 'Maybe she could bring Mr Champagne for his birthday.' she silently thought. 'Yes! Now that was a plan!' As she started to hatch her secret present for the man she loved Amy smiled. 'What a plan!'

CHAPTER THIRTY TWO

As they walked into The Resin Bar Amy's mouth flew open in surprise.

'Wow!' She exclaimed. 'Jesse come and look in here.' As she peered through the glass door Amy gasped once more. 'Jesse, look! Rope swings!' She was unable to contain her excitement and didn't care that the woman behind the counter was looking at her strangely. 'I'm sorry.' Amy said addressing her directly. 'It's my first time in Amsterdam and well……'

The woman smiled kindly at Amy.

'People are always amazed and a little crazy when they first visit us.' She remarked. 'Now what can I get for you guys?'

'Oh I'm not sure.' Turning to Jesse she hoped he would take the decision out of her hands and choose.

'I'll sort it out babe.' Jesse said. 'You go and grab us a seat.'

Walking through the glass door Amy entered the seating area whilst Jesse completed the sale.

The walls were painted a vibrant green. Along each wall jade leather seating with a variety of comfy cushions beckoned to Amy. As she made herself comfortable she glanced around in fascination as she noticed how the rope swings hung on enormous, chunky chains from the ceiling.

As Jesse walked towards her he wore a beaming smile. Placing their drinks and marijuana on the table he immediately sat on one of the swings, his long, lean legs dangling either side. Pushing the toes of his converse on the wooden floor he began to sway gently to and fro.

'Sick!' He gushed. 'This is sick!' The expression on his face made Amy smile, her heart quietly singing as she watched him and felt her love for him ooze from her every pore.

Amy smiled, happy that he was happy. Watching him closely she reached for her bag, removing the camera; she snapped a picture of him smiling. 'Fuck he is a handsome bastard.' She thought as she secretly studied him. His silky hair was tousled, his sexy eyes were alive, his mouth wore the almost permanent smile that had possessed him since they had landed in Holland. His perfectly arched eyebrows rose as he caught her starring.

Embarrassed she quickly looked away, casting her eyes to her feet; she began to fidget with the hem of her blouse.

'Your turn to skin up.' Jesse said as he continued to sway gently.

As she slowly recovered Amy reached for the paraphernalia that she needed to make the joint. Her fingers and mind occupied she glanced once more in his direction. Meeting his intense green eyes she blushed.

'No shenanigans.' She playfully scolded as he deepened the look the way only Mr. Champagne knew how. 'Behave!' She pleaded. 'I really can't cope you know!' As the heat began its journey through her body she rose from her comfortable seat.

'Where are you going?' Jesse asked an innocent look on his face.

'To the toilet, I need some "Me" time.' Amy replied handing him the grinder, marijuana and rolling paper. 'Can you do this please whilst I go?' She asked. 'My fingers won't work for some strange reason.'

'Mmmm, "Me" time sounds interesting, can I come?' He teased ignoring her question.

'No!' She responded, a playful smile on her lips. 'It's called "Me" time for a reason and I need a lot of it since I met you!' She huffed playfully as she reached out and touched his face.

'Awwww please let me come with you.' He begged sticking out his bottom lip.

'Jesse, you are bad!' Oh how she wanted him.

'Let me show you how bad I can be.' He winked sexily at her.

'I am going alone to the toilet now, I will be five minutes.' Grabbing her handbag Amy stomped off towards the back of the shop, the sound of Jesse's laughter at her embarrassment making her blush even more.

Resting her head against the cool tiled wall Amy tried to control her breathing.

She couldn't get enough of him but she also couldn't handle him, his eyes, his sodding, perfect, green, sexy fucking eyes. Her heart was thumping away in her chest as the image of him swam before her.

'Fuck! What is wrong with me?' She said to herself. 'Get a fucking grip woman!'

Turning on the cold tap Amy placed her wrists under the flowing water. As she felt her body begin to cool down her heart rate slowed a little. How could someone so young create such intense emotions? Was it magic? Did he possess some sort of mystical powers?

'Well it certainly feels as if I am under his bloody spell.' Amy spoke quietly to her reflection as she tidied up her hair. 'I mean, how does he do it? Sex is one thing but….. he is in here.' She said touching her chest lightly. Composing herself fully Amy retrieved her discarded handbag before heading back out into the shop.

Jesse was already smoking the joint he had finished making. Handing it to Amy he reached out to brush the hair back from her eyes.

'We need to get some food.' He declared. They hadn't eaten since they boarded the plane and as if wanting to get in on the conversation, Amy's stomach howled nosily.

'I think my stomach agrees.' She giggled as it once again rumbled.

'Let's finish up here and we will go and eat.' Jesse responded.

'So what do you think of Amsterdam so far Mr. Clayton?' Amy asked as she began to collect their belongings from the table.

'Amazing.' He replied.

'Just like you.' She whispered to him. 'Just like you.'

CHAPTER THIRTY THREE

Their time in Amsterdam passed quickly. As they explored the streets Amy's utter amazement grew with every passing shop and window. When daylight faded The Red Light District was light up beautifully and as they had walked along the canal Amy practically gawped at the women flaunting their bodies as they plied their trade.

Arriving home Amy had immediately scoured the internet to look for Jesse's birthday present. After carefully researching the different hotels she booked a two night break as her gift to him. Selecting earlier flights this time to make the most of their short vacation Amy inputted her card details. She couldn't wait to tell Jesse. She would have to give him notice of course but as the excitement ran through her she could no longer contain her delicious secret.

Reaching for her mobile phone Amy typed out a text.

'Hi Sexy Eyes. I am not telling you why but can you make sure you are available two days after your birthday please. xx I love you xx' Pressing send she waited for his reply, praying that he would be able to get the time off work.

'Hi baby, how long for? And why? xx' He replied.

'Three nights and don't be nosey! xx Love ya Sugar Lips. xx'

As she heard her phone beep she debated whether to let him stew for a while. Feeling guilty she picked it up and read his message.

'Please babe, where are we going? xx and love you too xx.' He wrote back.

'It's for your birthday. Please trust me, it's a surprise. xx' She replied hoping that he wouldn't put too much pressure on her to reveal the details. She wanted it to remain a surprise but knew that if he questioned her she would give in and spill the beans.

'Ok then but you know I don't like surprises. xx' He joked.

'Tough! xx' Came her one worded reply.

As his birthday approached she revealed her gift to him.

'You're joking!' He almost squealed, his deep, manly voice rising in excitement.

'No.' Amy giggled. 'I think we both fell in love with Amsterdam and so whilst we were in The Resin Bar I decided to do this for you.'

Grabbing her tightly Jesse wrapped his muscular arms around her, drawing her close. Placing his finger under her chin he raised her head so his eyes could meet hers.

'Thank you.' He whispered as he planted a kiss on the tip of her nose that sent tiny thrills straight to her heart.

'You're welcome.' Amy replied standing on her tiptoes so she could return his kiss. Feelings of love and trust coursed through her as she briefly met his eyes.

'A simple kiss on the end of my bloody conk and he has me swooning.' She silently reprimanded herself. 'I simply have no self-control where he is concerned.' She thought. 'My heart is most definitely on my sleeve!'

Jesse had loved his birthday present and both declared they wanted to visit a third, fourth and fifth time.

As the weeks past Amy grew used to having Jesse around as they spent more and more time together. Chloe and Bethany accepted him with open arms, content and happy that their mother seemed to permanently wear a smile on her face. She had slowly introduced her wonderful man to her two daughters, taking her time to make sure her girls were ok with everything. Her independence was something that she had begun to treasure and enjoy as she had embarked on her new single life but having a kind, caring man to hold you when the going got tough was heaven. Jesse ticked all the boxes, he was almost perfect.

'Almost.' The words echoed around her head. 'If only he was a little older or she a little younger.......

Whenever he stayed at home her bed would feel lonely without him. Finding it difficult to sleep she would cradle his pillow to her, inhaling his scent deeply into her nostrils until finally she was able to drift off into a troubled sleep.

The vivid, horrific nightmares visited her less and less and she was thankful that Jesse had never witnessed her have one. Oh how she thought those words too soon!

'Do you fancy going to the cinema? xx' He text.

'Yes!' She replied. 'What do you fancy watching? xx'

'We can decide when we get there; maybe get a bite to eat first? xx' He responded.

As they sat and watched the film Amy gripped tightly to the side of the arm rest as a scene played out before her, the villain placing a plastic bag over his victim's head, slowly suffocating the air from his body.

The flashback was quick as it invaded her brain and she winced in silent agony as she remembered Paul doing the exact same thing to her. Reaching for her hand Jesse squeezed it lightly sensing that something was amiss he turned in his seat and looked at her.

'Are you ok?' His words were spoken in an almost whisper, his eyes busily searching her face.

'I'm fine.' She responded as she tried to control her breathing not wanting Jesse to witness her pain or the feelings that she was now wrestling with silently.

No further words were necessary. Jesse knew almost everything about Amy's past now as she had gradually opened up to him as her trust for this wonderful, special man deepened. As she flinched beside him he guessed correctly that she was reliving some awful trauma she had suffered at her ex-husband's hands.

As the first streaks of light signaling a new day began to light up the dark, night sky Jesse woke to find Amy pitching about on her side of the bed, her arms and legs moving rapidly as she appeared to fight off her unseen attacker. She cried out, her voice trembling and laced with fear.

'Please no, please don't.' She repeated over and over.

'Stop. Please.'

Jesse couldn't stand to see her like this. Gently he reached for her, touching her arm softly.

'Amy.' He called softly, trying to wake her from the torment she was suffering. 'Amy. Amy.'

Somewhere, deep inside her nightmare filled mind, Amy heard his voice calling out her name.

Cradling her closely Amy fought to banish the images as her brain slowly awoke and she realised she was safe and secure in Jesse's arms.

'I'm sorry.' She sobbed.

'You're safe Amy.' Drawing her closer to him, he cocooned her tightly forcing the last of the horrific images from her trembling body.

As he held her Jesse became overwhelmed with feelings of sadness for Amy. In the short space of time that he had known her she had revealed so much and he had been especially horrified when he had asked what the scar was on her stomach.

'What's this?' He had asked as he gently ran his finger along the small scar as they lay spent after a particularly long sexual marathon.

'Nothing. I don't know.' She had replied, her hand reaching down quickly to cover the blemish.

Gently he removed her hand and touched the white mark with his fingertips.

'Ok, you don't have to tell me.' He had replied, his eyes searching deep within hers, knowing that she was hiding some awful truth from him.

Amy had immediately jumped up.

'Let's go for a walk.' She said as she threw on her dressing gown.

Sensing that the topic was not up for discussion Jesse had gone along with her fake jovial mood. After he went home Amy had sat for hours agonizing over whether to be truthful with the man she loved.

'I was stabbed.' She quietly said when Jesse returned later that day.

'I had a feeling.' He replied, taking her into his arms, holding her tight.

Jesse finally understood how bad her life had been. Beatings, repeatedly being raped and used, being stabbed, not to mention the almost constant verbal abuse that had left her a crumpled, frightened wreck. She was so tiny and vulnerable, almost like a little doll.

'It was a chisel.' She openly revealed holding tightly to him, her head buried into his chest, as she divulged a little more of her past to the amazing man who she loved and trusted with every part of her.

'Ok baby, you don't have to relive this, I understand. Sssshhh.' He gently coaxed as he stroked her hair.

He amazed her, so young and yet so understanding. Amy knew she had made the right choice when she had decided to allow herself to love him, how could any woman possibly not love this wonderful man she secretly thought.

CHAPTER THIRTY FOUR

'You up for another adventure Sexy Eyes? xx' Amy text.

'What do you have in mind Sexy Bum? xx' Jesse replied.

'Remember how I told you about the thatched cottages with the jacuzzis? Well we are going later. xx' A smile played happily on her face as she waited for his reply.

'Hell yeh! xx'

'Ok, well I will pick you up in about an hour. Is that ok? Xx'

'See you in an hour. Can't wait! xx' He text back.

Just over sixty minutes later the pair where on their way. As they flew up the motorway in Amy's nippy Ford Fiesta the conversation was funny and light.

'I can't wait to get there.' Amy squealed with excitement.

'Me too.' Jesse replied flashing his oh so sexy eyes at her.

'Behave! I am driving.' She laughed, desperately trying to quell the way her secret place was responding to his gaze.

Reaching out Jesse began to lightly stroke down the side of Amy's neck, his fingertips grazing her earlobe.

'Oh Jesse.' She murmured as she felt her head rest into his hand. As the car veered off into the right hand lane Jesse abruptly withdrew his fingers.

'Not a good idea whilst you're driving I think.' He chuckled.

'No, not a good idea at all.' Amy playfully scolded. 'May I suggest that if you want to arrive in one piece, you keep your hands to your side of the car!' She laughed.

As they drove into the car park the pair whooped in delight. White washed stone cottages with thatched roofs stood before them. They were surrounded by fields but off to the left Amy spotted the canal which appeared to be full of moored barges. She could hear ducks quacking and as a particularly vocal group came waddling across the tarmac Amy and Jesse burst out laughing in unison. As Amy opened the boot to retrieve their bags she sneaked a glance at Jesse.

God he was so handsome.

'You're hot!' She stated as she watched him finish his cigarette whilst casually leaning against the car.

'And you're sexy.' He replied, stamping out the butt before bending to retrieve it. 'I can't wait to get you in the jacuzzi.' He sexily threatened throwing the finished cigarette into a nearby bin.

'Bring it on Clayton!' She seductively replied. 'Give me your best.' With a wink Amy walked towards the reception.

The double executive room was amazing, the jacuzzi and wet room even more so. Tasteful pictures adorned the walls and a super queen sized bed beckoned to them. As Amy took in her surroundings, committing them to her memory, she spotted the large mirror which hung opposite the bed. Turning to Jesse she smiled.

'Oh.' Her finger pointed towards the enormous piece of glass.

'Oh.' Repeated Jesse. 'Now that could be fun.' He declared a sexy look in his eyes.

'Mmmm.' Amy dreamily replied as delicious, naughty thoughts took over. 'I am going to go and fill that jacuzzi.' She couldn't wait to try it out; she had never sat in a jacuzzi before, never mind have wild, passionate sex in one with an irresistible, sexy, hunk of a man.

The warm water filled the jacuzzi and as Amy poured in the bubble bath she watched in fascination and then horror as the foam began to multiply at an alarming rate as the powerful jets churned the water around.

'Jesse.' She called. 'Shit Jesse!'

'What's the matter?' He asked appearing in the doorway. 'Oh, I see.' He laughed. 'Bloody hell Amy how much did you use?' Reaching for the button Jesse turned off the flow of water, silencing the feisty jets.

Taking off her shoes the pair began to scoop the bubbles out of the jacuzzi, throwing them on the floor.

'Do you think they will all disappear?' She asked Jesse as she looked around her at the foamy chaos giggling hysterically. She could feel the bubbles tickling her ankles as she padded around the bathroom, trying to get rid of the mess she had created.

'Yeh, it's a wet room.' He replied. 'Oh you brought candles.' He added pointing to the purple wax objects that were dotted about the room.

'I thought it would be nice to sit in the jacuzzi, have a smoke and watch that brilliant flat screen TV.' She said, her hand sweeping out towards the television above the jacuzzi.

'Now that is a plan!' Jesse agreed scooping another handful of bubbles out of the tub.

Half an hour later the two relaxed whilst enjoying their smoke of marijuana in the jacuzzi, the candles casting a seductive glow around the large bathroom. Taking a sip of her wine Amy gazed lovingly at Jesse.

'Wow! This is....' As Jesse brought his lips down onto hers, silencing her words, she closed her eyes, her mouth responding immediately to the silky touch of his mouth.

'I want you.' He breathed. Drawing back he looked into her eyes, a penetrating stare that clenched at her heart. The mixture of cannabis and alcohol making her brave she tried to meet his sexy gaze.

'I want you too.' She replied in a hushed, sexy tone.

As her arms encircled his neck she sank her fingers into his hair, drawing his mouth once more to hers. As her tongue began to explore his mouth she shifted her position slightly until she could feel the powerful jets on her sex. Leaning back and spreading her legs Amy felt the forceful stream of water connect with her clitoris.

'Oh......My......God.' She stuttered as she felt the first stirrings of her impending climax.

Pulling himself away from her Jesse watched with complete fascination as Amy surrendered herself to the water. Reaching for her nipples he traced their contours with his fingertips, sending waves of desire throughout her as he increased the pressure making her gasp with pleasure.

As the orgasm took over her Jesse bent his head. Taking her right nipple into his mouth he sucked and flicked his tongue over the erect bud, his fingers weaving their magic on her left one until Amy fully exploded, moaning loudly whilst calling out his name.

'I want you.' He said, reaching for her.

As the final swells of her climax left her body Jesse thrust into her hard sending her toppling over the edge once again. She clung to him, the water splashing violently around as her orgasm raged, her fingernails digging into the soft skin of his back she cried out his name over and over again.

CHAPTER THIRTY FIVE

Lying in his arms on the enormous, comfortable bed Amy felt as if she was in heaven. The way he touched her, the way he kissed her, the way he looked at her…….

'Do you fancy listening to some music babe?' He lazily asked as his fingertips drew lazy patterns over her bare skin.

'That would be nice.' Amy replied dreamily.

As he rose from the bed Amy observed him, her eyes cast downwards in case he caught her.

She adored watching him, the way he moved with an almost catlike grace as his naked body made its way across the room towards the dark wood desk where he had previously placed his laptop.

'What do you fancy?' He asked, turning around to look at her.

'You!' She replied courageously, stretching her body enticingly.

Laughing Jesse turned his attention back to selecting some music.

'All in good time Miss Lucas.' He replied throwing her one of his sexy Jesse looks.

As the first strains of the wonderful music played Amy rested her head on her arms and allowed the strangely addictive notes to wash over her. Deep within her she felt herself stir once again, her passion growing with every sultry note that was played.

'What's this?' She dreamily asked as her longing for him began to mount along with the tempo of the tune.

'Massive Attack, Paradise Circus.' He whispered as he watched her body move in time with the beat of the music as he lay back down on the bed.

'Well, it's turning me on!' She declared as she reached out for him.

Throwing her one of his "looks," Jesse reached for her, drawing her tightly to his chest.

'I love you Amy.' He breathed as his mouth began to explore her lips and neck.

'Oh Jesse, I love you too.' She murmured. 'I don't think you realise just how much I do love you.' Amy quickly buried her head in his chest, afraid that her brave, outspoken words would scare him. She knew that the way she loved him was very powerful, it made her gasp whenever she allowed herself to think about it. The intense feelings she held for this special and amazing man had slowly overtaken her life but deep, deep within the confines of her brain and heart lurked the truth and no matter how hard she fought and tried to forget it, it was always there, poking its finger of fun at her accusingly. If only she could totally forget the difference in their ages. If only she could be totally free to love him the way only she did. Amy had given him her heart, body, mind and soul and was totally his.

As his lips sought hers he kissed her deeply, a kiss that stopped her heart for a fraction of a second, a kiss that only Jesse knew how to deliver, a meeting of lips that she matched with the love that was cradled for him deep within her heart.

Their bodies became one as hands, lips, feet and torsos entwined, the melody that turned Amy on so much, still playing on repeat in the background.

Pulling herself away from him gently she looked briefly into his eyes.

'I have a surprise for you.' She quietly whispered whilst tracing her index finger along his bottom lip.

'And what is that?' Jesse grinned taking hold of her finger and promptly putting it into his mouth where he began to swirl his tongue deliciously over the pad.

'Wait there.' She replied removing her finger and placing a small kiss on his soft, full lips.

Bending to pick up her overnight bag Amy winked at Jesse before disappearing into the bathroom. She had bought the sexy lingerie a few days ago and as she drew the sheer red fabric down over her body she glanced at her reflection in the large mirror that ran down the back of the closed door. Reaching for the high heeled, red suede shoes she carefully placed her feet into them, holding on to the edge of the sink for support. Once again she checked out her reflection as self-doubt began to stab at her.

'Stop it!' She hissed at herself. Sticking her tongue out cheekily at her reflection she quickly retrieved the tiny sliver of silver metal from inside her purse. Bending once more she secured the chain around her ankle, its delicate heart rested lightly on her right lateral malleolus.

Taking a much needed lung full of air Amy slowly opened the door to find Jesse lay back on the bed, his eyes closed as he listened to the music that played from his laptop.

'Hi.' She murmured as her self-confidence plummeted in a crashing heap around her stiletto encased tiny feet.

Sensing what she was feeling Jesse rose from the bed and strode casually towards her, an amazingly sexy look in his beautiful green eyes.

'Wow!' He said. 'Amy…….'

'Do you like it?' She asked shyly, her eyes cast down to the floor.

'I love it, oh…my….god…..those shoes!' Standing back Jesse took in fully the bashful woman before him. 'They are so sexy, you are so sexy.' He murmured as he reached for her hand to guide her back to the bed.

'I'm glad you like it.' She responded as she felt her self-confidence slowly begin to return.

Jesse tenderly grasped first her left foot and then her right planting tiny, succulent kisses along the exposed part of her skin where it disappeared into the foot of the extremely high shoes.

'What's this?' He asked, his green eyes burning straight into hers as he twirled the silver anklet around. 'I like it.' He added. 'Do you know what would look perfect just here?' He asked pointing to where the tiny heart lay on her ankle bone, a tattoo.'

'Really?' She asked. Amy had never considered adorning her body with permanent art work but as the idea slowly sank into her brain she embraced it. 'Mmmmm I think I agree.' She responded giving into the sensations he was creating with his fingers and lips on her feet.

With an almost heart breaking slowness Jesse trailed his fingers up her leg, lingering as he connected with her secret place. As he placed his fingers at her entrance Amy moaned as she opened up, ready to accept him. Never taking his eyes away from her Jesse began to move, long, languid motions that had Amy withering and moaning beneath him as he explored her dark, wet place. Unable to meet the intense gaze of his beautiful eyes she shut her own; concentrating on the spectacular feelings that swirled around her body.

As her breathing escalated Jesse abruptly withdrew his fingers only to replace them with his lips and tongue. Oh how she loved him doing this to her. At first she had been embarrassed when his head had disappeared between her legs, now feeling alive and sexy, she watched in the mirror adjacent to the bed as he brought her close to the orgasm that her body and mind now craved.

'I love you.' He breathed before burying his tongue deep inside her sending her crashing into a climax like she had never felt before. As she exploded around his tongue and fingers she called out his name.

'Jesse, I…. love…. You…..' Came her rasping words as she rode the waves that engulfed her.

Sliding up her body he positioned his erect cock and drove into her with a passion that completely matched her own. Pulling himself back so he was positioned on his knees he reached for her feet, the red suede stilettos looked so small in his big, masculine hands as he raised her legs high and wide so he could thrust deeply within her.

Amy's eyes were wide, her breath caught in her throat as he moved himself inside her.

'Breath.' He instructed.

Taking a large gulp of air Amy filled her lungs. His powerful cock filled her as he continued to bring her even closer to yet another climax. As the brink descended upon her Jesse withdrew himself.

'Please…. don't.' She pleaded. 'Make me come Jesse, please……' Amy begged.

Turning her gently over onto her stomach Jesse lay against her, the skin of his chest against the skin of her back. He grasped her hands tightly above her head, his free hand moved down, caressing the soft flesh of her behind.

'I think I remember you saying "spank me," Amy.' He whispered in her ear whilst gently nibbling on her earlobe.

Startled Amy held her breath.

'Shit!' She silently thought. 'Why the fuck did I feel it was necessary to play sexy games!' She demanded of herself.

'Are you ok?' Jesse asked, his breath felt warm on her neck.

With a steely determination Amy swallowed hard.

'I'm fine baby.' She whispered. 'So you want to spank me do you?' She enquired. The temporary flash of fear she felt as he had uttered the words vanished as he moved to look at her. 'I know you would never hurt me.' She spoke quietly, her voice the merest whisper as she saw only love and wanting in his sexy eyes.

'Amy, I would never hurt you, I don't know how anyone could.' His lips sought hers and as she lost herself once more Amy felt her body relax.

Jesse made love to her like never before whilst the melody continued to play on repeat. Giving into the feelings and sensations once more Amy closed her eyes, giving herself completely to her very own personal Mr. Champagne.

CHAPTER THIRTY SIX

'So you fancy the idea of giving my arse a good slapping?' She joked as they lay sharing another joint whilst listening to music. Amy felt relaxed and happy, her fleeting apprehension totally forgotten. She knew Jesse, she knew the man he was, he would never hurt her.

'Mmmm, I would like to try it.' His eyes burned into hers; reaching for her glass of wine Amy avoided his intense, alluring stare.

'What else do you fancy?' She bravely asked throwing every fear to the back of her mind as she fought with her emotions. She wanted to please him, give him everything he craved and desired.

'Role play.' Startled, Amy sat bolt upright in the bed, spitting her wine out in shock. Laughing Jesse patted her back whilst she choked on the fruity, alcoholic liquid.

'Role play hey? What sort of role play?' Her stomach was in knots as she felt tiny shivers of fear run up her spine as her hands tried to rub away the rose stains that the spilt wine had left on the bed linen.

'What the hell did he have in mind?' She silently thought as the icy fingers of terror began to take hold of her completely.

'A naughty secretary.' He sexily smiled.

Amy had been with Paul for twenty years and his brutal attacks and rapes had left deep, weeping scars. It was moments and words like these that sparked off the anxiety that she had buried months before, bringing the horror of her past life flooding back to her.

'NO!' She screamed silently. 'Jesse is good, Jesse isn't Paul, he would never hurt you.' She tried in vain to reassure herself as she tried to shake off the flashbacks that began to flood into her head.

Rising from the bed she padded over the dark red carpet to retrieve the wine bottle. Pouring herself a fresh glass she took a large gulp before turning back to Jesse.

'Come on you silly moo, you can do this.' She silently scolded. 'Look at him; he hasn't got a violent fibre in his handsome, young body!'

'A secretary….' She paused as she tried to slow her raging heart.

'And what would Mr Clayton like his naughty secretary to do?' She questioned, the icy fingers refused to let go, clinging hold of her, waiting for his answer.

'Well, we would book into a hotel then you could go and get changed and I would then love you to knock on the door.' He said a sexy smile on his lips, that "look" in his eyes.

'And?' She asked trying to keep her face impassive and hide the fear that was busily lurking in the background.

'Well….. you would walk in, I would sit at my desk and then you would show me what you were wearing.'

'You would be able to see what I was wearing.' Amy responded a puzzled look on her face as she took another large mouthful of wine, swallowing it quickly.

'I mean underneath you tit!' He chuckled. 'Your stockings and underwear.' He said sexily.

'And then what?' She asked. She knew she was firing questions at him but she desperately wanted to hear his answers all at once. This was foreign to her and Amy knew she was going to have to draw every ounce of courage she had to even continue the conversation.

'Then I would interview you for the position.' He replied, that "look" still present in his eyes, a sexy smile on his lips.

'And how would Mr Clayton interview me?' She cheekily responded, the icy fingers beginning to disappear as she watched his beautiful face closely.

'By sucking my cock!'

'Oh, and I am guessing that if I take you to blow job heaven I will secure the vacancy.' She played along, her confidence growing a little more with every passing minute.

'Yes.' He hissed as he watched her slowly and deliberately reach down and begin to stroke her foot.

'Who knew?' She murmured. 'Who knew that a pair of feet and some sexy shoes could affect you the way they do.'

'It's your feet.' He replied. 'They are tiny and perfect and soooo sexy and those heels……'

'You like the heels do you Mr Clayton?' She asked perching her bottom on the very edge of the desk.

'Yes.'

Leaning back slightly on her arms she lifted first her left foot and then her right. As she twirled her ankles, pretending to inspect them, she heard his sharp intake of breath.

'Come here.' He demanded.

Amy scurried over to the bed, glad to be in the safety of his arms once again. Her flirty actions had eventually caused her to blush vividly.

'So what would the boss do after I have sucked his cock?' She mumbled her face against his chest.

'The boss would then love to tie your hands, blindfold you and give you multiple orgasms.' He replied squeezing her to him.

Trying to keep her breathing even Amy closed her eyes.

'Fuck he wants to tie me up!' Her common sense screamed at her. 'Avoid, avoid, avoid.'

The first time her husband had raped her she had fought like an alley cat; trying to kick, punch, scratch and bite him, anything to end the horrific ordeal he was putting her through. She had screamed as loud as she was able to as his vulgar words had embedded themselves firmly in her brain. When he finally punched her in the face to silence her screams he had sent her into a welcoming unconsciousness. As the flashback assaulted her, her hand instinctively went up to the scar on her face.

The second time he tied her hands tightly but Amy already knew not to fight and so lying back, devoid of all emotion, her eyes screwed tightly shut, she allowed him to use her body. Now Jesse wanted to tie her hands to bring her pleasure, would she be able to separate the two, she silently thought, was it even possible?

She loved and trusted this man with every part of her, her heart was screaming 'don't be fuckin stupid,' her brain 'be careful.'

'Ok.' The merest whisper came from her frightened mouth that she was sure would betray her. 'I know you would never hurt me Jesse.' She carefully said, planting a light kiss on his chest.

'It will be fun and I guarantee you will enjoy it.' Jesse replied, oblivious to the demon wrestling that had just occurred in her mind.

'If I don't like it will you untie me?' Amy asked in a small, almost childlike voice as she continued to bury her face into his chest.

'Of course!' He replied. 'Amy are you ok?' He gently added.

'I'm fine.' She answered, taking a deep breath and leaning up on her elbows so she could see his face. 'So I now know about the secretarial position you have open, what other role play would you like to try?' She asked knowing that Jesse was beginning to sense something; she fought to feel a little braver. Jesse was dragging her into unfamiliar waters and as she questioned him some more Amy silently prayed she was strong enough. Digging deep she churned around the ideas and began to realise that role play was perhaps part of a healthy sexual relationship and the man beside her loved her, he wouldn't hurt her would he? No, Amy trusted him. 'Tell me please.' She quietly encouraged.

'Are you sure you are ok?' Jesse repeated a concerned look on his face.

'Jesse I am fine.' She replied taking hold of his head in her hands she looked into his eyes, hoping he would understand, too afraid to speak the words of truth for fear of losing him. She wanted to please him, she wanted to explore her sexuality but she was afraid. He knew her husband had raped her, the intimate, horrific details he did not. 'Tell me.' She asked again in what she hoped was a braver voice.

'Well the secretary then a police woman, oh now we could have some fun with that.' He laughed.

Feeling a little braver Amy began to explore his ideas.

'A police woman?' She chuckled. 'Do you want arresting and handcuffing babe? Now that could be fun.' She laughed. 'Anything else?' She asked her enthusiasm increasing by the second as she began to relax.

'A maid. Now that is kinky.' He grinned.

'And what about a nurse?' She threw at him, winking.

'As long as you have a stethoscope around your neck.' Jesse laughed. 'Mmmm kinky, very kinky.'

Reaching for her Jesse drew her back into his arms, planting a sweet kiss on the end of her nose.

    'I love you Amy Lucas.'

    'I love you Jesse Clayton.'

CHAPTER THIRTY SEVEN

'The hotel is booked for Wednesday Sexy Eyes. xx' Amy text.

'Sweet. I'm looking forward to this. xx' He wrote back.

Once they had returned from the beautiful thatched cottage Amy had immediately rang Jen.

'Are you busy Jen?' She had asked. 'I need to see you, I need some advice.'

'What's the matter Amy? Are you ok?' Jen replied, concern clearly evident in her voice.

'I'm fine, I just need some advice, I have kind of gotten myself into a situation!' Amy knew the decibels in her voice were getting higher and higher.

Thirty minutes later the pair where sat at Amy's dining room table.

'You look worried. Tell me Amy, what's the matter.' As soon as she had opened the door Jen knew that something was amiss with her little friend.

Taking a large gulp of air Amy opened her mouth, the words tumbling out in chaos and as Jen listened a smile gradually began to spread across her face.

'Don't be so fuckin soft!' Jen cried. Sensing her friend's distress she lowered the tone of her voice. 'Amy, listen to me please. It is normal, this is something men and women enjoy, they experiment, explore. Hey, if you don't like it then you tell him honey but I guarantee that once you try role play you will fucking love it!'

'Really?' Amy questioned, still unconvinced.

'Look Amy what could possibly happen to you?' Jen asked laughing.

The look on Amy's face stopped Jen from speaking any further. Standing quickly she walked around the table, taking hold of her friend she embraced her tightly.

'Oh Amy....Amy.... You don't need to be afraid, he is a good man, Jesse wouldn't hurt you.' Jen tried to reassure her some more.

'Jen, I know he is a good man and the dressing up isn't the issue here, I mean I wear sexy lingerie most of the time, an outfit isn't going to be much different. I'm shit scared of being tied up Jen…. And you know why….' She added in a small voice.

'I know, I know, beautiful lady.' Jen said as if she was cooing at a baby. 'You need to speak to Jesse Amy, he will understand.'

'I'm not so sure Jen. He knows about my past but not the details, I mean come off it Jen do you honestly think he wouldn't run a mile in the fuckin opposite direction!' Tears began to flow down Amy's cheeks, her eyes two pools of desperate misery as she looked at her friend. 'He's too young to take on my past.' Amy wailed.

'Amy, listen to me. You don't have to tell him the details; you don't have to reveal all that. Just talk to him, please for me.' Jen pleaded.

'Ok.' Amy meekly replied not knowing how the hell she was going to do this. 'I know he won't hurt me Jen, it's just…..'

'Let it go Amy before it destroys you, destroys you and Jesse.' Amy knew the words her friend spoke were the truth but could she really bury the anxiety that was slowly taking over her body.

'I'll talk to him tonight.' She stated. 'I know I can do this, I just have to relax about the whole thing.'

'Yes, you do. Have a few puffs of the magic plant.' Jen replied laughing. 'You gave enough to that bastard; it's time to take control again Amy. How long has Paul got left by the way?' She asked seriously, referring to his prison sentence.

'I'm not sure Jen.' Amy replied. 'I should imagine he will be out soon, Vicky said she would ring me so I'm forewarned.

In Jen's eyes, Paul had received a very lenient sentence. Her brave little friend had refused to press charges or even discuss the rapes and so the scumbag was laughing all the way to the prison gates knowing he would only serve half of his three year sentence.

'He can't hurt you anymore Amy.' Jen said her voice the merest whisper.

'I know Jen.' Amy said, the tears flowing down her sad face.

'Be strong my little friend, be strong.' Jen hated Paul for the years of torment and abuse he had put her friend through, seeing her like this brought the horror that she had suffered to the surface for everyone to see. 'So what is your poa?' She asked, trying to change the subject.

'I don't know.' Amy replied, wiping her tears with the sleeve of her jumper. 'I will talk to him tonight.' She added.

'Good! Make sure you do Amy, he won't hurt you, I promise.' Her words of reassurance were followed by a steel like embrace. 'YOU… CAN….DO….THIS.' Jen stated, accentuating each of her words.

'I know, I know.' Amy laughed. 'I promise! Let me grab my phone, I'm sure I just heard it beep.'

Scurrying upstairs she retrieved her phone from the dressing table in her bedroom and noticed that Jesse had left a couple of message and tried to ring her.

'Shit.' She muttered as she opened his texts.

'Hey sexy bum, how are you today? xx'

'Are you busy? Xx'

Typing out a quick reply she hurried back down the stairs to Jen.

'Hiya sexy eyes, sugar lips. Sorry left my phone upstairs and didn't hear it. Are you ok? xx'

Her phone rang almost immediately.

'Hello sexy bum.' His voice was like rich, smooth velvet to her ears and had an almost immediate calming effect on her jangled nerves.

'Hello handsome, are you ok?' She asked.

'I'm good. I was wondering what you are up to tonight?'

'Nothing much, do you fancy coming up and I will make you some dinner.' Amy was aware that she was nibbling on her fingernail as their impending conversation swirled around her brain.

'Sure, what time?' He asked enthusiastically.

'Whenever you want sexy eyes.' As she listened to his low, sexy voice she allowed herself to belief that everything would be ok. 'Jesse, I need to talk to you later.' She stated, her eyes screwed tightly closed.

'Are you ok?' He asked. Jesse could detect the underlying anxiety in her voice. 'Amy?...'

'I'm fine.' She responded. 'I just need to speak with you, it's nothing heavy.' She was trying to reassure him. 'Nothing heavy, liar!' She silently reprimanded herself.

'Ok.' Well I will be there about 6ish, is that ok?'

'That's fine. I'll see you later handsome and Jesse…..' She added before she hung up the phone.

'Yes.'

'I love you.' She stated in a quiet voice.

'I love you too Amy.' He answered. 'See you later.'

Jen watched in complete fascination as her friend's face changed as she spoke to Jesse on the phone. One minute she was biting her nail, a worried look on her angelic face, the next she was beaming, the twinkle back in her eyes.

'You really do love him don't you?' Jen asked her friend.

'Oh Jen, yes I really do. He is almost perfect.' Amy stated dreamily as her mind floated off.

'Why almost Sweetie?' She asked as she watched the pain flood back into Amy's face.

'Almost….. almost…..' Amy said wistfully. 'If he was older he would be perfect.'

'You obviously have something a wee bit special Amy, cherish it.'

'We were always meant to say goodbye Jen and it hurts, it really does, it's here every minute of every day.' Amy said placing her hand over her heart. How the hell am I going to cope when it ends?' The tears appeared once more as Amy began to reveal her worries to her friend. 'I mean, look at me Jen and none of your bullshit, look at me! Amy's voice rose as she swept her hands before her. 'I guess I am ok for now but shit Jen some young, hot girl is going to come along one day and he will be gone. I have to prepare myself for it because when it happens I know my heart will break.' She sobbed.

'Oh Amy….' Jen took her friend into her arms, stroking her silky chestnut hair to comfort her.

'I have churned this over so many times Jen, it took a long time to let him in but he broke down my walls so easily, he is so easy to love. I would do anything, give everything for that man to be happy and I know there will come a time when I will have to walk away.' She said sadly.

'And what if he doesn't walk away Amy? Have you even considered that?' Jen replied.

'Jen, be reasonable. He is going to want a family, babies of his own, he is a very special person and if he feels one half of what I feel when he meets the woman he wants to spend the rest of his life with then I will gladly walk away knowing that the man I gave everything to is content, at peace but most of all happy. He has changed me so much, changed my life Jen and I am so glad I gave him my heart. I will always love him even if he will break my heart.' She added, the tears running down her face as she began to prematurely mourn the loss of him.

'Never say never.' Jen replied. 'Amy live for now Sweetie, you have had a rough deal for years, now is your time, seize it, make the fuckin most of it for Christ's sake!'

'I will Jen, I promise.' Amy replied, the doubts now taking over her every thought. 'I guess you never know how long something will last.' She questioned thoughtfully. 'I mean, I could have met someone nearer my own age, fallen in love and he then died on me! I suppose nothing should be taken for granted.' Amy paused as she digested the words she had spoken. 'Shit! Why have I never thought of it like this before! God I can be such a moron at times!'

'That's my girl.' Jen said smiling sweetly at her friend. 'Take what is in front of you; cherish it and hold it close to your heart but most of all enjoy it for as long as you can. You deserve this Amy, you deserve someone like Jesse to love you be it for a while or forever.'

'I will! I fucking will!' Amy stated, a new found determination sat firmly on her shoulders. 'I am going to do this, I am going to let him tie me up and pleasure me, Jen I can do this!'

'Yes you can Sweetie, you just have to dig deep and find that little soldier in yourself.'

'Yes ma'am.' Amy retorted as she saluted her friend. 'I am so glad you are my friend Jen, you don't know how much your words calm me. Thank you.' She whispered taking hold of Jen's hand. 'I love you.'

'I love you more.' Jen replied. 'Listen, will you be ok now, I have to go and pick the munchkin up from school.' She said referring to little Caitlin as she put on her leather jacket.

'I will be fine.' Amy said. 'In fact I will be fanfuckintastic.' Her confidence was slowly soaring. 'If I can take twenty years of nothingness and pain then I'm sure I can stand being tied up and pleasured.' She grinned cheekily.

'You go girlie.' Jen screeched fist pumping the air. 'You are beautiful here.' She said pointing to where Amy's heart lay beneath her clothing, 'and here.' She finished pointing to her face.

'Thank you.' Amy breathed in response.

Hugging her friend to her closely Amy thanked her once again before walking with her to the door.

Shutting the front door after her friend Amy leaned against the wall.

'Dig deep Amy, dig deep.' She said out loud. 'You can do this.'

With a determination she thought was impossible Amy went upstairs to get ready for the man she loved, Jesse.

CHAPTER THIRTY EIGHT

As she ran the bath Amy pulled out her writing pad and favourite pen. She wanted Jesse to know, when the time was right, that she couldn't have possibly loved him anymore or any better than she had. She had given him everything and so turning off the water she sat down to write him a letter from her heart.

"To My Darling Jesse

I love you very, very much. If you are reading this letter then I have walked away from you knowing you are happy with your life. This, my love, is my final farewell to you.

I had rebuilt my life and was content being on my own, then, I opened the door to you and the first thing I noticed were your amazing eyes. No one has ever had an effect on me the way you do. You turned a sensible woman into a nervous wreck from the first moment I laid eyes on you. □

Falling in love with you was so easy, learning to trust you, just as easy. I have said it before to you, you are an amazing, special man Jesse and even though I tormented myself with doubts for weeks I am so glad I met you and allowed myself to feel what I do for you. When I am with you I feel complete, when you are inside me I am overwhelmed with such intense feelings and emotions that I am unable to describe them, when I am not with you I feel as if a crucial part of me is missing. I gave you my heart some time ago but gradually and gladly I gave you everything I am, everything I feel. The icicle that I had firmly stabbed into my heart melted as my love and trust for you grew with every minute that ticked by.

You have changed me and my life so much Jesse and I want to thank you so much for that. I love the way you make me feel, the way my heart, my body responds to you. You make me feel alive, sexy and very brave. Thank you.

I have fallen, fallen hard and deeply in love and I hope and wish for you that you will find love again, a powerful, intense love like the one I feel for you. I want happiness for you darling. I know you will find that special one because you yourself are so special. You will always have my heart Jesse; I gave it willingly and freely.

I feel honoured to have known you and so thankful for every second I have spent with you. My love, the love I feel for you is so intense, so mind blowing, something I have never felt before and something that I want you to know I cherished and held close to my heart every single second of every single day and I will continue to do so until my heart stops beating.

My past is my past but I need you to know Jesse that in no way is my past the reason I fell so in love with you! I need you to trust me babe, trust what I say and how I feel but most of all trust in yourself. I fell in love with you, the most special man, amazing person I have ever known and I feel so privileged and lucky. I trusted in what I felt Jesse and every second that I have spent with you has not only helped me to heal but has helped me make some beautiful memories that I will cherish forever.

You are so right darling when you say you have a "knack," you certainly do!!! A knack that has blown me away, a knack for making me crumble into a heated mess at your feet!!! Its simple Jesse, I adore you.

I never thought I would be able to trust another human being again, let alone a man but you taught me that there are beautiful, sincere and trustworthy people out there and once again I will say it, I feel so lucky to have known you and had you in my life Jesse.

Thank you for being you. Thank you for every milli- second I have spent with you. Most of all thank you for allowing me to love you the way I do.

I will never forget you Jesse; never forget your eyes or that special "look" you always gave me. I will never forget your smile, the way it reached your eyes or the way your hair flopped down over your forehead. The way you kissed the tip of my nose and made me laugh and smile, thank you Jesse. Most of all I will never forget how it felt to be held in your arms, my hand over your heart.

Have a happy life my love and know that I will always be around for you, no matter what.

My heart and soul are yours now and forever.
All my love
You're Amy
Xxxxxxxxxxxxx"

As she wrote the poignant words to the man who had her heart she cried, silent, heart breakingly, sad tears cascaded down her face as she wept prematurely for the love she knew she would eventually loose. Her heart would break, she knew that but for now she loved him and he loved her. For Amy she knew that no man would ever replace Jesse, her heart was his until it no longer beat.

Wiping the tears away she re-read her letter before sealing it in an envelope.

"Jesse – The reason I believe in love." She scrawled before stowing it away in her drawer for safe keeping.

CHAPTER THIRTY NINE

Jesse arrived as Amy was putting the finishing touches to the chilli she had prepared, his knock on her front door sending tiny shivers of both fear and love up her spine. She had made a promise to Jen and she intended to keep it, how she was going to reveal her darkest horrors to Jesse she didn't know but she knew she needed to let him know how she felt. The role play in itself didn't bother her, that would be fun; it was the binding of her hands that she feared the most. Since meeting Jesse her world had changed, she had changed. Gone was the broken, frightened woman, in her place a courageous female who was now stepping out into an unfamiliar but somehow exciting sexual world.

'Hi.' She demurely whispered as she stood on her tiptoes to kiss his irresistible lips.

'Hi.' Jesse responded drawing her to him. 'Have you had a good day?' He questioned smiling at her.

Fuck! She couldn't tell him the truth, not yet, she needed more time.

'Yes, Jen came round and we had our girlie session.' She laughed hoping that he wouldn't be able to detect the hint of nervousness that she could feel in her own voice.

'How is she?' Jesse asked. 'I bumped into Rick earlier; he's gone into town with a few of our mates.'

'She is fine, still in love.' Amy chuckled. 'Are you ready to eat?' She asked turning her attention back to the stove.

'Only if it's your pussy.' He saucily replied.

'You are sooooo bad Clayton.' She jested turning around to wag her index finger at him playfully.

Reaching for the wooden spoon to give the chilli a stir she pivoted around to the stove on her tiptoes.

'That's so cute.' She heard him say. Turning around to face him she noticed he was looking down at her feet.

'What's cute?' She asked glancing down to see what had caught his attention.

'You, you are always on your tiptoes. When you wash the dishes you are on them, when you are cooking, making a brew, it's funny; I have never seen anyone do it before, you even stand on them in the shower babe.' He chuckled.

'It's because I'm a short arse.' She laughed. 'I guess it's all those years dancing, it's kinda natural to me.' She said a little more seriously, smiling at him softly.

'Well it's cute.' He laughed, standing up.

'And what do you think you are doing?' Amy said, pointing the wooden spoon in Jesse's direction in a bid to halt his steps. He was walking slowly towards her, that "Jesse look" in his sexy green eyes. 'Stay right there!' She commanded her tone unconvincing. 'Jesse I am serious.' She finished, turning around and putting her back to him.

'Mistake!' She heard him mumble into her ear as his hands encircled her waist.

'Jesse.' She whispered as his fingertips trailed south, grasping her behind firmly.

Quickly he turned her around so she was facing him. Rising on her toes she looked up at him, her eyes filled with love.

'I want you.' He said quietly. Picking her up Jesse placed her gently down on the work surface. 'Here.' He added sexily, his hands all over her.

Pushing her hands into his hair she pulled him passionately towards her, her lips so eager for his. As her tongue connected with the inside of his mouth and he deeply returned her kiss she almost purred with contentment, she had never been kissed like this before. Every time he caressed her lips with his own she felt new emotions run throughout her body and mind, each kiss was always the perfect kiss to Amy.

'So perfect.' She murmured as he grazed his lips across hers. 'Every time it's so perfect.' Jesse reached for her hair; tilting her head to the side his lips assaulting her neck sending quivers of desire through her down to her secret place.

Wrapping her legs around his waist she drew him closer, their lips meeting once again. She knew she was ready for him as her need to feel Jesse inside her took over.

'I want you Jesse.' The desire was heavy in her voice.

Pulling her down from the cool marble surface, he turned her around pressing his erect cock into the small of her back.

'Can you feel how hard you make me Amy?' He whispered into her ear. 'I want you too.' She felt him pull back and began to turn around. 'Don't turn around, stay there babe.' He softly instructed as she heard him removing his clothes. She felt naughty and exposed as she stood resting her elbows on the work surface, her skirt around her waist. 'I love that you never wear knickers Amy.' Once again he pressed against her, this time he was naked, his stiff, beautiful cock against the bare skin of her behind.

'Please.' Amy panted trying to reach for him so she could pull him towards her.

Pressing her back against the surface Jesse thrust himself into her making Amy gasp with desire as he connected with her deep inside.

'You love me being deep inside you, don't you?' He sexily asked as he continued to drive his cock in and out of her.

'Yes.' She hissed as she felt the orgasm approaching. The light slaps on her behind temporarily stunned her but as he quickly replaced the flat of his hand with the feather light tracing of his fingertips she came violently, grinding herself back onto him she screamed out with passion as convulsion after convulsion tore through her body.

Jesse continued to pummel her with his cock until his own desire overtook and he came fiercely, emptying himself deep within her as she called out his name, her own climax as furious as his.

'Are you ok?' Amy had collapsed onto the floor and was now cradled by a panting Jesse.

'Yes.' She whispered, enjoying the feel of his arms around her. 'Wow! That was.....'

'I know.' Jesse squeezed her tightly. 'I think you like having your arse spanked Miss Lucas.' He giggled quietly.

'Sssshhh.' Amy replied as she buried her face into his chest to hide her embarrassment.

'What's the matter?' Jesse laughed as he tried to lift her face knowing she would be blushing furiously.

'Don't.' Amy pleaded holding on to him tightly.

Laughing Jesse tried to stand whilst holding her in his arms. Amy began to giggle as she playfully fought with him, desperate to keep her embarrassment hidden. As he gently placed her on the cool, tiled floor she instinctively came up onto her tiptoes, her eyes cast downwards.

'Let me look at you.' Jesse words were gently as once again he tried to lift her chin.

Trying to search her eyes with his own he finally realised how shy Amy really was.

'Are you shy?' He asked gently, his finger still under her chin.

'Yes.' She mumbled as she did her best to avoid his gaze. 'Jesse please.' Releasing her chin Jesse encircled her with his arms.

'Can I have some chilli now?' He chuckled quietly. 'I'm starving!'

'Of course sir.' Amy pulled away from him and curtseyed glad that he had let the subject of her embarrassment drop. 'Would you like a drink Jesse?' She asked as she straightened out her clothing before she put the finishing touches to their meal.

'Please babe.' Jesse shouted. He was now sat on the sofa in all his naked glory flicking the TV remote.

'Jesse!' Amy squealed as she walked into the living room. 'For God's sake will you please have some pity on me and put some bloody clothes on. Please.' She added closing her eyes as she felt the blush begin to take over her once again.

'How was this possible?' She silently thought. 'How can I want him so badly when I have just had the most earth shattering, fanfuckintastic orgasm ever? I need help!'

'What?' Jesse responded, an innocent but very hot look on his handsome face.

'You know what!' Amy declared as she pointed at him. 'You're… you're a torment!' Huffing she stomped back into the kitchen her skin on fire once again. She could hear Jesse laughing, clearly enjoying the blushes he was causing. 'I'll get him back one day. Yes Mr Clayton, one day I will be brazen and confident enough to strut my feckin stuff around the house naked. Yeh that will show him! She silently declared.

CHAPTER FORTY

Amy found it difficult to eat her food that night knowing the impending conversation was not too far away. Playing over the scene that had occurred only an hour ago in the kitchen she felt herself begin to blush once more. She had actually enjoyed it, the slight stinging sensation his hands had caused on her bare skin had quickly disappeared when his fingertips had caressed the faint pink marks his print had left.

'It turned me on.' Shit! Did she actually just say that out loud? Amy froze waiting to see if Jesse had heard.

Seconds ticked by as she silently watched him, just as she felt the last minute bits of air leave her lungs he spoke.

'I know you did.' His voice was low as he continued to eat his dinner whilst watching TV.

Feeling a little braver Amy sat up straight and looked at him.

'I mean, I really enjoyed it, it turned me on Jesse.'

'I heard you the first time babe.' He replied, his eyes fixed firmly ahead.

'Please look at me.' She said timidly. 'Jesse.' Turning slowly he met her eyes and she inhaled sharply. 'I would like to do that again, that orgasm…….' Her words trailed off as she had to look away from his penetrating stare. She wanted to reassure him but most of all she wanted him to know how she felt. 'I love you.'

'It turned me on too Amy but you have to know that I would never do anything to hurt you.' Jesse placed his plate on the floor and reached for her petite hands. 'I love you Amy.' As his lips grazed her knuckles she silently berated herself.

How could she have doubted him? How could she have doubted herself? Jesse understood her completely. He loved her, with she hoped, was the same intense passion as she felt for him. He wanted to please her, take her to new sexual heights, not hurt her. What a fool she had been not to trust in him. Reaching for him she placed her lips lightly at first on his.

'Thank you.' She whispered into his mouth as she felt the final piece of her heart open to him.

Their hands reached up in unison as fingertips disappeared into hair their lips met. Jesse kissed her deeply again and again, his lips and tongue making her writhe with pleasure.

'So close.' She secretly thought. 'So close.' Every time he placed his mouth on hers she would feel the beginnings of an orgasm. 'If only he would kiss me a while longer.' Amy knew that it was only a matter of time until Jesse could literally make her come with his kisses.

She loved the way his mouth felt on hers, the feel of his soft lips as he took possession of her own. The way his fingers held her hair when he kissed her, the way he stroked her neck running his fingers down into the cup of her bra until he almost touched the nipple. Jesse would tease her in his own delicious way until she would literally beg for him to take her.

Lying back on the sofa she gazed at him.

'I want to feel you.' She murmured. 'I want to touch you.'

Jesse had wrapped a towel around his waist whilst he ate his dinner and as Amy reached for him she burst out laughing.

'Well I think someone is very, very happy.' She giggled. His erect penis was standing proud. 'We should name him.' She murmured a cheeky grin on her face as she snaked her hand around his cock.

'What would you like to call him then?' Jesse asked chuckling.

'Bruce or should I say Brucie.' Amy stated a satisfied look on her face.

'Bruce?' Jesse asked. 'I don't get it?' His eyes were puzzled.

'The Boss!' Amy huffed. 'Bruce Springsteen, The Boss, your cock is The Boss.' She laughed. Both Amy and Jesse liked to listen to Springsteen and so the name was very apt.

'Now what about you?' Jesse asked, a sexy grin played on his lips. 'I know Lulu!' He declared.

'Lulu!' Amy guffawed. 'Lulu! Now I don't get it.'

'Well she is a singer and she is little like you.' He laughed. 'Lulu, that's a good name, I like it!' Jesse said proudly,

Laughing Amy reached for him once again. Taking his cock she slowly bent her neck until her lips were only millimetres from the tip of him.

'Would Brucie like to come out to play with Lulu?' She whispered, blowing gently on him whilst moving her hand slowly up and down the length of him.

Jesse reached for her, gently lying her down on the sofa.

'Brucie would love to come out to play with Lulu.' He groaned bringing his lips down onto hers.

She was ready. She loved him kissing her, taking her almost to the beginnings of a climax with his lips on hers, not touching her secret place until he positioned himself at her entrance and thrust deep inside her. That was how she wanted him now.

'Fuck the foreplay.' She hissed. 'Please just give me Brucie!'

She saw only raw passion on his face as he thrust himself into her. Trying to meet his eyes she felt herself begin to plummet over the edge as his green stare penetrated into her very soul. Somewhere from a once foreign place deep inside, she felt the volcano erupt as the spasms of her orgasm raged through her. As her heart and sex united she surrendered to the powerful emotions that swamped her giving herself to Jesse completely.

'I love you.' She cried as he massaged her deep inside, squeezing the last droplets of orgasm from her.

Raising her legs to his shoulders he accessed her darkest place and as he violently erupted inside her she clasped him tight as her own orgasm took over her once again.

'I love you so much.' They said in almost unison as they collapsed on the sofa.

Lying with his head on her breast Amy began to stroke Jesse's hair. Closing her eyes she gave in to the sensations of powerful love and trust that washed their way around her body, entering her heart to stay there forever. She should never have doubted this man. This kind, gentle, caring human being that had entered her life for a reason. He had helped her heal, taught her how to love and trust but most of all he taught her how to experience a myriad of new emotions and feelings. As she sighed softly she felt her heart expand as it silently made room for him.

'My heart is yours.' She murmured softly.

CHAPTER FORTY ONE

'You all set?' She asked an eager look on her smiling face.

'Yip.' He replied. 'Let's go.' As they walked to the front door Amy turned to smile at him.

'I'm excited.' She gushed, blushing furiously.

'Me too.' He laughed locking the door before placing the keys in his pocket.

Amy had been both looking forward to but dreading this day. Part of her was so eager to please the man she loved and she knew that him binding her hands would only bring her gratification. He didn't want to hurt her; it was Jesse, sweet, caring, handsome Jesse. She had the kinky secretarial outfit stowed away in her bag along with stockings, suspenders and shiny black, high stilettos. The plan was to leave Jesse in the room whilst she went to get changed.

'You going to be ok all alone in here?' Amy seductively asked her hands all over him as soon as they opened the door to their room.

'If you don't go I am going to end up ruining you here and now!' He hissed as she knelt on the floor, her hands poised seductively at his buckle.

'I can't wait to feel you in my mouth and taste that big hard cock of yours.' She teased bravely. Standing up she collected her bag, flinging it over her shoulder she left the room without another word. As she walked down the carpeted corridors she couldn't help but smile, she was nervous but there was also a sweet anticipation coursing through her veins as she imagined his sexy eyes and those talented hands and lips running over her body, their sole goal to bring her pleasure.

Amy had already seen where the public toilets were situated when they had checked in at reception. As she walked towards her destination she silently prayed that no one would be using them. Opening the heavy, old oak door she peeked inside.

'Phew, vacant.' She whispered as she walked in.

Selecting the cubicle at the end Amy shut the door and placed her bag on the closed toilet seat. Reaching for her phone she sent Jesse a text.

'Operation Naughty Secretary is underway. xx'

As she carefully put on the sheer, black stockings her phone beeped.

'That's my girl. xx' He wrote back. Smiling Amy took a deep breath before changing into the rest of the outfit.

Stepping out of the cubicle she inspected her reflection in the mirror. Her cheeks were flushed, her eyes bright and as she smoothed down her black, tight pencil skirt she felt the first stirrings of desire knowing that in minutes she would be back in the room with the man she loved. Reaching into her bag she drew out some hair clips, laying them out in front of her on the counter. Drawing her thick, chestnut locks into her hands she wound it around, securing it with the pins as she went until a neat chignon was formed.

'You can do this!' She told her reflection as she adjusted the black blouse, opening another button so her cleavage was on show.

With a deep breath Amy opened the door and began the short walk back to their room. She could feel her heart hammering away in her chest, her blush clearly evident for all to see.

'Calm down!' She quietly scolded herself as she stood outside the door, her hand poised ready to knock. She felt sick, her stomach was in knots. What if he didn't like what she was wearing?

Forcing herself to calm down she knocked on the door and waited.

'Hello.' He said as he opened the door.

'Hello.' Amy shyly replied as she watched him walk away from her and sit in the chair by the large mahogany desk. 'Fuck, I have to walk to him with him fucking watching me.' She silently thought. 'Oh fuck!'

Taking another deep breath Amy walked slowly towards him, his eyes were busy roaming all over her as he took in the sexy, tight fitting outfit.

'Wow.' He exclaimed. 'You look sexy.'

Amy smiled a soft, sweet, sexy smile. Standing inches away from him she slowly lifted the tight fitting skirt, parting her legs suggestively to reveal the tops of her stockings, turning slowly she allowed him to inspect her from behind as she bent slowly, running her hand up the sheer black material that encased her legs she was rewarded by his sharp intake of breath. As she turned she looked into his green eyes which smouldered with intense passion.

'Does Mr Clayton approve?' She seductively asked casting her eyes to her feet. 'Are you nervous?' She added. Secretly she hoped he was because her nerves were on edge, she knew her hands were shaking so before her legs gave way she hitched her skirt up a little further and straddled him, her hands immediately reaching up for his hair.

'Sexy, so sexy.' He murmured as she caressed his skin with her lips and tongue. 'Yes, I'm a bit nervous.'

'Me too.' She whispered as she felt his hands grasp her behind. God help him if I wasn't nervous Amy silently thought as she felt the desire for him grip her violently.

'You have one sexy arse!' Jesse stated. 'A very, very sexy arse.'

'And you are sexy everything.' She mumbled as she placed her lips on his.

Grabbing her by the waist Jesse pushed her back a little.

'Wow!' The look on his face banished all Amy's nerves quickly as she read the lust written there. 'Wrap me up.' He instructed.

Encasing him with her legs he stood sitting her down on the desk. Clinging to him she refused to let go.

'Let go baby.' He asked as he gently reached for her arms to loosen their grip.

Reluctantly Amy unwrapped her legs from around him. Tentatively she reached out with the toes of her shoes until both her limbs connected with the floor. His fingers reached out, caressing the exposed skin of her chest lightly with his fingertips. As they swirled around she threw back her head moaning loudly.

'Your skin is so soft.' He murmured as his lips sought hers. Suddenly he pulled away and stepped back.

'Don't.' She pleaded, her arms reaching out for him as she suddenly felt exposed.

'I just want to look at you.' He breathed with desire.

As he moved towards her once again she grabbed him, wrapping her arms tightly around his neck in a bid to halt his inspection of her.

'Steady on babe.' He said his hands reaching for hers to try and loosen the hold she had on him again.

'I'm sorry.' Amy murmured. 'It's just…..' The words lay unfinished as he once again kissed her. She felt his fingers on the buttons of her blouse, as he undid the last one Jesse bent his head to kiss her bare skin, his fingers seeking her nipple which lay hidden in the cup of her black lacy bra.

Pulling away from her once again she watched as Jesse went to the chest of drawers. Opening the top one he removed two silk scarves, one was a pale, summer blue, the other pink and she immediately recognised them as her own.

'When did you take these?' She asked giggling nervously.

'Yesterday.' He replied. 'I thought they would be soft enough for your wrists.' As he walked back towards her she felt herself freeze in fear. Unable to make even the slightest of movements she became frozen, glued to the spot, her eyes wide, her breathing unsteady as he casually sauntered across the room.

'I won't hurt you.' Jesse stated. 'I promise you will enjoy this.' He added as he stood in-between her legs, his eyes never leaving her face.

Forcing herself to relax, Amy drew a deep, cleansing breath. Looking into Jesse's eyes she felt her anxiety begin to slip away.

'I know Jesse.' She whispered, her black, stocking encased legs encircling him once again, her lips seeking his.

Picking her up Jesse carried Amy towards the bed, as he laid her down gently he reached for her hands.

'Are you sure?' He asked one last time, his eyes searching her face.

Nodding her head Amy offered her wrists to him.

'I am sure.' The words were gently and sincere as she spoke them softly whilst trying to meet his gaze.

Silently he bound her wrists together with the two silk scarves.

'Lift your head for me please.' He asked, his voice the merest whisper, a tender look on his face.

She trusted him completely so closing her eyes she lifted the back of her head off the pillow to allow him to put the blindfold in place.

CHAPTER FORTY TWO

Jesse certainly did have a "knack!"

Surrendering herself completely to him Amy gave into the amazing sensations that he was creating with his tongue, lips and hands. Unable to see him she never knew where his lips would touch next. Every sense appeared heightened, her body responding in a new, exciting, highly erotic way. As she felt the bed slightly shift she tried to reach out with her bound wrists.

'Don't leave me.' She pleaded. 'Jesse come back.' She was beginning to panic but as she heard the familiar notes from "Paradise Circus" begin to play Amy sank back relaxing whilst the beautiful melody drifted over her, the notes washing away her fears and doubts.

Returning to the bed Jesse slowly removed her skirt until she lay before him tied and blindfolded in just her stockings, suspenders and bra.

'If you want me to stop tell me.' He demanded huskily as he disappeared down her body.

The thrill that coursed through her was unexpected as his tongue flicked at her clitoris. Her senses were acutely heightened, his touches magnified. Gently shoving her legs further apart he continued to explore her with his mouth. As his fingers reached up and clasped her nipple she groaned loudly as her orgasm began to shudder through her body, saturating every nerve ending and fibre as it washed its way throughout her.

'Jesse......Jesse......' She called out as she came. It was agony not being able to touch or see him, to feel his hair in her fingers, to see his mesmerizing sexy eyes, even if it was for only a fleeting few seconds that she could hold his gaze for. Just as her orgasm was beginning to fade he thrust himself deep inside her causing her to topple once again over the precipice.

'I......love.....you...' She screamed as wave after wave coursed their way through her.

Withdrawing slowly from her Amy pleaded for him to put his cock once more inside her.

'Please Jesse…..please…..oh.' Amy's words were lost as Jesse once again began to pleasure her with his mouth, tongue and fingers.

'I love eating your pussy, you taste so good.' He murmured as he continued to flick his tongue at her clitoris making Amy writher beneath him. As the swells of yet another orgasm washed through her she screamed out his name, begging him to untie her wrists so she could feel his skin beneath her fingertips.

'Not yet babe, not yet.' He whispered into her ear as he plunged once again into her, his hard cock creating a path of fire deep within her.

'I love you Jesse.' She called out as she came violently.

Pulling the blindfold from her eyes Amy looked at Jesse with huge, bewildered eyes.

'And I love you.' His mouth once again claimed hers in a sweet, passionate kiss.

'I want you in my mouth.' She demanded. 'Please untie me Jesse.'

Reaching for her hands Jesse undid the scarves that had rendered her immobile.

'Did you enjoy that Amy?' He tenderly asked, searching her face carefully, afraid that he may see something he didn't want to. 'The scarves didn't hurt you did they?'

'Yes, I enjoyed it and no, my wrists are fine.' Her voice was timid and embarrassed.

'Now I know you like it we will do it for longer next time babe.' He sexily winked at her. 'I wanted to take it easy the first time.' Jesse knew more than she thought he did, he wasn't stupid; she was an easy and open person to read.

Bending she took him into her mouth and heard his sigh of contentment as she leisurely withdrew him before running her tongue around the very tip of his cock.

'You taste so good.' She murmured before taking him as deep as she could. 'I want to make love to your cock with my mouth.'

'Oh Amy….' His words trailed off as she grasped him tightly with her hand.

Bringing him pleasure was Amy's only goal. She loved having his hard cock in her mouth and boy was he at full salute today!

She continued to work her own personal magic on Jesse, her tongue and lips making him moan with desire as she sucked and licked him, savouring the way this delicious act made her feel. Tightening her grip on him she moved her hand faster and faster, her lips around the end of him, sucking, ready to taste the hot semen that was almost ready to make its escape.

'Do you want to try something?' Amy asked lifting her head to look at him, his cock still in her hand. 'Do you trust me?'

'Of course.' Jesse breathlessly replied, his sexy eyes hazy with lust.

'Come sit on the desk.' Amy commanded, standing slowly, Jesse's hard cock still in her hand.

Bending her head she took him again in her mouth. As she swirled her tongue around the bell shaped end she gently grasped his testicles pulling them gently downwards then back.

'Amy….' She knew he was close. 'Amy…..' Sucking hard she felt him explode into her mouth with a force that astounded her. Fighting back the urge to gag as his hot maleness assaulted the back of her throat she continued to suck and lick his cock whilst massaging his cupped balls, pulling them back softly. 'Aarrgghhh.,….' He shouted as she sucked the last drops of sperm from him and he collapsed back against the wall.

'Have I got the job?' Amy sexily asked whilst grinning at him, she loved making him come this way it turned her on in a big way and the little ball trick she had read on the internet seemed to have made Jesse come very forcefully, his orgasm lasting longer than usual.

'Yes….' He murmured his eyes closed as he recovered. 'Amy that was mind blowing!'

'My only wish is that you are feeling what I am.' She quietly whispered.

Amy lay blissfully content in his arms, her head resting on his chest. She could hear his heartbeat in the quiet room and silently marvelled at the strong, steady beat as it pumped his blood throughout his temporarily sated body. Her own heart was his for as long as he wanted her; she prayed that he wouldn't leave her anytime soon.

'This is my special place.' She said moving her fingers over the place where his heart lay beneath. 'Right here, in your arms.'

'Did you really enjoy your wrists being tied Amy?' He asked tentatively, hugging her closer to him.

Rising so she could look at him, her hand still above his heart, she spoke the single word meekly.

'Yes….' Her eyes immediately fell downwards as she fought with the new feelings and emotions that were coursing throughout her body and mind.

'I would never hurt you Amy.' His hand was lazily stroking the bare skin of her back.

'I trust you.' Another three little words of her own. 'The orgasms were….' Amy was unable to describe the feelings and sensations that she had felt whilst she had been blindfolded and bound.

Pulling her once more into his arms she rested her head.

'Tell me something about you that I don't already know Jess.' Amy said dreamily, her eyes closed.

'Like what?' Jesse replied.

'Tell me where you have been on holiday?' She asked wanting to know more about him and his life.

She loved their times like this, cocooned in his arms whilst they chatted about everyday things.

'The States, Amsterdam, Madrid, New Zealand and France.' He replied. 'Oh and Rome.' He added.

'New Zealand! I would love to go to New Zealand. I have relatives who live near Mount Ruapehu which is a big ski resort from June until October.' Amy said.

'Really! That's where I have skied, Mount Ruapehu, its beautiful Amy. I have some pictures on my hard drive, I will show you later.' He promised.

'I have always wanted to learn to ski.' Amy said wistfully. It had always been a dream of hers to visit Austria in the winter when the snow lay thickly on the ground. For years she had looked at pictures and marvelled at the beauty they held.

'I will teach you.' Jesse said.

'Really!' She exclaimed sitting up on the bed.

'Really.' Jesse laughed. 'We can go to the indoor slopes whilst you learn, it will be fun.'

Sliding her arms into his grey shirt Amy stood to fasten the buttons.

'You look sexy. The shirt suits you.' He stated as he watched her every move.

Grasping the collar with her left hand Amy bent her neck so she could inhale his scent.

'It smells of you.' She whispered. 'I love the way you smell.'

'You can have it babe. It's yours.' He replied smiling at her sweetly.

'Thank you.' She muttered shyly. 'Are you hungry?'

'Famished!' Jesse stated as he stood up and walked towards the bathroom.

'Can you put some clothes on please?' Amy begged. 'You're just too much.'

Laughing he reached for the white, fluffy bathrobe that hung in the closet. Putting it on, he tied the belt at his waist.

'Better?' He questioned, that special "Jesse look" in his green eyes.

'Not really.' Amy wailed. 'Fuck, what are you doing to me?' She added. 'You even look fuckin hot in a hotel bathrobe!'

Closing the distance between them he enveloped Amy with his arms, drawing her close to his chest.

'The same thing that you are doing to me.' He responded as he lifted her face to his.

'Naughty!' Amy was already on her tiptoes, her mouth eager for his. As he bent his head towards her, his lips tantalizingly close to hers, he kissed the tip of her nose. 'Aarrghh the special "Jesse nose kiss," she quietly thought. 'How can his lips on the end of my nose make my heart gush the way it does?' She silently questioned. 'Because you love him and he has your heart. You are his.' Her inner voice whispered in answer to her unspoken question.

CHAPTER FORTY THREE

Dropping Jesse off at his house Amy decided to drive straight home. She would talk to Jen on the phone that way she could conceal her embarrassment. When she and Jesse had first embarked on their love affair she had regaled her dearest friend with most of the details but as Amy slowly fell in love she kept the sexual specifics to herself not wanting what she felt for Jesse to be cheapened in any way. She trusted Jen and her friend had supported and been there for her as the affair had blossomed. Amy knew that they had a very special friendship and no matter what problem reared its ugly head both women understood that their loyalty to one another would always stand the test of time.

Dropping her bags onto the living room floor Amy reached for her mobile phone.

'I haven't got a clue where we are going and I don't really care. I do know that you are a very special man Jesse and I love you with every part of me. I love you. xx' Hitting the send button she bent to retrieve her bags before going upstairs to her bedroom.

'I have no idea either baby but I know we've got something special. Who knows where we'll be a year down the line so let's make the most of this perfect situation. I love you. xx'

His loving words brought tears to her eyes. She never wanted to say goodbye to him, she knew her heart would break.

Typing out her reply she hesitated before sending it.

'You made me cry.' She wrote. 'I love you so much; my heart is yours for as long as you want it. xx' Amy knew that she was his totally; her body, heart, mind and soul belonged to him. She knew she would be devastated when it had to end but for now she embraced the love she felt for him, holding it close. She would always love him, always be his, he had her completely under his spell.

'I love you too.xx' His reply brought a smile to her tearful face.

Feeling the way she did about Jesse, Amy knew that she could be content for the rest of her life. She would not be the only woman he loved the way he did her, but she knew that she would never love another man this way ever again.

'Once in a lifetime is enough for me.' She whispered into the air.

For the first time in a long time, Amy was happy, she knew that the dark cloud of misery would never be far away and no matter how hard she tried she could never quite dispel the feelings of sadness that followed her every day whenever she thought of Jesse. One day she would lose him, of that she was certain.

Sighing heavily Amy noticed a missed call from Jen and immediately dialled her number, her friend answering on the second ring.

'Are you ok?' Jen gushed in a panicked voice.

'I'm fine Jen… and wait for it….. I'm fanfuckintastic!' Amy was giggling like a teenager as all thoughts of sadness quickly disappeared, to be replaced with images from the night before.

'Thank God for that. You really are a remarkable woman, do you know that?' Jen stated.

'I trust him Jen, I let go of my demons and trusted him.' The rejoice in her voice was evident for the world to hear.

'I told you. Not all men are bad Amy.'

'I know.' Amy replied. 'I should never have doubted him. I feel as if I have somehow betrayed him Jen, betrayed his love and feelings for me.'

'Don't be stupid! You have a past Amy, a bad past that has scarred you deeply, I know Jesse is young but he isn't thick, he understands probably a lot more than you give him credit for and I have said this God's knows how many times to you Amy!'

Just as Amy was about to respond to her friend the house phone began to ring.

'I'll ring you back in a minute Jen, the house phone is going.' Amy said quickly as she reached for it.

'Hello.'

'Hi is that Amy?' Amy recognised the voice, searching her mind trying to place the familiar female voice she felt the colour begin to drain from her face.

'Yes, is that Vicky?' She asked. Her heart was hammering in her chest, her palms were sweaty and tiny beads of moisture began to develop on her upper lip.

'Yes Amy, its Vicky from the Domestic Violence Unit. Are you staying at home?' She asked.

'Yes, why?' Amy responded, the nausea sweeping throughout her in fathomless waves. Vicky wanted to visit for a reason and as the date registered in Amy's head she quickly spoke her response.

'Yes I'm home. Vicky I have to go, see you shortly.' Amy hung up whilst running to the bathroom. Leaning over the toilet she gave into the sickly feelings that were gripping her stomach and chest and vomited, tears running down her face as the panic multiplied with every second that past.

Half an hour later she heard the knock on the door. Walking slowly towards it she had an impending sense of doom as she spotted Vicky through the glass panel.

'Hi Vicky.' Her voice was small, afraid.

'Hi Amy. Wow! First of all you look fab.' She scanned the petite woman before her. Her hair hung in waves to her tiny shoulders, a chestnut mane that shone with health. Her body was toned and tanned and the way she moved was so different from the last time Vicky had seen her. Her head was held high, her shoulders back. Gone was the timid, shy woman she had sat with in court whilst she gave the evidence that was needed to send her husband to prison.

'Thank you.' Amy tried to smile. 'What's the matter Vicky?' She asked, not wanting to drag out what she already knew the policewoman was here to say.

'Let's sit down.' Vicky said gently. 'I think you know why I am here Amy.'

Perching her bottom on the very edge of the sofa Amy looked with wide eyes at the woman opposite her.

'He's been released.' She whispered in a frightened voice.

'Yes Amy. He is due to be released at 4pm tomorrow. I am sorry it is such short notice but I only found out myself this morning.' Vicky reached for the fragile woman's hands. 'You don't need to be afraid

Amy, you still have the restraining order, I went to court as soon as I found out and had it stamped for another two years. He can't touch you.' Vicky tried to reassure her client. She had been through so much and Vicky had tried to persuade Amy to bring charges against her husband for the rapes but she had refused and so the scumbag had gotten away with a light sentence.

'Amy, I have to say this to you, it's my job. You can still press charges against Paul for the rapes.'

'Please don't start this again.' Amy wailed. When she had been recovering in hospital from the horrific injuries she had suffered at his hands Vicky had tried to pressure her into giving a statement. Amy had rebuffed all Vicky's attempts to try and get her to spill the beans, her mouth staying firmly shut.

'Ok Amy, please calm down.' Vicky realised she had perhaps pushed a little too far. 'You have been so brave, don't let him being released from prison have a negative effect Amy, he can't come near you or the house.'

Amy knew her ex-husband, he would want revenge. She had gradually built a life for herself and her daughters and now she feared that she was in danger of losing everything she had fought so courageously for.

'I am going to leave you with my number again Amy. Store it in your phone. If he is stupid enough to come anywhere near you I want you to ring 999. Only when it is safe to do so do I want you to ring me.' Vicky was squeezing her hands tightly. 'Amy you are strong, he can't hurt you anymore.'

Tears ran down Amy's face as flashback after flashback assaulted her. She was afraid, no she was petrified.

'You say he can't hurt me anymore.' She whispered. 'Vicky you don't know him, you don't know what he is capable of.' Amy cried.

'Well press charges for the rapes Amy, send him to prison for a long time.' Vicky repeated hoping that Amy's fear would encourage her to speak out.

'No!' She replied firmly. 'No Vicky!'

'Ok.' Vicky replied standing up. 'You have my number Amy; call me if you need anything.' She said walking in the direction of the front door.

'Thank you.' Amy mumbled as the tears threatened once more. 'You have to understand Vicky, I have to protect the girls, he's still their father at the end of the day.'

'I know Amy.' Putting her hand on Amy's shoulder she made her promise that she would call if she needed anything.

'I promise.' Amy said as she walked with her to the front door.

Closing the door to the policewoman Amy leaned against it. As she slid down to the floor she wrapped herself in a ball, her sobs and cries filling the silent air as once again her past visited her, taking her back in time, the brave, sexy woman gone, in her place a weak and petrified wreck.

CHAPTER FORTY FOUR

'Open the door!' Jen was screaming through the letter box. After receiving the strange phone call from her best friend, Jen had floored the accelerator of her little car eating up the miles quickly. She needed to get to her friend.

'Amy will you please open this fucking door!' She hollered once more, banging on the letter box whilst ringing the bell.

As Amy unlocked the door Jen stood back and gasped.

'What the….. Amy what's the matter?' She grabbed her friend into her arms. Amy sobbed, her words a jumbled mess.

'He's…been….released.' She wailed. 'Jen…he's….been… released.'

'Who? Paul!' Jen tried to keep her voice low and steady as she tried to make sense of the words Amy spoke. 'Fuckin hell Amy.' Bundling her friend into the house Jen shut the door behind them.

'Lock it.' Amy cried. 'Lock it Jen.'

'Calm down Amy please.' Jen pleaded. She hated seeing her friend like this, broken, wrecked and afraid. 'Where's Jesse?' She asked taking hold of Amy's hands trying to calm her down.

'At work and I don't want him to know Jen. Please don't tell him or Rick for that matter.' She pleaded gripping Jen's hands tightly. 'Please Jen, I'm pleading with you, don't tell Jesse!'

'Amy he has a right to know.' Jen stated wisely. 'Paul is a dangerous man, Jesse needs to know, he needs to be aware.'

'He would never approach Jesse.' Amy responded. 'He can only bully and beat women.' She added quietly. 'What am I going to do Jen? I'm so scared.' Amy cried.

It had taken Amy a long time to break away from the violence that she once accepted as everyday life and even longer to find the courage to begin a new life. As she looked at Jen with eyes flooded with tears she felt a deep and lonely sadness run through her. It had been good whilst it lasted, at least she had known love and kindness for just a while……..

'Oh Amy.' Jen took her friend once more into her arms, holding her closely whilst she wept. 'When was he released?' She asked as Amy began to finally calm down.

'Not until tomorrow.' Amy replied trying to fight back the tears of misery and stop her tiny body from shaking.

'So we don't need to lock the door then. Have you still got the restraining order Amy?' Jen questioned.

'Vicky, the policewoman from the Domestic Violence Unit went to court today and got one for two years.' Amy replied.

'See! You are protected Amy, he really can't hurt you.' Jen was trying to reassure her little friend.

'Do you think a restraining order will fucking stop him?' Amy shouted. 'Will it fuck! Mark my words Jen he will come for me, come on be friggin honest, you know him, know what he is capable of.' She added breaking down once again.

'Well if he comes anywhere near phone the police straight away Amy. Can the police not put some sort of information on your address so they know what they are responding to?' Jen asked. Her own mind was in turmoil as a thousand thoughts ran through her brain. She needed to help and protect her friend; Jen hated seeing her like this. Amy had worked so hard, been so strong and for the last few months had finally found peace, witnessing her distress was tearing Jen apart.

'I don't know, I could ring Vicky I guess and ask.' Amy replied. Reaching for her mobile phone she noticed that Jesse had text her.

'Hope you are having a good day sexy bum. I will come up later after work. I love you. xx'

'Oh fuck!' Amy said throwing her phone onto the sofa as fresh tears ran down her face once again.

'What's the matter?' Jen asked, concern and pain written all over her face.

'Jesse, he wants to come up tonight. Let me just send him a quick message, is it ok if I tell him I'm going to visit you tonight?' Amy asked, knowing that lying to Jesse was the last thing she wanted to do but her love for him was too great; she had to keep this from him.

'Why? Why are you avoiding him? He is a good man Amy, he will understand.' Jen was once again trying to reassure her.

'He is too young to take on this, my past.' Amy stated miserably. 'Paul is a dangerous man Jen, I don't want Jesse near this, he means too much to me.' Again the tears began to fall. The two men she had been intimate with were so different. Paul was evil, a manipulative, controlling man who had brought her terror nearly every day of their twenty year relationship; Jesse well he was pure and innocent, kind, caring, loving. He brought only smiles and happiness. No, she definitely didn't want him tainted by her past.

'So what are you going to say to Jesse?' Jen asked stroking her friend's hands softly.

'Ok.' Amy relinquished. 'I will tell him that Paul has been released Jen but that's it. He has his own life to live, his friends, his family......'

'And he loves you Amy.' Jen added. 'He will understand. If Paul does decide to hang around then Jesse is much better being informed, to keep him in the dark would be wrong and dangerous Amy.'

Amy knew that the words her friend spoke were true.

'Let me ring Vicky.' Amy said reaching for the phone.

Jen listened carefully to the one sided conversation.

'So you can put a police marker on the property. Yes, that has reassured me a little. Thank you Vicky.' Amy concluded before hanging up. Turning to Jen she reached for her friend once again.

'Did you get the gist of the conversation Jen?' Amy asked. 'They will put some sort of marker on the house, any calls will take priority.'

'Does that make you feel a little safer Amy?' Jen asked, smiling softly at her friend.

'Yes, it makes me feel safer.' Amy responded to Jen's question. 'It's just...'

'It's just what?' Jen carefully asked. 'Tell me Amy.' She softly encouraged.

'Jen, by the time the police get here I could be dead......' Amy sobbed as raw fear overtook her once again.

'He wouldn't dare Amy, he knows you are no longer that weak, pathetic woman who put up with his shit and abuse for years, I mean Amy, think about it, you gave evidence and put the bastard in jail.'

'Precisely Jen, precisely. He is going to want his revenge.' Amy knew Paul, knew what made him tick, knew what made him mad. He had been sat in his prison cell with a lot of time to think about his life, about her and how he thought she had betrayed him.

'Listen to me Amy. He is getting old, too old for all his shit! I bet he has moved on, I bet he leaves you alone.' Jen stated a little unconvincingly.

'We'll see.' Amy replied. 'I guess only time will tell. At least I know he is being released tomorrow so I can prepare, make sure we are safe.'

'What are you going to tell Chloe and Bethany?' Jen asked. 'I know the girls don't want anything to do with him but they still need to know he is out.' Jen said wisely.

'I am going to speak to them later Jen, you are right, they do need to know their dad is being released.' Amy replied, her face so sad and fearful.

'What time are they due home?' Jen asked standing up. 'Is it ok if I make a drink Sweetie?' She added.

'Oh Jen, I am so sorry, where are my manners.' Amy cried. 'I'll make it, it will take my mind of all this.' She said sweeping her hands before her.

'You are going to be ok Amy.' Jen said squeezing her shoulder. 'You can do this, you can't let him beat you after everything you have fought for, come on girl, you fell hard but you fought harder!' Jen added passionately.

'You are right Jen. If I can survive twenty years living with the bastard I am sure I can survive another twenty living without him!' Amy declared.

'Now that's more like it, got to get you some spunk girl!' Jen replied smiling. 'Now text Jesse back will you whilst I make something to drink.'

'Thank you Jen.' Amy whispered. 'You really are a good friend to me.'

'You would do the same for me Amy.' Jen stated correctly. 'Now send the hot stuff a fuckin text will you!' She laughed picking Amy's phone up and handing it to her.

Amy laughed as she reached for her mobile phone from her friend's hands.

'Hiya sexy eyes. Sorry was having a girlie chat with Jen. Of course it is. See you later. I love you too. xx'

An hour later Chloe and Bethany burst through the front door.

'Hiya mum.' They shouted in unison as they walked into the house, their voices happy and carefree.

'I'm in here.' Amy shouted from the kitchen. Turning she spotted her two daughters and smiled broadly. 'Roast chicken dinner, is that ok?' She asked walking towards the pair and hugging them.

'Cool.' Chloe responded.

'Yeh!' Came Bethany's reply.

Twenty minutes later the three women sat around the black glass dining table.

'Girls I need to talk to you both.' Amy said. The nausea was rising once again. Placing her knife and fork down she looked at her daughters. 'Your dad is being released from prison tomorrow.'

'What!' They both screeched.

'Calm down girls.' Amy instructed. 'He is being released tomorrow; I thought you would both want to know.'

'Thanks mum but I personally don't want to know, I never want to lay eyes on him again!' Chloe said passionately.

'And I don't give a shit! Bethany added. 'He can go and rot in hell for me!'

'Are you scared mum?' Chloe asked concern on her beautiful face as she reached for her mother's hand.

'No!' Amy hoped she sounded convincing. Her girls were intelligent; she would have to be very careful how she acted around them both.

'Good, he's a looser!' Bethany added.

'Let's hope he moves out of the country.' Chloe said. 'Don't let him scare you mum, you have been so brave and you are the happiest I have ever seen you since meeting Jesse.'

Standing she drew both her daughter's into her arms.

'I promise.' She whispered her fingers crossed firmly behind their backs.

CHAPTER FORTY FIVE

Jesse's knock on the door sent Bethany running down the stairs.

'I'll get it.' She shouted knowing her mother was finishing writing a letter. 'Hi Jesse.' She grinned as she opened the door to him. 'My mum is upstairs in her room.'

Amy had slowly introduced the girls to Jesse and was relieved when the pair had declared him a hit. Both Chloe and Bethany thought he was wonderful as they watched their mother change before their eyes into a happy, smiling woman.

'Thanks Bethany.' He responded taking the stairs two at a time. 'Hi you.' He said as he peered around her bedroom door.

'Hi yourself.' She responded smiling at him warmly. Her day had begun so happy, she had awoken to find herself snuggled into Jesse's arms and as she watched him sleep she had studied his handsome face carefully. It was times like this that Amy loved, Jesse so blissfully unaware that her eyes were on him. She could really look at him when those bloody sexy eyes were closed! The shape of his almost perfect eyebrows, the way his wavy hair fell over his forehead, his nose, his soft lips.......

'Have you had a good day babe?' He asked flopping down onto the bed sending the cushions and throw flying through the air. 'I don't know why you have all this fancy shit on your bed.' He laughed, hurling a small cushion in her direction.

'Ermmm....' Sensing she was about to reveal something important Jesse sat up, his eyes on her face, the smile that played at his mouth slowly disappeared as he looked at Amy carefully.

'What's the matter Amy?' He asked softly. 'You look worried.' He added reaching over to stroke her cheek.

'I've got something to tell you.' She said in a small voice as she rested her face in his hand. 'Paul is being released from prison tomorrow.' Her eyes immediately fell to the floor.

'Hey.' He said lifting her face back up so he could read what was written all over it. 'Are you scared?' He asked gently.

'Yes.' She whispered. Amy had revealed so much to Jesse over the months she had known him but with Paul in prison she had felt free and able to pursue her dreams and let go of her past.

'I love you too much to let anything happen to you Amy.' He said quietly. Taking her into his arms he squeezed her tightly to him.

'He is a dangerous man Jesse; you need to know how evil he can be.' She murmured.

'I can guess Amy, I see it sometimes in your face, I can tell he hurt you badly.' Jesse knew far more than Amy thought, the scars on her body were one thing, it was the look of pain that he sometimes caught on her face that tore at him the most. She was a brave woman but as he studied her now closely he began to see how deeply afraid she really was.

'He did and yes I'm afraid, he can hit me but I never want him to touch me again Jesse.' She quietly cried.

'You mean rape you Amy.' He said softly noticing that she was again looking at the ground. 'Have you ever spoken to anyone Amy, I mean a counsellor or doctor?'

'Not really. Vicky, the policewoman who looked after me after the attack helped a lot, she knows mostly everything.' Amy replied, her voice the merest whisper.

'Would you do something for me and for you Amy?' He asked, hooking his finger under her chin, his green eyes soft, almost appealing to her as he reached out.

'I would do anything for you.' Amy whispered trying to meet his soft gaze.

'Would you go and talk to someone Amy? It will help you.' He stated, his fingertips softly stroking her cheek.

Amy had refused all offers of counselling not wanting to share her pain with anyone. She had done a good job thus far in re building her shattered life, she was strong, she could cope. This was a momentary blip, a weak and pathetic response to the news she had received earlier that day, after a good night's sleep she would be fine. No, she didn't want to share her past with anyone, especially not a stranger.

'I don't know Jesse.' She replied, not wanting to hurt his feelings.

Amy knew he was trying to help but she really didn't want to talk about her past, it was too painful.

'Please, for me.' He asked again softly. He knew he was taking advantage of her soft nature and her love for him but he desperately wanted to help her.

Removing herself from his arms she looked at her lover's face, his kind eyes, his gentle smile……..

'Ok.' She relinquished. 'I will do it for you.'

'No, for you.' He said gathering her into his arms once again. 'I am here for you Amy.' He added lovingly as he once again saw the pain in her eyes.

'Thank you.' She whispered feeling safe in his arms. 'Jesse.'

'Yes.' He answered.

'I'm scared of losing you, he is dangerous and I know he will come after me.'

'Amy please listen to me. You have told me all about your marriage, although I still feel that you are holding back on me. I could have walked away months ago but I didn't, I fell in love with you. I am glad I have helped you to heal, I want to be here for you.'

'Ok. Thank you.' She muttered, pressing herself into him, his words burying themselves deep in her heart. 'I love you so much.' He was so young yet somehow so wise. Her past, her world was foreign to him yet somehow he made it all seem better.

His lips claimed hers and as she felt his kiss deepen she clung to him, her fears put away for the time being.

'Where are Chloe and Bethany?' He breathed. He wanted her; he needed to take her pain away so she would forget.

'Chloe is out and I think I just heard Bethany leave. Hang on a sec.' Jumping up she picked up her phone. 'Yes, she has gone out.' Amy added as she read the text from her youngest daughter. 'She has gone to the cinema with her friends.'

'Come here.' He beckoned. His voice low and sexy, the "Jesse look" in his eyes. 'I have someone who wants to say hello.'

'And who might they be?' Amy giggled playing along with him as she felt the heaviness begin to disappear from her body and mind.

'Brucie!'

Reaching for the buckle of his belt Amy quickly undid it. As she moved to the side of the bed she extended her fingers, touching the button on his Levis briefly. Running her hands under his t shirt she sighed softly as they came into contact with the soft skin of his stomach. She needed his arms around her, she needed him.

' So "The Boss" wants to say hi?' She murmured as she continued to trace lazy patterns across his flat stomach. Moving her hand down she unzipped his jeans, her hand grazing his erect penis. 'Hi Bruce.' She whispered as her hand dove into his tight fitting black boxer shorts. Taking him in her hand she began to move his foreskin back and forth slowly.

'Oh babe.' He hissed. 'Please take my jeans off.'

Obliging Amy stood up; reaching for the waistband of his jeans she tugged them down taking his boxer shorts with them.

'I have a surprise for you.' Folding his jeans carefully she lay them on the floor before opening her wardrobe door.

'What is it?' Jesse asked excitedly as he watched her take out a white box.

'I think you will like them.' She stated as she took the lid off, hiding the contents from him.

'Let me see.' Jesse pleaded as he tried to look into the box.

'God you are so handsome.' Amy replied as she looked at him propped up on his elbow, a beaming smile on his face. Slowly she took the contents out of the box as she sat down on the edge of the bed. 'I hope you like them Jesse.' She said placing one in each hand to show him.

'Oh.....My.....God! Amy they are so sexy.' Jesse was now sat bolt upright on the bed. His wavy, dark hair flopping down onto his forehead as his eyes burned into her.

Placing the contents on the floor she watched his face closely as she slipped on the new, super high stilettos. Amy had always had difficulty buying "big girl's shoes," as she called them as she only had tiny size 2 feet. She had found a store on the internet that specialised in both small and large sizes and immediately written a rather extensive shoe shopping list.

What do you think?' She asked Jesse standing up and twirling first one ankle, then the other. The heels were enormous on the leopard printed shoes and they fit snuggly like a glove. As soon as the delivery man had placed them in her hands she had ran up the stairs, stripping off her clothes as she went. Amy needed to see what the shoes looked like and the jeans she had been wearing just wouldn't do, no she needed a skirt, a short skirt. Reaching into her wardrobe she pulled out the first one she saw and quickly put it on, the skin tight, black material clinging to her body in all the right places. Placing her feet gingerly into the outrageously high shoes she took baby steps towards the full length mirror that was on the back of the door, her mouth immediately gaping open as she had looked at her reflection.... her legs looked so long! As she had twirled carefully, trying to look from every angle, a sexy grin slowly graced her face; a goddess like sparkle adorned her eyes as an image of Jesse appeared before her, his green eyes burning with passion.

'Wow!' He exclaimed. 'Fuckin hell Amy they are sexy shoes.' He couldn't keep his eyes off them as he watched her delicately move her ankles. 'You are one sexy woman!' He stated huskily as he reached for her, gently dragging her towards him.

'I'm glad you approve.' She whispered seductively pushing him gently back down onto the bed. 'Now, are you ready for blow job heaven Jesse?' She seductively teased. All her fears and anguish had slowly disappeared to be replaced with a burning desire to feel his cock in her mouth.

'Oh yeh!' Jesse replied, grabbing himself. 'Come get my cock babe.' His eyes were two green pools of lust as he began to move his hand back and forth, beckoning to her to take him into her warm, ready mouth.

Standing at the side of the bed, close to his head, Amy slowly turned her back to him, bending over she reached for his cock. As she turned to look at him, her eyes seeking his for a few moments, she gently moved his hand away, claiming him as her own. Sweeping her hair away she kissed her way down his body until her lips opened wide to receive him into her ready mouth.

'Fucking hell!' She heard him gasp. Her short, bleached denim skirt finished just below her bottom cheeks, her tanned legs on show disappeared into the amazingly high shoes. 'This is defo one to commit to memory!' He stated as he ran his hands up and down the length of her legs.

Sighing Amy tightened her grip on his cock causing him to groan with pleasure. As she bent at the waist she took him deep into her mouth, her tongue and lips working in unison to bring him the gratification he now desperately craved.

'Oh baby, you know just how I like it.' He mumbled as she took as much of him as was possible into her mouth again, her lips softly holding him in place. Withdrawing him slowly she ran her tongue around his tip before plunging him once more into her wet, warm mouth. As she felt his fingers inside her she moaned softly, parting her legs a little more to allow him full access to her sex. Her mouth continued to pleasure him as she sucked and licked his erect cock whilst his fingers were inside her, massaging her, her pussy wet, wanting to feel the fullness of his hard cock. 'Come here.' Jesse moved his hands to her hips, guiding her onto the bed so her secret place was inches from his mouth.

'Oh Jesse.' She breathed as she felt his mouth on her, his tongue circling her clitoris, his fingers deep inside her. Hungrily she slid his cock into her mouth, her lips and tongue eager to please him. Matching his tempo she gripped him firmly with her hand whilst sucking the tip of him.

'Stop!' He hissed withdrawing his fingers and mouth.

'Jesse! Don't stop. Please.' She wailed as she felt her impending orgasm begin to slip away.

Moving himself from under her he swiftly lay her down on the bed, her legs wide apart ready for him. Positioning himself at her entrance he hesitated, his eyes burning into her.

'Please Jesse, please.' She whimpered her desire for him, her need to feel him inside her taking over every thought. 'Please.' She begged once more as she threw her arm across her face to block out the intense look in his eyes.

'Look at me. Amy, look at me.' He gently demanded, his voice huskily seducing her from where she hide.

Peeking from underneath her arm she gasped, his eyes were on fire.

'I can't.' She pleaded. 'Jesse please.' She begged grabbing a pillow to cover her face, his eyes too much for her to bear. It was an almost pleasurable pain that began in her heart, spreading deep within her until its intensity was such it caused her an agony she was unable to endure.

As she felt him glide slowly into her she let go. Wave after wave enveloped her, cocooning her in the ultimate sexual blanket as he plunged himself in and out of her, her internal muscles gripping him tightly as each contraction infiltrated her body.

Withdrawing from her suddenly she yelped out as she felt the void he had left, her body wanting more.

'No!'

'Stand up.' He ordered softly reaching for her hands to help her.

'My legs are like jelly.' She protested trying to lie back down, wanting him back in her arms, his cock inside her wet pussy.

'Up!' Jesse insisted trying to help her once again. 'There that's better.' He added as she stood before him. 'Now let's remove these clothes.'

Never taking his eyes away from her face he reached down to remove her top.

'No!'

'No?' Jesse responded cocking his head to one side, a puzzled look on his face. As he looked at Amy closely, took in the passion in her eyes, he knew what she wanted. 'I'll rip it off if you don't let me take it off.' He threatened a maddeningly sexy look on his face.

'Be my guest.' Amy replied nervously, biting down hard on her bottom lip as her inner confident self screamed out 'do it, do it!'

His lips were on hers, his tongue exploring the inside of her mouth. Amy reached for his hair, her fingers sinking into the soft waves as she pulled him even closer, wanting to feel a part of him on every inch of her body.

'You turn me on so much.' He whispered as he reached for her top, his lips once again assaulting her own. The buttons flew off easily as he tore apart the flimsy material exposing her bra. 'This is new.' His words were like velvet to her ears as he removed the remnants of fabric from her body, his lips trailing delicate kisses down the side of her neck. 'I like it.' He added as he ran his fingers along the top of the jade coloured, lacy cup. Looking up to capture her eyes he spoke softly. 'I hope you are going to let me remove this Amy? I don't want to ruin it, it's sexy.'

Nodding her head Amy watched him mesmerized as he slowly turned her around unclasping her bra smoothly, his fingertips a mere whisper on her bare skin.

'That's better.' He murmured, his fingers tracing the light marks that the bra had left on her soft skin. Every touch appeared to be in slow motion as she concentrated on the movement of his fingers, the sound of his voice. 'Put your hands here.' He instructed reaching for her arms and guiding them to the wall so they were positioned above her head. His hold on her wrists was light and as he trailed his hands down her arms and through her hair Amy heard the soft moans escape from her parted lips. 'Now for the skirt.' Running his hands tenderly down her back his hands encircled her waist before he reached around to undo the button and zip. As it dropped to the floor Amy leant flat against the wall, sticking her bottom out invitingly, spreading her legs just a little further apart. 'So sexy.' He murmured as his hands roamed all over her bare skin.

Feeling Jesse's presence between her legs she moved them a little further apart.

'Do you want me to leave the shoes on?' She asked in a breathless voice, her face to the side as she stood against the wall. Amy knew that as soon as he pushed his cock inside her she would explode.

'Yes! Just the shoes and the anklet Amy, so sexy......' Since leaving the thatched cottage Amy hadn't removed the silver chain, liking the way it felt at her ankle.

His words trailed off as he thrust into her, his hard cock filling her completely. Clasping both her wrists with one hand, holding them firmly above her head, his other reached around for her clitoris.

'Make me come.' She hissed between her clenched teeth. 'Please Jesse, fuck me and make me come.' Her need for him was overwhelming, her need to climax taking over her entire being as she throbbed for him needing the release that only Jesse could give her.

Again he withdrew himself.

'What, why! Jesse!' As she made to turn around he picked her up easily. 'Where are we going?' She asked as he opened the bedroom door.

'Shower.' He responded his lips seeking hers once again as he deposited her on the floor of the bathroom. 'These need to come off.' He stated, bending to remove the new shoes. 'They are sexy as fuck and I don't want to get them ruined although the idea of you in the shower with them on is driving me crazy.'

'Cold!' She said as her bare feet hit the black, shiny tiles that lay on the floor.

'Not for long.' Jesse responded a playful look on his handsome face as he reached behind the glass shower screen to turn on the shower. 'There, nice and warm.' He stated flicking the water from his hands in her direction, his cock standing proud, beckoning to her.

'Jesse!' She squealed as the freezing cold water hit her naked skin. 'It's fuckin freezing!' She was beginning to feel more than a little frustrated; she needed fucking not a shower!

Laughing Jesse adjusted the control so the water flowed warmer.

'There, it's perfect now. You getting in?' He said hopping into the shower dragging her with him.

The warm water cascaded over their bodies, reaching for the bottle of scented shower gel he squirted some into his hands before bending to her feet.

'Jesse.' She giggled as he massaged the foamy liquid into her feet. 'It tickles.'

'Relax.' He softly instructed as his soapy hands made their way slowly up her legs. 'You have really sexy legs.' Jesse breathed, kneading her flesh lightly before running the tips of his fingers up her inner thigh.

Amy was leaning against the white tiles of the wall, the steady stream of warm water mixed with his hands, created waves of delicious sensations throughout her. As Jesse ran his hands over her bottom, kneading the flesh between his fingers she wanted to beg him, plead for him to fill her with his hard cock. Pushing herself back onto the tiles she moaned loudly.

'I want you.' The words spoken so softly into her ear igniting a fire deep within her secret place as his lips grazed the side of her neck before bending to take her left nipple into his mouth. As his lips encircled it she felt the delicious connection begin with her sex, its power increasing as his mouth moved to the right, her body responding, so ready for him.

'Turn around Amy.' Jesse said reaching for the shower gel one more time.

'Jesse….' She breathed as his hands left her skin causing an almost pain like sensation. Her body craved his touch, she needed to feel his skin on hers, his cock inside her, then she would feel complete.

Amy stood against the cool tiles, her breasts pressed firmly against them, her head to the side as the water rained down on her body she waited for him to wash her back. Slipping his cock unexpectedly back into her she gasped as she felt him glide into her, her pussy wet and ready for him. As he thrust deeply she clenched her muscles tightly, holding him, feeling every single part of him inside her.

'Oh Jesse….' She moaned as she forced her hips backwards, impaling herself onto him so he was deep inside her.

Slowly he moved, teasing her, bringing her almost to the brink of orgasm.

'Jesse!' She wailed pushing herself further away from the wall in a bid to grind herself upon him.

Reaching his fingers around her he began to massage her clitoris, his cock building up the tempo driving her wild with desire. Feeling the first signs of her impending orgasm Jesse gripped her firmly around the waist, pulling her back onto him, his cock motionless and rigid deep inside her. As the swells began to rise she screamed out his name, crushing herself into him, gripping him with her pelvic muscles as they contracted fiercely.

'Jesse….. Jesse…… Jesse.' She repeated his name over and over as she rode the crest of her climax.

'Amy.' He shouted as his own climax overtook him and he spurted his warm semen into her, grasping her tightly until he was spent.

CHAPTER FORTY SIX

Lying in his arms on her bed Amy felt as if she had gone to heaven. Jesse had denied her for so long, teasing her until she thought she would explode but the orgasm she had only moments before experienced was still sending tiny ripples of sensation throughout her body.

'Do you feel better?' Jesse asked hopefully as he gazed at her peaceful face.

'Yes.' She breathed. 'Jesse you are a special man.' She stated softly, a gentle, contented smile upon her lips. 'You certainly have a knack.' She giggled.

'I'm glad I can take some of the pain away Amy. You don't deserve all this.' He replied as he stroked her bare back.

'Chloe is moving out.' Amy said wistfully. 'I will miss her.'

'Have they bought a house?' Jesse asked referring to her eldest daughter and her boyfriend Mark.

'No, they are renting whilst they save the deposit to buy.' Amy replied. 'It's a one bedroom apartment and Chloe says it's in a very beautiful, peaceful location.' Amy was grief stricken that her eldest baby was leaving home but knew that Mark would look after her. He was a good man and Amy loved him for the way he was with her daughter, so gentle and caring yet capable of controlling Chloe's sometimes impulsive nature.

'Where is it?' Jesse asked reaching for his cigarettes. 'Can you pass me the ashtray please babe.'

'Here.' She said handing him the ashtray. 'It's not far from where Mark lives now. Chloe said it's rural and you have to cross a little bridge to get there, it sounds gorgeous.' Amy replied enthusiastically. She would miss Chloe but at nearly 21 years old she knew that the day when she flew the nest was never far away. She had been with Mark since leaving school and Chloe loved him with all her heart and wanted to make a life of her own.

'Do the girls know about their dad being released?' Jesse asked as he lit a cigarette and inhaled deeply.

'Yes. Neither of them wants any contact with him Jesse.'

'That has to be up to them Amy, they are grown up.' He stated correctly.

'He will blame me.' She whispered, the fear edging back into her voice as she spoke the words that she knew Paul would have thought. 'His mind doesn't work normally; he perceives everything and everyone to be against him.' Amy needed Jesse to fully understand, it was her way of protecting him. Amy knew Jesse had been raised by a good family, his parents were professional people, and the likelihood of him ever coming across a person like Paul was foreign to her.

'You will be fine Amy, I promise.' Jesse was trying to reassure her; he wanted her to smile again.

'Thank you.' She whispered into his chest.

'So when is Chloe moving out?' He asked in a bid to distract her from her ex-husband.

'This weekend. I'm sad.' Amy stated. Squeezing her into his arms Jesse shifted his position so he could plant a small kiss on the tip of her nose. 'Are you hungry?' She asked.

'Starving!' Came his quick reply.

'I should have known.' She laughed as she began to peel herself from his embrace. 'I will go and make you something.' She said as she reached for the shirt he had given to her.

'That really suits you.' Jesse said. 'I know….' Bounding off the bed he disappeared, returning seconds later, her leopard print heels in his hands. 'I bet these look hot with the shirt.' He said holding them out to her, a sexy grin on his face that light up his eyes, eyes that wore the special "Jesse look" once again.

Laughing Amy arched her foot in front of her and looked down before looking back up to meet Jesse's eyes for a moment.

'You really like my feet, don't you.' She questioned.

'Yes, they are cute and tiny and sexy.' He replied, a massive grin spread from each corner of his mouth.

Holding on to the dressing table for support, Amy slowly slid her feet into the enormously high shoes, watching his facial expressions as she did so.

'What is it that turns you on so much?' She purred, placing her right foot onto the bed at his side.

'Sexy.' He breathed as his fingers ran down her leg towards the shoes. Slowly he moved his fingertips along where her foot disappeared into the shoe. 'It's this.' He quietly said continuing to run his fingers over the side of her exposed foot.

'No shenanigans!' Amy instructed removing her foot. 'You need feeding!' Without another word she walked towards the bedroom door, knowing he was watching her every move. 'Oh what's this?' She said bending to retrieve some imaginary object from the floor, her shirt rising as she did so revealing her bare arse.

'Amy!' Jesse hissed.

'What?' She responded innocently turning around so she was facing him.

'You know what!' He replied.

'Arrrgghhh Mr Clayton, it's payback time.' She chuckled as she took pleasure in watching him. 'Now you know how it feels.' She added in what she hoped was a sexy voice although every single nerve in her body was screaming for her to stop this outlandish and strange behaviour.

Jumping up from the bed Jesse lunged towards her. Squealing Amy escaped through the door taking the stairs as quickly as she could in the ridiculously high heels. As she stood on the bottom step he was behind her, reaching for her shoulders he prevented her from moving as he twirled her around so she was facing him.

'Fancy being fucked on the stairs?' He threatened sexily.

'No.' She responded, a playful look on her face. 'I think I have had enough for one day Mr Clayton but thank you very much for your very kind offer.......'

His mouth stopped her from uttering another word as he sat down on one of the stairs, bringing her with him.

'Food.' She murmured her voice becoming lost as his lips sought out hers.

'Lulu.' He murmured back reaching down in between her legs.

His thumb and fingers began to weave their magic. As he brought her closer and closer to orgasm she spread her legs further apart, wanting to feel him at her very core. Grasping his wrist, thrusting his fingers into her as far as they would go she gave into the wild sensations that tore through her body as her climax assaulted her with wave after wave of pleasure.

'Wow!' She said, gazing at him. Jesse wore a triumphant look on his face. 'You are looking mighty pleased with yourself there Clayton.' She remarked playfully as she came down slowly from the high of her intense orgasm.

'Happy to assist Miss Lucas.' He replied grinning at her. 'Now food!' He stated shoving her away from him gently before slapping her lightly on the behind.

'With pleasure sir.' She replied. As she stood she bowed before him, sweeping her arm out widely.

'Cheeky.' His response was filled with laughter.

Walking into the kitchen Amy wondered what on earth she could make him to eat. Rummaging inside the fridge and cupboards she selected various ingredients.

'Will an omelette do?' She shouted. Jesse was lay on the sofa watching TV.

'Why you shouting.' His voice startled her.

'Shit! I thought you were in the living room.' She declared. 'You scared me.' She giggled.

'Do you honestly think that the TV is the best thing to watch around here?' He questioned looking her up and down. 'You in that shirt and those shoes are much more interesting.' He grinned, the "Jesse look" in his eyes as he casually leaned against the doorframe.

'Behave! I need to concentrate.' She pleaded blushing a lovely, deep shade of red. 'How does he do this? Earth shattering, mind blowing fucking orgasms and I still want him!' She scolded herself silently.

Turning her attention to preparing him something to eat Amy pretended he wasn't sat just feet away from her. Jesse was sitting on one of the high backed, chairs, his elbows resting on the glass dining table, his chin perched on his hands, his sexy, green eyes following her every move.

Swallowing she turned to look at him.

'What would you like in your omelette?' She asked, her eyes avoiding his as her hands instinctively went up to her hair, making sure her fringe was in place.

'Errmm let me see.' He responded, a devilish, tormenting look on his face. He was enjoying watching her squirm with nerves and embarrassment.

'Jesse!' She pleaded quietly, sticking her bottom lip out a little.

'Errmm, I can't really decide.' He answered wickedly, the look never leaving his eyes as they swept from her tiny feet encased in the ridiculous high heels up to the burning skin of her flushed face.

'Well you shall get what you're given in that case.' Amy retorted putting her back to him once again.

Whisking the eggs viciously she added salt and pepper before delving into the refrigerator for the mushrooms, peppers, cheese and tomatoes. She could feel his eyes burning into her and knew that without him even touching her she would be wet and ready again for him.

'How the fuck does he do this to me?' She silently questioned herself.

'You ok there babe?' He cheekily asked, knowing that the mere sound of his voice would cause her more embarrassment.

'Ssshhh. Don't talk to me.' She muttered her back still to him as she chopped up the vegetables. 'Here, make yourself useful.' She said handing him the cheese and grater. 'Will you grate some cheese please?' She asked, avoiding his gaze.

'Of course ma'am.' He responded sexily, his eyes burning into hers. 'Look at me Amy.' He whispered.

'Jesse, stop it!' She half-heartedly demanded. 'I can't cope!' She stated sticking her bottom lip out at him in a mock like sulk once again. 'Seriously Jesse you make me dizzy!'

Jesse had a powerful effect on her from the moment she had laid eyes on him that day at her friend, Jen's. As the weeks and months passed by her symptoms only worsened. She was fine until he knocked on her door or she heard his low, sexy voice on the telephone, even his texts made her blush at times. Without even answering the door to his knock her heart would start hammering in her chest, the tiny beads of moisture gathering menacingly on her upper lip, ready to betray her to his green, sexy eyes. She was a mess. From the outside she looked like any other woman who was blissfully in love, the inside was a different matter. It wasn't just his eyes, she secretly thought, it's him, he has me under some weird spell. His presence in her life had sent her reeling and she was positive she would never completely recover from what she had fondly called her love illness - "Jesseitus."

'Are you ready for this cheese?' He asked, unaware of how dizzy Amy was actually beginning to feel.

'Erm... yes please.' She murmured refusing to meet his eyes as she reached for the bowl.

'Love ya.' He said, getting up suddenly and leaving the room.

'Fuck!' Amy exclaimed to herself. 'I'm going to pass out in a minute.' Turning her attention back to the stove she tried to concentrate on making the simple omelette.

CHAPTER FORTY SEVEN

'Well, did you speak to him?' Jen asked. It was 7am and the constant ringing of her mobile phone had eventually made Amy reach for it as she rubbed her eyes trying to wake up.

'Yes Jen, I did. Do you know what time it is? She asked a little grumpily.

'Hey sleepy arse, wake the fuck up!' Jen shouted down the phone. 'What did he say?' She continued.

'He was fine Jen, I told him that Paul was being released...... shit, it's today!' She exclaimed sitting bolt upright in her bed, the sleep she had been so crudely disturbed from forgotten.

'Now don't start panicking Amy, you are going to be fine. Did Jesse reassure you a little?' She gently prodded hoping that if Amy thought about Jesse she would forget about the bastard being released.

'Yes he did Jen, I will say it again, I don't know why I doubted him.'

'Because of his age.' Jen provided.

'Yes, I guess so plus he has been brought up so well Jen, he isn't used to nut jobs like Paul.'

'Everything will be fine Amy, you will see.' Jen's tone was light as she tried once again to reassure her little friend. 'Did Jesse stay last night?' She asked.

'No, he has work early this morning.' Amy replied. 'He is coming round this evening though.' She added.

'Good.' Jen replied. 'Right Sweetie I will leave you to wake up and speak to you later. Now don't go worrying all day, you are going to be just peachy.' She giggled.

'Ok Jen and thank you for ringing even if it is too friggin early!' She laughed in reply.

Pulling back the curtains Amy noticed the sky. Big, black clouds reached as far as her eyes could see, the rain was falling heavily.

'What a shit day!' Amy exclaimed to no one in particular.

Putting on her bathrobe she walked into the girl's bedrooms and noticed their beds made and un-slept in. It wasn't unusually for Chloe to stay with Mark but Bethany had gone out with friends the night before, where the hell was she? Reaching for her mobile phone she quickly dialled Bethany's number.

'Hello.' A sleepy voice answered the phone.

'Bethany where are you?' Amy asked the anxiety evident in her voice.

'I stayed at a friend's mum; I'll be home later, after work.' Bethany hung up the phone and Amy smiled as relief flooded through her and she imagined her youngest daughter falling straight back to sleep.

Walking down the stairs and into the kitchen Amy switched the kettle on for her morning cuppa. The ringing of her mobile phone had her running back up the stairs as she recognised the ringtone she had set for Jesse, "Baby I Love You" by the Ramones.

'Damn!' She shouted at herself. Just as she had picked it up he had disconnected the call probably thinking she was still asleep. Dialling his number she waited for him to answer his phone.

'Hi babe.' His greeting was warm and friendly and just what Amy needed. The silky tones of his voice almost wrapping themselves around her, cocooning her whilst making her feel safe.

'Hi sugar lips.' She replied. 'Sorry I was downstairs making a brew and by the time I got upstairs you'd rang off.'

'I thought you may be sleeping when you didn't answer.' He responded. 'How are you feeling baby?' He added his voice sexy and low.

'I'm ok.' She replied. 'I didn't sleep very well if I'm honest and then Jen woke me up at 7am with her morning alarm call!'

'She was probably doing the same thing as me.' He replied. 'Seeing if you are ok. Are you ok Amy?' He repeated.

Yes, honestly Jesse I am fine.' She crossed the fingers of her free hand behind her back, ashamed that she wasn't being honest with him, knowing that the words "I'm fine" were a simple act of bravado.

'Ok, well I am on my way to a job now; I finish about 6ish, is it ok if I come up?' He asked.

'Jesse, you don't have to ask.' Amy responded. 'You are welcome in my house anytime you like.' Amy knew it was his good breeding, his manners were impeccable.

'Next question.' He said. 'I am going to stay for a few nights Amy, if that is ok with you.'

'Of course it is but can I ask you why Jesse, if this is to do with Paul being released I will be fine, he daren't come near me.' Could she really keep up this act of courage? She silently thought. How many times would she have to lie to this wonderful man with the words "I'm fine?"

'Partly.' He replied honestly. 'But I also want to be with you Amy.' He added. 'I like sleeping beside you.'

'Ok baby. Well I will let you get on to your next job. See you later darling. Have a good day, I love you Jesse and thank you.' Amy was smiling as she closed her eyes and summoned his image to her mind.

'I love you too and try not to worry.'

'I won't.' She was doing a very convincing job as she kept her voice fresh and light. 'Bye babe.' She added before hanging up on him.

As she had lay wide awake the night before, her thoughts a scrambled mess, she knew what she had to do. Amy knew there was one thing she did well, protect the people she loved. For years she had shielded her daughters from the horrific truth until they grew and saw with their own eyes the agony that their mother endured on a daily basis. The strength her two daughters' had given her helped her to carry on until she couldn't stand the life that had been dealt to her anymore. She loved Jesse with every part of her and she knew she had to protect him also. He had helped her so much in the months that she had known him, yes; it was her job to protect him she had vowed to herself.

At just after 10am her landline rang, disturbing her from the pile of work she had lain out before her.

'Hello.' She said distractedly.

'Amy, its Vicky.' Amy felt her heart sink as she heard the police woman's voice.

'Hi Vicky.' She replied flatly as all her emotions suddenly left her body.

'Amy, Paul is being released at 11am not 4pm. The prison apparently has quite a few inmates to get rid of today so they have had to section off the times.'

'Shit!' The panic started to rise making her feel sick with worry. 'Ok Vicky, thank you for letting me know.' She added, desperate to get off the phone.

'Remember Amy, be vigilant, be careful but most of all don't let this destroy the new life you have built for yourself. You have got to be strong, you can do this, don't let him win.' Vicky wanted to go that bit further with Amy, she really felt for the little woman.

'I will Vicky and thank you.' Amy whispered.

Running to the bathroom she vomited violently into the toilet, the phone still in her hand. As she wretched and gagged tears flowed down her face. Never again would she be able to live the carefree life she had so easily adopted. Amy knew she was prematurely mourning its loss but it was inevitable, that she knew without the slightest doubt.

Brushing her teeth she inspected her reflection closely.

'Come on Amy, you can do this.' She told herself. 'Be strong, you have people to protect. No more tears, they show weakness.'

CHAPTER FORTY EIGHT

Settling herself back down Amy decided to forget about her problems and get on with the work she needed to complete by the close of business. When she had embarked on her single life she had trawled the internet for ideas to make some money. Jen had encouraged her to use her typing skills and so "Lucas Secretarial Services" took off. Amy had developed her business and now had a good set of clients who provided her with work on a daily basis.

The ringing of her mobile phone distracted Amy from the spread sheet she was diligently trying to work on.

'Hello.' She absent mindedly answered the phone, not noticing who the caller was.

'Bitch, you're dead. You are mine, I own you.' He hung up without waiting for a response.

'No!' She screamed. 'No!' Clutching her mouth she ran for the toilet, vomiting violently until she collapsed in a heap on the cold, tiled floor, her mobile by her side.

It rang again.

'You are mine, I own you, I'm coming to collect what's mine!' Again he hung up.

'Please no!' Amy cried. 'No!' Flashback after flashback assaulted her as she vomited once again. Visions of him stood over her, his fists clenched ready to punch her in the face flew through her brain.

Once again her phone rang, again a withheld number.

'What!' She screamed.

'Amy, what's the matter?' Vicky's voice vaguely registered somewhere deep inside her brain.

'Vicky, help me please.' She cried.

'Amy hang on.' Vicky replied. 'I'm listening to you Amy but I need to make a call, bear with me, tell me what happened, I'm listening.' She repeated trying to reassure her as she reached for the other phone on her desk. 'It's Vicky; I need a unit to attend…..'

'Vicky, he isn't here.' Amy shouted down the phone, hoping the policewoman would hear her. 'Don't send anyone round; it's a waste of time.'

'Hang on one sec.' She heard Vicky say into the other phone. 'Amy what has happened, take deep breaths and tell me.' Vicky knew she had to listen carefully to what Amy said now, her training had taught her well, this could be a trap. Amy could really need help but at the last moment been prevented from completing the call.

'He...rang...me.' She whimpered. 'He said he owns me and he wants what's his.' Vicky made the decision that Amy wasn't in any immediate danger so ended her call for a unit.

'It will take me twenty minutes to get there Amy, will you be ok 'til I arrive? I can send a unit round.'

'No Vicky, don't please. I'm just upset; I can wait until you get here.' Amy tried to calm herself down by controlling her breathing. 'It scared me Vicky, I wasn't expecting it.'

'He isn't allowed to contact you at all Amy!' Vicky declared. 'Right, I am going to put the phone down, I will be with you shortly.'

'Ok.' Amy replied hanging up the phone.

Fifteen minutes later Vicky knocked on the front door the shock clearly evident on her face when Amy opened the door and she saw the tiny, wrecked woman before her. She was deathly pale, her hands shaking uncontrollably. Taking her into her arms Vicky tried to comfort the distraught woman.

'Amy he can't hurt you.' Vicky softly cooed.

'Don't be so fucking pathetic!' Amy shouted, pushing the policewoman from her. 'You don't know him!' Her shaking finger pointed at Vicky. 'I have always tried to tell you how dangerous he is Vicky, even when I was in hospital and you came to see me, why won't you understand.' She pleaded. 'He's dangerous.' The tears flowed once more down her face. 'I should never have left him...'

'Amy, listen to me.' Vicky said firmly, grasping her by the shoulders. 'You did the right thing, you ended twenty years of abuse, you are a strong woman.'

'He will never leave me alone.' She wailed. 'Vicky, what am I going to do?'

'I'll tell you what you are going to do shall I?' Pausing Vicky smiled gently at the woman before her. 'You are going to go upstairs, wash your face and brush your hair. I will put the kettle on then we will sit down and talk this through.' Vicky replied assertively. She needed Amy to calm down so she could find out exactly what had happened, only then would she be able to work out which was the best way to proceed.

Nodding Amy made her way upstairs to the bathroom. She knew she looked a mess but as she glanced at her reflection in the mirror she recoiled in horror. Gone was the happy, smiling face, the twinkle in her eyes, instead a pale, frightened woman looked back at her, her eyes to pools of blackness. The reflection starring back at her looked too familiar, Amy the survivor had disappeared, in her place Amy the victim stood, a sad almost desperate expression on her face.

'Fuck him!' She shouted at her reflection, anger was slowly replacing her fear.

'Are you ok Amy?' She heard Vicky shouting up the stairs.

'I'm fine Vicky.' Amy shouted. 'I'll be down in a minute.' Running the water she brushed her teeth and washed her face. Marching into her bedroom she picked up a brush and hastily ran it through her hair before gathering it up into a knot and securing it with a clip.

'Done!' Amy declared as she walked down the stairs. Vicky was perched on the end of the sofa, a notepad on her knee.

'You look better.' She smiled softly. 'I've made a cuppa.' She added pointing to the two steaming cups that she had placed on the sideboard. 'Now, take a deep breath and tell me what happened Amy.' She finished, patting the seat next to her.

Sitting down Amy inhaled deeply, trying to control her raging emotions.

'I was working when my mobile rang.' Amy paused biting her lip, the anxiety written all over her face. 'I reached for it not bothering to see who was calling, I said hello and then heard his voice.'

'What did he say to you Amy?' Vicky asked, keeping her voice deliberately low.

'I can't remember exactly just that he is coming back to collect what is his.' Amy softly cried. 'I'm scared Vicky.' She added.

'Did you say anything to him?' Vicky questioned.

'No, I froze.' Amy replied. 'I need to change my number; god knows where he has managed to get it from.' Amy began to search her mind as she mentally went through the people who had her mobile number.

'The terms of the restraining order are that he isn't allowed to contact you directly or indirectly, ringing you is direct contact Amy and I would like you to do a statement for me so I can arrest him.'

'No Vicky, I'm not making a statement.' Amy declared passionately. 'I can't go through anymore of this Vicky.' The pain in the tiny woman's face brought tears to the usually hardened police woman eyes.

'Yes you can! You are a lot stronger than you give yourself credit for Amy. Remember the court case?' She was trying to gently remind Amy that deep inside herself she had the courage to see this through. 'You were petrified yet you gave the evidence that was required to send him to prison.'

'Precisely!' Amy shouted back. 'Fucking precisely Vicky. I sent him to jail; he will never forgive me for that.'

'You sent him to jail for putting you in hospital Amy.' Vicky's voice was gentle as she spoke the words of truth.

'I shouldn't have done it. You don't understand Vicky.' Amy pleaded. 'I should have stayed, I was his wife.' She wailed as the sobs rose to an almost hysterical pitch as she flew back to her past as it tightened its hold on her.

'I do understand Amy, I work with women like you every day, it's my job. I may not be in an abusive relationship but I have been trained to help.'

'I know.' Amy replied. 'I'm sorry for swearing and shouting at you, none of this is your fault, you have always helped me, I'm so sorry Vicky.' She repeated guiltily.

'It's fine Amy, don't worry about it, I can assure you I have been shouted at by bigger and uglier people than you.' She joked, trying to lighten the atmosphere and perhaps take some of her fear away.

'I don't want to make a statement Vicky. He has just been released; he probably acted in a moment's haste.' Amy knew she was trying to convince herself, never mind the policewoman. 'I panicked, let's see how things go, if he continues to call me I will report it Vicky, I promise. He isn't stupid; he knows if he withholds his number you won't be able to prove it's him'

'Have you told Chloe and Bethany? I think they need to know Amy and if push comes to shove I can ask my superior if he will allow your phone to be traced. It isn't often they do that sort of thing if I'm being honest Amy, it's usually reserved for big drug busts, but I can always try if you want me to.' Vicky asked.

'Yes, they know their dad has been released from prison today, neither of them want any contact with him, I will no doubt get the blame for that as well. Amy added sadly.

'You need to be strong Amy, for yourself, for your girls. You have done a marvellous job up to now; don't let him ruin what you have worked so hard to build up. You are a changed woman; you look different, act differently. Gone is the woman that was manipulated and afraid. Be strong Amy, you can do it.' Vicky kept her voice deliberately low, her words soft but spoken slowly, hoping they would find their way to the woman before her.

'I won't Vicky, I was shocked, I really didn't expect him to ring me.' Amy responded knowing that she was going to have to dig very deep within herself to fight this one.

'Well you just bear in mind that he isn't allowed to contact you at all Amy. Even if he asked someone else to contact you that would be breaking the restraining order.' Vicky advised.

'Ok. I wasn't prepared for this Vicky.'

'I know Amy and believe me I have met characters like Paul before, he doesn't faze me, I will do everything within my power to protect you and your family Amy.' Again Vicky tried to reassure the petrified woman at her side.

'Thank you.' Amy reached for her mobile phone as it beeped. 'Let me just check this.' She added turning her attention to the message.

'Hi sexy bum. Just on my lunch, wanted to check you are alright. xx'

'Shit!' Amy exclaimed rubbing her forehead anxiously with her hand.

'What's the matter?' Vicky asked noticing the concern that had briefly flitted across Amy's face.

'It's Jesse….. I have to protect him too Vicky.'

'Amy, you don't have to protect anyone! Your girls are young women, Jesse is a grown man and I am bloody sure he can look after himself. It may be a good idea to show him a photograph of Paul so he knows what he looks like, that way he can be vigilant too.' Amy had already mentioned the new man in her life and Vicky secretly hoped he was strong enough to see this through and wouldn't walk away leaving Amy on her own to fight the monster that was her ex-husband. Vicky knew it wasn't his responsibility but the woman before her had changed so much and she knew that Jesse had to be the main cause of the miraculous transformation.

'Good idea.' Amy responded. She was softly chewing her fingernail, debating what to reply to Jesse. 'This isn't his problem though Vicky, it's mine.' She said reaching for her phone to send Jesse a quick reply.

'Hi sexy eyes, I'm fine, swamped with work. Steak for dinner. Hope you are having a good day. I love you. xx' There, that should convince him she was ok, she secretly thought.

'Are you sure you don't want to make a statement Amy? I could have his arse hauled back into prison by the end of the day, he is on probation.' Vicky asked again, hoping she would change her mind. Secretly Vicky thought Amy was stupid, the bastard had repeatedly beaten and raped her for years yet she had only been willing to give a statement about the assault, no amount of persuasion could convince Amy to press charges against the monster for rape. Deep down Vicky knew she was petrified of the scumbag; no amount of talking had convinced her to change her mind.

'Let's see how things go Vicky please.' Amy asked. 'He is bound to be annoyed today but he has had all this time to think about his actions, you never know.' Amy added hopefully, knowing she was trying to convince herself not the policewoman.

'Ok Amy, well if you need anything ring me but remember if it's an emergency dial 999.' Vicky stood up; putting on her coat she picked up her bag before strolling to the front door.

'Oh, there is one more thing that you may be able to help me with.' Amy asked, remembering what Jesse had requested of her the night before. 'Would you be able to set me up an appointment with a counsellor please Vicky?'

'Of course I will Amy and I am so glad you have decided to reach out and get help. I will make some calls when I get back to the station and give you a ring. In future Amy I am going to ring you on your landline, I will only use your mobile number if I can't get hold of you. If Paul rings again, answer it and try and write down what he says and include the date and time please.' Vicky advised.

'I will.' Amy replied. 'Thank you.' She added sweetly, ashamed that she had shouted at the policewoman who only wanted to help her.

'Stay in touch Amy, I will ring you later when I have an appointment for you. Keep your doors locked, your keys on you at all times. You know the drill Amy.' She added. 'You are a strong woman, keep your wits about you, you can do this.' Vicky finished, stroking Amy's arm briefly.

When Amy had been well enough after the attack she had attended a women's defence class where she began to learn different ways to protect herself. She knew her tiny stature wasn't in her favour and so taking all the information in and committing it to memory she progressed through the classes quickly. Purchasing a baseball bat she carefully hid it away, praying that she would never have to use it.

Locking the door, Amy placed the keys in her pocket before walking slowly up the stairs to her small study.

Sitting down at her desk, her head in her hands she allowed herself to weep.

'I'm not going to allow him to do this to me anymore.' She declared to herself, turning her attention back to the work that she had been disturbed from earlier with a vigour she knew would only be temporary.

CHAPTER FORTY NINE

'Where are Chloe and Bethany tonight?' Jesse asked as he waited for his dinner.

'Chloe is with Mark; Bethany is with her boyfriend, Adam until Sunday.' Amy replied as she stirred the creamy sauce she was making to go with the steak, vegetables and potatoes. 'Have you had a good day at work?' She asked.

'Yeh, busy but good, I'm exhausted.' Jesse replied. 'So have you heard from Vicky today?' He added, his eyes on her, watching her every move as he tried to assess how she was really feeling.

Turning her attention back to the sauce she closed her eyes. Shit, she really didn't want to lie to him, she loved him, trusted him but her need to protect him was greater.

'Only to make an appointment to see a counsellor.' She replied, hoping that he would let the subject drop.

'Oh Amy.' He was behind her in seconds, enveloping her into his arms. 'I'm so proud of you.' He whispered.

Her heart was hammering in her chest, she was lying to the man she loved. She had grown to trust Jesse and respected him deeply but her need to protect this wonderful man was greater.

'I guess I know that I need to talk to someone.' She replied, hoping he wouldn't be able to see what lay behind her eyes.

'It will help.' He replied squeezing her once more before sitting back down at the table.

'Why does he have to be so bloody nice to me, I'm lying to him for fuck's sake.' She silently thought as feelings of guilt began to stab at her.

As promised Vicky had made some phone calls and managed to get Amy an emergency appointment. She was due to see a woman named Brenda the next morning at 11am.

'So when do you go?' He asked.

'Vicky managed to get me an appointment tomorrow morning at 11.' She replied, smiling at him softly.

'Are you going to tell the counsellor everything Amy?' He gently prodded. 'I think it's important that you do.'

'Yes.' She whispered. 'Oh, I nearly forgot, Vicky asked me to show you a picture of Paul; she thinks it is important because he is out of prison now. I will have to go up into the attic though, all the photos are stored up there, I'll get them after we have eaten.'

'Ok.' He replied turning his attention to the photographs Amy had displayed on her kitchen wall. 'I have looked at these so many times but never asked you who this is?' He asked, pointing at the frame that held a photo of Amy and another woman.

'That's Deborah.' Amy said. 'It was taken the night before..... sorry.' She said stuttering.

'The night before what Amy?' Jesse asked noticing her discomfort and the pain that was so obvious in her eyes.

'The attack.' She whispered. 'It was her birthday, we had all been invited but Paul refused to go, he had been in a bad mood all day. He didn't want me to go.' She continued. 'But it was my friend's birthday so I went with Bethany.' The pain was too much for Jesse to bear, reaching for her he snuggled her close to him.

'I know it's painful for you to speak about these things Amy but it will help you. I'm not a professionally, that's why I mentioned a counsellor, but I am here for you and will listen whenever you are ready to talk.' His face was in her hair, his words muffled.

'Thank you Jesse.' She replied moving to kiss his lips. 'I love you.'

'I love you too Amy. So, how come I have never met Deborah?' He asked.

'She moved abroad to Australia.' Amy replied. 'We stay in contact on Facebook and send the occasional text to one another.'

'Does she like living over there?' Jesse asked as he studied the photograph some more.

As she was about to speak the fingers of guilt began to poke at her once again.

'Well.' She started, swallowing hard. 'We kind of had fallout shortly before she left for Australia.' Amy revealed, wanting to tell Jesse the truth. 'After the attack she was a good friend but Paul had always tried to warn me about her, she is very two faced Jesse. Many a time we would be sat around the table in her kitchen listening to her slagging off her "friends" and Paul would always throw me one of his looks to let me know I had to be careful of both her and what I said to her, he didn't want me getting too close I guess, I suppose he was afraid that I may start talking.' Amy paused, the conflict in her mind playing dangerous games. 'Anyway, I found out that she was writing to Paul in prison, her and her husband, that to me was the ultimate betrayal, she even spoke to him on the phone and they apparently swapped messages online although why they allow inmates to have computers I will never know. Let's face it Jesse, they are in prison for a reason!' Amy could feel the passion building up in her voice as she thought about how her friend had betrayed her.

'You are better off without her, friends like her you don't need Amy.' Jesse stated.

'I know Jesse.' She replied wistfully. 'I always thought she was a friend, now I know different. It hurt at first but now I don't really think about, in fact, this can come down.' Reaching for the framed photograph Amy promptly removed it from the wall placing it face down on the glass dining table. 'Now, let's eat.' She declared, trying to change the subject.

'How are you really feeling?' Jesse asked as they ate their dinner. 'I mean because Paul has been released today, are you ok?' His hands reached out across the table for hers.

'Yes, I'm fine Jesse.' Amy replied smiling at him before casting her eyes downwards towards their hands, temporarily mesmerized as she watched his fingers graze lightly over hers. 'It took me a long time to re-build my life Jesse, I refuse to let him wreck what I have fought so hard to achieve.' Amy said releasing her hands from his and reaching out for her glass of wine. 'I can't let him beat me.' She added taking a large sip of the cool liquid.

'No you can't Amy.' Jesse replied taking hold of her hands as she placed the glass back down. 'Let's eat then I will go in the attic and get the pictures for you, then I want to ruin you.' He added, the "Jesse look" back in his sexy eyes.

Blushing furiously Amy picked up her knife and fork.

'Stop looking at me!' She pleaded as she brought the fork to her mouth. 'Please Jesse.' She grinned, as the blush took over her body. Would she ever get used to the penetrating, sexy gaze of his beautiful green eyes? She asked herself. She knew the answer, no.

'What's for dessert baby?' Jesse mischievously asked as he placed the final fork full of food into his open mouth.

'Me!' She shot back bravely, instantly regretting it when she saw the look in his eyes. 'Jesse!' She pleaded as his eyes burned into hers and she had to look away, shrugging her chestnut hair around her face to try and shield herself from him.

'That was a bit forthright of you Miss Lucas.' He commented laughing, reaching forward to sweep her hair away from her face.

'Stop laughing at me.' She giggled, enjoying the touch of his fingertips on her face.

'I'm just not used to it, it's good.' He replied a little more seriously. 'I hope to see more of the courageous, outspoken Miss Lucas.' He added cheekily, his fingers drifting down towards her neck.

Resisting his touch she slowly drew her chair back just far enough to prevent him from reaching her.

'Pft! It's your entire fault you know.' She said pointing her index finger at him. 'You make me dizzy, you drive me crazy; I can't think when I'm around you. I think you are some sort of magician or hypnotist.' She declared chuckling. 'That's it!' She squealed with delight. 'You have hypnotized me and put me under some sort of love spell.'

'And here was me thinking it was my eyes.' He replied laughing.

'Stop it!' Amy playfully scolded as he gave her his special look again. 'I seriously can't cope.' She added wiping her hand across her forehead in mock exasperation.

'Sorry.' He said sticking out his bottom lip at her.

'You will be Clayton!' She threatened friskily. 'One day I will get you back, that I promise!' Her face was the colour of rich, summer strawberries as her skin flushed and her heart beat wildly in her chest as she moved her chair forward once again.

'We shall see.' He replied shifting his position in the chair.

'Jesse!' Amy squealed as she felt his hand glide up her thigh underneath the table.

'What babe?' He replied an innocent look on his face as he threw her "his look."

She had no hope of retaining any normal sort of thought process; she was a mess, a complete and utter mangled ball of blushes.

Removing his hand Jesse placed it back on the table, his fingertips almost touching hers.

'Later. I haven't finished with you.' He declared his eyes full of wanting and lust.

'See! There you go again, you are doing it again Jesse!' Amy cried as she tried to control her racing heart.

Looking at his handsome face smiling at her she scowled at him briefly, a warm smile quick to replace it as her eyes met his.

'Right, I'm going to go up into your attic now babe, is there anything particular I am looking for or is there anything else you need whilst I'm up there?' He asked as he stood up.

'They are right near the door, you will see them on the right as you stick your head in and no babe I don't think I need anything else.' Amy replied. 'I will wash these.' She said pointing to the dishes that stood by the sink. 'Do you want a drink or anything else to eat baby?' She asked Jesse, a warm smile on her still blushing face.

'A beer would be good please sexy bum.' He replied as he disappeared from the room.

'One beer coming on up.' Amy said jovially to his retreating back.

As she washed the dishes Amy sighed heavily. She had hated lying to him but she would do anything to protect this man she loved. He was innocent and pure and she wanted him to remain that way, not tainted by her ex-husband's evil ways. 'Yes.' She silently reassured herself, she was doing the right thing. The beeping of her mobile phone disturbed her train of thought; reaching for it she noticed a missed call from a withheld number and a text from Jen. Ignoring the call she opened the message.

'Hi Sweetie, sorry stuck in work until 10pm. I'm worried about you, are you ok? Has the dickhead been released or did they see sense and lock away the bastard for good! x'

Typing out a quick reply updating her best friend Amy turned her phone on silent. If Paul wanted to play his games he could do it when Jesse wasn't there. 'Jesse, where the hell is he' she thought.

'Jesse.' She called up the stairs.

'I'm in your bedroom.' He shouted back.

Running up the stairs she found him sat on her bed surrounded by photographs.

'You look unhappy.' He said sadly as he held out a photograph to her.

The picture was of her and the girls in Corfu and as Amy inspected the image she hardly recognised the woman starring back at her.

'Shit, I look ill despite that wonderful tan.' She said unhappily as she looked at the picture closely.

.'Is this him?' Jesse asked handing her another photograph.

'Yes.' She said quietly. 'That's him.' The whisper was small as she handed the picture back to Jesse.

Her eyes immediately fell to the ground.

'Can we put these away now please Jesse.' She asked the pain there for all to hear in her voice.

'Of course baby, I'm sorry.' He replied taking her into his arms.

'Don't say sorry, this needed to be done.' She replied snuggling closer to him. 'I love you Jesse.' She whispered into his chest.

'I love you too baby.' He replied, squeezing her to him. 'You are going to be ok, you know that don't you?' He asked.

'Yes, I suppose so.' She replied half-heartedly.

'No suppose so, you will be ok Amy.'

Lifting her head she glanced at the photographs scattered on her bed.

'I feel sick.' She whispered.

Jesse spread out his arms wide and scooped the pictures up placing them back in the containers quickly.

'Thank you Jesse.' She said reaching for him once again. He was so young yet so strong. 'You make me happy.' She added quietly.

'Good.' He replied. 'Right let me get these back into the attic then you are mine Lucas.' The "Jesse look" was back.

'Jesse……..'

'Yes.' He replied, putting the containers down onto the bed before turning to look at her as he sensed a shift in the tone of her voice.

'I do love you.' She responded. 'I have never felt this way before.' She was nervously playing with a thick strand of her hair, wrapping it around her finger again and again.

'There are reasons for that baby.' He replied, a soft smile on his lips.

Standing Amy looked at him, studying his face carefully, trying to read what lay beneath his eyes.

'What do you mean there are reasons?' She asked a puzzled look on her face.

'You know what I mean Amy. I am the first man to come along after…..' He paused not sure how to proceed as the look of intense hurt on Amy's face registered to him.

'Hey, listen to me.' Amy said. 'I love you for you, for all the right reasons and none of the friggin wrong, do you hear me.' She knew she was raising her voice and hated the stunned expression on his face but she needed him to know that what she felt was real, not some rebound teenage thing or a desperate need to be loved. She remembered the words she had wrote in her farewell letter to him, never expecting to have to speak them out loud. 'My loving you the way I do is nothing to do with my past Jesse. It's you.' She said pointing her finger at him. 'You Jesse. You are a wonderful, kind, gentle man who in my eyes is perfect, now that's the reason I fell in love with you, do you understand?' She asked feeling a little cross and upset with him. She could feel the tears beginning to form in her eyes and as she blinked they slowly fell down her cheeks.

'Ok, ok, baby.' He cooed as he took her into his arms.

Pushing him away from her Amy stood back, increasing the distance between them. Why the hell didn't he understand? Did he really think that she was that pathetic?

'Do you really think that little of yourself Jesse?' She asked turning the tables on him as her anger grew. 'Do you not think that the way you have been with me, the way you talk to me, make love to me, even fuck me made me fall in love with you? You are a special man, a wonderful man and YOU and only YOU are responsible for the way that I feel.' Now the tears were flowing freely, she was angry….. no she was hurt. Jesse had really hurt her…….

'Ok baby, I'm sorry.' He mumbled as he tried to wipe the tears from her face before taking her into his arms, holding her close.

'Ok.' Amy sniffled as she began to relax in his embrace. How could she make him understand? Ok her past was shit, no scratch that, her past was fucking shit but that was then, Jesse was her now and she hated the fact that now she felt as if it somehow cheapened what she felt for him.

Gradually she had let down her walls and allowed the icicle to melt and although she had fought it every inch of the way and doubted herself so many times, she had done so willingly knowing she was giving her everything to a man who treated her right. Why couldn't he see that? She wondered. 'Please Jesse, please understand.' She silently prayed.

'Are you ok baby?' Jesse asked softly, his arms holding her firmly.

'Yes.' She said burying her face into his chest. 'I love you, do you hear me Jesse, I love you? You make me feel alive and sexy and brave……..'

'I know Amy, I know and I'm sorry, I love you too baby.'

CHAPTER FIFTY

'Will you light the candles please sexy eyes?' She asked, throwing the lighter to Jesse.

Amy loved her bedroom being bathed in candle light, the soft luminosity they gave off always made her feel gooey when Jesse was around.

Peeling off her top Jesse let out a whoop.

'Woo, you got it!' He said excitedly.

'Yes.' Amy replied. 'Do you like it?' She asked as she undid her skirt and let it drop to the floor.

'Yes.' Jesse hissed, his eyes raking over her body.

The neon bra and French knicker set practically glowed in the candle light against Amy's tanned skin. She had searched everywhere for a sexy yellow underwear set after asking Jesse what his favourite colour was. It had taken nearly two months of almost constant internet searching and shopping to finally track one down.

'Would you pass me my leopard shoes please Jesse.' She asked sexily. 'I think they would look ok with this, what do you think?' She asked demurely.

'Erm YEH!' He declared, shooting off the bed to open her wardrobe door. 'Here.' He grinned, handing them to her. 'I don't know why you bothered to put them away.'

Turning around Amy bent slowly, placing the shoes on the floor. Hearing Jesse's sharp intake of breath, she lingered twirling the silver anklet, positioning the delicate little heart at her ankle bone.

'Oh......My......God.' She heard him say.

Smiling to herself and spurned on by his obvious desire for her, she stood up slowly, reaching for the dressing table she steadied herself, lifting her left foot seductively, arching her instep and pointing her toes. Looking over at Jesse she saw his eyes fixated on her feet.

'I won't get you back hey.' She secretly thought. 'We shall see Mr Fuckin Sexy Eyes!'

Placing her foot unhurriedly into her shoe she bent at the waist once more. The tight French knickers she wore strained across her arse as she ran her fingertips down her leg.

'I like these shoes.' She murmured, standing back up slowly. 'Do you like these shoes Jesse?' She asked, turning her neck slightly so he was in her view. Bringing her index finger up to her lips Amy stuck out the tip of her tongue and flicked it before letting it slowly drop to rest on her bottom lip. Again she heard him gasp.

'Come on you can do this.' She silently screamed at herself as she felt her self-confidence begin to slip. 'Come on Amy, he is clearly enjoying it.' She didn't want to blush so closing her eyes she repeated the seduction with her right leg, fighting the image of Jesse's green eyes from her mind she forced herself to concentrate.

'Yes, I really do like these shoes.' She whispered as she removed the clip from her hair, her chestnut locks falling heavily around her shoulders. Making her way over to him as he lay on the bed she unclipped her bra, removing it as she sat down at the side of him.

'I love your hair like this, all wild.' He said sinking his fingers into the soft strands. Gripping her gentle he brought her mouth down to his. With one touch of his lips he took away her last traces of anger and hurt at him.

'I love you Jesse.' She mumbled as his lips continued to graze hers, sending ripples and shivers of desire down her body, straight to her secret place.

'I know you do baby.' Deepening his kiss he was rewarded by a low groan from Amy.

'For you.' She softly whispered running the back of her hand gently down his face. He was so handsome. 'All the right reasons, none of the wrong, always remember that Jesse.'

As his lips trailed a fiery blaze down Amy's neck he shifted her gently along the bed, positioning himself over her. Wrapping her legs tightly around him, drawing him closer to her, she sank her fingers into his hair, bring his lips towards hers. She adored being close to him, his skin on hers igniting a passion in her she thought was impossible.

'Take these off.' He instructed, pulling away from her. His fingers ran along the waistband of her knickers and as he reached her side he dipped the tips in, trailing them back along her burning skin. 'I like them but they need to come off.' He whispered as his lips followed his fingers journey. Moving swiftly he stood beside her, reaching for the waistband he quickly removed them and his own clothes before lying back down, his lips once again on her body.

'Roll on your side.' He breathed in her ear before grasping her chin to bring her lips tantalizingly close to his. 'I want you.' His eyes burned into hers. Reaching her arm up Amy gripped him by the hair forcing his lips onto hers.

'The perfect kiss.......' Amy murmured. 'Oh Jesse.....' His lips devoured hers; cutting off her words, silencing her apart from the small moans that escaped her mouth as she gasped for air and prayed her heart wouldn't stop beating.

The bittersweet pain began to spread across her stomach, reaching up clasping her heart tightly, refusing to let go as her desire for him increased and her body and heart opened up, welcoming him in.

Placing his hand on her shoulder, Jesse gently rolled her away from him so she lay on her side, her back to his chest. His hands roamed over every available piece of flesh to him as his lips ran up and down her neck Amy pushed herself back into him, sighing softly as she felt his erect manhood come into contact with her body. His lips never left her neck as he placed himself at the entrance to her secret place, lifting her leg gently he eased himself into her, pulling her backwards, cocooning her to him.

'Oh...... Jesse......' She cried as she convulsed around him, the penetrating orgasm overtaking her entire being as he continued to kiss her neck whilst gently pushing himself in and out of her, the rhythm ant agonisingly slow, creating wave after wave of pleasure as her unrelenting climax overtook every part of her.

'I love you.' He breathed into her ear as his lips gently kissed the lobe. Wave after wave crashed through her as the orgasm faded only for another to begin building as he placed his leg between hers, grinding her onto him, his cock hitting her deepest, darkest place.

'Jesse......' She screamed out his name as he increased the tempo, thrusting into her deeply sending her over the edge once again.

'Jesse…. Jesse… Jesse…' She repeated grasping for him, clinging to him as the passionate storm continued to rage her body.

'Amy….' He moaned loudly, emptying himself into her. 'Fuck…..' He shouted, his own orgasm taking over him as he continued to move within her, massaging her inner walls, making her climax once again.

'You are an amazing lover.' She said dreamily as her head lay on his chest, her leg thrown over his. After taking a shower together they had quickly returned to bed, Amy eager to snuggle back up into Jesse's arms.

Squeezing her to him he raised his head causing Amy to look up at him.

'I love you.' He said kissing the tip of her nose.

'I love you too.' She whispered, shifting her position so she lay on her side looking at him. 'Good night sexy eyes.' Planting a kiss on his lips she smiled at him softly.

'Good night darling.' He replied stroking her face before turning onto his side, his back to her. 'Cuddle me.' He murmured as his eyes began to close.

Snuggling into him, her arm resting on his shoulder Amy closed her eyes and welcomed sleep, knowing it would come easily with Jesse beside her.

CHAPTER FIFTY ONE

'Urgggh…..' Amy reached for the alarm clock, turning it off as the shrill noise assaulted her sleepy senses.

'Jesse.' She cooed gently, stroking his shoulder to try and wake him up. 'Jesse.'

'Mmmmm.' He mumbled.

God he is difficult to wake up, Amy silently thought. Grinning to herself she thought of the perfect way to wake the man she loved. Sliding slowly under the duvet she reached for Jesse's cock, guiding him into her ready, warm, wet mouth.

'Good morning Brucie.' She murmured as she heard Jesse begin to softly moan.

Pulling back his foreskin to reveal his tasty tip she clamped her lips around him, sucking hard, moving her hand slowly up and down the length of him before grasping him tightly as he grew in her hand and mouth.

'Babe.' Jesse's voice was low as his hands became lost in her hair.

Taking him deep into her mouth she withdrew slowly, sucking him, pulling the foreskin back as she moved her hand. Jesse moaned loudly as she moved her hand tightly back down the length of his cock once again sucking his tip hard before swirling her tongue around him.

'Good morning.' She breathed looking up at him as he peered at her underneath the duvet.

'Good morning babe.' He responded, his sexy eyes glazy with lust and sleep. 'This is a nice way to wake up.' He groaned as Amy flicked her tongue out, teasing him. 'Suck me babe.' He panted as Amy continued to torment him. 'Please.' He begged, his hands tightening in her hair.

Sinking her mouth down onto him she took him to the back of her throat before withdrawing slightly so she could wrap all her fingers around him once again. Amy wanted to feel him entirely in her mouth but he was too big and she hadn't quite managed to control her gag reflex just yet.

'I love doing this to you, I love sucking your cock.' She murmured looking at him, meeting his eyes for a few agonising seconds. Reaching for his testicles she stroked them softly, kneading them gently as her mouth claimed him once again.

'Oh baby.....' His hands reached out for her pulling her on top of him. 'I want to be inside you.' He said running his hands up her stomach and cupping her breasts.

Rising on her knees, she guided him to her, pausing for a brief moment she braved his eyes as she sank on to him slowly, enveloping him with her warmth and wetness.

'Jesse.' She breathed as she began to move on him, holding him with her inner muscles at her entrance before plunging herself down on to him, grinding so he was deep within her.

Reaching for her Jesse cupped her breasts before running his thumbs over her nipples making them stand proud and erect, the sensations he was creating connecting directly with her sex.

Sitting up he took first one nipple, then the other into his warm mouth, teasing the little buds with his tongue and lips, sucking them, harder and harder as he mouth slowly came awake, causing Amy to whimper in ecstasy. Wrapping her in his arms together they began to move, Amy crying out his name whilst clinging to him as she came violently, Jesse following her with his own climax as she gripped him tightly, her muscles contracting as the orgasm took over her.

'Wow!' Jesse exclaimed, his breath coming in short pants as he held onto her tightly.

'I know.' Amy murmured, her face resting at the side of his neck. 'Each time it gets better. I think we have had the most perfect sex and then we make love again and it's even better, even more amazing.' She said.

Wrapped in his arms she glanced at the clock that stood on her bedside table.

'Shit! Jesse have you seen the time? Crap!' Reluctantly she began to peel herself away from him, her bottom lip sticking out.

'It's fine.' He laughed kissing the tip of her nose. 'I don't start until ten this morning.'

'What…. Oh.' Amy replied. 'Does that mean I can have an extra-long cuddle then?' She asked hopefully.

'Of course.' Jesse laughed lying back down on the bed taking Amy with him.

Snuggling into his arms, her back to his chest she closed her eyes.

'This is my new special place.' She murmured kissing his arm that held her lovingly.

Squeezing her to him Jesse mumbled in her ear.

'After cuddles can I have something to eat?' He asked chuckling.

'Yes.' Amy giggled with him. 'What do you fancy?' She asked sticking her bottom back into him. 'I'm not getting fresh.' She laughed. 'I just like being close to you.'

'Getting fresh…..' Jesse laughed. 'I haven't heard that one before.'

'Well you have now.' She chuckled. 'What do you fancy to eat Jesse?' She asked a little more seriously. She wanted to make sure he had his breakfast before he went to work.

'Your pussy.' He laughed gripping her to him playfully. 'Ermm any cereal will do babe but only after we have finished our cuddle.' He squeezed her to him and Amy closed her eyes, luxuriating in her love for him and the warmth and peace it created throughout her body and mind.

An hour later Amy was stood at the front door waiting for Jesse to turn his car around so she could blow him a kiss. Nervously she glanced up the road as thoughts of Paul briefly flashed through her mind.

Pulling up outside the house Jesse wound down his window.

'Good luck when you go to see…' He gave her a knowing look not wanting to broadcast her business on the street in case anyone was listening. 'Oh and I have something to show you later.' He had a massive grin on his face.

'Thank you Jesse and what?' Amy replied a smile on her lips.

'You will see later. I love you.' He shouted before driving off in his old, Renault Clio.

'Shit!' Exclaimed Amy. Now she would spend the rest of the day wondering what Jesse was so obviously excited about.

Shutting the door with a huff she marched upstairs to her room. Opening the drawer of the cabinet beside the bed, she took out her phone and switched it on, waiting patiently for the blackberry to fire up, she drummed her fingernails on the wood.

'You are bad, no you are naughty, no you are very fucking naughty! Now I am going to not get any work done or be able to concentrate because I will spend the day wondering what the hell it is that you appear so happy over and want to show me! I am mad but I still love you sexy eyes. xx' Amy hit the send button.

'Bloody shit!' She shouted into the air.

The phone beeped.

'Aww sexy bum don't be mad. You will see later but until then get some work done otherwise you will be a naughty secretary and I will have to spank your arse! Love you too babe. Have a good day and good luck again. xxx'

The tiny tingles that fluttered in her stomach suddenly dived between her legs as she remembered how the sting of his palm when he had spanked her had felt, followed by the gentle caresses that had tantalizingly had her craving for more.

'Fuck!' She shouted. 'Fuck, fuck, fuck!' What was he doing to her! A text, a simple bloody text and she was blushing like an idiot, her face and chest a burning shade of crimson as naughty, wicked thoughts flooded through her brain. 'What's happening to me, I'm turning into some sort of sex fiend!' She wailed to herself.

Jumping up Amy went to her wardrobe. Opening the door she hastily picked a pair of old, battered jeans and her favourite pale blue t shirt that had one of her favourite bands names blazed across the front; The Ramones. Scrabbling into them she reached for a pair of flat, pale blue pumps. As she reached out to grab them she noticed the red shoes that she had worn at the thatched cottage.

'Better not forget about you.' She said stroking the black velvet ribbon that sat on the front of the shoe. Jesse had loved the high, red, suede stilettos, maybe it was time for them to come out and play, Amy thought as she slid her feet into the pumps. Grabbing her clip from the dressing table she shoved her phone into the back pocket of her tight fitting jeans and gathered her hair up in a knot. Securing it with the clip she glanced at her reflection in the mirror, pulling tiny strands out at the sides so they hung gracefully at her earlobes before flicking her fingers through her fringe to make sure it was in place. Opening her jewellery box she took out the gold studs with the tiny sapphires and placed them in her ears.

'Done!' She declared to her reflection as she gathered her car keys and bag, ignoring the rattle of her mobile phone as it vibrated in her pocket.

CHAPTER FIFTY TWO

'Hi, I'm here to see Brenda.' Amy smiled at the attractive, blonde, young woman who sat behind the reception desk. 'Amy Lucas.'

'Take a seat please; I will let Brenda know you are here.' She smiled back. Amy tried not to gasp as she noticed the girl's teeth. Her two front ones were missing and as Amy looked into the girl's eyes she knew how she had lost them without her having to reveal her story. In her eyes was the same pain Amy had witnessed in her own before Jesse came into her life and changed her so much.

'Thank you.' Amy smiled back, turning around and walking to the windows where the black and green chairs stood. Her phone was vibrating again in her pocket; reaching for it she noticed her fifth missed call of the day from a withheld number. As the muscles clenched violently in her stomach Amy felt the nausea rise, standing she looked at the blonde woman, her hand over her mouth. Pointing to a set of double doors the woman quickly buzzed Amy through.

'Shit!' She exclaimed to her reflection as she swilled her mouth to free it from the vomit that had wretched her body. Reaching into her bag she searched for some mints, popping one into her mouth she tidied her hair and walked out of the toilet to find a brown haired, fifty something woman smiling at her.

'Hi I'm Brenda, you must be Amy. Susan said you had darted off to the toilet, I hope you are ok?' She asked placing her hand on Amy's shoulder briefly.

'I'm fine, nerves I guess.' Amy lied. During the drive to the centre her nerves had played with her until she had almost turned around and gone home, it was only a text from Jesse that stopped her.

'I love you Amy. xx' Four words that he somehow knew she had needed at that precise moment. Cursing herself she had continued on her journey, remembering her promise to Jesse to be brave.

'Would you like to follow me?' Brenda asked smiling once again. Amy noticed she had a faint scar down the left side of her face and wondered if she too had been a victim. Reaching her fingers up

Amy ensured her hair was covering her own as they walked along the brightly light corridor. 'We are really informal here, at one time or another we have all suffered some form of domestic violence. The centre offers temporary accommodation along with intense counselling services and any other help that is needed to help women escape, be strong and stay away.'

'So you were a victim?' Amy asked quietly, a deep respect ran through her for the woman.

'I was a victim, yes Amy. Now, well no, I… am… not… a…. victim.' Brenda paused as she spoke each of the last five words. 'I am me, my own person, free to make my own decisions, choose my own paths. Here, would you like to sit down, make yourself comfortable.' Brenda pointed to the sofa that sat along one of the walls of the cream coloured room they had just entered. Posters hung on the walls and as Amy starred at one the colour began to drain out of her face. Before her was a woman, curled up in a ball, beaten and broken, the words "Hands are not for hitting" below her as she lay on what looked like a cold, hard floor.

'Does she remind you of you?' Brenda quietly asked. 'It's a very powerful image.' She added softly.

'Yes.' Amy whispered sinking down onto the pale green sofa, her head in her hands.

'Let them come Amy.' Brenda said. 'Let the tears come. Vicky didn't provide me with a lot of details Amy, she only gave me the bare essentials, name, number etcetera, when you are ready we will fill out this simple form.' She said putting a folder down on the table that stood in front of the sofa on the dark brown carpet.

Looking up Amy leaned forward picking up the folder and pen that lay at its side.

'Whilst you fill out the information we can chat if that is ok. I like to make notes Amy but only with your consent. They are completely confidential, I type them up myself and you can have access to them anytime you like.' Brenda was smiling softly at Amy, she had to proceed carefully, slowly, ease the information that was required in order for her to help this little woman and get her to talk. There was something deep within Amy's eyes that concerned her, a fear that ran very deep and as she pondered what her story was Amy looked at her, her blue eyes two pools of misery.

'Yes that's fine.' She responded, referring to Brenda's question over the note taking. 'I don't mind, I suppose you see quite a lot of women....' Amy's words trailed off.

'I do Amy and it helps me to remember every woman's story because every woman has their own personal tales to tell, their own sorrow and fear to overcome.'

'How do you stand it? I mean listening to all that misery every day?' Amy asked. 'Does it upset you?'

'Yes Amy, at times I do get very emotionally involved, especially when a woman has escaped but can't stay away because she is either afraid or still under the manipulation and controlling spell that their partners have them under. You, see, bruises heal it's the psychological damage from the verbal abuse that I personally have found the majority of women find the most difficult to overcome.'

'I can relate to that.' Amy said softly glancing at the form to make sure she had included all the details that were required. 'Here, I've finished.' She added handing the folder and pen back to Brenda, a small smile on her lips.

'Thank you Amy.' Brenda said. 'Now do you want to tell me a little about yourself, you don't have to go into too much detail today, just some background information if you prefer. We will take things very slowly, at your own pace that suits you best.' Amy liked Brenda. She appeared to be a very peaceful person but it was her face that Amy was drawn to, it glowed, yes; her face was kind and happy. Again Amy wondered what had happened to cause the injury to the side of her face that had left the faint, thin scar but she felt rude asking. Brenda had big blue eyes and her short brown hair hung in curls along her jawline. Her brown skirt sat at her knees and on her feet were a comfy pair of brown leather shoes, the laces tied perfectly on each one. Yes, she was an open and friendly looking woman and Amy wondered if with time she may be able to open up to this woman and confide her deepest, darkest secrets and fears.

'I was with Paul for just over twenty years.' She started. 'At first he was lovely; everyone said he was my Prince Charming.' Amy's eyes began to cloud over as she tried to remember the good in her husband. 'We had only been seeing one another for a few months when I was rushed into hospital; I had an infection in my fallopian tube.' Amy added. 'They had to remove it and the doctors told me that my left tube was badly infected and scarred and that I could probably never have children.' Amy gulped as she remembered the pain she had felt at twenty one years of age when she was told that she would probably never be a mother.

'I was referred to see a specialist but with a six month waiting list I kind of gave up hope. It was a few weeks after the operation that Paul hit me for the first time.' Amy paused as the flashback assaulted her. 'Could I have a drink please?' She asked meekly.

'Of course, what would you like Amy?' Brenda asked, standing and walking over to the kitchen area that was situated at the back of the room. 'Tea, coffee, juice?' She called out over her shoulder. 'And feel free to carry on whilst I make us a cuppa.' She added turning on the tap to fill the kettle.

Erm, coffee, one sugar and a splash of milk please.' Amy replied. Taking a deep breath she continued to tell Brenda about Paul's first show of violence towards her.

'We were sat watching TV; I had been really busy at work and was so tired. The gas fire was on and I started to doze off......' Amy's voice trailed off as Paul's face appeared before her. Shaking her head violently she screwed her eyes shut to block out the horrible image. 'I'm sorry, give me a minute please.' Amy said taking a large gulp of air.

'Take your time Amy.' Brenda softly encouraged.

'I remember being so tired and warm from the fire, my eyes began to close and the next minute he grabbed me by the hair and lifted my head, slapping me hard with the back of his hand.' Silent tears began to form in Amy's eyes as her hand came up to her face, remembering the way his hand had felt on her cheek. 'It hurt, it really hurt.' Amy added. 'I ran into the bathroom and locked the door. I remember I was sat on the floor, in front of the bath and I was so scared. My face was hurting, burning almost, but I didn't want to look in the mirror. Paul was outside crying, he kept saying sorry over and over again so I ended up opening the door and he dragged me into his arms, sinking to his knees in front of me, gripping me so tightly. He told me he loved me so much and that I was his, he wanted to love me for the rest of my life and that he didn't mean to hurt me. I should have left him then....' She trailed off. Amy was looking at the floor, unable to look in Brenda's direction as feelings of shame washed over her.

'What happened next Amy?' Brenda coaxed.

'I forgave him!' Amy declared fiercely. 'I was a stupid idiot and I forgave him.'

'Why did you forgive him Amy, because you loved him so much?' Brenda asked.

'No.' Amy said quietly. 'Because I couldn't have children....'

'What do you mean you couldn't have children?' Brenda responded not daring to move as Amy began to cry.

'I was so young; I couldn't have children, who would have wanted me?' Amy was wailing as huge tears ran down her face as she remembered the misery she had felt as a young woman. 'Paul said no one would want me.......' Her anguished voice tore at Brenda's heart.

'And so the manipulation began Amy. Can you see that now?' Brenda asked hopefully.

'Yes.' Amy whispered. 'He knew what he was doing I guess right from the start, my not being able to have babies just played right into his hands.'

'Yes, that's correct Amy. Now, I am a little puzzled if I'm honest.' Brenda paused as she hoped that she had written down the information correctly. Amy was beginning to open up to her; she didn't want to blow it, gaining the little woman's trust was the most important thing, only then could she work with her, help her.

'What?' Amy asked, reaching for a tissue from the box that stood on the table.

'Vicky told me you have two daughters. Now if I have got it wrong I deeply apologise Amy.' Brenda said the concern evident in her voice.

'I have.' Laughed Amy, wiping the last of the tears away. 'I eventually saw a specialist about four months later. I stopped taking the contraceptive pill because, well, I just didn't see the point anymore. Anyway, I walked into the doctor's office, he asked me some questions and then told me to lie down whilst he examined me. I remember being really nervous and feeling sick but as he felt my stomach he looked at me really funny and said I had to go and have a scan before he went any further.' Amy paused, reaching for the drink that Brenda had placed on the table for her.

Amy went on to tell Brenda how she had lay really still whilst they had scanned her stomach, the radiographer calling for a doctor. Neither of them would tell Amy what was the matter until her own doctor had walked into the room and announced that she was twelve weeks pregnant!

'My, now that's a story!' Brenda exclaimed, a beaming smile on her cherub like face.

'I know!' Amy responded. 'Twelve weeks pregnant, I was so happy Brenda. I remember driving home so excited, dying to tell Paul. He was asleep when I got in; he hadn't come in until about 4am so was tired. I jumped on the bed to wake him up because I was so blissfully happy, I mean, I was having a baby!' Amy paused, a slight smile playing at her mouth which was suddenly replaced with a misery that made Brenda gasp.

'What happened Amy?' She prodded gently.

'He punched me in the face and sent me flying off the bed into the wall.' Amy cried. 'I was pregnant with his child......' Again her words were lost.

Grabbing another tissue, Brenda handed it to the weeping, broken woman before her.

'He told me to get an abortion, that he didn't want, "an ugly, useless slag" carrying his child.' Amy sobbed as memory after memory flooded into her brain and the words tumbled out.

'Oh Amy.' Brenda could feel the tears beginning to form in her own eyes as she began to understand Amy's pain.

'He was ok in the end though.' Amy added. 'He hit me a few times during the pregnancy, nothing major.'

'Hitting you full stop was wrong Amy, pregnant or not.' Brenda remarked.

'I know that now.' Amy replied. 'Brenda please try and understand, I thought I could never have children, I thought no one would want me. Then I find out I am pregnant, I was trapped…..'

'Amy you never have to explain yourself or your actions to anyone. At the time you did what was right for you. Always remember that.' Brenda added. 'So what about the other child?'

'Chloe is my first; she was such an easy baby, never cried, always happy.' The smile was back on Amy's face, the love clearly evident in her eyes as she spoke about her eldest child. 'Then Bethany came.' Amy added. 'Now that one was totally different.' She laughed lightly. 'From the moment she was born she was a hand full, a wilful little mare.' Amy added smiling tenderly. 'Her birth wasn't easy though, I didn't see her for two weeks after she was born and ended up with a hysterectomy after they delivered her.'

'Did Paul hit you during the second pregnancy Amy?' Brenda asked carefully. Amy was revealing so much about herself, she seemed almost desperate to talk to someone.

'Yes….' A deep pain registered in Amy's face and eyes as she remembered a distant memory. 'Bethany was actually my third pregnancy, I was pregnant before her but Paul beat me and I lost the baby….'

'Do you want to carry on Amy; you have told me such a lot today?' Brenda gently enquired.

'Yes, I want to carry on.' Amy replied determined to make Brenda understand why she had endured so much. 'I came home and told Paul I was pregnant, I was so happy, I mean, there I was believing I could never have children and I was pregnant again…. He beat me really badly and I lost my baby.' Amy was opening up and revealing her pain as Brenda continued to gentle encourage her. 'It was two months later that I got pregnant with Bethany. It wasn't an easy pregnancy but I was pregnant again, I was convinced that yet another miracle had happened. It was actually the first time I reported Paul to the police after he sat on my stomach and punched me in the face but I never followed it through.......The day after the beating I began to bleed so they rushed me into hospital where I stayed until I had her by emergency C section. She was 11 weeks premature.' Amy added. 'I had to have a hysterectomy because they couldn't stop the bleeding and I guess the rest is history, I was well and truly trapped then. What use was I, two kids, no womb and 25 years of age?' Tears of desperate misery ran down Amy's face as she sobbed for the loss she had suffered at such a young age.

'Amy.' Brenda said gently. 'Amy you have told me so much today, the more you talk, the less pain you will feel.' She added.

'Thank you, it feels good to share this with someone.' Amy responded reaching for Brenda's hand. 'Thank you.' She whispered. 'And thank you for understanding. I know that some people wonder why I stayed for so long, I wish they could understand......'

'Don't thank me, thank yourself Amy and remember, you had your reasons, you never have to explain them to anyone. You are obviously a very strong woman to have endured what you have, even though I know only a very, very small portion. I hope we develop a bond and we see each other regularly so that I may help you to fully heal.'

'Thank you Brenda.' Amy said reaching for her mobile phone. 'Have you got my mobile number? She asked noticing she had a text.

'Yes thank you.' Brenda replied noticing the massive smile that had taken over her client's face. 'Good news?' She enquired, pointing to the blackberry that was sat in Amy's hands.

'It's a friend.' Amy looked at Brenda closely, yes, she could trust her, she silently thought. 'I was single for just over a year, I had to give myself chance to heal Brenda. I never wanted another man in my life but I met someone who has completely turned my life around and upside down. He is wonderful and treats me so well...' Amy's voice trailed off once again, this time with happy memories as Jesse's handsome face flashed in front of her. His text was short but the few words reached her heart, making her smile.

'Yo sexy bum, hope you are ok and being brave. Love ya sexy mama. xx'

'You can tell me all about this mystery man as we get to know one another Amy but I will say it made me smile and happy to see you smile, especially after what you have revealed to me today.' Brenda smiled warmly at Amy.

'Thank you Brenda.' Amy responded. 'So, how often do I need to see you?'

'I would say once a week but that is entirely up to you Amy. I am going to give you my office and mobile number so if you just need someone to chat to you will be able to contact me. I want to be your friend Amy, I want to understand.'

'Thank you again. I seem to be saying thank you a lot to you.' Amy laughed. 'So next week, same day, same time, is that ok with you?' Amy asked.

'Yes and remember if you need anything in the meantime, call Amy.'

'Thanks again.' Amy repeated, hugging her new friend to her. 'See you next week.' She called as she left the room still smiling as she thought of Jesse's text.

CHAPTER FIFTY THREE

'How did it go Amy?' Jesse asked. She was just putting the finishing touches to the casserole that she had made for their tea when her phone rang.

'Good, I like her.' Amy told Jesse. 'Her name is Brenda and I think I could open up to her.'

'I'm so proud of you baby.' He said softly down the phone to her. 'I will be about an hour, is that ok? I just need to pick something up on the way.' Jesse added.

'Thank you and sure, what do you need baby?' She asked curiously.

'Never you mind sexy bum. I will see you in a while. Love ya.' Hanging up the phone he didn't allow Amy time to respond.

'Pft! xx' Amy text with a winky face.

'Love you. xx' He text back.

'Love you too. xx' She replied turning her attention back to the stove and the mountain of work that was waiting on the table to be moved to her office.

Glancing at her watch she decided to do some work on the spread sheets before Jesse arrived. Dinner was a one pot wonder tonight and was sat cooking away on a low heat in the oven so, grabbing a glass of juice Amy walked up the stairs to her small office, her mobile phone ringing as she climbed.

'Hello.' She answered her voice light and breezy as she distractedly wondered what Jesse wanted to show her.

'Fucking slag, I will pay you back bitch. I own you.' He slammed the phone down.

'No!' Amy wailed swallowing hard to stop the rush of vomit that was threatening to escape from her stomach.

The phone rang again.

'Slag, you are dead, you belong to me. Animal fodder, that's what you'll be.' Again he ended the call, this time Amy was unable to stop the wrenching, vomiting over the floor as she tried to make her way to the bathroom. Collapsing on the cool, tiled floor she cried, huge crests of sadness and fear washing throughout her body. She was afraid, very afraid. The number was withheld and Amy knew it was pointless reporting the calls to the police, they would arrest him, question him, release him and then Paul would be really mad. No, she would just try not to listen to his evil words, she silently thought, reaching for her toothbrush to clean her teeth.

'Shit.' She exclaimed as she noticed the time. Running down the stairs she gathered the roll of kitchen towel and the disinfectant from the cupboard under the sink and raced back upstairs to clean the vomit up before Jesse arrived. Satisfied that there wasn't a single trace, she quickly light an incense stick before sitting down at her dressing table to repair her streaked make up.

The ringing of the doorbell sent her flying down the stairs once again. As she saw Jesse's handsome face in the glass of the door she smiled, her heart doing a little leap in her chest, the phone calls forgotten for the time being.

'Hi sexy eyes.' She said, opening the door to him, her best smile plastered firmly on her lips.

Hi babe.' He replied bending to kiss her softly on the lips. 'How are you?' He asked, standing back to look at her.

'Good.' Amy lied, her fingers crossed behind her back. 'Now what's this thing that you have to show me?' She asked, changing the subject as her excitement grew by the second as she looked at his handsome, happy face, etching it into her brain to erase the bad memories as far away as possible.

'Come with me.' He said reaching for the door keys that still lay in her hand.

Opening the front door he stepped out and to the side.

'Wow!' Amy gasped as she looked at the shiny, black BMW that sat behind her little car on the driveway. 'Is that yours?' She asked, turning to look at Jesse whilst pointing her finger at the gorgeous car.

'Yep.' He replied, a massive smile on his face, his sexy eyes on hers.

'Jesse, it's......' Amy walked towards the vehicle, her fingers trailing lightly along the pristine paintwork. 'Beautiful. No, it's sick!'

She shouted jumping up and down. 'Can we go for a drive?' She asked walking back to him, her eyes hopeful.

'Of course.' Jesse replied, locking the front door and handing the keys to Amy. 'Come on, let's go.'

Amy followed him to the car.

'Oh my word!' She exclaimed as his opened the door and the interior was revealed.

Black, sumptuous, leather seats beckoned to her behind and as she sat down and gracefully swirled her legs around she took in the rest of the inside of the fancy vehicle.

'Jesse, it's amazing.' She said as he switched on the engine and the cockpit lit up.

'I'm glad you like it.' He responded, turning around to kiss the tip of her nose. 'Now where would ma'am like to go?' He asked chuckling.

'Where ever the kind sir wishes to take ma'am.' Amy laughed in response.

The BMW Mark 5 Series covered the miles smoothly and easily. Amy rested her head on the thick leather that cushioned her at just the right angle whilst listening to The Cranberries playing on the state of the art sound system. As the melody "Dreams" washed over her Amy closed her eyes and sang softly along to the lyrics.

'Though my life is changing every day in every possible way………..'She sang. 'I want more, impossible to ignore, impossible to ignore. They'll come true, impossible not to do, impossible not to do. And now I tell you openly, you have my heart so don't hurt me…….' Her soft voice sang along, oblivious that Jesse was watching her whilst driving. 'Cos you're a dream to me……' Opening her eyes she saw him look away quickly, his sexy eyes back on the road. 'I love this tune.' She said dreamily.

'Me too.' He replied glancing at her briefly. 'So, what do you think of my new car?' He asked.

'It's sweeeettttttt!' She declared laughing. 'It suits you.' She added. 'A handsome car, for a very handsome man and the smell, it's wonderful, new.' Her hands gripped the side of the leather seat, her fingers sinking into their softness.

'What's for dinner?' He asked. 'I'm starving.' He added chuckling.

'Beef stew and dumplings.' Amy replied laughing with him. Reaching out for his hand she stroked his fingers before laying her hand on his thigh, ignoring the vibrating phone in her cardigan pocket. She wasn't going to allow Paul to spoil this special moment as Jesse drove them back to her house. She was happy, the smile that she wore was genuine as the pair made small talk and chatted about Chloe moving out that weekend.

'Are you sad?' Jesse asked in reply to Amy saying she was going to miss her eldest baby.

'I am. I'm happy for her, happy that she has a good man to look after her, I'm happy that she has found love and appears settled but I'm sad that she is leaving home, I'm really going to miss her.'

'What about Bethany?' Jesse asked. He wanted to keep the conversation light, avoiding any topic that concerned Paul for the time being. He wanted her in his arms when they spoke about him so he could ease her pain a little. He hated the way her eyes clouded over and the distant look appeared whenever she was reminded of her ex-husband not to mention the way she hide behind her hair, her eyes cast downwards at the floor.

'She seems happy enough with Adam, he's a good man, he loves her to pieces, I guess only time will tell with those two.' Amy replied. 'They have good foundations to make it work because they were such close friends before they took a shot at a relationship.'

'What will you do when Bethany leaves home?' Jesse asked.

Amy looked out of the window, deep in thought she considered his question carefully, remembering her forgotten dreams. Turning to look at him, their eyes briefly met.

'I have a dream.' She said her voice small.

'Tell me.' Jesse softly encourage, turning the music down a little.

'I would love to spend 6 months in New Zealand at Mount Ruapehu.' She knew her dreams were ridiculous but they had kept her going as she endured the torment of her marriage. When things had got really tough, Amy would hide herself away in her thoughts, disappearing into her dreams, where Paul was a distant memory and her life was full of mountains and sunshine.

'Sounds like a plan to me.' Jesse responded smiling at her tenderly. 'Do you need anything from the shop on the way home?' He asked. 'Cigarettes, wine, chocolate?' He laughed.

'No, I'm fine.' Amy giggled with him. 'I love you Mr Clayton.' She said squeezing his thigh, her fingers gliding up towards his groin.

'Amy!' Jesse hissed as her fingers brushed over his cock.

'What Jesse?' She asked innocently, casting her eyes downwards in what she hoped was a very sexy and seductive way.

'Don't do that!' He hissed again through his teeth. 'Fuck you are so sexy, wait til I get you back home.' He playfully threatened.

'Bring it Clayton, bring it.' She played back. 'I have my own little surprise for you after dinner.' She chuckled, squeezing him through the soft material of his pants.

CHAPTER FIFTY FOUR

'So do you want to talk about today?' Jesse asked gently as they sat at the dining table eating the delicious beef stew that Amy had prepared earlier. 'Is there any of this mash left?' He added pointing his fork at the creamy, sweet potato that he had almost polished off.

'Sure.' Amy replied, passing him the white, ceramic serving dish. 'Help yourself.' She added smiling at him warmly.

'So, do you?' He asked again.

'Yes.' She replied, wanting to confide in him, the man she loved but realising she needed to hold back some of the more horrific details so she could protect him. He was young and innocent and she didn't want him tainted by her past in anyway. 'We didn't really talk about much today.' Amy offered. 'She asked me about the girls and the first time he hit me.' Her words trailed off as she remembered how upset she had become whilst talking to Brenda.

'You don't have to tell me Amy, all I need to know is do you think she can help you?' Jesse replied softly, reaching for her fingertips and taking them in his own.

'Yes Jesse, I do.' Pausing for a moment Amy thought about Brenda. 'In fact I really do think this is going to help.' She added a positive smile on her mouth.

'Good.' Jesse responded as he shoved a forkful of the stew into his mouth. 'This really is good.' He grinned.

'Thank you.' Amy replied. 'And thank you for encouraging me to seek help Jesse.' She said standing and walking around the table to give him a hug. 'Thank you.' She whispered again as she planted a small kiss on the back of his neck.

'Will you remember something for me Amy?' He asked standing, his meal forgotten as he enveloped her into his arms. 'Tears are not a sign of weakness.' He paused, his hand stroking her hair softly. 'They are just a sign that perhaps you have been too strong for too long Amy.' Reaching for her chin, he lifted her face, his eyes on hers. Blinking Amy searched his face for a moment.

'You are one of a kind, do you know that?' She said, placing her hand flat over his heart. 'I love you so much Jesse.' She added removing her hand and laying her head down in the exact same place.

'I love you too Amy.' He replied, squeezing her to him.

'Finish your dinner.' She whispered, reluctantly peeling herself away from him, sitting back down on her side of the table.

'What's for dessert?' He asked, the "Jesse look" appearing in his sexy eyes.

'What would you like?' She asked her voice deliberately low.

'Your pussy.' They said in unison, dissolving into fits of laughter.

'Predictable Clayton.' She whispered.

'Oh really Lucas!' He shot back, the "Jesse look" now blazing brightly in his eyes.

'Stop it!' Amy scolded as she felt the blush begin. 'Damn!' She exclaimed as she felt the tiny beads of moisture begin to build on her upper lip. Scrapping back her chair she rose, moving quickly to the sink. Turning on the cold tap she let it flow for a few seconds before plunging her wrists underneath the freezing water.

'You ok babe?' He chuckled, enjoying her discomfort and the effect he had on her.

'Get lost!' She huffed back as she closed her eyes and concentrated on making her blush disappear. 'I can't cope!' She wailed like a two year old. 'Seriously Jesse, I'm a mess whenever you are around!'

Jesse never said a word; he didn't need to as his eyes burned into her face.

'Stop it!' She pleaded once again as the heat began its journey to her secret place. 'Oh fuck!' She exclaimed. 'I give up!'

Amy could hear Jesse laughing but refused to look in his direction. She heard his chair moving as he stood up and closed her eyes, concentrating on trying to control her breathing, knowing that at any second he would be behind her, pressing himself up against her......

'I'm going to watch TV.' He announced.

Opening her eyes Amy looked at him.

'You're bad.' She whispered moving to collect the dirty dishes from the table to try and keep her mind occupied, her thoughts off

Jesse and his bloody sexy, magnetic eyes.

Filling up the bowl with hot, soapy water Amy began to do the dishes, gazing out of the kitchen window, her thoughts a million miles away.

'Sexy!' She jumped as his arms went around her, his lips on her neck.

'Oh.' She said softly as his hands travelled down her body, resting on her flat stomach. Pushing gentle back she rested against him, her eyes closed as he continued to caress her neck with his lips. 'Jesse.' She breathed, her arm reaching up to the back of his neck.

Placing his hands lightly in the small of her back, Jesse pushed her against the kitchen sink, his hands drifting down, underneath her short skirt.

'No knickers again Amy.' He hissed as he moved his hands over her bare behind, running them around the front until he connected with her secret place. 'And so wet and ready for me.' He added as his finger sank into her, the pad of his thumb creating a steady rhythm on her clitoris.

'Jesse.' She softly moaned as he placed another finger inside her, gently easing them apart in her moist, aroused sex.

Gripping hold of the edge of the sink Amy gave into the delicious sensations he was creating with his talented fingers and thumb, her climax building steadily as he massaged her inner walls.

Remembering her surprise for him she softly grabbed his hand, pulling herself away from him reluctantly.

'I have something for you.' She said softly, turning around to look at him. 'Wait here.' She instructed walking away from him towards the stairs.

'Come back, I haven't finished.' He stated, a look of shock on his face, she had been so close and then pulled away.

'Five minutes.' She said holding up her hand to him, her fingers splayed apart indicating the few minutes she needed alone.

'Ok.' He said sticking out his bottom lip as he plonked himself down on the sofa.

'Oh Jesse.' She said giggling. 'I promise that bottom lip will soon disappear.' Without another word she walked slowly up the stairs, avoiding the intense stare of his sexy, green eyes as he glared at her.

Walking into her bedroom she quietly closed the door behind her before walking over to her wardrobes. The package had been well hidden in an old handbag, reaching to the back she pulled the black, leather bag towards her. Opening it she collected the items she had previously stowed away from the prying eyes of both Jesse and the girls.

Reaching for the red suede stilettos she placed them on the bed beside her surprise before quickly removing her clothes.

'Hi.' She said sweetly as she stood on the stairs gazing down at him lying on the sofa. Jesse looked towards the sound of her voice, jumping up as he took in what she was wearing. 'Do you like it?' She softly asked, her self-confidence gradually slipping away as she made her way down the stairs.

'Yeh.' He whispered, his eyes all over her, a smile erupting on his face as he looked at her shoes. 'The red ones.' He breathed walking towards her.

The nurses outfit fit her snugly, the white, tight material strained across her chest, the zip pulled low enough so her cleavage was on show. On her head she wore a little hat which had the same red cross that was also on the uniform dress; around her neck a plastic toy, red stethoscope.

'Nurse Lucas.' She introduced herself quietly, her nerves jangling about her body, the blush a deep red on her cheeks and décolletage.

'I'm really poorly.' Jesse replied, falling back down onto the sofa, his eyes closed, his body still.

'Well I guess Nurse Lucas needs to examine you thoroughly.' She giggled as the nerves pitched about in her tummy.

Jesse was silent as she walked over to the sofa, his eyes remaining closed.

'Now, where shall I start?' She said quietly, nibbling softly on the nail of her index finger. Jesse opened his eyes briefly, gasped as he looked at her sucking her finger, then closed them again quickly. 'I think here.' She added bending to touch the soft waves on his head.

Running her fingers through his hair she reached for a cushion. Throwing it on the floor she sank to her knees beside him. 'Well Mr Clayton, your hair looks in good health.' She continued, her fingers softly touching his forehead as she brushed the hair from his face. 'I love the way your hair feels in my fingertips.' She breathed.

Jesse was still, his breathing low as he lay with his eyes still closed. Bending Amy planted a small kiss on his soft lips; drawing back she traced the outline with her fingertip. 'Your lips look a little sore; I think they need kissing very thoroughly Jesse.' Bending her head once more she kissed him, her tongue seeking out his as she gently prised his lips apart with her own. Responding to her, Jesse kissed her back. 'Oh no Mr Clayton.' She playfully scolded sitting back on her heels. 'Patience patient.' She added trailing her fingers over his eyebrows and down the side of his face towards his neck, bending her head once more she followed their path with her lips, gently turning his head to the side to allow her full access to the soft skin.

'Now can you tell me where the pain is?' She asked sexily. She liked Jesse's eyes closed, that way she could concentrate more on pleasing him with the role play. His eyes made her nervous, their hold difficult to fight.

'All over nurse.' He responded in a whisper, the mock pain in his voice causing her to laugh.

'Ok, well I think a full body examination is in order Mr Clayton, let's get this problem sorted for you.' Her hand stroked him through his pants causing him to gasp with desire. 'Keep your eyes closed.' She softly instructed. 'Unless I ask you to open them.' She smiled at him; Jesse was totally unaware that she was studying his handsome face. 'Perhaps I need to do role play more often.' She secretly thought. 'I can look at him without blushing when those friggin sexy eyes are closed.'

Running her hands underneath his green t shirt she spoke to him softly.

'Sit up please so I can remove this.' Her fingers rested at the hem. Jesse opened his eyes and gazed at her before sitting up.

'I like this.' He whispered as she drew the fabric up his lean, tanned torso.

'Lie back down please.' She instructed, ignoring his words and eyes.

Reaching for his buckle she undid the brown, leather belt swiftly.

'Now for the pants.' She breathed, pulling at his waistband. With deft fingers she removed his trousers leaving him lying on the sofa in just his white, snug fitting, boxer shorts, his erect cock beckoning to her silently.

Stroking her hands down his chest she heard him gasp as they lingered over his hard manhood. Withdrawing slowly she reached for the stethoscope placing the buds in her ears. Jesse opened his eyes and watched her with fascination as she pretended to listen to his heartbeat.

'I'm afraid I have some bad news Mr Clayton.' She said seductively. 'It appears I can't find a heartbeat.' Her eyes drifted to his cock as she licked her lips teasingly, the tip of her tongue caressing the soft skin as she felt her own desire building within her. 'Let me try it this way.' She added bending her head and resting it over his heart. 'Aarrgghh, that's much better, I hear it beating.' She said dreamily as she felt his hands begin to travel up the back of her legs.

'You are one sexy woman!' Jesse declared, the passion in his eyes almost frightening her, it was that intense.

Swallowing hard Amy stood before him slowly.

'I need to examine the rest of you.' She grinned, moving towards his feet.

'It tickles.' He chuckled, trying to free his feet from the meticulous inspection she had embarked on.

'This little piggy went to....' She began laughing with him as he pleaded for her to stop. 'I take it we have very ticklish feet Mr Clayton.' She laughed, moving her hands up his legs at a deliciously slow pace.

Jesse was squirming under her touch, his cock straining against the tight fitting material of his shorts. Pushing her fingertips under the waistband she let her fingers slip down, briefly touching him.

'Amy.' He breathed as her hand encompassed him tightly. 'Oh

babe.'

'Sssshhh, close your eyes.' She softly ordered as she seized the material, slowly pulling the shorts down his legs. 'Lift your bum.' She asked. Obliging, Amy removed his boxers, throwing them onto the carpet. 'Much better, much, much better.' She softly cooed as she reached for him once again. She was amazed how far she had travelled, gone was the meek, shy, nervous woman, in her place a siren that craved his touch. Jesse had created this woman before him, his pleasure her only aim. She knew she was wet, ready for him but this wasn't about her, she silently thought, no this was about Jesse and his pleasure.

Sinking to her knees she slid her hand around him, grasping him tightly as she brought her lips down.

'Oh…..My…..God.' He gasped as her tongue and lips worked in unison with her hand. 'Amy…..'

'Do you want me to stop?' She teased, her tongue gently flicking the tip of his cock, her eyes trying to meet the smouldering gaze of his.

'No!' The one word practically sizzled as he spoke it.

Amy needed no further encouragement. Sinking him once more into her mouth she continued to pleasure him with her tongue and lips.

'Stop!' He demanded, dangerously close to orgasm.

Holding him tightly in her hand she removed her mouth, looking at him once again.

'I love doing this to you, you taste so good. Do you know how much it turns me on that I am giving you so much pleasure?' She breathed, bending her head to kiss the tip once again. 'Turn over please.' She asked, placing her hands on his chest.

Jesse did as he was instructed, lying flat on his stomach, his head to the side.

'You are so handsome.' She breathed as she gazed at him. 'You're back looks fine but perhaps you could do with a massage.' She added. 'Be back in a sec.' Amy added, kicking off the red, high suede stilettos.

'Why you taking your shoes off?' Jesse asked pouting.

'So I can get up the stairs and back down again in record time baby.' She laughed.

Running up the stairs she quickly picked up the baby oil from her dressing table before taking a spare sheet and a towel out of the linen cupboard. Bounding down the stairs she stood before him, watching him quietly.

'I'm going to put this on the floor; I want you to lie on your stomach please.' Amy asked watching him rise from the sofa in all his naked glory, his hard, steel cock at full salute. 'Thank you.' She added as he lay down on the black sheet and towel that she had lain down to cushion him and protect the carpet from the slippery oil.

Picking up the shoes she placed them near his head. Lifting her right foot first because his face was turned that way, she arched and pointed her instep and toes before slowly placing it in the shoe. She heard him gasp, her feet only a few inches from his face.

'Turn your face the other way.' She softly instructed. Reaching for the left shoe she repeated the seduction over again knowing that she was pampering to his secret fetish in just the right way.

'Your feet.' He whispered, his breath catching in his throat as he moved his hand to touch the red shoe.

'No, no!' Amy said softly. Lifting up her left foot she placed it softly on his back, trailing the heel of the extremely high shoe up and down the smooth skin gently.

'Oh.' She heard him moan.

Removing her foot she picked up the baby oil and straddled him. Warming the liquid in her hands she slowly rubbed them up the length of his back, her fingertips digging deliciously into his muscles as she worked out the kinks in his shoulders.

Moaning softly Jesse shifted his position slightly.

'Are you comfortable?' Amy asked, afraid she was hurting him.

'Just adjusting Brucie.' Jesse chuckled, resting his head back onto his forearm, his eyes closing.

'Turn over.' Amy asked softly, removing herself from him.

Sinking beside him on the floor she once again took him into her mouth.

'I want you.' She whispered as she looked at him, the tip of his cock between her lips.

'Fuck Amy!' Jesse exclaimed. 'Don't look at me like that when you have my cock in your mouth!'

'Now you know how it feels.' She quietly said.

'Yes Mr Fuckin Sexy Eyes Champagne, now you know how it feels!' She silently declared to herself, her hands clapping furiously together in her brave imagination.

His hands were on her in a second, pulling her to him, his lips devouring hers causing her to gasp and moan with pleasure. Taking his lips away from hers suddenly Amy's eyes flew open in protest.

'Please.' She begged, trying to bring his head down to hers as she snaked her fingertips into his hair in a bid to avoid his intense gaze. 'Jesse.' She pleaded.

'Now you know how it feels hey.' He mocked her gently. 'I don't think so Nurse Lucas.' He added as he brought his lips down on to hers once again.

Melting into his kisses she silently conceded to him. She would never win with Jesse; his sexy eyes would always be just too much for her, especially when he looked at her in his special, Jesse way.

CHAPTER FIFTY FIVE

'I want you.' Jesse demanded his hands and mouth all over her body.

Turning, she positioned herself so she was on all fours, the stethoscope dangling down from her neck, her knees resting on the plump cushion she beckoned to him enticingly with her naked behind.

'I want you too.' She moaned as she felt him guiding himself towards her, his steel cock nudging her entrance gently. 'Jesse.' She gasped as he glided into her wet pussy, filling her completely, stretching her deliciously, his hands clasped firmly at her waist.

'Talk dirty to me.' He hissed.

Pausing for a split second Amy digested the words he had spoken. What did he mean?

'What do you want to hear?' She replied almost silently, her heart hammering in her chest as her desire began to edge away.

'Tell me to fuck you.' He whispered.

Amy felt herself clamp shut. Her secret place, her heart, her mind and her soul closed, refusing to budge as his words sank in slowly.

'I can't.' Amy replied her voice low and traced with fear.

Sensing she was in distress Jesse pulled out of her abruptly. Reaching for her he pulled her backwards into his arms.

'What's the matter babe?' He softly asked.

'Nothing Jesse.' She lied. Taking a deep breath she made to turn around. 'I'm fine.' She assured him as their eyes met for a brief second. 'Really, I'm fine Jesse.' She repeated her hands in his hair. 'Kiss me.' She asked softly.

His lips crashed down onto hers, his kiss banishing the scary images that his words had induced without him even knowing. Forcing his lust spoken words out of her mind she relaxed as his hands began to explore her again, his fingertips inducing moans of pleasure from her.

Moving back onto all fours Amy sighed softly as he entered her gently, his hands a mere whisper at her waist.

'Oh Jesse.' She breathed as the passion began to build inside her once again.

Withdrawing himself until only the very tip of his cock remained inside her, he stilled himself. Reaching around her his fingers sought out her clitoris.

'Jesse.' She cried as her orgasm began to wash over her.

Thrusting himself deep inside her he grabbed her by the hips, pushing his cock as far as it would go, grinding her back onto him so she could feel his testicles against her.

'You love my cock being deep inside you Amy, don't you?' He said as she came violently, her orgasm flowing through her body, taking over her entirely as she contracted around him, pushing herself back onto him, wanting all of him inside her. 'Oh babe.' He whispered as she gripped her pelvic muscles tightly around his rock hard cock as his flat palm connected with the bare skin of her arse cheeks.

Jesse continued to thrust himself into her, his own desire building as he continued to spank her behind.

'I want you in my mouth.' Amy panted, her voice filled with lust and desire.

'Not yet.' Jesse replied huskily, removing himself from her slowly.

'No.' she wailed as she felt the void he had left. 'Jesse.' She begged, reaching for him.

'No!' He answered. 'I haven't finished with you yet.'

Reaching for her shoulders he gently pulled her back until she was on her knees, her back pressing into his bare chest.

'I love you so much.' She murmured as his hand reached up to the front of her neck. 'Oh.' She moaned as he splayed the digits on his hand. The four fingers of his left hand gently rested at one side of the front of her neck, his thumb on the other. 'Jesse.' She breathed, the simple movement causing her to gasp with desire.

With an almost painfully slow, feather light touch, his other hand reached into the nurses uniform, grazing the side of her breast sending shivers of pleasure throughout her lust filled body. As she rose even further on her knees she pressed herself back onto him, his bare skin feeling like heaven against hers as his lips brushed down the side of her neck.

'I want you inside me.' She breathed, her chest rising and falling rapidly as her breath came in short bursts.

Standing Jesse lifted her up easily into his arms.

'Where are we going?' She squealed as she felt her feet leave the black carpet as his strong arms carried her easily.

'Upstairs!' He replied kissing the tip of her nose.

'Don't drop me.' Amy giggled, enjoying the feel of his arms around her.

'I won't.' He promised, tightening his grip on her as if to provide some reassurance. 'There.' He said plopping her down carefully on her red stilettos as they entered her bedroom.

Reaching up she threw her fingers into his hair, her hunger for him sated for only a moment when he touched her lips with his own.

'I love this.' He said, standing back and admiring the little kinky outfit. 'But it has to come off now.' He added sticking out his bottom lip.

'I'm sure Naughty Nurse Lucas can come play again.' She said, closing her eyes as his hand reached for the zipper.

'Open your eyes Amy.' He softly asked.

Reluctantly she opened first one eye, then the other, Jesse laughing as she peeked at him from underneath her fringe.

'Look at me Amy.' He repeated again, his soft, sexy voice beckoning to her.

Meeting his gaze she gasped as always, his eyes were on fire!

'Jesse.' She whispered as the blush began to make its way over her face. Hooking his finger under her chin he kissed her nose again before raising his other hand to sweep her hair back from her face.

'I love it when you do that.' She nervously giggled, referring to his soft kiss on the tip of her nose.

'And I love you.' He responded, his voice deep and sexy as he reached for the zipper once more.

Peeling the zip down slowly Jesse revealed her bra.

'This is nice.' He murmured as he trailed his fingers over the cups of the new cream bra which was edged in delicate lace. 'Very nice.'

Reaching around her back he deftly unclasped the bra with one hand.

'Very clever.' Amy murmured.

'I have a knack remember.' He replied, smiling at her tenderly.

'You certainly do.' She responded her own voice filled with a deep, lustful longing for him.

Laying her down on the bed he gently lowered himself towards her, nudging her legs apart with his own.

'Jesse.' She moaned as he entered her. 'I love you.'

'I love you too.' He murmured as he increased the tempo causing her to cry out with pleasure as once again her orgasm raged through her.

'Now can I taste you?' She asked demurely as the final swells left her body.

Pulling slowly out of her Jesse planted a small kiss on her lips.

'I love the way you feel inside me.' She whispered, smiling at him. 'Now give me Brucie!' She demanded playfully, reaching for him.

As her hand wrapped around his stiff cock Amy heard him gasp loudly. Gripping him tightly she began to move her hand up and down, letting her wrist do the work, her thumb grazing the ridge of him as she continued to build up the pace.

'Put me in your mouth.' Jesse demanded his voice the barest whisper.

Allowing her eyes to meet his she slid down his body, his cock still in her hand.

'I think Brucie needs some TLC.' She said sexily, her open mouth calling to him as she took on the role of Nurse Lucas once again. 'Let me make him all better.' She sighed running her tongue around his navel.

Her tongue and lips wove their magic, her hands working together until Jesse was practically writhe ring beside her. Raising her head she met his eyes once again.

'Please babe.' He pleaded. 'Put me back in your mouth.'

Shifting herself away from him she stood beside the bed, gazing down at him lovingly.

'Where are you going?' He asked, confusion written all over his handsome, young face.

'You'll see.' She responded, moving his legs gently apart and sitting between them, facing him.

'Kinky!' Jesse declared as she stretched out her legs, placing her stiletto clad feet at each side of his head. 'Wow!' He mumbled, running his hands over the shoes and her legs.

Hoping that she could pull off this new position she bent carefully, extending her neck down until his cock was back in her mouth.

'Oh….my…..god….' Jesse shouted as she took him deep. His hands holding onto the high, red, stiletto shoes as she continued to assault him with her tongue and lips.

'I want to taste you.' She said huskily running her tongue around his tip before taking him deep once again.

'Oh babe.' Jesse responded. 'I'm gonna come.' He shouted as she grasped him tightly with her hand, her mouth sucking him to orgasm.

The warm, salty liquid exploded into her mouth, swallowing she gagged as more of his thick, male liquid shot into her mouth.

'Shit!' Jesse shouted as his climax reached its peak. 'Babe……'

Sucking the final droplets out of him, Amy looked up slowly and smiled.

'It's all about the shoes.' She whispered.

'Yes.' He sexily responded, his eyes dazed. 'It's the shoes.'

CHAPTER FIFTY SIX

'Wow!' Jesse exclaimed again as he lay back on the comfy bed. 'Amy, that was…'

No further words were necessary as Amy cuddled up to him, bringing her body close to his.

'Well, I think the patient has made a full recovery.' She giggled, luxuriating in the pleasure she had just brought the man she loved.

'Can I ask you something Amy?' Jesse asked his voice low as he shifted position to reach for his cigarettes and lighter.

Immediately sensing that he was about to ask her something that would cause her to blush, she attempted to bury her face into the pillow.

'Yes.' She whispered feeling the knots beginning to tie themselves in her stomach.

'Before, downstairs, I got a bit lost in the moment Amy, I'm sorry if I hurt you in anyway.'

Looking puzzled Amy raised herself onto her elbows, searching his face carefully.

'Hurt me?' She asked perplexed.

'When I asked for you to say that you wanted me to fuck you.' Jesse revealed cautiously, not wanting to upset her.

'Oh Jesse, is it ok if I don't talk about it?' She asked, praying that he wouldn't be offended that she didn't want to share the truth with him.

'Ok.' He said, his voice small, a small tinge of disappointment evident in the single word he spoke.

'One day Jesse I hope I will be able to talk about my past freely, without it causing any pain, for now I can't baby, I hope you understand.'

'Of course I do.' He responded, squeezing her to him tightly. 'I won't run you know.' He added at the end.

'Thank you.' She quietly replied. 'I need to go and brush my teeth darling.' Amy added rising reluctantly from his arms and the bed.

Putting on her dressing gown she blew him a kiss before walking out of the door.

Shutting the bathroom door behind her she leant against it. How could she reveal the truth? She questioned herself silently. The first time Paul raped her he had punched and bitten her relentlessly because she had refused to give into his demands.

'Tell me to fuck you, you cunt!' He had screamed at her, his saliva running down his chin, his beady, evil eyes roaming wildly over her body as he had pulled her hair violently, spitting in her face. 'Tell me to fuck you I said!' It was only when he punched her really hard that she had slipped gratefully into unconsciousness. She had fought with every ounce of strength she had but it just wasn't enough to get him off her and make the terrifying ordeal disappear.

Returning back to the bedroom Amy smiled at Jesse, removing her robe before she took her place beside him once again.

'I know you won't.' Amy whispered to Jesse referring to his not running away. 'I just can't speak about it just yet but I want you to know that you did nothing wrong Jesse.' Looking at him she saw sorrow in his eyes. 'Jesse! Are you listening to me, you did nothing wrong.' She repeated taking his face into her hands she kissed his lips softly. 'I love you and I know you would never do anything to hurt me Jesse, I trust you.' She added.

'Why won't you tell me?' He prodded softly.

'Oh Jesse.' She thought. 'Lovely, kind, caring Jesse who only knows good.'

'Amy.'

'Jesse, I can't.' She whispered as tears began to form in her eyes.

'Ok.' He responded. 'But you need to know Amy that I love you and want to help you and eventually I hope you are strong enough to tell me whatever it is that you are holding so close to you.'

'I will, I promise.' Her voice was so small as she curled herself tightly into him trying to force the images of her ex-husband from her brain.

She had changed, her life had changed and it was all down to the man whose chest she was lay on. He had helped her to heal so much, she just hoped that the final few hurdles would be as effortless as falling in love with this wonderful man had been.

'Is Chloe all packed and ready?' Jesse asked, sensing that he needed to change the conversation.

'She is.' Amy said sadly. 'Are you working on Saturday by the way?' She asked.

'Yes, why babe?' He responded. 'We've had a big job on all week that has run over.'

'I said I would drive up with Chloe and the boxes she has packed, I'm dying to see the apartment.' Amy's voice sounded a little happier.

'I will probably finish about 2ish if you want me to come and help.' He offered kindly.

'I'm hoping we will be finished by then.' Amy replied. 'Do you fancy going for a meal tomorrow night?' She added. Chloe and Mark had discovered this fantastic little Mediterrean restaurant which they swore served the best steak they had ever tasted.

'Sure, where did you have in mind?' He asked.

Amy told him all about the restaurant that was situated in the middle of nowhere, deep in the open countryside that was only a few miles from Amy's house.

'It's a very traditional looking pub with open fires and cosy seating that overlooks the fields beyond, let me ring and book a table.' Reaching for her mobile she quickly text Chloe.

'Hi baby cakes; do you have the number for that restaurant please.? Hope you are ok. Love you xx.'

'Do you want anything to eat or drink?' She asked turning her attention back to Jesse.

'Please, a brew would be good.' He responded, cheekily slapping her on the arse as she went to leave the room.

'Kinky!' She said as she threw on her bathrobe, placing her mobile phone in the pocket before opening the door. 'Won't be long baby.'

Once in the kitchen Amy removed her phone and looked at it, six missed calls from a withheld number.

'Shit!' Amy exclaimed.

'What's the matter babe?' She jumped at the sound of his voice, not expecting him to be behind her.

'Shit! Jesse, you scared the hell out of me.' She said as she clasped her hands together to stop them shaking, the colour draining from her face as she looked at him.

'Christ! I'm so sorry Amy.' The look of horror on his face tore at her heart. 'I'm so sorry.' He mumbled into her hair as he took her into his arms. 'Are you ok.' Stroking her back he tried to calm her down and stop the trembling that had now taken over her entire body. 'Amy.....' His words trailed off as she sank to the floor. 'Amy.... Amy....' He called repeatedly. 'Shit, Amy, please wake up.'

As she slid away from him to the floor he reached out, his arms cushioning her as she connected with the hard ceramic tiles.

'Amy.....'

'Jesse....' She whimpered as she fought to regain consciousness as his voice delved into the deepest part of her mind, summoning her back to him. 'What happened?'

'I think you fainted, fuck Amy, I am so sorry.' His handsome face was full of distress.

'Hey, you did nothing wrong Jesse.' She reached out, stroking his face, trying to reassure him.

'But I scared you.' He replied.

'Jesse, it's me....' She responded quietly. 'You're not to blame baby.' She added.

'I love you.' He said, his lips seeking hers.

'I love you too Jesse.' She answered, melting into his arms knowing that she needed help badly to banish the demons of her past forever.

CHAPTER FIFTY SEVEN

'Jesse.' Amy called up the stairs. 'The table is booked for 8pm, is that ok with you?'

'That's fine babe.' He shouted down. 'I won't be a minute.'

'Ok, well your food is ready.'

Walking back into the kitchen she picked up her mobile phone as it vibrated on the work surface.

'Hello.' She whispered to the caller who had withheld their number.

'Get him out of my house, now! I'm going to fucking kill you Amy. You remember, you belong to me slag and I am going to take back what's rightfully mine.'

Hanging up the phone she screwed her eyes shut tightly, Paul was obviously watching the house. Flying up the stairs she bumped into Jesse who was just coming out of the bathroom.

'Where's the fire?' He asked laughing as she hurried around her bedroom, throwing on a pair of jeans and a blouse before slipping her feet into her converse. 'Where are you going babe?' He added the fainting attack still weighing heavily on his mind as he watched her rushing around in obvious distress.

'I've ran out of bloody milk!' She declared, her face a picture of concentration as her fingers struggled to tie the laces of her shoes.

'What do you need milk for?' Jesse asked. 'If it's for a brew it doesn't matter babe, I will have juice.'

'Don't be silly.' She replied, standing on her tiptoes to plant a hasty kiss on his lips. 'I'll only be a minute.'

Leaving a bewildered Jesse in her bedroom she picked up her car keys before taking the stairs two at a time.

'Won't be long.' She called as she opened the front door.

Locking the door behind her she pressed the control to unlock her car.

'Shit!' She exclaimed as she realised that Jesse's shiny, new BMW was parked behind her car. 'Guess I have to walk.' She said, setting off down the road at a quick pace, petrified knowing that her psychopathic ex-husband was obviously in the vicinity and spying on her.

As she went around the corner Amy bent at the waist, unable to contain it any more she vomited violently into the bushes as she finally allowed the fear to overtake her. As the last heaves left her body her phone began to ring again.

'I'm coming for you bitch. I'm taking back what's mine. First I'm going to rape you then I'll chop you up in pieces and dump you for the animals.' Again he hung up.

Clutching her phone to her chest Amy's eyes looked wildly around, he was watching her, she was sure, she could feel him.

Again her phone rang.

'What!' She answered bravely. 'What do you want Paul?'

'You know what I want bitch.' He responded. 'You went to the police, I'll pay you back. I've had a lot of time to think about what you did to me slag and how I'm going to get rid of you oh and remember this Amy..... I'm not interested in your little man; it's you I'm after!'

Relief flooded through her body as she listened to his vile words, he didn't want Jesse or the girls, he was after her. The three people she loved more than anything in this world were safe from this evil man.

As her phone rang for the third time she shouted out as she answered it.

'Fuck off!'

'Amy! What the hell!' It was Jesse, her distress was so great that she didn't even register that the ring tone she had assigned to him in her blackberry had played.

Her world came crashing down around her tiny feet as she heard his words but was unable to respond.

'Where are you?' He demanded. 'Amy, where the fuck are you?!'

'Around the corner, I'm coming back.' She quietly replied hanging up the phone, astonished to hear Jesse raise his voice to her but immediately understanding why.

How the hell could she get herself out of this one? She silently thought as she walked the short distance back to her house whilst looking wildly around, her eyes scanning her surroundings, her ears listening for the slightest sound.

Jesse was stood in the hallway as she unlocked the front door, his mobile phone in his hand, a worried look on his beautiful face.

'What was that all about babe?' He probed gently fighting the urge to take her in his arms. He wanted to see her face, watch her eyes, something was very wrong and he was desperate to know what was upsetting her so much.

'I thought it was Debs, she rang me a couple of times.' Amy lied.

Carefully searching her eyes Jesse knew she was lying to him.

'Ok babe, as long as you are alright.' She was obviously lying to him for a very good reason, he silently thought as he decided to play along with her, accepting what she told him to be the truth.

'I'm fine.' She responded brushing past him into the house and climbing the stairs.

Locking herself in the bathroom she reached for her toothbrush and the paste, brushing her teeth vigorously she spat into the sink and noticed pale red streaks of blood.

'What......' She murmured inspecting her mouth in the mirror. A tiny cut was visible on her gum line where she had brushed too hard. 'Shit.' She muttered.

'Are you ok in there?' Jesse asked, knocking at the door.

'I'm fine.' She shouted back as she tried to control her hair with the clip, her mind shooting off in every direction as she tried to summon the courage to walk out of the bathroom and face Jesse.

Ten minutes later she opened the door to find him sat on the top stair, his eyes locked on hers the moment he saw her.

'Now, do you want to tell me the truth Amy?' His voice was low, his eyes burning into hers.

Casting her eyes to the floor she fought back the tears that were threatening to flow.

'I'm fine.' She repeated.

'Amy I know you and I know when you say "I'm fine," that you are lying. Now please will you tell me what the hell has happened to upset you so much, is it Paul?' He added.

'Yes.' She whispered her eyes cast downwards towards the floor.

Jesse was by her side, his arms enveloping her in an instant.

'What's happened baby, the truth please.' Jesse asked gently.

'Jesse I don't want to lose you.' She pleaded softly.

'I'm going nowhere.' He replied, cocooning her with his body. 'Please tell me Amy, I can't help you if you keep holding back.'

'Can we go and sit down please.' She asked meekly, her eyes still on the floor.

'Of course baby.' He responded, lifting her into his arms and carrying her into her bedroom. Placing her down gently on the bed he sat at her side, her hands in his. 'Tell me.' He gently coaxed, brushing her hair back from her face.

'Paul has been ringing me.' She began quietly. A battle was slowly raging through her heart and head as she fought silently with her feelings. She needed to protect Jesse but he knew her too well.

'Have you told the police?' Jesse asked his eyes to pools of concern as he looked closely at Amy.

'No Jesse, they won't be able to do anything.' Amy replied sadly.

'What do you mean? You have a restraining order; he's still on bloody probation.' Jesse could feel his temper begin to rise as he looked at the broken woman before him.

'I have to prove he has called Jesse, he withholds his number.' Amy explained. 'Yes, they can arrest him, haul his arse into a police cell, question him but then they would have to let him go and then he will be mad as hell Jesse, I just can't do it until I can prove it so I can make sure they lock him away.' She cried.

'Ok baby, ok.' He gently cooed trying to take away her pain. 'I won't let him hurt you Amy.' He added reassuringly.

'Thank you Jesse.' She replied in a soft, low voice. 'He scares me, he can hit me but I don't want him to ever touch me again!' Her voice rose as the words tumbled out.

'Rape you Amy.' He said quietly.

'Yes.' She whispered.

'Oh baby.' He said, squeezing her tightly to him. 'What has he said to you?'

As Amy recited Paul's words to Jesse she felt him stiffen at her side.

'I'm sorry.' She mumbled, she didn't want to lose him, he meant too much to her.

'Why are you sorry?' He asked. 'Amy, none of this is your fault; you certainly don't deserve to be treated this way.'

'He will never leave me alone; I'll never get any peace.' She wailed as the tears flew down her sad face.

'Can I ask you to do something for me Amy please?' Jesse asked softly.

'Yes.' She responded, her voice low and afraid.

'Always tell me the truth, don't hold anything back, I'm going nowhere Amy.'

'Ok.' She replied.

'Promise.' He asked.

'Jesse, I can't promise.' She responded, the pain in her voice tore at him as she carried on. 'I want to protect you.' She whispered. 'I love you, I need to protect you.'

'Oh Amy......' He wanted to take her pain away, make her forget. 'You don't need to protect me baby.'

'You don't know him Jesse, he is evil. I don't think for one minute that he has an axe to grind with you, in fact I know he doesn't, he told me.'

Jesse's ears pricked up as she spoke the words softly to him.

'Why what did he say?' Jesse asked gently.

'He said and I quote, "I'm not interested in your little man." He doesn't want you or the girls Jesse; it's me he's after.'

'Well he can't have you!' Jesse responded his voice filled with passion as his need to protect her took over. 'You have to be strong Amy; you know it's in there somewhere.' He added squeezing her to him.

'You don't know him Jesse.' She pleaded, trying to make him understand. 'I've been strong for so very long Jesse, I can't do it anymore.'

Paul didn't act like "normal" people. Amy remembered how he had behaved when he had fallen out with a friend. He had stalked her relentlessly, following her to the school when she took her son, the supermarket, watching her house for hours. He always carried a large hunting knife stuffed down the back of his jeans when he had been in stalker mode.

'You are not like him Jesse, you are complete opposites.' Her desperate need for him to understand took over her. 'Jesse, he is evil, he won't think twice about getting his revenge, oh, he will plan it meticulously, even draw diagrams, but if Paul wants something, he usually finds a way to get it.' She thought about the pieces of paper she had found at the back of the drawer when she had returned to the house after the attack. Detailed drawings of his friend's and her daughter's houses with arrows pointing to places where he could hide and watch them unseen.

'Amy, I will repeat myself, I'm going nowhere. I'm not easily frightened Amy, I understand what you are saying but really, don't worry about me. I'm not going to let anything happen to you.'

'Ok.' She mumbled quietly. 'He is a bully Jesse who can only hit women and children..........'

'Trust me please. Your nightmare life with him is over.'

Closing her eyes Amy allowed herself to dream of her escape. Her and Jesse stood on top of the beautiful mountain in New Zealand. Yes, that was her dream. She silently thought. Far, far away from Paul and all her problems.

CHAPTER FIFTY EIGHT

'How you feeling sexy bum? xx' Jesse's text arrived as Amy was pulling her car into the parking lot at the centre. He had a "knack" of knowing just the right time to send his messages.

'I'm good sexy eyes. Just going in to see Brenda now. I love you. xx' She text back, turning her phone on silent as she opened the heavy glass doors that would take her into the foyer of the building.

'Good luck. Remember dig deep baby. I love you too. xx' His texts always made her smile. Amy knew that the smile she wore everyday was the one that Jesse always left her with. With Jesse she had peace, if only her past would stay firmly locked away......

For an entire week Amy had endured Paul's calls. Most of the time he hurled abuse down the phone at her but over the last two days he had remained silent. That scared Amy more than his vile words, knowing he was lurking about somewhere, ready to pounce. She noticed that a pattern began to develop; Paul never rang when Jesse was at the house. This only made Amy more nervous and aware as it confirmed to her that he was definitely watching her and the house.

'Hi, I'm here to see Brenda.' Amy said to the young girl sitting behind the reception desk. 'I'm Amy by the way, Amy Lucas.' She smiled warmly before taking a seat.

'I will let Brenda know you are here.' The receptionist said. 'My name is Rebecca.' She added smiling back at Amy.

'Pleased to meet you Rebecca and thank you.' Amy replied reaching for her mobile phone as it began to flash.

'Hi mum, have you got a spare extension lead, TV wire isn't long enough? Love my life mum, I am so happy. Xxxx'

Amy smiled, Chloe and Mark had moved into their new apartment the previous weekend. Amy had driven up with Chloe and her boxes and suitcases, immediately falling in love with the peaceful location. Leaving the main road they had travelled along a country lane before crossing a tiny bridge that ran over a stream. The little village was remote but very beautiful. Stone, terraced cottages ran along the side of the stream and as Amy turned around the corner, after the crossing the bridge, she spotted a tall, wooden stall that had a variety of produce lay on it and an honesty box for customers to leave their money after they had purchased goods.

'That's so cute!' Amy had squealed. 'An honesty box!' She was amazed at the trust the owners had placed on their customers in this enchanting tiny village.

'I love it here.' Chloe had replied. 'I'm going to be so happy mum.'

Pulling up at the side of the stall, Amy reached for her eldest child.

'I'm so happy for you Chloe.' She had murmured as she embraced her tightly. 'You are wise and so beautiful, both inside and out.

'I'm going to miss you mum.' She whispered, the tears brimming in her wide, dark eyes.'

'I'm going to miss you too Chloe.' Amy breathed. 'Right let's get your stuff to your new home!' She added, wiping away the tears from her own face. She was going to miss Chloe, they had always been close. From the first moment Amy had held her in her arms the bound had been strong, a deep, unconditional love and respect had grown quickly and as Chloe had grown, Amy had watched with silent fascination as her little girl became a strong, stunningly beautiful, independent woman.

Every window in the young couple's new apartment had spectacular views of open countryside, trees and the stream and as Amy had looked out of the kitchen window she squealed with delight.

'Chloe, come quick, look at your neighbours.' She had called excitedly.

The two women giggled as they watched the two sheep lazily graze on the grass of their front lawn.

'I wouldn't spend any money on flowers for there.' Amy said pointing her finger through the window at the lawn. 'And I don't think you will have to get the mower out much.' She giggled. 'Chloe it's fantastic, I love it.' Holding her eldest daughter in her arms as they said their goodbyes had Amy in floods of tears again, tears of happiness but also tears of sadness, sadness that her baby was so grown up and leaving her. Glancing around the apartment at the unorganised chaos

Amy felt her heart swell, Chloe had done well for herself, she would be fine, she had chosen well.

Sending her eldest daughter a quick text in reply Amy stood as she noticed Brenda walking towards her.

'Hi Amy, how are you?' Brenda asked, her friendly face a welcoming sight.

'I'm fine.' Amy responded smiling back at her.

'Good, would you like a drink?' She asked as they walked side by side into the now familiar room.

'Please.' Amy replied as she sat down on the sofa, placing her handbag at her feet.

'You look nice today.' Brenda remarked as she looked at the smiling woman.

'Thank you.' Amy replied. Her black, skinny jeans hugged her body, on her feet a pair of pale pink, flat ballet pumps. Her blouse was different shades of pink and blue checks, the short sleeves finished off with tiny buttons. Amy never wore much makeup or jewellery but Brenda noticed the dainty gold bracelet on her wrist and the tiny studs in her ears.

'I like your blouse.' She responded. 'The colours suit you.' She added. 'So, how has your week been?'

Amy paused as she remembered her promise to Jesse to tell Brenda the truth.

'Shit!' Amy replied forcefully. 'No, forget that, it's been really shit!' Amy began to fidget with the hem of her blouse, her eyes clouding over as she looked at Brenda. 'The day Paul was released from prison he contacted me, every day since he has rang my mobile, withholding his number, shouting abuse down the phone at me.'

'How does that make you feel?' Brenda asked as she placed the steaming mugs of coffee onto the coffee table before sitting down on the sofa next to Amy.

'Scared, nervous, really afraid.' She replied. 'He is watching the house, watching me.'

'How do you know Amy?' Brenda asked a worried look on her friendly, open face.

'Because, he never rings when Jesse is there.' Amy said in a small voice. 'Well, he has once but Jesse has bought a new car so perhaps he didn't know....'

'Who's Jesse?' Brenda asked, cutting off Amy's words.

'Someone I met last year. Someone who changed my life so much......' Her words trailed off as a vision of his sexy eyes entered her mind. As the blush made its way across her face and chest, Amy smiled.

'Well, well well.' Brenda laughed. 'Is this the man you mentioned briefly to me last time? I'm guessing from the look in your eyes and the tone of your voice that Jesse means a lot to you Amy.'

'Yes.' She whispered. 'I love him so much.' She added, meeting Brenda's kind blue eyes with her own. 'He has changed me so much, helped me so much, he is an amazing and very special man Brenda. She finished smiling.

'Wow!' Brenda exclaimed, truly happy for the little woman who had been through so much.

'It took me a long time to let him in; it was so painful Brenda, learning to trust a man again isn't easy.' Amy said wistfully. 'I really do love him Brenda.'

'I can see that Amy, it's written all over your face and anyone looking into your eyes would see it immediately, I am pleased for you. I don't know your full story yet but you deserve him.' Brenda was smiling, her hand resting on Amy's knee. 'So tell me what Paul has been up to?' Brenda added squeezing Amy's knee lightly.

Immediately Amy's face changed, gone the smile and sparkle that had light it up so brilliantly at the mention of Jesse's name, in its place an expression of a deep and hurtful sorrow.

'He says he wants back what is his.' Amy whispered her words so small and scared.

'And what belongs to him Amy?' Brenda gently probed. 'Has he got any belongings still in the house?' She asked.

'No, he means me.' Her voice was hardly audible as she answered Brenda's question. 'He said he is going to take back what belongs to him, rape....' Amy stuttered, unable to say the last word fully. 'Me and then chop me up and fed me to the animals.'

'What?' Brenda exclaimed. 'Amy have you told Vicky?' Brenda asked referring to the policewoman from the Domestic Violence Unit.

'No.' Amy said in a small voice. 'I need proof. If I don't have proof then all they will do is arrest him, question him and then release him and he will be really mad then. The day he was released from prison he rang and I panicked and rang Vicky but I need evidence Brenda, I need to be able to prove it.'

'Amy, he isn't allowed to contact you in any way, shape or form.' Brenda stated. 'He is breaking both his probation and the terms of the restraining order.'

'I know Brenda and when I have proof I will report him. I promise.' Amy responded.

'Ok, but Amy, don't struggle, don't be afraid. These sessions will help you but, you and only you.' She said pointing her finger gently in Amy's direction. 'Can do this Amy, no one else. Time is a great healer but you have to be strong and vigilant. Be careful Amy.' Brenda was concerned as she witnessed Amy crumble before her.

'I'll be fine.' She replied, angrily wiping the tears from her face with the back of her hand.

'So, do you want to tell me a little more about this wonderful Jesse?' Brenda asked sensing that the mere mention of his name would bring Amy's thoughts back to the present.

Immediately Amy's face changed as she closed her eyes and summoned his image to her. She had been doing it a lot over the last few days, drawing strength from him even though he wasn't physically present. If she imagined hard enough she could visualize his face, see his eyes, the reassuring smile on his lips until she would blissfully land in her secret, special place.....

'He's younger than me.' Amy dreamily responded, wondering what the other woman's reaction would be.

'How young?' Brenda asked a kind smile on her face as she smiled at Amy.

'Almost half my age.' Amy whispered, suddenly wanting the other woman's approval.

'Age is a number Amy, it's irrelevant.' Brenda replied.

'It makes me doubt the whole thing Brenda. I met him late October last year and from the first moment it was his eyes. He has the most magnetic, sexy eyes I have ever seen and I felt drawn to him from the minute I laid my own eyes on him. I was a wreck Brenda, a complete bundle of nerves, every time he looked in my direction I could feel myself blush.' She laughed, remembering their first meeting. Pausing she looked at the expression on Brenda's face expecting to see a look of accusation or disgust.

'Carry on.' Brenda encouraged, a warm and friendly smile still on her face. 'This is exciting Amy and so wonderful for you.'

'He contacted me on Facebook and then by text, after getting my number from my friend Jen, and I guess the rest is history.' Amy laughed. 'It was supposed to be a…..' Amy struggled with the words suddenly feeling a little ashamed.

'Go on.' Brenda softly encouraged again.

'Well, it was supposed to be a one night stand, two adults having consensual sex, I guess it was what I needed at the time, part of the healing process I guess. I hadn't had consensual intercourse for over four years.' Amy stated laughing as the shocked look on Brenda's face registered with her. 'Yes, four years.' Amy repeated. 'A long time, a lonely time.'

'I can see in your eyes that there are reasons for that Amy and we will explore them as we go along but for now I really want to hear about this fabulous, young man.' She giggled.

'I had the most amazing, mind blowing sex that first night.' Amy wanted to be honest with the kind woman who had already helped her so much and was beginning to feel like a real friend. 'Here was me thinking he would be some sort of fumbling idiot who basically just wanted his kicks and a pat on the back from his mates for bedding an older woman. I thought it would be easy, you know, having sex again and then saying goodbye but he was so much more, is so much more.' Amy said dreamily. 'It's his eyes and his kind heart; it's just him full stop.'

'My oh my!' Brenda exclaimed. 'Amy, I can honestly say that I don't think I have ever seen anyone so blissfully in love before, he must be special to have captured your heart.'

'He is Brenda, he is very special. I fought against my feelings, not only because of my past but because of his age but eventually I decided to just go with it, enjoy him, enjoy us. Our paths crossed for a reason Brenda and I guess I know what that is now. He has my heart.' Amy added, her face shining radiantly with the feelings she had for this wonderful, young man.

'How does he feel about Paul being released?' Brenda asked wanting to know more about Jesse. The last thing Amy needed at this time was to be hurt again. She loved the way Amy's face shone whenever Jesse's name was mentioned so hated bringing Paul back into the conversation.

'Jesse knows so much about me, over the months, as I feel in love with him, I opened up a little. He probably knows more about me than anyone else Brenda. At first I hid the calls from him but lying to the man I love was so hard, but I would have carried on to protect him until he caught me out.' Again the tears began to flow as Amy remembered the phone calls from Paul.

'What do you mean, he caught you out Amy?' Brenda gently probed.

'Paul rang a couple of times so I made an excuse saying I needed to go to the shop. Once I was out of the house, Paul rang again, threatening me, then Jesse rang and I shouted "fuck off," thinking it was Paul again, so he knew something was wrong.'

'And how did he react?' Brenda said reaching for her cup of coffee. 'Here, do you want yours?' She asked offering Amy one of the mugs.

'Thanks.' Amy replied as she took hold of the white cup. 'Kind, caring, typical Jesse.' Amy responded. 'He said he won't let Paul hurt me......' Amy starred at the haunting posters on the wall, her mind a million miles away as she wrestled with the images before her, trying to bring Jesse back to her so she could once again be in her safe space.

'He loves you and wants to protect you Amy, that's good, that's normal.' Brenda softly replied. 'Well, Jesse seems like a wonderful man Amy, forget about the age, have fun, love him, enjoy him.'

Brenda advised. 'He is a grown man; you have nothing to be ashamed of.' Handing her a small card Brenda asked Amy to read it.

"The woman came from the man's rib. Not from his feet to be walked on. Not from his head to be superior, but from the side to be equal. Under the arm to be protected and next to the heart to be loved."

'This is beautiful.' Amy whispered as tears began to form in her eyes.

'Keep it, cherish it, take it out every now and then and read it.' Brenda responded. 'You are a brave and lucky woman Amy.' She added.

'I know and I am.' Amy replied dragging her eyes away from the little card back to Brenda. 'I have to protect him though.' She whispered.

'Protect him?' Brenda replied. 'From Paul?' She asked

'Yes.' Amy whispered her eyes cast down to the floor.

'When was the last time Paul contacted you Amy?' Brenda asked.

'I've had three calls this morning, all silent.' Amy replied.

'Ok.' Brenda responded, writing something down on her pad. 'So, now I know all about the wonderful Jesse what else would you like to talk about Amy?' She asked smiling.

'I don't know.' Amy replied, a puzzled look on her face. Surely Brenda should be the one leading her. She silently thought.

'Last time, you told me about the first months of your relationship with Paul and the first time he hit you. Do you want to carry on from there?' Brenda gently encouraged.

Knowing it was time to fulfil her promise to Jesse Amy took a deep breath as she began to open up once again. She was taking baby steps; tiny, fragile steps towards her future, a future that she prayed would finally free her totally from her past. Closing her eyes she inhaled deeply, summoning Jesse's image to her so she was safe and secure in her special place.

'When the girls were small he hit me all the time, he didn't care where, my face, back, legs, arms. I had constant bald patches and my head was so sore where he pulled out clumps of my hair.' Amy paused taking a sip of her drink. Closing her eyes she fought with the visions that began to flood into her mind. 'After I had Bethany I was very poorly, physically and mentally.' Amy admitted opening her eyes slowly to look once more at Brenda. 'I always thought deep down that Paul was responsible for Bethany's premature birth and my hysterectomy after.' She said quietly, reaching for a tissue to wipe the tears that had begun to fall away.

'I don't understand Amy.' Brenda replied, reaching for her hand to offer some comfort.

'Paul sat on my stomach when I was just a couple of months pregnant; he punched me in the face, causing this scar.' She said quietly as she raised her finger to her temple. 'When I went for the scan they said I had something called placenta preavia, it's where the placenta lies across the cervix making it impossible to have a natural birth. I ended up with a c section and then the hysterectomy because they couldn't stop the bleeding. I really shouldn't blame Paul, I will never know if him attacking me caused it, but….' Amy paused again, the words getting stuck in the back of her throat. 'I have always secretly blamed him.' She added, the tears cascading down her sad face. 'I have always wondered "what if." What if he hadn't attacked me, what if he hadn't sat on my stomach, what if he hadn't put his hands around my neck and tried to strangle the last breath out of me?' Amy was becoming hysterical as her past once more came to haunt her. 'I don't know whether I can carry on with this.' She wailed referring to the counselling sessions. 'It hurts too much Brenda.' She added sobbing uncontrollably.

'I know Amy but talking about your past will help with your future, how you cope.' Brenda replied softly. 'Do you want to carry on?' She asked.

Taking a deep breath, Amy once again remembered her promise to Jesse. She knew that in order to fully heal she needed to confront the horror of her past and share it with someone. Looking at Brenda Amy smiled sadly, taking another huge gulp of air.

'That's when he started to get really violent.' Amy continued quietly as the memories flooded her brain making her wince in silent agony as each one haunted her separately. 'I became really ill, mentally ill, I was very depressed. I felt trapped Brenda, two babies and nowhere to go. I could have gone to my mother's but Paul would never have allowed that. I spent my days looking after my family, not going out much and so that became my life.'

'Oh Amy.' Brenda cried. 'It must have been awful for you.'

'It was. Do you know something Brenda? I can't even remember one day of the twenty years where my day wouldn't be filled with some form of abuse. He didn't hit me every day, it was the words..........' Again the flashbacks assaulted her. 'He said I was weak and useless, then he started using the hysterectomy to taunt me, telling me I was his because no other man would want me, I was scarred for life. I will never forget his near constant words to me Brenda. "Look at you, what man would want you, a scar on your belly and your head fucked up, you're useless to anyone, including me!" It hurt, it really hurt and I believed him.' Amy was crying openly now, big, fat tears running down her face, her eyes and face shrouded in hurt and anguish.

'Jesse.' The one word spoken from Brenda's lips brought a tiny smile to Amy's face. As Brenda watched the small woman before her she noticed the misery begin to fade away and knew that Amy had already travelled a long way on her journey to a new life.

'I know. I know that now but back then I didn't Brenda. Even now I catch my reflection in the mirror and wonder what it is that Jesse sees when he looks at me.' Amy was revealing her innermost feelings, her deepest fears. 'All those years ago I was very young, easy to manipulate I guess; Paul had me exactly where he wanted me.' Amy continued. 'I went back to work and tried to put the hysterectomy behind me.' Amy paused, her eyes clouding over once again.

'What's the matter Amy?' Brenda softly asked.

'That's when he first used me.' She whispered. 'I discovered some money missing from the petty cash; small amounts had been disappearing for a couple of weeks. Eventually I got to the bottom of it and had to suspend one of my staff.'

'Where did you work Amy?' Brenda questioned gently.

'I had a good job; I was the PA for a CEO.' Amy said, answering

Brenda's question. 'I sent Paul a text to tell him I would be late home.' Amy stopped once again as she fought with her emotions. Closing her eyes she continued. 'When I walked through the front door I saw him pacing and he looked really angry…..'

'Carry on.' Brenda encouraged softly.

Opening her eyes Amy sighed…..

'He attacked me, said I was a slag, threw me on the floor and then……..' Amy was distraught as she remembered the first time her husband raped her. 'I fought, I really fought Brenda but he was too strong……' Amy paused again as an image of him looming over her flashed before her eyes. 'I really did fight and when he finally punched me in the face and knocked me out I welcomed the blackness Brenda…… I wanted to die.' She cried. 'He hurt me so much……'

Brenda was amazed at this little woman's bravery. She had endured so much over such a long period of time; she was stronger than she thought.

'You are such a brave woman Amy.' Brenda said, conveying her secret thoughts to the woman at her side.

'I don't know about brave.' Amy replied. 'Stupid and naive more like.'

'Amy, at the time you felt trapped and anyone listening to your story would understand. I see lots of women and at times I get more than a little frustrated when they arrive battered and bruised only to return to the violence a few days later. It may have taken you a long time but you got there in the end.' Brenda so desperately wanted Amy to understand just how brave she had been, she had an enormous amount of courage, Amy just needed to believe.

'I just wish I could turn back the clock, go back to the time before I met him.' Amy said wistfully. 'But then I guess I wouldn't know what I do now and I wouldn't have met Jesse.' The tiniest of smiles played at her mouth and eyes as she forced Paul from her mind, Jesse and his sexy eyes flying into her brain saving her from the anguish and horror of her past once again.

'That's true Amy.' Brenda responded. 'Well, I think we have covered a lot today, do you want to rest now, we can continue next week?'

'Please, I feel totally drained.' Amy responded as she reached for another tissue to wipe the last of her tears away.

As she walked back to her car after hugging Brenda and promising to see her the next week, Amy thought about her life.

'Yes, I've made some really crappy decisions.' She thought. 'But, my life is so perfect now.'

Getting into her car she reached for her mobile phone as it rang.

'Tick tock, tick tock. Your clock is ticking Amy. You're dead!' Paul.

'Fuck you!' She shouted back. 'Come and fucking get me you fucking retarded prick, come on big man, you know where I am you sick fuck! I don't belong to you anymore, do you fucking hear me you rapist piece of fucking scum!' The words were out before she could stop them. 'Come on!' She screamed.

'I love it when you're angry, it makes me hard, I think I'll have a wank.' Amy down the phone, opening her car door she vomited over the tarmac. As the last dregs violently left her body she heard her phone ringing again. Jesse.

'Babe are you ok?' He asked as he listened to her anguished sobs on the other end of the phone. 'Amy where are you, I'm on my way.' His words wouldn't register in her foggy brain. 'Amy!' He shouted. 'Answer me.'

'Jesse.' She whispered.

'Amy where are you?' He asked again as he paced up and down the office. 'Amy, please tell me where you are, are you in danger Amy?' Jesse was trying to keep his voice calm as he listened carefully for her reply.

'At the centre, in my car, I need to go home.' She cried. 'No I'm not in danger.' She added quietly. 'I just need you Jesse.'

'I'm on my way, stay there!' He ordered as he picked his keys up from the desk and ran out of the office. 'Cancel my job please for this afternoon; I'll be back in a couple of hours.' She heard him shout. 'Are you still there Amy?' He asked as he raced towards his car. He knew she needed him but the reason why he was desperate to find out.

'Yes, I'm going to drive around the corner Jesse, I need to get away from here.' Amy replied referring to the centre.

'Ok baby, I am going to hang up now because I'm driving. Stay in your car, I won't be long.' The phone went dead in her hands.

CHAPTER FIFTY NINE

'Amy.' The soft way he spoke her name slowly dragged her out of the dark hole her mind and body was in.

'Jesse.' She whispered as she felt his arms around her, lifting her from the car.

'We'll leave your car here.' He stated as he walked effortlessly towards his car with her in his arms, the door already open. 'Baby.' He cooed as he sat her down in the passenger seat and fastened her seat belt, moving her hair back from her face he gasped at the anguish and pain in her eyes.

She was a mess, a small, crumpled wreck.

'Jesse.' Again she spoke his name, shaking her head in a bid to clear the mist.

Amy watched as he shut the door and walked around the front of the car. Opening the driver's door he quickly sat beside her, his hands reaching out.

'What happened babe.' He asked, stroking her hair in a bid to try and soothe her.

He had witnessed her in pain before but this was something new, he didn't recognise the woman before him.

'It's Paul.' She said. 'He rang me again.' Her voice was so small.

'What did he say Amy.' Jesse asked, reaching for her hand as he fastened his own belt.

Releasing her own belt Amy quickly opened the door, vomiting once more. She could feel Jesse's hands lightly rubbing her back as she continued to wrench, her stomach cramping violently as another wave hit her.

'I'm sorry.' She whispered wiping the back of her hand across her mouth. 'Have you got anything to drink please?' She asked meekly.

'Here.' Jesse passed her a small bottle of water. 'Drink some of this.' He added, his fingers brushing back her hair and tucking it behind her ear.

The cool liquid felt good as she swilled it around her mouth before spitting it out onto the tarmac. Drinking thirstily she looked at Jesse.

'I'm sorry.' She repeated timidly.

'Amy what's happened.' He asked gently, afraid at what he saw in her eyes.

'Paul, he rang, it was awful.........' The remainder of her words were left unspoken.

'What did he say to you Amy?' Jesse asked, stroking his fingers over hers, trying to calm the petrified woman who he loved.

'I lost my temper. He said I turned him on being angry......' She paused as she felt the nausea begin to wash over her again. Taking a large gulp of the water she swallowed. 'He said I was making him hard, that he was going to masturbate.' The sadness and fear on her face cried out to Jesse.

'He said what?!' Jesse shouted. 'Sorry baby.' He said as she jumped. 'I didn't mean to scare you, I would never hurt you.' His hand reached out to stroke her cheek lightly.

'I know. Well, he didn't exactly say masturbate..... he said wank.' Moving quickly, Amy leaned out of the car door as she vomited once more.

'Let's get you home.' Waiting until she had finishing wrenching Jesse started the car, his hand holding firmly to hers.

The drive to her house seemed to take forever and as Jesse turned to look at her whilst stopping for a red light he gasped as he fully took in the change in her. As soon as the light changed he floored the super-fast car getting her home in record time.

'Why don't you go and lie down on your bed for a while.' Jesse gently encouraged as soon as they walked through her front door. 'You look exhausted babe.'

'I won't be able to sleep Jesse.' She replied. 'But I am going to go upstairs and wash my face, brush my teeth and sort my bloody hair out.' Her chestnut locks looked wild as she caught sight of her reflection in the mirror. 'Oh my god!' She cried. 'I look a mess.' Flinging her hands over her face she escaped up the stairs. 'Won't be long.' She called to Jesse as she disappeared from his view.

Fifteen minutes later she walked down the stairs, a different woman.

'You look better.' Jesse smiled. 'The colour is back in your face, you were deathly pale babe.' He said reaching for her and pulling her into his arms. 'I love you brave lady.' He whispered.

'I love you too Jesse.' She replied as she buried her face into his chest. 'I need a cigarette!'

Opening the patio door Amy walked into the little garden and lit the cigarette she had grabbed from her packet.

'That's better.' She declared as she inhaled deeply. 'Much better.' She added as she blew the smoke from her lungs. 'I need to escape Jesse.' Her eyes met his briefly. 'I can't live like this anymore.'

'Where would you go Amy?' He asked trying to read what she was thinking.

'I don't know Jesse.' She replied, a faraway look in her sad eyes. 'Perhaps New Zealand……..'

'Are you leaving me?' He quietly asked, his eyes searching out hers.

Looking at him she paused, the cigarette close to her mouth. Turning she looked for the ashtray and stubbed it out before slowly walking back to him.

'No, I could never leave you, not yet.' She whispered looking into his green eyes. 'I love you Jesse.' Standing on her tiptoes she planted a small kiss on his soft lips. 'Very much.' She added laying her head on his chest, feeling safe in his strong, young arms.

'I love you too Amy.' He replied as he enveloped her closely, pressing her into him, wanting to make her feel safe and secure.

'I'm yours for as long as you want me.' She mumbled into his chest.

Amy meant every word she spoke. She adored this wonderful, special man who held her so tightly, her heart wasn't her own, it was his. She had entrusted him with it knowing she would never love another the way she loved Jesse.

'Bethany's leaving.' She whispered her voice muffled as she stood protected in Jesse's arms.

'What? When?' Jesse replied, drawing back a little, knowing that this would affect Amy deeply.

'She is going to live in America for a year Jesse. I'm going to miss her but maybe this is my opportunity, maybe this is my chance to escape for a while.' Her mind was in turmoil as she fought with her need for peace and her love for Jesse. Snuggling back into his arms she sighed heavily.

'Everything will be ok.' Jesse reassured her, gently stroking his hands down her back.

'I need peace Jesse.' She murmured. Amy knew her love for Jesse was enough to keep her by his side, was it strong enough to survive Paul, that was the question...........

CHAPTER EIGHTY

'What time are we leaving Bethany?' Amy shouted up the stairs.

'Ten minutes mum.' Her youngest daughter called back.

Bethany was all packed and ready to go. At eighteen years old she had grown into a beautiful young woman with a fierce passion for life. Her closest friend had emigrated six months previously and Amy knew that Bethany had found it hard without her closest confident. They had been friends since nursery school and talked almost constantly on Skype and so when Bethany had hurtled down the stairs, crashing into the kitchen, screaming with excitement that she was going to live in America for a year Amy was already prepared for her youngest daughter to fly the nest. Deep in her heart and stomach Amy knew that Bethany would probably never come home to England again.

Amy remembered the conversations that had followed and Bethany's tears as she had mental fought with the chance of a lifetime, a year in America, and her boyfriend, Adam. Slowly Bethany had fallen in love and as the days had passed Amy had watched as both her daughter and Adam began to mourn their love as Bethany's remaining time in England gradually ticked away.

'Adam, have you thought about going with Bethany to America?' Amy had asked after watching them both get upset for the fourth time that night. 'Bethany is it possible that Adam could go with you, would your friend be ok I mean and could all the paperwork be sorted in time? It's worth a shot, worth thinking about.' Amy had added.

For the first time in her life Amy knew what "real" love felt like. Remembering her own torments, that Jesse was simply on loan to her, she urged the two youngsters to think about the possibility. Love was often cruel, snatching itself away prematurely; they really needed to think very carefully.

The two young lovers had smiled at one another, both disappearing out of the room only to return half an hour later announcing that Adam was going with her youngest child.

'Hurry up Bethany!' Amy shouted as she glanced at her watch.

'You are cutting it fine young lady.' They had just thirty minutes to get to the airport. 'Bethany!' She screamed once more up the staircase.

'Coming, coming, bloody hell mother, keep your knickers on!' She laughed as she came down the stairs dragging yet another suitcase.

'Bethany, how much stuff do you need?' Amy asked looking at the bags and cases scattered over the living room floor. 'You have three cases and two bags!'

'Have you seen how much stuff I need to take mum? I'm going for a whole year remember.' She replied looking exasperated.

'Ok.' Amy sighed realising it was perhaps a bit too late to start nagging her daughter now. 'Let's go.' She added, reaching for one of the cases, hoping that they would all fit into her car.

'Will you be ok mum?' Bethany asked as they sped along the motorway, Amy pushing the car to its limits to try and get her daughter there on time.

'I'll be fine baby girl.' She replied smiling at her youngest daughter. Neither of her daughters knew about the phone calls from their father, Amy as always wanted to protect them. She had spent a lot of time feeling guilty for the lives her daughters had grown up in. The constant violence and abuse that she tried her best to hide from them had slowly turned on them as they had grown.

Over the weeks since his release Paul had continued in his relentless torture becoming braver and braver as time went on. Amy was literally afraid for her life, knowing it was only a matter of time before he accomplished what he so obviously wanted. She found that she was spending more and more time shut away in the house, petrified of venturing out on her own, knowing that he was watching her, stalking her. Amy began to realise that a very familiar pattern was beginning to develop, she was once again lying to her children, protecting them, after all, it was her job……

'I'm not sure I want to leave you.' Bethany sobbed as she saw the signs for the airport.

'You are young and beautiful Bethany; this is a wonderful experience for you. I will be fine; I'm a big girl you know.' Amy laughed trying to reassure her second born child. 'I'm so excited for you, you are going to see new places, meet new people, oh Bethany, I really am happy for you.' Amy gushed. 'And remember if you don't like it you can always come home.' She added.

'Thanks mum. I really like Jesse you know, he makes you smile. You have changed so much since you left him.' Amy knew she was referring to her father. 'I wonder what he is doing now?' Bethany said quietly. 'Eww forget I said that!' She added forcefully whilst shaking her pretty head.

'Bethany, despite what he did he is still your father baby girl and if you wanted to see him or perhaps talk to him on the phone I would support you.'

Secretly Amy was glad neither of her daughters wanted any contact with Paul, she didn't trust him with her babies, no matter how old they were. During the violent years of her marriage it became one of the major reasons that had kept her by Paul's side, she knew that once they were over 16 he couldn't touch them, no court in the land would force her girls to see their father if they chose not to.

'I never want to see him again mum, Chloe doesn't either.' Amy knew Bethany was speaking the truth on her sister's behalf. Chloe had completely switched off where Paul was concerned, pretending she had never had a father.

'Ok, I just needed you to know Bethany darling.' Amy smiled at her daughter. 'We're here.' She stated excitedly. 'Look, there's Adam, let's get you checked in baby girl.' She added switching off the engine and opening her door. 'I'm going to miss you Bethany.' She whispered as the two women collected the luggage from the boot of the car.

'I'm going to miss you too mum. I have set up your Skype account so we can talk every day.' Her arms were around her mother in an instant as they both felt the tears they had tried so hard to fight back begin to erupt.

'No tears now!' Amy said as she reached out and brushed the moisture from her daughter's face whilst trying to dry her own. 'You are going on an adventure.' She squealed as she opened the back door of the car and heaved Bethany's last case out. 'I love you so much Bethany, be wise, be good but most of all have an amazing time.' She added enveloping her daughter into her arms for one final hug. 'I'm going to miss you so much.' She whispered.

'Oh mum.' Tears were flowing down her youngest daughter's face. 'I'm going to miss you too but I know you will be fine with Jesse, he will look after you.' She smiled.

Loading the luggage onto a trolley the two women walked towards Adam.

'Look after my baby girl for me Adam please.' Amy whispered as she gave him a final hug.

'I will Amy, I promise.' He replied stepping back allowing Amy to hug her daughter in her arms one last time.

'I love you Bethany.' Amy whispered into her youngest child's hair. 'Have a wonderful time beautiful girl.'

One man and two women walked into the airport, only one walked out, her tears flowing down her face as feelings of loneliness and abandonment washed through her.

CHAPTER SIXTY ONE

Opening the front door of her empty house Amy sighed heavily, it was so quiet.

She had gradually grown accustomed to Chloe's absence; Bethany's would hit her hard. As she wandered through the house she made her way up the stairs into her youngest child's bedroom. Sitting on the bed she finally allowed the tears to flow freely, huge sobs filling her body as she remembered Bethany as a baby.

Born prematurely she had spent the first weeks of her life in the special care baby unit; she was so tiny with her little legs sticking up under the blankets. Slowly she had put on the weight that was needed to go home and when the day finally arrived a very anxious, young Amy had cradled her baby to her breast as she walked out of the hospital for the first time in 20 weeks.

Now she was all grown, a beautiful young woman with long, thick, chestnut hair, like her mother's and enormous brown eyes that seemed to look right through you. Both her daughters were petite, although the pair stood a little taller than their mother.

Amy loved her daughters with every fibre in her body and had spent all of their lives trying her best to protect them. Chloe was blissfully happy with Mark; Bethany and Adam would be in the air now on their way to a new and exciting life. With a heavy sigh Amy stood up and walked from the room, with one final glance she shut the door behind her, the lonely tears coming once again.

Strolling into her bedroom she noticed Jesse's shirt that he had given her weeks before. Slipping off her clothes she shrugged into the cool cotton before lying down on her bed. Reaching for the pillow where Jesse had laid his head, she drew it closely to her, inhaling his scent before wrapping herself around it in a foetal position and closing her eyes.

The ringing of her mobile phone jarred her from the troublesome sleep she had fallen into.

'Shit!' She exclaimed as she glanced at the clock on her bedside table. It was nearly 4pm. Grabbing the phone she noticed it was Jen.

'Hello Sweetie, how are you?' The sound of her friend's voice made Amy cry once again as the sleep left her mind and her thoughts came charging back. Bethany was gone.

'Fucking miserable.' She replied.

'I'm guessing our little Bethany is in the sky as we speak.' She responded.

The two women talked almost every day on the telephone; Jen was her closest and dearest friend, her confident and ally. Amy knew that without her she would never have dared to meet Jesse, her gentle persuasion and encouragement had spurned her on, making her feel brave and when the doubts had flooded her mind, Jen had always been on hand to make her feel better and ease the conflicts away.

'She is. My beautiful little girl is flying across the world Jen.' Amy responded sadly. 'I have an empty nest.' She wailed.

'Awww Sweetie, you will be fine, you have Jesse.' The mention of his name brought a soft smile to Amy's face.

'I know.' She replied. 'Jen....' Amy paused. 'I have had an idea.'

'What?' Jen asked.

'Well, both the girls have gone now; I don't know why I don't make a new life for myself, somewhere completely new.' Sitting up in bed, she threw back the covers as a plan began to formulate in her now wide awake mind.

'What! So you are planning on leaving too?' Jen shouted down the phone.

'Yes, Paul is still hounding me Jen. He followed me yesterday and nearly ran me off the road. I tried to take a picture on my mobile phone so I could go to the police but I was so scared and panicking that I dropped it. He really wants to kill me Jen; I don't think I will ever be totally free of him.'

Paul had gradually given up on the phone calls when Amy refused to speak to him. Whenever she received a call from a withheld number she would answer but say nothing, if he then spoke she would promptly hang up the telephone. Eventually, with gently persuasion from Jesse, she had changed her number, a number that she had changed when she had escaped. She often wondered where Paul had obtained her new number from……. Debs perhaps?

Amy began to notice that things had been moved in the garden during the night, a plant pot here, an ashtray there. He even rang the doorbell late one night which had Amy a wreck as she sat alone in her living room, huddled up on the sofa. She knew it was Paul, she heard him call out quietly to her, his voice evoking deathly fear throughout her. Jesse stayed most nights but when her bed was empty she would stay awake all night, listening for every sound, afraid of her own shadow as she sat in her bed with the lights on.

'Amy you can't carry on living like this anymore, you are going to end up a basket case.' Jen said, worried about her little friend.

'I know Jen.' Amy responded. 'I need to get away, make a new life for myself.' As she paused she knew she needed her friend. 'Jen, I know I need to leave but I can't.' Amy finished crying softly.

'Why can't you?' Jen asked knowing what the answer would be before Amy replied.

'Jesse. It would break my heart Jen.' Amy was crying softly as once again she fought her mental battles. Peace or Jesse, she couldn't have both.

'You never know Amy, you never know.' Jen whispered down the phone. 'Ask him, see what he says.'

'I'll think about it.' Amy sniffled in response.

The two women chatted for almost half an hour as Amy plotted and planned, her excitement growing by the minute as she shared her dream with her best friend.

'I've got to go now Sweetie works a calling. I will text you later. Love you Amy and stay strong beautiful lady.' Jen hung up leaving Amy with her thoughts.

'Yes, I am going to escape.' She silently thought. 'Far away where he can't find or hurt me anymore.'

As she finished formulating her escape she walked into her office. Sitting down at the desk she turned on her laptop.

Hello darling,

I wanted to share my idea of a perfect escape with you.

MY PERFECT ESCAPE BY AMY LUCAS

As she gazed out of the window of her study, her fingers poised on the keypad the final words for the letter sprang from her mind.

'How her life had changed.' She silently thought as she reached for the smouldering cigarette from the ashtray that was perched by the side of her. Gone was the broken, frightened woman, in her place a brave blissfully happy and contended female.

Jesse had changed her and her life so much. Gradually she had allowed the walls that she had so diligently built fall down until they lay, wrecked, beneath her feet. She had given herself completely to him, she was his.

At first it had been painful, the difference in their ages always at the front of her mind but as time had passed Amy no longer cared as she gave into the feelings he created whenever he was around or she thought of him.

His eyes, those sexy, magnetic, mesmerizing eyes. Even after all this time she still found it hard to meet his gaze. When he looked at her, in his special "Jesse way," she would feel the heat begin to spread throughout her body until with an almost unbearable, sweet agony; she would have to look away.

Putting the finishing touches to her letter she turned off the laptop and padded across the thick carpet into the kitchen.

'He'll be back soon.' She hugged herself……

Amy had hatched 'Her Perfect Escape.' Mount Ruapehu was where she wanted to be, far, far away from England and all her unsolved problems.

'She knew she would never go, she couldn't leave him, no until he was ready to say goodbye. Amy knew she could easily love this man for the rest of her life, the amazing, special man who she loved with all her heart, body, mind and soul, the man that despite his young age had changed her and her life so much. The man whom she belonged to, for as long as he wanted her. She knew they were always meant to say goodbye and so with every passing day she made her memories, committing the smallest things to her mind. His smile, the way he looked at her, his touch…..

'I couldn't escape, I couldn't leave you. Not yet.' She said quietly as she lay with her head on his arm.

That night as he slept beside her, his hand resting on her waist she dreamt of him leaving her. As she relived the thoughts her unconscious mind had placed upon her the next morning silent tears ran down her face and so she decided to write him a story and reveal her most secret of dreams to the man she loved.

'I want to escape to Mount Ruapehu with you. I want to breathe the air with you.' She wrote.

'You have always wanted to travel……'

'You can tell everyone you are travelling for 6 months and come with me to Ruapehu. You can ski whilst I dream.'

'I want to love you, look after you, dream with you but most of all I want to feel peace with you.'

She had explored so much with him and even though she was older she had experienced a lot of firsts with Jesse. The way she loved him, the places they had been, Amsterdam….. not to mention the role play and other kinky goings on…..

He made her feel alive and sexy, brave and courageous and she didn't want it to end not yet…….. He made her feel as if she could conquer anything, no obstacle was too large anymore.

'Please come with me.' She had pleaded.

'Yes.' Jesse had replied.

'You can go home whenever you want. I just want to share my first time in this special place with you because you are so special to me.

'Let's do it!'

And so the two journeyed to Mount Ruapehu in New Zealand………

The closing chapters forgotten for the time being…..

I love you Jesse, my heart is yours. I am yours.

Now and forever

You're Amy

Xxxxxxxxxxxxxx

Reading it over Amy sat back, her finger poised on the enter key.

'Done!' She shouted as she hit the key. 'No turning back now.'

CHAPTER SIXTY TWO

'Be there in ten babe. xx' Amy felt the nausea begin to rise almost immediately as she read Jesse's text.

'Shit! Shit! Shit!' She shouted, nervously pacing back and forth. Kicking off the high heeled shoes she continued to verbally curse herself.

Why the hell had she sent that email? Why was she deliberately torturing herself? Was she some sort of sadist, intent on causing herself grief and misery for the rest of her stupid life? This was it; he was coming to tell her goodbye. This was the last time she would see Jesse, the very last time she would see his eyes.

Hearing his knock on the door she shoved her feet back into her shoes before hurrying down the stairs. Wiping her fingers across the top of her lip to remove the nervous moisture, she plastered her best smile onto her face, gulping hard to fight back the waves of sickness.

She had always promised to walk away when the time was right, for Amy it wasn't, but she knew that once Jesse read her email he would walk away from her. She had reached out to him, wanting to feel peace with the man she loved but deep within her heart Amy knew she had asked too much of him.

'Hi sexy bum.' He said, picking her up as soon as she opened the door to him. 'How's your day been?' Placing her down on the sofa, Jesse removed his shoes before joining her, a sexy smile on his lips. 'Did Bethany and Adam catch their flight ok?' He asked as he reached for her hands.

Amy was confused. The smile she had fixed on her mouth as she had opened the door to him was still firmly in place. As she searched his face she looked for a clue, the slightest give away as to how he was feeling. Nothing………

'Erm… we just made it on time.' Amy replied feeling the mask gradually slip away as she studied Jesse carefully and still found nothing. As she looked into his eyes she felt her mouth begin to move, the genuine smile was back in place. Perhaps he hadn't read the email yet......

'So, we have the house to ourselves Amy.' His voice was husky and low as he brought her closer to him.

Inhaling deeply Amy committed his scent to memory. As she straddled him, her hands in his hair, her lips seeking his she silently vowed to remember every touch, every kiss but most of all every look.

'You are wearing the shoes.' Jesse sexily murmured as his lips met the bare skin of the side of her neck. 'Wrap me up baby.' He asked, scooping her up into his arms as she placed her arms around his neck, her legs around his waist.

'Yes.' She whispered, burying her head into the side of his neck, nibbling his earlobe softly. 'I love you so much.'

'I love you too Amy.' He replied as he placed her gently onto the bed. As he removed his clothes Amy watched, again committing every movement, every look to her mind.

'You seem so serious.' Jesse said softly as he joined her. 'Are you sad?' He asked, his fingers undoing the buttons on her blouse as her fingers disappeared into his wavy hair.

'Yes.......' Amy gasped as Jesse peeled back her blouse, his fingers seeking out her nipple.

Pulling him towards her their lips met Amy's passion so intense she felt as if her heart was on fire. Jesse swiftly removed the rest of her clothes until she lay before him naked apart from the high, red, suede stilettos with the black velvet bow.

'Make love to me.' She whimpered as she fought back the tears. This was the last time she would feel him inside her, their bodies united............

Feeling his hands travelling slowly up her legs Amy sighed softly, closing her eyes she allowed the sensations to wash over her body as his fingertips connected with her sex.

'I love you so much.' She called out as the first waves of her orgasm crashed through her, Jesse moved quickly down her body, his mouth joining his fingers. As they worked together, deliciously torturing her secret place she felt another climax building, this one deeper, as she opened up to him. 'Oh.....Jesse......' She wailed as sensations and feelings swamped her tiny frame and mind, the orgasm penetrating every fibre of her being as he plunged himself into her. Contraction after contraction gripped his cock tightly as she clung to him, calling out his name, her fingernails embedding themselves in the soft skin of his back.

Pushing his fingers into her hair, he groaned loudly, bringing his lips once more down onto hers.

'I love you too.' He moaned, his lips trailing a blazing path over the side of her neck. 'Turn over.' He whispered, withdrawing himself slowly from her.

Lying on her stomach, Amy waited, her eyes closed, for her lover to join her. As she felt his skin connect with hers she moaned softly, parting her legs as he gently nudged them with his own. Reaching for her hands he gathered the two easily in one of his, pinning them above her head, his other hand guiding his cock to her wet and ready entrance. He glided into her, her inner muscles immediately reacting, grasping him as they welcomed the fullness.

'I love it like this.' Amy moaned as she felt the first stirrings of another climax begin to take form. She felt so close to him, their skin touching, his cock buried deep inside her, his lips on her neck and the side of her face. Forgetting her sadness completely she welcomed her orgasm, surrendering herself totally to it, to Jesse, as he clung to her, his own climax raging, his sperm shooting deep within her. Amy's heart was open, her body alive, every sense heightened as her internal muscles continued to incubate him tightly, holding him, never wanting to let go.

She knew she would forever remember him, his touch, his smile, his gentle way. Jesse had her heart. Most of all Amy knew, without a doubt, that she would never, ever forget the way he looked at her, his eyes. Those sexy, mesmerising, magnetic, green eyes..................

EPILOGUE

'Yes.' The one word she had prayed she would hear.

As she had lain beneath him, the final waves of her orgasm slowly fading, he whispered the single word into her ear.

'What?' She didn't dare to move.

'Yes. Yes to New Zealand.' Gently he had kissed the side of her neck before rolling onto his side taking Amy with him.

Remaining as still as possible Amy closed her eyes. Could she dream? Dare she dream? Was it possible that Jesse really wanted to go with her?

'Really?' Her voice was timid and small.

Sliding out of her slowly Jesse kissed her shoulder before leaping over her, his smiling face inches from hers.

'Yeh, let's do it!' His excitement was contagious as Amy jumped up, a wide smile beginning to spread on her mouth.

'Ok.' She gulped. 'Let's do this. Let's go to New Zealand!'

Now Jesse was sitting beside her, holding her hand as they soared into the sky on the Virgin airplane, their destination Auckland, New Zealand.

'I love you sexy eyes.' She whispered as she squeezed his hand.

'I love you too sexy bum.' He replied, his green eyes blazing into hers.

Resting her head back on the thick leather headrest Amy closed her eyes and listened to the sounds of the familiar tune that played from Jesse's IPod, a tune that she had made her own as the words meant so much to her and her life with Jesse, the man she loved with every single part of her.

"I'll be your dream, I'll be your wish, I'll be your fantasy. I'll be your hope; I'll be your love, be everything that you need." Truly, madly, deeply by Savage Garden.

"I will be strong; I will be faithful cos I'm counting on a new beginning, a reason for living, a deeper meaning."

"I want to stand with you on a mountain, I want to bathe with you in the sea, I want to lay like this forever...................

Opening her eyes she looked at Jesse.

'So handsome.' She thought. 'So completely and utterly perfect and for now I am his.'

For the first time, in a long time, Amy felt totally at peace as she soared hundreds of miles above the earth, her problems far away, left behind without a moment's hesitation. As she looked at Jesse her eyes met his beautiful, green, sexy ones.

'I love you.' She mouthed.

'I love you.' He mouthed back.

For Amy most of her life had been a battle, the last twenty years being the hardest. As she closed her eyes she briefly thought about her past. Never again would she feel a man's hand connect with her face, his foot with her body. Never again would she be a victim. No, Amy was a survivor.

Turning her face towards Jesse she saw him watching her. Reaching out she removed the ear bud before taking both his hands in hers, her fingers stroking them, her eyes following their every move. Jesse hands were good; he would never use them to hurt her. Looking up at him her blue eyes met his green ones and lingered……..

'Thank you Jesse.' She whispered looking down at his hands once again. 'My life has changed so much because of you.' She added meeting his eyes once again. 'I adore you.'

Bringing her hands up to his lips he kissed each one tenderly.

'We are going on an adventure Amy and I'm happy and honoured that you want me to share this with you.' Amy felt the tears of happiness begin to form in her eyes.

'The perfect escape.' She whispered, touching her lips softly to his.

As she drew back from him she laughed as her eyes met his, the "Jesse look" was there, beckoning to her, making her blush from head to foot.

'The perfect escape and a lot of hot, kinky sex!' Jesse added, stroking her hair back from her face.

'Bring it on Clayton. Bring it on!' She replied laughing, her blue eyes holding his sexy, mesmerizing green ones until he was forced to look away for the very first time.

THE END

Would you like to see your manuscript become a book?

If you are interested in becoming a PublishAmerica author, please submit your manuscript for possible publication to us at:

acquisitions@publishamerica.com

You may also mail in your manuscript to:

PublishAmerica
PO Box 151
Frederick, MD 21705

We also offer free graphics for Children's Picture Books!

---

www.publishamerica.com

Lightning Source UK Ltd.
Milton Keynes UK
UKOW042238211112

202575UK00002B/7/P